NOW AND THEN

MARY O' SULLIVAN

POOLBEG

This book is a work of fiction. The names, characters, places, businesses, organisations and incidents portrayed in it are either the product of the author's imagination or are used fictitiously. Any resemblance to actual persons, living or dead, events or locales is entirely coincidental.

Published 2020
by Poolbeg Press Ltd.
123 Grange Hill, Baldoyle,
Dublin 13, Ireland
Email: poolbeg@poolbeg.com

A catalogue record for this book is available from the British Library.

ISBN 978178199-358-3

www.poolbeg.com

About the author

I am lucky enough to live near the coast in beautiful West Clare, Ireland. Until 2006 I worked as a laboratory technician, wrote a column for a local newspaper, composed poetry and short stories, and daydreamed about becoming a published novelist.

Since the 2006 publication by Poolbeg Press of my first novel, *Parting Company*, I have devoted my time to writing.

My published novels include *As Easy as That*, *Inside Out*, *Ebb and Flow*, *Under the Rainbow*, *Time and Tide*, *Fire and Ice*, *Thicker Than Water*. I have also written a collection of short stories – *Full Circle and Other Stories* – which is available online.

Acknowledgements

I am very grateful for the support I have received from so many people, both in writing *Now and Then* and in bringing it to publication.

Firstly, my gratitude to Poolbeg Press for accepting this novel. Special thanks to Paula Campbell, editor Gaye Shortland and David Prendergast.

A big word of thanks to Siobhan Moloney, who read early drafts and told me to get on with it when I was dithering.

Thank you, Paul O'Sullivan, for your astute suggestions and insights. Thank you especially for your trip home from NZ to surprise me on my birthday. It was special.

Thank you, Anne Fleming and Mary Malone, for reading my manuscript and for your encouragement.

Thanks is such a little word to say to my family for all the support and love they have shown me, but I'll say it anyway for my husband Sean, my sons Paul and Owen, and my sister Anne. Love you always.

Appreciation to Lotte Sutton and Alice Twaite for your support and very welcome visit to Clare.

For Siobhan Moloney, a token of thanks for the support and encouragement you have given me during the writing of this book and always being there with a listening ear.

NOW

CHAPTER ONE

Sunday 9th December 2012

Murmurs wash over me. I want to cover my ears, to hide from judgement and speculation. My breathing quickens, sweat breaks out on my forehead, my hands begin to shake. Signs I have been taught to recognise. Eyes closed, I force my breathing to slow, shakes to steady, fear to slither back to its hiding place. But the guilt stays. It is an integral part of me, encoded in my DNA. I am Leah Parrish, the sometimes fearful, always guilty one.

I hear the tap-tap of Cora Sheehan's shoes as she strides towards the backstage room where I am waiting. She is the person who organised my visit to this County Kerry village hall. I get the welcome aroma of coffee as she pushes the door open with her elbow, carefully balancing a tray in her hands.

"You did say no sugar, didn't you?" she asks as she busily sets about placing cup, plate and milk jug on the trestle table in front of me.

I nod. I dislike sweet drinks. Almost as much as I dislike the wobbly trestle tables, folding chairs and echoing timber floors in every village hall and community centre I have visited during the past two years.

"It's filling up nicely outside," Cora says.

"Good," I hear myself say.

"We advertised your visit in the parish newsletter and the local paper so we're expecting a fair turnout."

Of course there will be a crowd. There always is. An entertainer, that's what I am. A curiosity. Yet this torture is self-imposed. Nobody except myself to blame for the humiliation.

"The screen and projector are set up on stage for you. Anything else you need, Leah?"

"No, thank you. Just something to rest my laptop on. A table, a lectern. Whatever."

"It will be ready and waiting for you. Well then, I'll leave you to get your thoughts together. Five more minutes enough for you?"

"Yes, thank you, Cora. Would you close the door on your way out, please?"

"Fine, I'll give you a call before I go on stage to introduce you. Just a few words. They all know who you are."

As the door shuts I can no longer hear the murmuring voices from the hall. I reach into my bag and take out the notebook. The one with the green leather cover. I rest it on top of my laptop. It reminds me why I'm here.

I fish in the bag again and find my phone. There are new messages and emails. Ignoring them, I swipe the photo icon. Suddenly, there they are, grinning at me. The twins Josh and Anna and their big brother Rob. My heart, so full of love for my children, seems to swell and fill the room. A knock sounds on the door and it immediately opens.

"Time to start now," Cora says. "Are you ready?"

I take a last glance at my children. At their happy grins, trusting gaze, their joy in life. Switching off the phone, I turn to Cora.

"I'm ready. Lead the way."

I stand at the side of the stage as Cora introduces me. I can pick out faces in the front rows. Some leaning forward, waiting to catch a glimpse of me. Taking a deep breath, I walk onstage to join Cora at the podium provided. She goes, leaving me alone to face my audience. I put my laptop down, place the notebook beside it, and log onto my PowerPoint. Out of the corner of my eye, I see a flash of colour as the first photo of my presentation appears on the screen.

"Thank you all for coming along this evening. I appreciate you giving me the opportunity to talk to you. Let me take you back to two years ago. I was married to Ben, mother to two-and-a-half-year-old twins and a five-year-old boy. I also ran a hairdressing salon in Paircmoor, the rural village we had moved to from Dublin."

I can see several heads nod. They already know the details of my life. Or think they do. I click on the next frame. As it flicks on screen, I pause, straighten my shoulders, clear my throat and take myself back two years to Leah's Salon in Paircmoor village.

THEN

CHAPTER TWO

Thursday 25th November 2010

Mags was doing it again. She was taking a phone call, leaving the client sitting with her root treatment half done. My fault. I was never assertive enough with her, maybe in deference to the fact that she was older than me. Or perhaps I was just an incompetent boss. As she rushed towards me, I braced myself for another drama.

"Leah! Emergency! Claire's had an accident. I must go. Now!"

My first reaction was annoyance with Claire and her constant need to have her mother dance attendance on her, especially during work hours. We were busy. I could not spare my only trained stylist to babysit her twenty-seven-year-old daughter. Yet again.

"What kind of accident?" I asked.

Mags' lower lip was quivering, her eyes filled with tears.

"A van rammed into the back of her car. She can't move."

I didn't need to hear anymore. I could see the scene – a hysterical Claire causing chaos, demanding attention. I nodded to Mags.

"Go on."

She was already racing out of the salon, muttering

apologies as she went.

"Try to get back here if you can, please!" I called after her.

She waved a hand without turning. I knew then she would not be back until the morning.

I looked at Tina, a work-experience student I had agreed to take on for two months. She was leaning against the reception desk, a blank expression on her face. I'm not sure whose idea it was to send her to a hairdressing salon but, judging by her lack of interest, it clearly wasn't Tina's. However, she was all I had now.

Minnie Curran, she of the abandoned root treatment, cleared her throat. Of course, she was about to complain. And the child whose hair I had been cutting was starting to get restless. The arrival of another customer, early for her ten o'clock appointment, was not what I needed just then.

"Tina, would you seat our ten o'clock and give her some magazines, please?"

To my relief, Tina peeled herself away from the desk and went towards our customer.

"What about my roots?" Minnie Curran asked me.

"I'll be with you as soon as I can, Minnie."

"I need to go to the bathroom," the child said and wriggled off the seat before I could stop her. She tripped over the towel I had draped around her, fell and began to cry.

As I helped her up, I felt my phone vibrate in my pocket. I glanced at the screen. It was my husband, Ben. I switched off my phone and put it back in my pocket.

I had a chaotic, understaffed hair salon to sort out. Ben would have to wait.

Ben gave up leaving messages for Leah. Obviously, she was too busy to take a call. Entrepreneur that she was. Clawing her way onto the Paircmoor commercial Who's Who list. Gaining respect in the community they had moved to only two years before. Garnering pity for her circumstances. His lack of circumstance. His joblessness.

The baby monitor was silent, so the twins were still napping. If he stopped feeling sorry for himself, he could get something done before they woke. Assuming there would be an internet connection today. The service was hit-and-miss in the Paircmoor area. Mostly miss. Not the ideal location to set up an e-business. He clicked on his browser and was relieved when his home page opened. He logged on to his email. Nothing new. He had been so certain the Maine souvenir company would have placed an order by now. It was tempting to contact them, to ask if they had reached a decision yet, to offer them a better deal. He visited his website. There had been twenty visits since last he checked. If interest in his product was money, he would be making a living. Hell, he would be making a fortune. Enough to fuck off out of the prison that was Paircmoor.

He shut down the computer and, standing up, took a key from the top shelf, inserted it in the keyhole of the left-hand drawer of his desk, and opened it up. Taking out the few loose items, he removed the false bottom, then lifted out his diary and sat down at his desk, pen in hand.

Thursday 25th November 2010, he wrote. *Same old shit. Leah too busy to answer my calls. The twins asleep. Rob in school. No update on business front. Losing hope now that*

The baby monitor sounded. One of the twins was up and about. Ben guessed it would be Anna. He replaced his diary in its hideout and locked the drawer. He would come back to it later. He always did. It was his place of refuge.

His non-judgemental friend. When he reached the twins' bedroom he saw that Anna was standing up on her bed, challenging life to come and get her, then running across to her twin brother's bed to shake him awake. Even at two and a half years of age, she was as driven as her mother.

Ben tried Leah's number once more. It went straight to her chirpy voicemail. He would have thrown his phone against the wall if he could afford to replace it, and if he didn't now have to make lunch for the twins. Because his wife was too busy washing strangers' hair to look after her own family.

His angry stream of thought was halted abruptly by a cry of pain. He lifted his eyes from his phone, just in time to see Anna pinch Josh on the soft flesh of his tummy.

"Stop, Anna! That's very naughty. You're hurting Josh!"

"Him won't get up," she said.

"But you mustn't hurt him."

Ben sat on Josh's bed and took the crying child into his arms. Anna clambered onto his knee.

"I sorry," she said, rubbing Josh's face with her fingers.

Josh stopped crying and smiled at his sister. If Anna was like her mother – and she was in her delicate blonde beauty, deep blue eyes, her boundless energy – then Josh, dark-haired, brown-eyed, compliant little Josh was his father's son. Ben held his son closer, as if he could protect him from the hurts and pain life would inflict on him.

Anna stared at Ben for a moment then gently touched his cheek.

"Why you sad, Daddy?"

Why? Why? Why you sad, Ben Parrish? Just because you were made redundant from your swish architect's office? Just because you, and practically every other architect who hasn't emigrated from Ireland, has fallen foul of the economic crash? Just because you know in your heart the business you are trying to launch is dead in the water before it starts? A joke. Born out of desperation. Just because you are now being supported by your wife? Financially, that is.

He kissed Anna on her blonde hair.

"I'm not sad, you goose. I'm just hungry. What do you two say to pancakes for lunch?"

She slithered off his knee and raced towards the kitchen. Ben reluctantly eased Josh's warm little body away from him.

"Come on, Josh. Goodness knows what your sister will get up to in the kitchen."

Josh, wise beyond his two and a half years, shrugged. An acknowledgement that he could never second-guess his sister's next move.

Ben took his son's hand and led him to the kitchen where Anna had dropped a carton of eggs on the floor.

It was Ben's turn to shrug his shoulders. An acknowledgement on his part of both defeat and acceptance.

"What do I owe you?"

I knew by the way she narrowed her eyes that Minnie Curran was issuing a challenge, not asking a question. I glanced at the clock. The cuckoo clock Ben's mother had brought back from one of her skiing trips to Switzerland. It looked out of place in the salon but at least I didn't have to listen to the blasted bird and its hourly mechanical clatter at home.

"It's quarter past twelve," Minnie Curran said.

It was. The old biddy had been here since half past nine. She was the last of the morning customers to leave. She had her bag open but no sign of purse or money in her hand. I nodded. I would have to take this one on the chin, no matter how much I needed the cash. I mustered a smile, false but functional.

"I apologise again, Minnie. As you saw, the delay was unavoidable because of Mags being called away."

"Well, I've missed my lift home. You know I live six miles the other side of the village."

I needed to ring Ben to know how the children were. I especially needed to be rid of moaning Minnie Curran who was already preparing to spread the word about the bad service in Leah's Salon.

"Please accept my sincere apologies, Minnie. I won't be charging for your root treatment today. I hope to see you here again soon."

She squinted at me for an instant. I thought she was going to ask me for a taxi fare. Suddenly she smiled and the usual affable Minnie came to life.

"That's very kind of you, Leah, if you're sure. Between you and me, Mags Hoey has her daughter spoiled. She had no right to leave you in the lurch."

I caught her by the elbow and gently steered her towards the door. It opened just as we got there and Tina sloped in. Refreshed no doubt after her break in the village café. Though I had to admit, much to my surprise, she had pulled her weight since Mags left. She had even managed to shampoo and condition without scalding or drowning customers.

It was starting to rain. Needles of icy cold, wind-driven rain swirled around Minnie and her newly styled hair. She stepped back in, fumbling with scarf and umbrella.

"Bother!" she said. "Why does it have to lash just now?"

"Yes, it's a bad day," I answered, holding the door open

long enough for Minnie to fix her scarf and accept that she did indeed have to face the weather.

Free of Minnie, I checked the appointment book. One o'clock was the next wash and blow-dry. A break at last.

There was no sign of Tina, She had obviously gone into the little canteen in the back of the salon. Probably leaning against the kitchen counter there instead of against the reception desk. I picked up my phone to ring Ben but Tina called from the canteen. I sighed and went to see what she wanted. Maybe she needed me to clear a counter space for her to lean against.

I had a precious mug. My very own Stephen Pearce mug. It sat on the counter now, steam rising from the freshly made coffee inside. Beside it was a plate on which sat a cream-filled chocolate éclair. Tina pulled out a stool.

"I thought you could do with this, Mrs Parrish. You had no break since morning."

It hit me then, how long it had been since anyone had done something nice for me. At the same time, I was struck by the realisation that I gave people no reason to believe their kindness would be welcome. Leah the almighty, managing home and business with efficiency. I no longer recognised myself. Who was inside my mind, spewing all these bitter thoughts, judging some people, misjudging others? How could I expect support from Ben when I offered him none? Even Mags – I hadn't bothered enquiring how her daughter was doing since the accident this morning. And this trusting young girl, Tina. I had dismissed her as worthless. How arrogant. How shallow.

"Tina, this is so thoughtful. I appreciate it very much."

"Enjoy. I'll mind the salon until you're ready."

She walked out the door in that elegant way I had

thought of as affected, but now recognised as a natural grace. How many other things had I got wrong? How far off track had I come? How far away had I pushed my husband?

I took a sip of coffee and rang Ben.

CHAPTER THREE

Not for the first time Ben cursed the fiddly buckles and belts in the children's car seats. Tying Josh in was easy but keeping Anna quiet for long enough to secure all the bits and pieces was a challenge.

"We go for Rob now?" she asked when at last he had both of them strapped in safely.

"Rob," Josh echoed.

The twins idolised their older brother.

"*Robbie, Robbie!*" they chanted in unison as Ben switched on the engine.

Rob was five and had started primary school that year. The daily journey to collect their big brother was the highlight of the twins' day. As he carefully guided the jeep down the narrow lane from Cowslip Cottage, Ben noted, as he always did, that he hated the house name. Like everything else, Leah's opinion had prevailed. She said it had been named one hundred years ago and tradition must be respected. Besides, she informed him, cowslips had the most delicately beautiful perfume she ever smelt. None of this stopped Ben thinking 'Cowshit Cottage' every time he saw the age-worn stone plaque on the front of their home.

The primary school was built on the outskirts of the village. Out past Leah's salon. The twins waved, as they did every day when passing the place where their mother spent most of her time. Ben frowned, remembering her phone call just before he left the cottage. Being summoned to a 'talk' by Leah was ominous. It would most probably be about money. Or lack of it.

"Ellen," Anna said, clapping her hands together as they approached the school.

Ben smiled. Ellen's car was parked in her usual spot outside the school gates. Right beside her Nissan was a vacant space which was generally accepted as Ben's by now. When Ben had parked, the riot of colour that was Ellen jumped out of her car. She was wearing a lime-green raincoat, rainbow-coloured wellingtons and her dark curls spilled out from underneath a pink floppy hat. She was, as ever, smiling as she opened the passenger door of the jeep and hopped in.

"How are my favourite twinnies?" she asked, turning to the children in the back seat.

Anna leaned forward and reached a hand towards Ellen.

"I think she wants to touch your hair again. And –"

Ben suddenly stopped talking, forgetting the words he had been about to say, admitting to himself, that he, not his daughter, was the one who needed to touch Ellen's hair. He had a fleeting image of himself stroking her face, breathing in her perfume. He recognised it as a fragment of a dream he had hidden in the safety of his subconscious. A dangerous, unsettling dream. He blinked to clear it away quickly, as if Ellen could see his shame. She was looking at him, concern in her green eyes.

"Ben? Are you alright?"

Alright? What the fuck did that mean? Had he been alright pre-Paircmoor? When every day had a focus, a worthwhile reason to get up. When he had a respected role in the life of a vibrant city, establishing his career with Walton, Walton and Meade architectural firm. When he had ambition. Self-respect. A future.

Ellen was looking at him with concern. He attempted a smile.

"I'm fine, Ellen. Still waiting to hear from Maine but, like they say, no news is good news. How about you? Any developments on that exhibition in Dublin?"

"Yes. No. Well, something's come up –"

"*Me, me!*" Anna shouted. "*Take me out! Him must get out too!*"

Ellen laughed. "First things first. We had better free this pair before little madam has a tantrum."

Ben checked the time on the dash clock. "It's almost time for Rob and Finn to be out anyway."

They took the excited twins to the gate of the school yard, where other parents were waiting for junior class to be released. Ben nodded and smiled in reply to the many salutes. That was Paircmoor for you, salutes, smiles, stares and invisible barriers that said keep your distance, you're not one of us. Perhaps that was why he and Ellen had forged a friendship. She too was an outsider.

The school doors opened and a stream of little people wearing blue-and-navy uniforms poured out. Finn led the charge and raced towards his mother. He had Ellen's dark hair, her smile and those sparkling green eyes. Impossible to say if he resembled his father in any way. Ellen and her son lived alone and never mentioned anything about their personal lives before they had come to Paircmoor from England.

Ben looked to the back of the group. That's where he knew he would find Rob. Taller than his classmates. Ambling along. Content in his own company. Anna ran towards her older brother. A smile lit Rob's face as he caught his sister's hand and brought her to the gate.

Ben, busy putting the twins back into their seats and Rob into his booster seat, did not get a chance to talk to Ellen again. She wound down her window as she reversed out of her parking space.

"What I have to tell you will hold until tomorrow. See you then."

"Same time, same place," he said.

It was their joke. Their private joke.

She waved and drove away. The colour went out of his day.

I checked that the immersion was off, dryers and straighteners unplugged, towels loaded in the laundry bag for washing at home, floors swept clean for the morning. Everything was in order. Thanks mainly to Tina. I could not have managed today without her. I turned the door sign to CLOSED, then switched off the lights.

Standing in the dimness of the salon, I breathed in the quiet. This was my favourite time of day, especially if I'd been busy. It was when I could pat myself on the back and say, yes, I had made the right decision in opening the business. In leaving my children. My stomach muscles clenched, a physical reaction to the emotional pain I rarely allowed myself to acknowledge. It wasn't as if I had abandoned Rob and the twins. I would be seeing them shortly, would be putting them to bed, listening to the stories of their day, reading to them. They were being cared for by their father, not some stranger whose job it was to mind the children of busy parents. But yet, my heart ached with the knowledge that they were growing up without me there to hold them when they cried, to kiss away hurt, to laugh with them and show them the wonders of nature, to protect them from the dangers of life.

I eased onto one of the leather salon chairs. Headlights from passing traffic played on walls and ceiling, then left me in blacker darkness.

I wrapped my arms around myself, then relaxed into the darkness, holding my secret close.

Cowslip Cottage was five kilometres outside the village of Paircmoor along a picturesque winding road, bordered by mountains on one side and forest on the other. I sensed, but could not see, the shapes of hills and trees looming in the black night as I drove home. The nearer I got to the cottage, the more slowly I drove. Yes, Ben and I had to talk. Not bicker. Not a one-way conversation with him silent and me laying down the law. Not a repeat of the upsetting shouting-match the last time we tried to really communicate beyond shopping lists and duty rotas.

I slowed down even more as I approached the skew bridge. It was narrow, humped, and spanned a deceptively docile stream. I had seen the water rage and surge up onto the road in the bad storms last winter. Sometimes I believed Mags' stories about a workhouse that had once been on the banks of the stream, and that the restless ghosts of the dead poor still haunted the area.

As I turned the car into the laneway we grandly called our avenue, I faced the truth I was reluctant to admit. I was unfair to Ben. Just as Mags managed her daughter's life, I organised Ben's life for him, telling him how to be a stay-at-home dad, what the children were to wear and eat. I had little or no interest in his new business. That worked both ways as he had scant regard for my salon, despite the fact that the income from it was putting food on the table. And there I went again. Judging. Condemning without knowing all the facts. But neither did Ben. Tonight, when our children were in bed, I would have to tell him.

I switched off the engine, gathered up my handbag and the salon laundry, took a deep breath and stepped out of my Mini. As I approached the front door the sound of a car sweeping up the front avenue startled me. I knew by the speed, the very arrogance of the way it hurtled into the gravelled front yard, spewing chippings as brakes were suddenly applied, that my plans for this evening were now scuppered.

The very last person I wanted see waved to me. The front door opened and the outside light flooded the yard. Ben stood there, ready to welcome the visitor. His. Not mine.

"Why didn't you warn me your mother was calling?" I whispered to him.

"I didn't know," he said and that was probably true. Della Parrish had a talent for turning up uninvited at the most inconvenient times.

"As far as you're concerned, Leah, there is no good time for her to visit."

He got that right. I passed him by and went to see my children.

Della Parrish was the epitome of a glamorous gran. Nothing of the stereotypical rounded, cuddly grandmother about her. She insisted the children call her Della, as if in denying grannyhood she could also deny the passing years. I had to admit she was very generous to the children. And also to Ben. She had bought and insured the jeep he drove. In Dublin she had paid our mortgage when we could not. I knew she could afford to do so, but we might well have been homeless without her help.

The three children rushed into the hall as I came in, led of course by Anna. I smiled, as I always did, when I saw her peculiar way of bobbing along, her blonde curls bouncing. So full of energy that she created a force field around her and dragged Josh and Rob along in her wake. I stooped down, ready to gather her in my arms.

"Must see Della," she told me as she and the boys sped past, leaving me to haul myself tiredly up from my stooping position.

In the kitchen, I put their abandoned suppers in the fridge, then went to the utility to put on the salon wash. Judging by the pile of mucky little clothes on the floor near the machine, Ben had been gardening with the children again. All good, healthy and educational, if only he could manage to put their soiled clothes into the machine instead of on the floor in front of it. He seemed to think that was a domestic chore too far for him, but not for me after my long day at work.

Back in the kitchen, I heard excited squeals from the children and knew that Della had played her usual Lady Bountiful routine and had come laden with gifts for them. Rob was first in, waving a new game for his junior computer.

"Look, Mom! Della brought me this. My very fave!"

He kissed me quickly on the cheek, then ran to his room, clutching his precious game close to his chest. There would be no need to follow. He could manage that little computer so much better than me. The only problem would be getting him to turn it off at sleep time.

Josh arrived in next, a shiny, red, remote-control car in his hand. He put it down on the floor and then ran over to me, his arms raised. I picked him up and held him close, his head nestled into my neck.

"Wov you, Mom," he whispered.

"I love you too, Josh," I said, conscious that words could never, ever express the depth of love I felt for him.

He wriggled out of my arms and picked up the control pad of his new car. In a matter of seconds he had figured out how to work the forward and reverse controls without any help from me. I shook my head, wondering, not for the first time, if babies were now being born pre-programmed with tech-savvy brains.

A swishing sound accompanied by the tap of high heels approached. Anna and her grandmother stood just inside the kitchen door, backlit by the hall light. I stared at the pair of them. Awestruck by their beauty, I noted the strong resemblance between my daughter and mother-in-law. The likeness was not physical. Anna looked like me. Petite and blonde. Della was tall, auburn-haired. Imposing. The resemblance was in their posture, the proud tilt of the chin, the straight backs, the utter self-belief.

Anna was hopping from foot to foot now, waving the wand of the princess costume Della had brought her.

"I Princess Anna, Mom," she said.

"And so you are," I said, smiling at her. "Did you thank Della for your present?"

"Princess give her magic," Anna said, waving her wand at her grandmother.

Della laughed and hugged Anna. "You did, my princess.

Now, you have supper with your mom while I go have a private talk with your dad."

Bitch, arrogant cow, I thought as Della turned without saying one word to me and went back down the hall towards the sitting room.

"I do you magic, Mom," Anna said as she waved her sparkly wand in my direction.

I smiled at her. I needed all the magic I could get to sort out the mess that was my life.

CHAPTER FOUR

I stood outside the door of our sitting room and hesitated. Etiquette demanded I knock. Della had made it very clear that her conversation with Ben was private. But this was my home. How dare they shut me out? I could compromise by kicking the door to satisfy my anger, while at the same time being mannerly enough not to burst in unannounced on their secret chat. Tempting. Common sense won out. I tapped on the door, then opened it quickly. My husband and his mother were seated side by side on the couch. Both turned towards me with slightly surprised expressions on their faces as if they had forgotten I too lived there.

"Sorry to intrude," I said. "The children want to see you both before they go to sleep."

I turned my back on them. As I reached the kitchen I heard Della make her way towards the children's bedrooms.

Ben came into the kitchen.

"Are you not going to say goodnight to the kids?" I asked.

He dropped onto a chair at the table and hung his head, much like Rob did if he had misbehaved.

"Ben? What's wrong?"

He looked up at me and I caught a glimpse of panic in his eyes. Ben never panicked. He was cool. Sometimes too cool. I leaned closer to him.

"Has she said something to you? Done something?"

"Mum? Of course not! When has she ever done anything but help us?"

I managed to bite my tongue and not to mention the thousands of insults she had thrown in my direction since first I had met Ben. Her youngest son. Her baby. An architect like Gavin Parrish, his late dad. Doing the Parrish family proud in every way, except in his choice of bride.

"Supper?" I asked, going to the fridge to get the food Ben had not touched earlier.

"Not for me, thank you."

"I brought Sachertorte, Ben. Your favourite. You'll have that?"

I turned around to see Della standing beside Ben, a cake box in her hand. He smiled up at his mother.

"How could I refuse?"

Just like you refused supper, I thought, then almost laughed at the pettiness of the competition between Della and me. Let her have her fancy-chocolate-cake victory. At least she had brought a smile back to Ben's face.

"Sit down, Leah," she said so imperiously that I automatically sat at the table across from Ben. "We have something to tell you, but first I'm going to make you both cappuccino and cake."

I was too taken aback to protest about the cappuccino. Caffeine after six in the evening was guaranteed to keep me awake for most of the night. But instinct told me that whatever the Parrish mother and son were about to tell me would steal my sleep for a lot longer than a few hours. I looked at Ben but he deliberately avoided eye contact with me. So I sat and watched my mother-in-law potter around our kitchen, opening drawers and presses, tutting occasionally.

Cake and coffee served, she sat down beside Ben.

"Eat up and enjoy," she ordered.

"Not until I know what all the mystery is about," I said.

I sat back, wondering where I had found the courage to challenge Mother Parrish. Her nose twitched, exactly as it had done the first time Ben introduced me to her. It was such a tiny movement only I was aware of it. The momentary flare of Della's delicately shaped nostrils had told me she had got the stench of poverty and ignorance from me. Obviously the intervening years and three grandchildren had not changed her opinion. I noticed her nod in Ben's direction, giving him permission to speak.

He swallowed a mouthful of the famous cake and at last looked me in the eye.

"Leah, Mum's going to the U.S. tomorrow. Over to see Hugh."

I waited. There had to be more. Della made bi-annual trips to see her eldest son in California. A big shot in Silicon Valley. Married to Piper, a banker's daughter who also did something lucrative in finance, when she wasn't lolling by the pool at their seven-bedroomed villa. Ben was shuffling his feet underneath the table. He cleared his throat but no words came out. Della was being suspiciously silent.

"So, Della's going to see Hugh?" I prompted.

More throat-clearing and foot-shuffling from Ben before at last he blurted out the words that had been stuck in his throat.

"You know Piper, Hugh's wife? Well, her brother is a developer. Zach Milberg. *Really*, *really* big. He's done federal buildings and libraries, shopping malls and tower blocks. A legend in the US. He employs thousands in his company."

I put up my hand to stop him as it suddenly dawned on me where this might be going.

"Let him finish," Della said.

"Well, the point is," Ben continued, "that Piper's brother, has read my CV and –"

"Damn it, Ben! You mean you sent your CV to him and never said a word to me? How could you?"

"He didn't," Della told me calmly. "I did."

That figured. I would not give her the satisfaction of showing my hurt. I was angrier with Ben at that stage than with Della. I leaned across the table and touched his arm, forcing him to look me straight in the face.

"Did you agree to this?"

"Yes."

"What are you thinking? Surely you're not serious about working in the States?"

"Well, there's no goddamn work, here is there? I can't be a nanny for the rest of my life, Leah. Don't you understand that?"

I felt my breath catch in my chest as if I had been punched. I sat back and stared at Ben. At my husband of six years. I saw a stranger.

"So, a nanny, is it? That's how you think of looking after your own children."

"They're yours too. I don't see you doing much looking after."

A smile flitted across Della's face. She sat a little taller, obviously proud that her son had cut his wife down to size.

"You hardly want him to waste his years of study and his qualifications," she said to me.

Her smug, superior expression made me feel like slapping her. How she would love that. Proof that she had always been right about my lack of class. But tough titty to you, Della. Mam, the kind and gentle woman who had reared me on her own, had taught me to hold my head high and be proud of who I am.

"What I expect, Della, is that any decisions affecting our family situation are made by Ben and me. Without interference from anybody else, including you."

I heard Ben's sharp intake of breath. What was wrong with him? Could he not see that Della was using his jobless situation to win back the control she had lost when her son married me? He glared at me. I would have glared back but I found myself very close to tears.

"I'm sure you didn't mean that, Leah," he said. "You know Mum is just trying to help."

"By setting you up in the States? How does that help? What about the children? The cottage? Our life here?"

Della played a canny game. She smiled at me, her head tilted slightly to one side as if to say she was very puzzled, but willing to try to understand me.

"That's the whole point, Leah," she said. "What life here? This economy is going to take at least five years to recover. And possibly another ten for Paircmoor to catch up after that. Do you want your children to grow up without opportunities?"

"I don't want them to grow up without their father," I said as I pushed back my chair and stood.

Ben stood also and faced me.

"Why do you assume that I would go and leave my family behind? Is that what you want?"

Now he asked me what I wanted. Now that Della had

set everything in motion. Past experience told me she would already have all the details in place in order to get her own way. Ben was right, I had assumed he would go and leave me behind. All our hopes and promises to each other, our grand visions of an idyllic childhood in rural Ireland for Rob and the twins, even our love, meant nothing when his mother could so effortlessly manipulate him into wanting to fly off to the States. Probably as a passenger on her broomstick. I felt tears sting my eyes and did not want to give Della the satisfaction of seeing me cry. I took a deep breath.

"Della, please tell my husband exactly what commitments you have made on his behalf. And if the children and I are included in your scheme."

I went towards the door. Then before I could stop myself, I turned around to Ben.

"For God's sake, grow a pair of balls, Ben. Stand up for yourself and your family. About time you cut the apron strings."

I twirled on my heel and left the kitchen, knowing I had allowed my temper lead me into Della's cleverly laid trap. I had vindicated her low opinion of me and further alienated Ben. I went to bed. Alone.

I gave up on the idea of getting any sleep. It was three o'clock in the morning. The house was still, yet echoing with the creaks and groans of a hundred-year-old home whispering its history into the darkness. I had heard Della noisily start up her car before midnight. I listened in vain for sounds of Ben coming to bed. I could picture him, still sitting at the kitchen table, shoulders drooped, head bowed. Or maybe that was the wrong image. Perhaps he was online, researching his new job, his new home, his new life in California. I tossed and turned until I was suffocating under the weight of worry. I got out of bed and went to check on the children.

Tiptoeing into the twins' room, I almost tripped over Ben's feet. He was sitting on the chair just inside the door. The chair with gold-brocade upholstery and ornate Queen Anne legs. It had been so right when we had lived in our big home in Dublin, but looked pretentious in the cottage. Ben's long legs were sprawled out, his chin on his chest and his mouth slightly open as he slept. So typical of him, just closing his eyes to the problems, dodging difficult conversations.

The nightlight cast a dim glow around the room, laying shadows on the planes of the twins' faces, highlighting Anna's blonde curls and Josh's extraordinarily long lashes. Even in sleep, Anna was restless, moving her arms, rolling from her back onto her side. A little smile curved her cherub mouth. She's playing with the angels my mother used to say. I heard the chair creak and turned back to look at Ben.

"I'm sorry, Leah," he whispered and held out his hand towards me.

I hesitated for just a second. He looked so vulnerable with his hair tossed and his eyes sleepy. I was tired. God, I was so tired, and I was facing getting up again in a couple of hours to organise another day for the children. And the salon. It was not the time to have the Della and America conversation. Or the other conversation I must soon have with him. But not yet. I took his hand and smiled.

"Let's sleep," I said. "It will all look better in the morning."

CHAPTER FIVE

Friday 26th November 2010

After I dropped Rob off at school, I rushed to the salon, hoping Mags might be there. When she did not turn up by nine thirty, I rang her. No reply. I was going through the list of appointments to see how best I could organise the day with only Tina to help, when Mags rang back.

"How's Claire?" I asked.

There were sounds of sniffling, then sobs.

"Mags? Are you alright?"

"Claire is . . . she might be . . . she may never walk again."

Shocked, I flopped onto the nearest seat.

"But I thought it was just a minor accident. A tip at traffic lights."

"It was. And she was wearing her seat belt. Nevertheless she's in agony. She can't move with the pain. We'll just have to hope and pray."

Mags sounded genuinely terrified for her daughter's future.

"When will you have a definite diagnosis?" I asked.

"She's having a CT scan this morning."

"I'm so sorry, Mags. Let me know if there's anything I can do to help."

"Thank you, Leah. I hate letting you down but Claire needs me now. Even more so when she is discharged from hospital."

"When do you expect her home?"

"Later today."

Ah! My initial instinct had been right. Mags was overreacting to a minor injury. I was glad for Claire's sake. Experience also told me that it would be pointless trying to tie Mags down to any work commitment while she was milking the drama of the accident.

My instinct and experience were not working as well when it came to understanding my husband. The chaos of the early morning routine at Cowslip Cottage was not conducive to having in-depth discussions, but this morning I sensed a subtle difference in Ben. A defensiveness. Resentment against me I had not felt before. Was that why he had apologised to me in the early hours of the morning? A warning that battle lines had been drawn? With my mother-in-law holding the balance of power.

The arrival of another customer brought my thoughts back to work. Back to earning enough money to keep a roof over our heads.

Ben sat at the messy table and watched the children play. It was ten o'clock. The table was not yet cleared after breakfast and the twins were still in their pyjamas. His neck was stiff from the hours he had slept last night in the Queen Anne chair meant for show, not comfort. Josh was working busily at the play cooker while Anna had taken over her brother's remote-control car. So what now on nature versus nurture, Ben wondered. Josh saw his dad as the homemaker and was learning by example. Anna saw her mother drive off to work every day and she was following suit in her two-year-old way. Did Anna not have an instinct to nurture, Josh to protect? Were their life paths now decided because Ben had lost his job and stayed at home while Leah went out to work?

Josh had a very piercing cry, as if he hid a stock of utter misery underneath his good humour, then let it all out at once in a banshee-like wail. His cry rang around the kitchen as Anna steered the remote-control car at speed over her brother's bare toes. Ben felt tempted to sit down on the floor beside Josh and howl with him. Instead he yelled at Anna.

"*For Christ's sake, Anna! Stop that at once!* Why do you always tease him? He's your brother. You should be kind to him. And Josh, would you ever stand up for yourself!"

They stared at him. His two precious babies. Anna's face crumpled and Josh, in shock, stopped wailing. Tears glistened on their cheeks as they moved close together and put their arms around each other. Ben imagined this was how they had spent their nine months in the womb. Protecting each other in their dark, prenatal world. It was probably how they would spend their lives. Always guarding each other from dangers – such as an angry, shouting father. He had never raised his voice to them before. Neither he nor they knew how to cope now that he had, for the first time ever, lost his temper with them. He wanted to scoop them up in his arms, to kiss away their tears, to tell them how much he loved them. He stooped down to their level and reached out. Josh flinched and Anna tightened her hold on her brother.

Dismayed by their reaction, Ben sat back on his heels.

"Daddy should not have shouted at you," he said. "It was a mistake and I am very, very, sorry."

They stared at him, still clinging together. He saw hurt in Josh's eyes, a spark of defiance in Anna's.

"You make Anna and Josh cry," she accused.

"I did," Ben agreed. "That's why I'm saying sorry. But don't you remember, Anna, it was you made Josh cry? You hurt his toes with the car."

She hung her head. Josh took a side-step away from her. Great bloody parenting, Ben thought. Now he was ruining the special relationship between the twins. He remembered his mother's words of last night. Staying here, burying himself in this jobless, hopeless environment was denying the children the future they deserved. The future he deserved too. He was a far better architect than he was a stay-at-home father.

Anna suddenly dropped to her knees, then mimicked Ben by sitting back on her heels facing her brother.

"I very, very sorry, Josh," she said. "I kiss your toes better."

Lying flat, she wriggled her way over to Josh and kissed his toes.

Ben smiled. Maybe he was not too bad a dad after all. He had taught them the need to apologise when you were wrong. A good life lesson. Except when someone thought you were wrong all the time. Especially when that someone was Leah.

"Group hug!" Anna ordered.

He held out his arms and the twins came to him. He pulled them close to him and wondered how he could ever leave them, even for a little while. Just until he got settled in the US, his mother had said. Just until all the visas were sorted.

"It's for the children," she had advised. "They will thank you when they enjoy the opportunities America has to offer. Look at Hugh."

Indeed. Look at Hugh Parrish, the paragon. No wonder Ben's neck was aching. It wasn't from falling asleep in the silly chair but from a lifetime spent looking up to his older brother. It was even more difficult now that Ben had fallen on his ass, career-wise, while Hugh was climbing to ever more dizzying heights of success.

Ben glanced down at the blonde and dark heads snuggled against his chest and made a silent vow to do whatever it took to protect Anna and Josh and solemn little Rob. Always.

The doorbell rang. Anna was up and running before Ben had even risen from his knees. He noted the untidy kitchen as he walked through and hoped whoever was outside did not want to come in. The bell rang again just as he got to the hall. He opened the door and the rainbow colours of Ellen Riggs shone in the greyness of the drizzly morning.

Ben looked at her in surprise. The only other times she had been there had been to drop Finn off when he had come to play with Rob. The boys were at school now so why was she here?

Anna threw herself at Ellen and grabbed her hand.

"Can you read stories?"

"I'm pretty good at reading," Ellen said, laughing. "But I must talk to your daddy first. How's that for you?"

Ben watched as Josh took Ellen's other hand and for one moment the treacherous thought crossed his mind that life would be so different if Ellen was their mother. What would it be like to wake up to that radiant smile, those sparkling eyes, her dark hair spread on the pillow, her lithe body curled into his?

"Come on in," he invited her, shamed by the realisation that she would see the chaos in the house.

"We're a little behind this morning," he said as he led the way in. "I'm afraid the place is a mess."

"We sad first but we all sorry now," Anna piped up.

Out of the mouths of babes, Ben thought, as he cleared a space at the table and pulled a chair out for Ellen. Except that Daddy is still sad as well as sorry. And what was he to do now? The children must be washed and dressed, the kitchen tidied, but Ellen said she had to talk to him? Fuck! He couldn't even organise domestic affairs. How did he think he could go to the US and convince Zach Milburg that he was capable of making decisions involving hundreds of thousands, millions, of client money? He looked from his pyjama-clad children to unfinished cereal congealing in bowls. A band of tension tightened its grip around his head. Ellen was staring at him, a puzzled expression on her face.

"Are you ill, Ben?"

"No. I'm fine, thank you. If you'll excuse me for a few minutes, I'll get the children settled."

He took Josh and a protesting Anna and sat them in front of the TV in the lounge. He loaded their favourite *Baby Einstein* CD. It was his tried and trusted technique when he needed to have ten uninterrupted minutes.

When he got back to the kitchen he put on the kettle, cleared the table and, being Irish, chatted to Ellen about the weather. He made them coffee and sat across from her, knowing that he was staring but unable to stop. It was as if Ellen was a figment of his imagination and he feared she would vanish at any moment.

Aware he was behaving like an adolescent, he spoke abruptly.

"You mentioned yesterday you had something to tell me."

She nodded, then put both her hands around her coffee

mug. Her long fingers looked elegant, even wound around the Mickey Mouse mug he had inadvertently given her. Artist's hands. He could imagine those fingers deftly moulding the pottery pieces for which she was internationally renowned. Gently running through his hair and –

"I'm leaving," she said.

Leaving? Why? When? The questions ran silently along the tension band around his head. He could not, would not voice them. He did not want to hear the answers.

"Finn needs to have more contact with his father. They both want that."

So, there was the why. Finn's father. Who was he? She was watching him, waiting for him to say something but his questions continued their silent laps inside his head.

"I have my work to consider too," she added. "I need to be based in the UK. The logistics of exhibiting internationally from here are daunting. That situation can't continue either. Not if I want to build my pottery brand."

For the first time Ben saw a gleam of ambition in her eyes. Her work was a top seller in Irish design shops and upmarket stores. But it sounded as if that was not enough. She wanted more. More money. More fame.

"How will Finn feel about leaving his friends in Paircmoor? To go where? Where are you moving to?"

"London. And you know Finn. He'll make friends anywhere. He's excited about going."

"Why there? I thought you loved country life. The fresh air you always talk about. The starry night sky devoid of light pollution. The wildlife. The inspiration you said it gives you."

"Because that's where my husband has his practice. It's not just Finn missing him. I do too."

Husband! The shock punched Ben in the gut. She belonged to someone else. Of course she did. Someone she missed. Someone with a 'practice'. Someone successful. Employed. In control. In charge. A real man.

"What does he do?" he asked. "Your husband."

"He's a plastic surgeon. Harley Street."

Of course he was. Ben could picture this man. Tall, just a hint of silver in his dark hair, surgeon to the rich and famous. He would nip and tuck and look after Ellen, preserve her very special beauty. He focussed on Ellen's long fingers again now. No jewellery. No wedding ring. She followed his gaze.

"I don't wear my rings because of work," she said. "Doesn't make me any less married."

Even though he was six foot two, Ben felt small. Insignificant. He had been so stupid to fantasise about the beautiful woman sitting across from him. It had been delusional to believe he had any claim on her, just because she passed the boring wait outside the school gate talking to him and they had brought the children on a few outings together. His forte seemed to be in setting himself up for rejection and failure. His shoulders began to pain. *Stress, stress, stress*. He knew this because he had gone to the doctor asking for medication for his aching shoulders. Instead Dr Kelly had kindly, but firmly, pointed out that it was Ben's brain, his emotions, his mind, his very soul, crying out for ease from the constant pain of failure.

"When are you going?" he asked.

"Tomorrow."

"Tomorrow! So soon."

"No point in hanging around once the decision has been made."

He nodded. That's exactly what his mother had said last night. No point in hanging around Paircmoor. In fact, that's what everyone said, with the exception of Leah. His wife saw this godforsaken spot as the centre of the world. He could not bear Ellen to think he belonged here.

"Actually, I'll be leaving soon too," he said. "An opportunity has come up to work in America. Reams of paperwork involved with visas and permits but it will be worth it."

As he spoke the words, he realised he meant them. He must go. The blackness that filled the very core of his being seeped up from the soil of Paircmoor. It was sucking him down into its boggy land, shackling him with knotted roots.

"Oh, I'm so glad, Ben! You need an outlet for your talents and it appears it will be quite a while before this country is up and running again."

She was smiling at him, glowing, her eyes sparkling. The muscles in his arms twitched with their need to reach out and hold her.

"That reminds me," she said. "Your new project. Any news on that?"

"It's a total fuck-up," he said.

He saw a cloud pass over her lovely brightness and thought his swearing had offended her.

"I'm sorry. Excuse the language, Ellen. It's just that I've put so much work into promoting it and now I realise it was never a viable idea. I don't know why I thought there would be a market for quality scale models of historical Irish buildings."

"I'm so sorry, Ben. It's a niche market and would take a long time to build up."

It was a talent of hers to imply without bluntly stating.

The word *idiot* never passed her lips, but Ben heard the implication loud and clear.

She stood up and pushed back her chair.

"I'd better read that story I promised the children. I'll ask Anna to get her book."

He bowed his head, not wanting to see her walk away. Not wanting to see her take the colour from his life. Not wanting to be left alone with the cold blackness enveloping him from the inside out. He wondered why she had left her husband in the first place, only to go back to him now.

He heard them laughing in the lounge, his precious babies and the woman who should have been his. As he sat there he knew, deep within him, that this was his fate. On the outside. In the cold. Needing to belong but not knowing how to bridge the gap between himself and happiness.

CHAPTER SIX

The cuckoo sprang out of its clock housing, forcing me to grit my teeth at the racket it made. I found it hard to believe that it was already five o'clock. The day had sped past as Tina and I worked our way through the busy Friday bookings. I was admitting by now that the girl had a flair for hairdressing and a natural talent for dealing with customers. When her work experience was over, I fully intended offering her Saturday and holiday work. Unless she reverted back to being a total slouch when Mags returned. If Mags returned.

I stacked that problem in the back of my mind for now, concentrating on the up-style I was doing for Viv Henderson – Lady Paircmoor as she was referred to locally. And with good reason. The Hendersons were Paircmoor royalty, controlling anything worth having in the area. They owned the garage, grocery shop, pub, hardware store, and the post office now run by the eldest Henderson daughter, in addition to a sizable farm where they raised cattle which ended up for sale in their butcher shop. In fact, I rented the salon from them. It had somehow become part of the leasing contract that I style the matriarch's hair every week.

Viv never offered money for my work and I always felt unable to ask.

I held the hand mirror up so that she could see the French plait I had done for her. As she patted her hair and preened, the door of the salon suddenly burst open. In the mirror I saw Minnie Curran rushing towards me. I twirled around.

"Minnie! Slow down! What's the matter?"

"*Look at me! Look at my scalp, at my forehead!*"

With a move as dramatic as her entrance, Minnie whipped the scarf from her head. The mirror slipped from my hand to crash onto the tiled floor. She had no need to shout. The scalp inflammation was apparent, even through her hair. I immediately linked it to the delayed colour treatment she had here yesterday. And so, obviously, did she. Her forehead also showed an angry red rash. The skin was glistening as if ointment had been applied. Had she been to a doctor? Was she building a case against me?

My stomach muscles contracted so violently I thought I would be sick all over her. I became aware that Tina was brushing shards of broken mirror into the dustpan. Harbinger of seven more years of blasted bad luck. I was annoyed with Mags for lathering Minnie's head with hair dye and then abandoning her. I was angrier at myself for not knowing if I had rinsed the dye out in the recommended time or not. I had been under pressure because of being short-staffed. That I knew. Had I left Minnie waiting so long with the dye in her hair that I burned her? Would my insurance cover me if it was my fault?

I was usually a strong woman, for me and for my family, but now my legs began to shake. Judging by the interested stares of Viv Henderson, the news would be all around the village in no time. With embellishments, of course. The truth in Paircmoor had magnetic qualities, attracting exaggerated and downright false particles of gossip to itself as it spread through the parish.

"What are you going to do about it, Leah?" Minnie demanded.

Yes, indeed. What was I going to do about it? Offer to pay medical expenses? That would be admitting liability. But then, again, I probably *was* liable.

"I'll be with you, Minnie, when I've finished with Viv. Tina, would you make a coffee for Mrs Curran, please?"

"Don't try to fob me off with coffee, Leah Parrish," Minnie said. "I'm not moving from here until you take responsibility for the damage you've caused."

Minnie seemed to have taken root so firmly in the middle of the salon that it would take an excavator to shift her.

"I don't mind waiting," Viv Henderson said.

I knew that much was true. She wanted all the gory details. I was not going to give her that satisfaction.

"Actually, there's no reason for you to stay, Viv," I said, removing the protective cape from around her shoulders. "You're done."

Viv stood reluctantly. As I walked towards the door with her, it opened from the outside. Ellen Riggs came in. The famous potter. The woman Ben often spoke about. His school-run friend. Tall and willowy, she had magnificent hair framing a face best described as perfect. Ellen herself was a work of art, beautifully presented in designer clothes. Even though Ben had not admitted his infatuation with this paragon of feminine appeal, I knew instinctively she was special to him.

"Have I come at a bad time?" she asked as she looked around at Tina with dustpan in hand, Minnie Curran and her multi-coloured forehead and scalp, me attempting to steer Viv Henderson out the door.

"Not at all, Ellen. I'll be with you now. We're not taking any more appointments today though."

"That's alright. This is a personal visit, not business."

My stomach lurched again. Given the direction the day had taken, whatever brought Ellen Riggs here was bound to be negative.

Viv Henderson was still standing by the door. Listening. I was getting to the stage where I would gladly kick her out.

"Take a seat Ellen, please. Viv, good evening. I'll see you again next week."

"I don't know about that," she said, as she and her free French plait sailed off.

I closed the door and leaned against it for a moment. Just long enough to ease the ache in my lower back and to do what I always did in times of crisis. I called on my mother to help me. A long-distance call to wherever the energy that had been Mam was resting. Cancer had ended her journey here, but nothing, not even death, could break our bond. I briefly closed my eyes and drew on her strength.

The tinkle of broken mirror being tipped into the bin galvanised me into action. It seemed to have an effect on Ellen also as she stood and walked towards me. She was carrying a bag. It was tied with cream-silk ribbon and had a ceramic scarlet poppy flower stuck in the middle of the bow. Very beautiful and artistic just like the woman carrying it. I felt compelled to note every detail as she stood in front of me. As if this was a moment I would remember forever. I shrugged off the ridiculous thought.

"What can I do for you, Ellen?"

"I called to let you know that Finn and I are leaving. We're going back to London."

At least this was one problem solved. I would not have to worry about my husband making an idiot of himself over Ellen Riggs and her ethereal beauty. I checked my expression to be sure it was suitably regretful.

"We'll be sorry to see you go, Ellen. Especially Rob. He will miss Finn. When do you leave?"

"Tomorrow. We made a quick decision. Just like Ben."

It happened again, the nausea and the shaking legs. What in the hell was she talking about?

"Like Ben. What do you mean?"

She took a step closer to me.

Minnie Curran took a step closer to us both.

"He told me about America. About the opportunities there. I hope it works out for all of you. This gift is to say thanks to your family for your kindness to Finn and me. Good luck with your move."

She handed me the bag with the silk ribbon and, without seeming to rush, she left the salon in a flash. But not as quickly as it took Minnie Curran to reach me.

"No wonder you don't care about the damage you've done to me," she said. "Don't think I'll let you run off to the States scot free. You'll pay for what you've done, Leah Parrish!"

Then with far less elegance than Ellen, Minnie flounced out the door, forgetting her scarf.

I felt weighed down with questions. What had Ben told Ellen about the job offer in California? Was he seriously considering leaving here to dance to his mother's tune on another continent? Without even discussing it with me. What about us, me and the children? And was Minnie Curran really threatening legal action?

I managed to get my jelly-like legs to walk me to a chair. I eased onto it and began to shake. My head, too full of panic and unanswered questions, bowed down. I heard Tina moving around in the kitchenette. I had forgotten about her. I was just about to tell her to go home when she came towards me, a mug of coffee in her hand. My mug. My Stephen Pearce. She handed it to me.

"Drink that up, Mrs Parrish, while I talk to you."

I muttered my thanks and did as I was told. It was like we had reversed roles and Tina was the adult while I was a vulnerable teenager.

She pulled up a chair and sat beside me.

"I have something to tell you," she said.

No! Not Tina too. Not another kick in the backside.

I nodded to her to continue.

"You know I'll be assessed on my work experience when I go back to class."

"Right."

"So, the point is, I've been taking notes so that I don't forget any details."

"Yes. Go on."

"Remember you changed supplier for dye products? It was Mags' first time using that brand, so she carried out patch tests before she used it on anyone. Including Mrs Curran."

I sat up a little straighter. I should have remembered this. I had instructed Mags to test all clients for allergic reactions before using the new brand. It was just a dab of the product behind the ear and a twenty-four hour wait to see if any adverse reaction developed. Unfortunately, I did not follow up with Mags. I had trusted her to tell me if there was any problem.

"And? When did she test Minnie?

"Last week when Mrs Curran was here for a wash and blow-dry. The result was negative. No rash. No itch or redness. Mrs Curran herself said so. Look, she made a note in the ledger you keep for client hair-dye mixes."

I looked at the page she held open. Sure enough, there was the information, dated and signed. Better still, Tina switched on her phone and showed me a photograph she had taken of Mags applying the patch test.

I took a sip of coffee and felt its warmth trickle through me.

"I did ask Mrs Curran's permission to take the photograph," Tina said as if I had objected. "I explained to her that I would have to do a presentation when I went back to school."

So, Mags and Tina could both testify that Minnie herself was satisfied she was not allergic to the dye. The blame was still down to me. I must have left it on too long.

"Would you know, Tina, how long the dye was on Minnie's roots?"

"You had the timer on. My memory is that you rinsed her off when the alarm sounded. Sorry, I was too busy to log anything. But does it matter? She's not allergic to it anyway and Mags can confirm that."

I nodded. That was true. What happened to Minnie's scalp and forehead then? Yes, it was good that the skin test had been done but there was still a problem to be faced. I would have to ring my insurance company for advice on handling the situation. Or maybe not. Not until the situation was clearer. Just what I needed. Yet another problem.

Tina was watching me, solemn-faced.

I smiled at her.

"Thank you, Tina. You've been a great help. I appreciate it very much."

"That's nice of you to say, Mrs Parrish."

"Call me Leah, please. Off home now. And I don't want you worrying about this, Tina. It's my responsibility to sort it."

I could see her shoulders relax with relief.

When she had left I continued to sit there, finishing my coffee and trying to get control of the panic welling up inside me.

I opened the bag Ellen had given me. Inside, nestling in swathes of pale-lavender tissue, was an exquisite vase. An Ellen Riggs piece. I knew from reading about her work how valuable this must be. Precious, just like I suspected she was to my husband.

With huge effort I got myself out of the chair and prepared to face home. This was it. No more procrastinating. Tonight, when the children were in bed, Ben and I had to sit down and talk.

About America.

About Ellen Riggs.

About the most important thing of all.

CHAPTER SEVEN

Ben was alone in the kitchen while Leah put the children to bed. Her nightly maternal duty. She had left Ellen's vase on the countertop in the kitchen, in between the toaster and the breadboard. Careless. He picked the vase up and placed it in the centre of the table. He sat in front of it, sipping his tea and absorbing every detail of the artwork. Ellen hand-painted her pottery before glazing and giving it the final firing. She had told him about the process. And about her love of the poppy flower because of its vibrancy and the daisy because of the smile on its face.

As he examined her work, he knew she had made this specifically to remind him of the conversations they had about wild flowers and arts and crafts and life and death. They had spoken about everything as they waited outside the school gates. Except of course, her marriage to the tit-and-bum surgeon and his to Leah. Ellen had been cold today. She blatantly did not feel the sadness of their parting. She had actually offered him a handshake when they said goodbye for the last time outside the school gates. As if they were nothing more than business partners. But he had to accept that anything else, such as a kiss, would have been inappropriate. He reached out and touched one of the scarlet poppies. He imagined the concentration on Ellen's face as she had painted it, the –

"What in the hell was Ellen Riggs doing in here today? Anna has just told me she read a story for them. Why didn't you say?"

He looked from the beautiful vase to Leah. She was glaring at him. He shrugged. What could he say? That his precious time with Ellen was none of his wife's business.

"She just called to tell us she's leaving. Pity."

"A pity? Why?"

Ben put his arms on the table and laid his head on them. He squeezed his eyes shut. Inky darkness settled around him. He allowed himself to hide inside it for one healing moment. But Leah's voice pierced his protective cover. She was small, but her voice was not.

"Why did you tell Ellen about the States when we've not even discussed it? Where did she get the idea that you're all ready to go? Apparently I'm emigrating too. And the children. Did it just slip your mind to tell me? Ben! Talk to me!"

She was standing over him now. He could hear her intake of breath between sentences, the bracelets she wore clinking against each other as she gesticulated. That was Leah. Always talking. Always waving her hands about.

"Ben, would you please lift your head and look at me. If the children behaved like this, I would put them in the bold corner."

He tried not to be angry with her, to admit to himself that Leah was his reality while Ellen had been his fantasy. And that there was no escape. He opened his eyes and slowly lifted his head.

"I *am* in the fucking bold boys' corner," he said. "It's where I live."

"Stop feeling sorry for yourself and answer my question."

"Okay, there's a job waiting for me in San Francisco pending a meeting with Piper's brother. So what do you say to that?"

She was silent. No criticism. No terse order. But there was reaction. He saw it in her eyes.

"We did tell you last night. Why the shock?"

"Of course I'm shocked, Ben! It sounds as if it's a done deal. You and Cruella plotting together and –"

"*Don't* talk about my mother like that. We need help and she's giving it to us."

"How? By splitting us up? Is she moving to California with her two sons and her socially acceptable daughter-in-law? What about our children, Ben?"

"Shit, Leah! This *is* for the children. What future do you think they'll have here? And you're being unfair yet again. My mother idolises the children. She would never do anything to harm them."

Ben stood to face Leah. She hovered as if not sure of what to do next. He frowned. Suddenly this vulnerable woman bore little resemblance to his self-assured wife. She bowed her head but not before he saw a lone tear trickle down her face. He put his arms around her.

"Don't cry, Leah. Please don't cry."

As he held her close he felt her body shake with sobs. He stroked her hair and rocked her gently, as if she were one of the children in need of comfort.

"You'll see," he murmured. "It will all work out for the best. The children are young enough to relocate without difficulty at this stage. They'll adapt really quickly and –"

She pulled abruptly away from him. The Leah look was back on her face. Disdain, anger and behind it all a deep disappointment. Her eyes were red-rimmed, tears glistened on her cheeks, but yet she was ready to lash him with her disapproval.

"What about Rob? He's just settling into school here and you want to drag him away. The twins are booked into kindergarten for next year. And my business. What about that? I've worked my butt off to build the salon up so that we can at least eat, and you dismiss it without a thought. You certainly inherited your mother's arrogance."

Ben shook his head as he stared at her. When had she become a harridan and he a . . . ? What was he now? A failed husband and father? An unemployment statistic. A doormat.

Leah was still ranting on, picking relentlessly at the last of his self-esteem. He was gripped by an urge to hit her, to land his fist on her mouth. Shocked by the force of his anger, he walked back until she was out of range of his already clenched fist.

"*Shut the fuck up!*" he heard himself shout.

Leah stopped talking. She looked terrified. Ben, bile rising up his throat in self-disgust, took a step towards her. She backed away.

"*Don't come near me! I'm warning you!*"

He stood still as she backed even further away.

"Give me a break, Leah! I apologise for shouting but, Christ Almighty, you never listen to a word I say. You organise me like I'm one of the children. Can't you see I'm suffocating here in Paircmoor? There's no –" He fell silent mid-sentence when he saw the kitchen door slowly open.

Rob's head, all tousled hair and sleepy eyes, peeped

around the door. As the child stepped into the room, he held his tattered security blanket in front of him like a protective shield. His bottom lip was quivering. Leah turned and held her arms open to their son. He ran to her and clung on.

"I heard shouts and bad words, Mom," he said. "I'm afraid."

Ben took a step forward to comfort his son, to explain. Leah glared at him over the child's head. There were no words spoken. They were not needed. Anger shone from her eyes, warning him to keep his distance. She turned and walked away with Rob, crooning softly to him, telling him Mom and Dad were just playing a silly game. The kitchen door swung shut and he could hear them no more.

The walls of the kitchen, the overhead beams, the counter, the sink, the stove, presses with cereals and ware, the kit and caboodle of everyday living, all began to bear down on Ben. He was dizzy, breathless, his heart thumping so loudly the sound seemed to fill the room. The beams spun until they were on the floor and the stove on the ceiling. Imprinted on everything was the image of Rob, his dark eyes filled with fear, his little chest heaving with sobs. Even as the words of apology and regret formed in Ben's mind, he knew Rob – gentle, sensitive Rob – would never forgive him and he could never forgive himself. Leah would make sure of that.

He picked up Ellen's vase from the table in an effort to get comfort from the beauty of the piece. There was none to be had. Ellen was just like the vase, beautiful on the outside, shallow inside. Reaching his arm back, he flung the vase as hard as he could against the feature brick wall around the stove. The crack of shattering ceramic steadied the spinning images in his mind and forced a gulp of air into his lungs.

He strode out into the hall, through the front door and into the dark of the night.

I sat at the side of Rob's bed with him on my lap, gently stroking his back, feeling the heat of his body through the fabric of his Batman pyjamas. My shoulder was damp from his tears.

"I was so afraid, Mom. Why did you and Dad play such a cross game?"

Why indeed? I had seen a new side to Ben tonight. A vicious, aggressive side. The cross game had frightened me too. I laid my chin on top of my son's head and encircled him in my arms.

"It was a mistake, Rob. It was a silly game and we will never play it again."

"Dad said a bad word. I heard him."

"Then he can't watch TV for two nights. That will teach him –"

There was a loud crash. The explosive crackle of ware smashing. Rob stiffened in my arms. Jesus! Had Ben lost his reason? The smash was quickly followed by the sound of the front door opening and banging shut. Rob was shaking.

"What's happening, Mom? Is an ogre coming into our house?"

His dark eyes were glistening with tears again, skinny little arms latched on around my neck as he clung tight. At that moment I felt a surge of hate for Ben as strong as my protective instinct for my son.

"No, Rob. Ogres are only in stories. They don't really exist. Your dad must have dropped his cup on the floor when he was putting it in the dishwasher. You know what a loud bang that would make on the tiles. He's just gone out now to put the pieces in the bin."

"Oh!"

Lies, lies, lies. I hated lying to him but what was I to tell him? He wriggled in my arms as he lifted his right hand and stuck his thumb into his mouth. He had not done that for two years now. There had been a time when I thought he would graduate from university with his thumb in his mouth. I felt his body relax as he sucked and I was glad he was finding comfort. Gently, I laid him on his bed and tucked him in. I continued to stroke his hair until his eyes closed and his breathing was deep and even.

I kissed him softly on the forehead and tiptoed out of his room.

The kitchen door was closed. The bang had been so loud, I knew something must have been hurled with force. The sound had reverberated with angry energy. What in the hell had he done?

I took a deep breath and opened the door. The floor around the stove was strewn with shards of painted poppies and daisies.

I stared at the remnants of the beautiful artefact. Like a shaman casting bones, I read my fortune in the shattered pieces. There the shard of scarlet poppy represented Ellen Riggs, here the sunshine heart of a daisy, the children. And the rest, the splintered and sharp bits were Ben and me, our past, our future, hurled against a brick wall and destroyed.

I shivered, then got the dustpan and brush and began the clean-up.

CHAPTER EIGHT

Not a sliver of moonlight or starshine pierced the heavy cloud cover. The sky was black, black, black. Even the air was dense, heavy, as Ben tried to draw it into his lungs. Out of the darkness a sudden gust of wind swirled, bringing with it rain.

He shivered. He had been in such a hurry to leave Cowslip Cottage behind that he had come out without a jacket. The rain soaked into his T-shirt and the wind slapped icy drops into his face. His T-shirt was white. Like a flag of surrender, waving as he walked towards the sea. Away from Paircmoor. Away from his family.

Five kilometres. That's how far he was from the coast.

He upped his pace, pushing against the wind and rain. The night got even darker as the road narrowed. The trees on either side meshed branches overhead to form a tunnel. They creaked and groaned as he passed underneath and occasionally dumped sprays of rainwater onto his head. He stood and shook his fist at the leafy arch.

"*Go on! Piss on me. Everyone else does!*"

The sound of his own voice came back to him out of the darkness. He laughed. Out loud. Hysterically. Then he began to cry. How had Ben Parrish ended up standing on this godforsaken road, drenched, frozen and in despair, threatening trees with physical violence? It was a nightmare. He had never lost his job. Of course not. He had worked too hard, been too talented to be thrown on the scrapheap. And he could not be living in the arsehole of the country, in a house he didn't like and couldn't afford to renovate. A has-been before he had really begun.

He started to run. His lungs hurt as he gulped breaths of the winter storm, his muscles ached, his heart thumped. He focused on reaching the end of the tree tunnel. That would be where he could leave the nightmare behind and stride into reality. His real life. His meaningful, successful life. He rounded a bend, one he knew well from driving the children to the beach. He was warmed for an instant by an image of that day when Ellen had come too and they had sat side by side on a rug and watched over the children playing in the sand. Ahead of him the trees still entwined branches over the road. The tunnel must end soon. Then everything would be alright.

The road widened and there were no more trees. Nor was there, Ben admitted, any new reality. The helplessness, the grieving for opportunities lost, the bitter taste of failure, were still burrowed into the very essence of his soul. This was it. His life.

He kept running. A car came against him, slowed then stopped. It was a silver saloon, driven by an elderly man of the helpful stranger variety. He lowered the driver's window.

"Bad night," he said. "Are you alright?"

"I'm fine, thank you," Ben told the Good Samaritan. "Just doing some marathon training."

He continued running towards the sea. To where he

knew with certainty he would find a solution to his problems.

One way or another.

Just as he thought he would never reach the coast, Ben caught a waft of brine on the wind and heard the rumble of restless tide. He knew if he continued on the main road it would take him towards the bleak Pouldubh Head. Instead he took the turn to his left, down a by-road, which brought him towards the beach. Tarmacadam soon gave way to gravel path. He stopped to catch his breath, leaning over, hands on knees. A dog barked and before he could straighten up, it came running at him out of the dark. He backed slowly away, afraid to make any sudden moves.

"*Pilot! Come here! You bad boy!*"

A woman, leash in hand came rushing forward, grabbing the dog by the collar.

"I'm so sorry," she said. "He's not used to seeing people out here this time of night. He won't bite you. He just likes to make a lot of noise."

She reached into her pocket, pulled out a torch and shone it on the dog. Ben almost laughed out loud. He had anticipated seeing at least a snarling Alsatian, teeth bared. Instead a Shih Tzu wearing a blue ribbon in its hair bounced on its legs as it continued the loud barking.

"Not to worry," Ben said. "I'm fine."

"All the same you must have got a fright. Would you like a cup of tea? Vera Sanquest is my name. I live in Cliff House, just over there." She pointed to her left.

"I'm good, thank you," he answered, deliberately withholding his own name, not sure whether this Vera was being nice or nosey.

Ben knew the house to see. It was the only one so near

the cliff edge. Ellen had speculated on whether it would fall into the sea in five years' time. Or two if coastal erosion continued as it was going.

"Well then, I had better take Pilot home. Looks like it's going to be a very bad night. Are you sure you're alright? Do you have far to go?"

"No, not far. Goodnight."

He walked back towards the road – the Paircmoor Road – and stood in the darkness until the circle of light from the Vera Sanquest's torch disappeared into Cliff House and she shut her front door. Then he headed back to the sea.

The cliff path sloped gently to the shore. Safe and comfortable to walk in the daylight but it was neither as Ben slid his way down in the pitch dark, the sound of surf pounding in his ears. Occasional flashes of white streaked the darkness as foam-crested waves rushed to shore and a buoy flashed intermittently far out to sea. He could easily lose his footing, batter his head against rocks, tumble into the sea below. Risks he was willing to take in order to reach his goal. Somewhere along the road from Cowslip Cottage, it had become urgent for him to find the cave he, Ellen and the children had explored on that precious day they had spent together on the beach.

Almost down to the beach, he discerned the rhythmic scrape of pebble and shell being sucked back into the powerful undertow. Fine spray misted his face. He licked his lips and tasted salt. He was shivering uncontrollably, the chilling wind seeming to blow right through him. He was cold to his core. Maybe he should have accepted that woman's offer of a cup of tea. A heat by her fire before setting off back home. Not home. That had been in Dublin.

Before it had been sold to an investor. Before it was subdivided into apartments and let out to students. Before Cowslip Cottage. And what would he tell the woman in Cliff House when she asked who he was, what he did, why he was out in a storm half-dressed, half frozen to death?

He stood still. A short flight of steps led from the cliff path onto the strand. He squinted his eyes and peered down. Stilled his breathing and listened intently. Was the tide incoming or ebbing? He knew he would have to turn left at the bottom of the steps and walk along under the cliff face for a minute or so before he could reach the cave. What if he got trapped by this raging tide and was dragged out to sea underneath tons of heaving water? Just when the possibility of a job with Zach Milburg offered the first glimmer of hope since his redundancy.

It seemed to him at that moment, poised between the security of dry land and the threat of a lawless sea, between unemployment and the hope of a new start in America, that he was already trapped by fate. He had missed every goal he had aimed for. Why should working for Zach Milburg be any different? Mum would champion his cause. So would Hugh, not because he cared about Ben but because Mum told him to. But Leah. She would dig her heels in. Against all the odds, a city girl born and bred, Leah was rooted in Paircmoor and was making sure the children were too. And yes, they had talked about moving here and he had agreed. But Paircmoor was just meant to be a breathing space. A place to lick wounds and heal. He had not anticipated a burying alive. He was drained by failure. Reaching the cave could be his last challenge and, by Christ, he was going to achieve it. He grabbed the handrail and put his right foot into the void.

Six minutes later, Ben found the cave. It had taken courage to walk that short distance, at one stage a wave washing over his feet as it bullied its way further inshore. He flopped onto a rock inside the cave and got control of his breathing. The coldness of the cave crept into his bones but at least he was sheltered from the biting wind. He heard a drip and remembered seeing fresh water from the clifftop seeping in when he had been here with the children. And Ellen. They had all called their names out loud, just to hear them echoing from the depths of the cave. It was hollowed out far back into the cliff, the roof getting progressively lower. They had stayed at the front, exploring the rock pools and finding little fish darting about. Gobies, Ellen had said. She had an encyclopaedic knowledge of nature. And a wonderful laugh. And a fuck-off, fabulously successful, husband. Why had he ever thought she could have been interested in a has-been architect with a wife, three children and no prospects?

He stood and stretched, his raised arms almost tipping the roof of the cave, wondering if bats were hanging there, sensing his presence. Could they feel his fear and know he was too destroyed by life to be a threat to them? The dark of the night seeped into the blackness in his mind, his heart, his soul. His arms dropped to his sides, forced down by the weight of despair. He recognised that this was his nadir. He was scraping the very depths of – of – of what? Depression, self-pity, or like Leah always said, selfishness?

A wave crashed onto the rocks a few feet away. A semi-circle of foam pushed into the cave. The tide was incoming. At a fast pace. In a short time he would be trapped here. Until the tide swept him out to sea. Until it filled his lungs with water and fed his remains to hungry fish. And it would all be over then – the constant feeling of inadequacy, the permanent knot of sadness in his throat, the dashed hopes, the rejections. All the unbearable things he had to battle every day. What were a few moments of panic and pain compared to the prospect of eternal peace from all that torment? Never again to dread waking to another day, to see the look of pity in peoples' eyes . . .

Never to see the children again. Not Rob, solemn and calm. So in need of protection. Not Josh, the sensitive little man. And Anna, precious Anna. A mini-Leah, feisty and full of energy. He tried to imagine how they would be without him. He was their main carer, their cook and chauffeur. They would miss him for a while and then they would forget him. Leah was young and attractive. She would remarry and the children would have a new daddy. A man to pick them up when they fell and cuddle them when they were afraid. Someone they could look up to, who would provide them with opportunities in life. Someone like Hugh. The successful brother.

A sob escaped him. He turned to look back into the cave but it was too dark to know if he could shelter safely there until the tide went out. And if he should even try. Perhaps his subconscious intention in coming here had been to throw himself at the mercy of the sea, and not, as he had told himself, to relive the day he had shared with Ellen. He thought he saw her emerge from the darkness. He blinked and she was gone. Back to her husband.

A huge wave crashed against the mouth of the cave. Now the decision was out of his hands. Water rushed in and washed over his feet. He felt so tired it was difficult to stand. He tried to take some deep breaths but his lungs continued to make shallow grabs for air. Numb feet made wading to the opening even more difficult. He stood at the mouth of the cave. To left, right and ahead, he was surrounded by heaving sea. The water was reaching for him, imposing its rhythm of ebb and flow on his breathing. On his thoughts. On his memories of a life begun in privilege and ending in disaster.

He walked into the back of the cave and found his rock. He sat and wrapped his arms around himself. Made no difference. He was already deathly cold. He began to feel drowsy and knew he must be hypothermic, that he should try moving to warm himself. He did not.

Ben Parrish closed his eyes and allowed the sounds of the wind and sea fill his head. Somewhere in the confused noise he thought he heard his mother call, reminding him that she had bought an air ticket to California for him and that she would ensure Zach Milburg offered him a job. Charity. Pity. Mum had not yet realised that successful entrepreneurs, especially of the billionaire variety, don't do pity.

He was too cold, too wet, too weary, too sad.

Too broken to fix.

Another wave lashed into the cave mouth.

CHAPTER NINE

The children's clothes were washed and hanging on the airer, salon towels in the dryer, dishwasher unloaded and the table set for breakfast in the morning. Next I had to make Rob's school lunch and mine for tomorrow. All the time I was working, I cursed Ben Parrish for his selfishness, his lack of character. The depth of my anger against him shook me. Yes, Ben had frightened me tonight but I could cope. Rob could not. I would not forgive him for terrifying our child.

School lunch made, I took the towels from the dryer and rolled them, ready for the salon in the morning. That brought my attention back to the problem with Minnie Curran and her allergic reaction. I had no doubt her spotted scalp and forehead were the talk of the village by now. I had intended asking Ben to contact his college friend, Joe, a solicitor, for some legal advice. All I could hope was that the evidence of the skin test being done would save me if Minnie brought a case against me. If not, I might as well close the doors of the salon immediately.

That thought made me ashamed. I was not a quitter. My children needed me to be strong for them. I went to their rooms and watched them as they slept: Rob curled up, still clutching his security blanket, Anna limbs sprawled outside her duvet, restless, Josh lying still on his sturdy little back. I was as bowed down by my responsibility to guide them into adulthood, as I was buoyed by my love for them. I gently closed their doors and left them to their dreams.

Going back to the now orderly kitchen, I put a mug of milk in the microwave to heat. My usual bedtime drink. Ben always had tea. Ben. He didn't seem to need as much sleep as I did. He always stayed up longer than I did. Doing work on his computer, he said. So what was the relationship between him and Ellen Riggs? Was this disgraceful tantrum because Ellen was leaving? Had he been having an affair with her? I shrugged off the idea. Logistics wouldn't allow for clandestine meetings and romantic trysts. Ben's day was totally taken up with minding the children. Other than a very occasional trip to see his mother in Dublin, he didn't go out in the evenings. How telling that I believed Ben was not having an affair, simply because he could not fit it into his schedule.

I took my hot milk to the counter and sat on a stool. First chance to relax since I got home. I was bone weary, my back aching even more than usual. Not good. Nor was the slight swelling in my ankles and hands. I should see the doctor. And talk to Ben, whether I wanted to or not. It was past time.

My phone was on the counter. I glanced at it and was startled to see that it was already after ten o'clock. I hadn't noticed how late it was getting. It must have been around eight when Ben left. Where in the hell was he for that length of time? He couldn't be with friends because he didn't have any. The bald fact was that he had made no effort to integrate.

Admittedly, trying to gain acceptance in Paircmoor was not easy. The indigenous population cherished their history, their generations-long links with the area. Their inalienable right to belong on the inside of the invisible wall they built, while blow-ins were consigned to the outside. I understood that. I also understood that he must be missing his old life. Like golf and theatre nights and dining out. But tough! I missed many things too because we could no longer afford them. The so-called friendships we had in the city had been shallow. No doubt about that. Even when we had still been in Dublin, the invitations to events had fallen off dramatically after Ben had been made redundant. Maybe people were being considerate, knowing we could no longer afford a social life. Or else they could not face the whiff of desperation surrounding both me and Ben as the national economic crisis deepened, hope of Ben getting another job faded, and finally the possibility of losing our Dublin home became reality. To her credit, his mother stepped in and paid the mortgage until we had sold our home and paid off the bank debt. Our house had been bought by an investor friend of hers. Putting us even more in her debt. And yes, much to my shame, I should be more grateful to Della.

I checked my phone again. I had no missed call from Ben. No text. So why was I sitting here, my thoughts getting more and more bitter, when I should be trying to find out where he had flounced off to. I went to the front door and opened it. It was a pitch-black night. I flicked on the outside light and saw that it was teeming with rain and the trees tossed in a strong gale. I hadn't realised how stormy it had become.

The car and jeep were both parked where we had left

them. I grabbed my coat and ran to the jeep. It was empty. No Ben sulking in the driver's seat or sprawled out asleep in the back between the baby seats. He was not in my car either.

I ran back in and checked his jackets in the hall closet. They were all there. Was he sheltering somewhere from the rain? Unlikely that he had gone for a walk or a run on a night like this. He didn't exercise much anymore. But then what did I know? The man who had thrown the exquisite vase with such violence, and shouted so aggressively at me, was not the Ben I knew. Unless. Unless I was completely wrong about his relationship with Ellen. Maybe he was going to London with her. Only one way to find out.

I pressed Ben's quick-dial number. His phone rang in the lounge. How stupid of me! I had assumed he was not in the house. Of course he was here, probably snoring on the couch. I hurried to the lounge. It was in darkness. I turned on the lamp. His phone was on the coffee table, the missed call message glowing on-screen, his house keys sitting beside it. But Ben was not there. I ran then from room to room, getting increasingly more panicky. It did not take long to realise that he was not in Cowslip Cottage.

In the kitchen I scrolled through my contact list. Who in the name of God could I ring? I hesitated at Della's number. His mother would know where he was. She was probably directing his every move. Except that she was most likely landed in California by now. I moved on to Ellen's number. It was in my phone because of the friendship between Rob and Finn. We had swapped numbers just in case either child needed their mom in a hurry. Ironic that I wanted to contact her now because my husband might have needed Ellen too. The thought of the affair that I had dismissed so glibly gained traction by the second. I had been wrong in thinking Ben had no friends here. He had Ellen Riggs in all her blasted perfection. I was the friendless one. Mags Hoey would come closest but, if she was not an employee, we probably would not have any contact.

I pressed the phone icon and suddenly realised I didn't know what to say to Ellen. I could hardly ask if my husband was in bed with her or if he was about to run away with her. Her voicemail came on, with a '*Sorry, I am busy but please leave a message*' greeting. I ended the call. I was pretty sure in that moment that she was busy with my husband. Then I immediately rang again. And again. Still nothing but that generic voicemail.

I stood there, paralysed with guilt. Every working day I allotted myself play time with the children, laundry time, food prep for next day and a precious thirty minutes with a mug of hot milk and some TV before bed. I had never thought of Ben time. Or Ben and Leah time. Sundays and Mondays, my days off, were set aside for family outings and house-cleaning. On my orders. Ben was right. I put him in the same category as the children. Organising his time, telling him what to do and how to do it. Never asking how he was coping. Having no interest in his scale-model scheme which I assumed to be a ridiculous waste of time. Not caring as long as it was not costing too much money. No wonder his head was turned by Ellen Riggs. My milk sat on the counter untouched, slowly developing a crinkly skin on top as it cooled.

If I had tried harder to understand Ben's frustrations, we might not be in this situation. I shook with fear at maybe having to face the future on my own, but also with an all-consuming anger at his selfishness for putting me through yet more worry. I wanted to sit down and cry but where would that get me? And what if I was wrong and Ben was not with Ellen? He could be in trouble, lying injured on the road, the rain pouring down on top of his broken body. Should I ring the gardaí? I could imagine how that conversation would go when I told them he had been missing just over two hours. How pathetic would I look when they found him with his girlfriend, arms around each other, all ready for a shining new life together?

Ben had been right about one thing. Cowslip Cottage was in a bleak and isolated area. No neighbours nearby to hop over and mind the children while I searched for him. No one to offer advice and support.

I turned to Mam then and cursed her roundly for dying. I needed her more than ever but she was off doing her afterlife thing in heaven or in nothingness. Like a possessed woman, I begged her out loud to give me a sign, anything, a feather floating through the air, a whisper of a breeze across my face. Anything just to let me know that she was still looking after me.

My phone rang. Ellen's name flashed on the screen. Mam had given me my sign. I stood and stared, wanting so much to grab the phone but terrified to hear what she had to say.

At least I would know.

One way or another.

CHAPTER TEN

Vera Sanquest opened the front door of Cliff House when she saw the lights of her husband's car approach. She waited impatiently in the hall for him to park and lock the car. No point in trying to get him to hurry. Walter Sanquest was not for rushing. She pulled her cardigan more tightly around her as she waited. It was a vicious night with cold rain, swept by swirling winds. Typical for November.

"What kept you so long?" she demanded as Walter walked to the door. "You said you were going into Paircmoor just for milk. Did you have to milk a cow yourself?"

"I met John Sweeney and went for a pint with him. So what? And don't bother with your drink-driving lecture. It was only one pint."

"Never mind that now. There's a man. A young man. He went away and came back again and I haven't seen him come up the path. I was just about to ring the Coast Guard."

He stood looking at her in puzzlement.

"I haven't a notion what you're talking about, Vera. Come in out of the cold and shut the door. All the heat will be going out and the price of oil is gone up. Again."

She blocked his way as he made to step inside.

"Listen to me, Walter. I met this man when I was walking the dog. He looked troubled. He had no coat. I asked him to come in for a cup of tea but he refused."

"Jesus! You invited him in, not knowing who he was! That's dangerous, Vera!"

"Will you stop interrupting? He pretended to walk towards Paircmoor Road but when I came into the house, I saw him come back and head down the cliff path to the strand. He hasn't come back up. Now, do you understand?"

"Oh! How long ago was this?"

"I'd say maybe an hour and a half. And before you ask, I've been on the lookout all the time and there's been no sign of him since."

"How do you know? It's a pitch-dark night. How could you see him from here?"

"He was wearing a white T-shirt. I was just about able to see him going down to the cliff path. I would have gone and called him but you know I'm nervous when the tide is in. Especially in a storm."

Walter wasn't listening to her. He was remembering the young man he had met on the Paircmoor road. Wearing a white T-shirt in the lashing rain, breathless and slightly manic. He had stopped to ask if he was alright but had pegged him as one of those fitness fanatics who thought it healthy to push your body to its limits and beyond.

Walter nodded. Yes, that must be the man he met. He cocked his head, with his good ear, the left one, turned in the direction of the sea.

"Tide's turned," he said. "It's on the way out now. I'll get a torch and boots and go have a look below on the strand."

Vera sighed. She had been afraid this would happen. Many years ago, when they had both been young and strong and the children had filled Cliff House with their energy and love of life, Walter had rescued a family trapped by high tide in the infamous pirate cave on the strand. He had lived in hope since of a repeat performance.

"Walter Sanquest, you silly old man! Don't even think of being a have-a-go-hero! That day is gone. I'll ring the Coast Guard now."

She was talking to his back. He was already heading for the shed where he kept his boots and waterproof coat. She went back into the house and tucked Pilot into his basket by the kitchen stove. In the utility room she put on her coat and boots. They were still wet from her walk with Pilot but that didn't matter once they were dry on the inside. She pulled on her woolly hat, put her phone into her pocket, got her torch, then went out and closed the front door behind her.

Outside the gate, she stood for a moment. A beam of light wavering below her told her Walter was almost at the cliff path. She said a silent prayer to her angel to keep them both safe and to the disturbed young man's angel to bring him peace. Wherever he was.

Then she switched on her torch and followed her husband.

I was shaking as I picked up my phone to answer Ellen Riggs' call. I had planned on exactly what to say. How to ask questions without sounding desperate. Or angry. Now, as I heard Ellen's cultured tones, words failed me.

"Leah? This is Ellen. How may I help you?"

How about sending my husband home, you patronising bitch? How about you just feic off to London and never come near my family again?

I had to breathe deeply in order to bury my angry thoughts.

"This *is* Leah, isn't it? Speak to me or I will cut the call now."

Shit! She thought I was a heavy breather. And I was, because I was smothered with panic. Words began to escape me. I tried in vain to make them sound sensible.

"Sorry for ringing you so late at night, Ellen. It's just that I was wondering if . . . Could you tell me . . . Have you . . ."

"Leah! Whatever is the matter? Just calm down."

"Sorry. Sorry. It's Ben."

"Ben? What's happened? Has he had an accident?"

I hesitated again, wondering if Ellen was playing a clever game of bluff or if she was as genuinely puzzled as she sounded. The thought entered my mind that I should be grateful if he was safely with Ellen rather than involved in an accident. I pushed the silly idea away. I was nowhere near being so kind-spirited. Only one way to find out.

"Is he with you, Ellen?"

There was silence. It spoke volumes to me. I imagined them in bed, Ellen propped up by pillows, wearing a silk negligee, her phone on speaker so that Ben, lying beside her, could listen in. She would look at him, an eyebrow arched, a smile on her lips. They would both supress a laugh as they listened to the dreary old wife. The abandoned one. The one who had never been good enough.

"I don't understand, Leah. Why would your husband be with me?"

"Because I don't know where else he would be. He doesn't know many people here and I think he's upset about you leaving. You didn't answer my question. Is he with you now?"

There was no silence this time. Her words came strong and clear.

"He most certainly is *not.*"

The disdain in her voice told me that Ben had never stood a chance with her. He was not in her league any more than I was in his.

"I'm sorry you and Ben seem to be having some difficulties, Leah, but I must be up early in the morning to catch a flight. I hope you find your husband soon. Goodnight."

I held my phone in my hand for several minutes after she had cut off my call. I could hear rain lash against the window panes and the high-pitched whirr of the gale down the chimney. The possibility that Ben was out in the storm, with no coat or hat, was fast becoming a probability. I thought again about ringing the gardaí. The call would have to be transferred to the barracks in our nearest town, twenty kilometres away. The local station in Paircmoor had been closed long before we moved here. They would probably tell me ring back in the morning. I would not expect them to send a patrol car all that way to search for someone who could not yet be officially listed as missing.

I put the kettle on to make coffee. I would not sleep tonight anyway and my brain needed the caffeine boost. I heaped two spoons of instant into my mug and took a sip of the dark brew, feeling energy surging through me. Now I could make a plan. I wanted to jump in my car, go out and search the village, the woods, the highways and byways for Ben. To find him huddled underneath a hedge, or maybe in one of the ruined cottages which peppered the Paircmoor landscape. I would put my arms around him and tell him I loved him. A good plan except that I could not follow it through because of the children.

I paced the kitchen, trying to impose some logic on my thinking. Ben had left here with no coat, no phone, no key.

That meant he intended being gone just a short time. Or it could mean he had somewhere to go for the night. Or that he had no intention of coming back and did not want to be contacted. He was not with Ellen Riggs. She had made that clear. He could not be sheltering in the salon because his key was here. Anyway he avoided the place like the plague. As far as I was aware, he was not on visiting terms with anybody in the area.

I stood still, realising that I knew lots of people here. Clients at the salon, parents of the children's peers, staff in the supermarket, garage and post office. Yet, now, when I desperately needed help, I had nobody to turn to. Mags Hoey was the nearest I had to a friend. But not quite. I never saw her outside of work hours.

A cold sweat broke out on my forehead. What had I done? It had been my idea to come here. I had pushed and pushed until Ben agreed. It was to be a fresh start. Security for the children. A healthy environment. And the children *were* happy here. But I had been so busy surviving that I had forgotten to check on Ben.

I picked up my phone again. Mags Hoey was my only option. I knew she would not yet be in bed because she would be watching the *Late Late Show*. I also knew she would not want to be dragged away from her daughter. She answered on the second ring.

"Apologies for ringing so late, Mags, but I am badly stuck for a babysitter for an hour or so. Any possibility you could oblige?"

"Leah! I needed to talk to you anyway. Have you any idea of the terrible things Minnie Curran is saying about you and your salon? She's going around Paircmoor with her spotty –"

"I can't deal with that now, Mags. Can you babysit? It's urgent."

"Oh, I hate to say no, Leah, but I can't because of Claire's condition. She could take a bad turn."

I heard some mutters, then quite clearly heard Claire tell her mother she was fine and would appreciate a little time to herself.

"Leah? It's a bad night. I'd be nervous driving out your way. Could you collect me?"

"No, sorry, I can't. Ben is not here. That's why I need a babysitter."

"Oh! He's away then."

"No. He's not. He's just not at home at the moment. I'd be very grateful, Mags, if you could help me out."

More mutters before she finally came back.

"Alright. I'll see you in about fifteen minutes. I must give Claire her medication first."

Fifteen minutes to lay out supper for Mags, make sure the children were tucked in and to decide where in the name of goodness I was going to start the search for my missing husband.

CHAPTER ELEVEN

Walter had noticed Vera's torchlight and had waited for her on the clifftop. As soon as they were safely down the cliff path, they shone their torches around the strand in an arc. Both were searching for sight of a white T-shirt. They saw nothing but a storm-ravaged beach.

"Big tide," Walter said, noting a frill of seaweed from the highwater mark along the cliff face. "Nobody could have stayed here when the tide was in."

"But I'm telling you he never came back up," Vera said. "Not on the path anyway."

"There's no other way."

"Exactly. Unless he was an expert climber, I suppose – but even if he was –"

"The cave," Walter said.

They struggled to walk as they faced into the wind, picking their way over stone and rock slippery with seaweed. Vera heard the angry voice of the receding tide and knew the young man would have been powerless against it. At the mouth of the cave she stood for a moment to get her breath back before following Walter inside. He aimed the beam of light into the cavern, to where the roof got lower and the darkness blacker. They began to walk forward, stooping in a crouch as the rock slanted downward.

They both saw him at the same time.

"Too late," Walter muttered. "Too bloody late."

The young man was in a sitting position on a rock, his back resting against the cave wall, hands dangling down, feet in a pool left by the outgoing tide. He was as still as the rock which surrounded him. Entombed him.

Walter cautiously pressed his fingers to the man's neck. He felt a flutter beneath his fingers.

"He has a pulse! Faint but still beating. We must get help. And quick!"

Vera handed her phone to Walter and then took off her coat. She nudged Walter out of the way and knelt beside the young man. He was tall. She reckoned about six foot two. She was a foot smaller. She had to lean him forward in order to wrap the coat around his back. The icy coldness of his body penetrated her fingers as she pulled the warm fabric around him. She lifted his hands and put them resting on his thighs underneath the coat, then moved his feet out of the pool and onto a flat stone she picked off the floor. She remembered reading somewhere that it's a myth to say most heat is lost through the head but she had no doubt that yet another study would prove that revisionist theory to be false. Trusting her instincts, she took off her hat and pulled it over his hair. Beautiful, thick, dark hair, now drenched and freezing to the touch.

The rock he was on was low and flat with plenty of space. Vera sat beside him. Out near the mouth of the cave she could hear Walter talk to someone on the phone, explaining what had happened, asking for a doctor and ambulance urgently. She put an arm around the young man's shoulders and drew him in as close to her as possible. She began to hum Brahms' Lullaby. Just like she used to hum to her children when they were small. She wondered if this man's mother had sung to him too, wishing him all the best life had to offer her child. Never for a moment thinking he would end up freezing to death in a cave. His T-shirt had Golden Gate Bridge, San Francisco, on the front. Was he a husband? A father? She hummed and rocked the barely alive young man in her arms as she remembered her own babies. How she used to watch their features relax into sleep as she sang to them. How she missed them now as they forged their own life paths!

"Jesus! You'll get pneumonia, Vera!"

Walter whipped off his big heavy jacket, draped it around her and pulled up the hood.

"Did you get a doctor?" she asked.

Walter huffed. She recognised the sound as his angry huff.

"It's a bloody joke! Cutbacks, cutbacks! Do you realise there's just one doctor on call to cover all this area? He's at the other end of the county now. Not his fault. He's just one man, but someone is to blame for the downgrade in service. It's as if lives outside the city don't matter anymore!"

"What about an ambulance?" she asked before he could continue his rant.

"Yes, they're sending an ambulance as soon as possible, whatever that means. Just as well we can depend on our neighbours. I called the Careys. Tim and his lads are getting ready to come down now. They're bringing a fold-up sunbed to act as a stretcher."

"Are you sure it's right to move him? We might do more harm than good."

"You're right, Vera. Moving him is risky. We'll have to be as gentle as possible. His pulse is steady now but a jolt could change that."

"Why risk it so? Isn't it better to wait for the paramedics?"

"He's not going to make it if we don't get him warmed up soon. The ambulance will be at the very least three quarters of an hour. This man hasn't got that much time."

She nodded, knowing better than to argue with Walter and his years of attending first-aid courses.

"Go up and get a coat for yourself," she ordered.

He ignored her as he found a space on the rock on the other side of the young man in the white T-shirt. He put his arm around the young man's shoulders. His hand found Vera's and their fingers intertwined as naturally as their lives had for the past fifty years. They cradled the young man between them.

It seemed to take forever to settle Mags Hoey into Cowslip Cottage. She kept interrupting with questions as I was trying to tell her about the children and what to do in the unlikely event that they woke up.

"Oh! That table lamp, Leah. Where did you get it? I've been looking for one just like it for ages."

"I brought it with me from Dublin. Now, if the children wake, tell them I'm gone to get cornflakes in the garage shop."

"Don't you know the garage is closed at this hour? What are you going to do about Minnie Curran?"

Ugh! As if I didn't realise the bloody garage was closed. And I didn't give a damn about Minnie. I gave up trying to tell Mags about the children. I steered her towards the sitting room and turned on the TV for her. As soon as she had the remote control in her hand, she stopped asking questions. I put the baby monitor on the arm of her chair.

"Right, Mags, I'm going now. I shouldn't be too long. Ring me if there are any problems."

I was answered by a grunt and a dismissive wave of the hand.

Outside I shivered against the cold blast of wind and rain as I ran to my car. I stopped at the end of the driveway and thought about where I was going to start the search. Two choices here: go left into the village or right along the coast road. I couldn't see why Ben would have gone right. It wasn't a night for heading to the seaside. Without a coat. I quickly turned left.

I stopped when I came to the bendy bridge, as the children called the stretch of road that forded the river near the site of the old workhouse. I grabbed the torch I always carried in the glovebox and got out. Flicking on the light, I shone it over the wall, down into the cascading water below. Swollen by rain, the usually gentle stream had become an angry monster. My hands shook at the realisation that Ben had been very upset when he left home. My eyes raked the shadows for any signs that my husband had been here. That he had stood where I was now and decided to climb down to the maelstrom below.

I shone my light on the banks. I remembered he was wearing a white T-shirt his mother had brought him from San Francisco, the Golden Gate Bridge emblazoned on the front. I had never liked it but was glad now that he had been wearing something easily seen in the dark. There was nothing below but the frothing water rushing from the hilltops. As I got back into the car I fancied I heard the cries of the workhouse ghosts carried on the shrieking wind. I shook off the silly thought of the restless dead and headed for the village.

Paircmoor would have been swallowed up by the dark night except for the lights shining from the pub. It was one of those traditional places with a grocery shop in the front and the bar at the rear of the building. I had been there several times to get a few last-minute groceries on my way home after work but never to have a drink. I parked and looked towards the lit-up building. It would be unlikely that Ben would be drinking here. Especially since his wallet was at home. But he could have money in his pocket and somebody could have given him a lift in. I pulled up the hood of my coat and got out of the car. I could see, through the display of tinned beans and washing powder in the window, that the grocery shop was empty but even over the howl of the gale I heard the faint sound of traditional Irish music coming from the bar. I hesitated for just a second. To hell with what anyone thought of me. I needed to find my husband.

I pushed the door open. An overhead bell clanged and a young woman appeared through a beaded curtain and stood behind the counter.

"Shop or bar?" she asked.

"Actually, I'm looking for my husband. Ben Parrish. He's tall, dark-haired. Wearing a white T-shirt. Have you seen him tonight?"

"I know who he is. He has twins. And a little boy named Rob. My son is in Rob's class. You're the hairdresser, aren't you?"

"That's right. Is he by any chance in the bar?"

"I'll check for you."

I breathed a sigh of relief that I didn't have to face into

the crowd of revellers. The volume of music rose as the girl opened the door into the bar and faded as it shut behind her. I tapped my foot impatiently as I waited, wondering how she was explaining my missing husband to people or if she was just going around peering into faces, or checking for white T-shirts.

The music blared again as the door opened. But it was not the young woman who appeared. Viv Henderson stood before me, complete with her free French plait. I should have remembered that the Hendersons owned the pub. Of course they did.

"So you're looking for your husband," she said. "I'm sorry. He's not here. I believe he's wearing a T-shirt? Not very appropriate clothing for this weather."

"He was out for a run," I said, hating the fact that I felt obliged to make up an excuse. "I'm worried he may have had an accident."

"Oh dear! It's not your day, is it, what with the incident with Minnie Curran's hair and now a missing husband."

Bitch! Despite an urge to thump Lady Paircmoor, I somehow managed to hold my temper in check.

"Thank you for your help, Viv. I'd better keep on searching."

I turned and dashed outside as quickly as possible, kicking the front tyre of the car with temper before getting in. The childish gesture helped. I drove the length and breadth of the village, crawling along and peering into doorways and the dark lanes that ran from the street to the backs of the buildings. That search did not take long and yielded nothing.

I knew Ben did not have a key to the salon, but I headed there anyway. It was cloaked in darkness. I got out of the car, unlocked the door and flicked on the lights. No Ben.

He had not smashed a window to gain entry or broken in the back door. The salon was cold and somehow threatening without the buzz of dryers and customer chat. I shivered, suddenly feeling that tremor of fear usually referred to as somebody walking over your grave. I shrugged. I wanted to be cremated and have my ashes scattered over the sea. Good luck to whoever was trying to walk over my grave. I locked up and went back to my car.

Where to now? It was after eleven o'clock. Three hours missing. Should I contact the gardaí, convince them Ben would not be gone this long unless there was something wrong? And there, as I sat in my car outside the dark salon, the realisation dawned. There *was* something wrong with Ben. In fact, everything was wrong in his life. He was undoubtedly hit hard by Ellen's departure. That had been the trigger, but not the main cause of his looking for an escape. Truth was he hated the cottage, Paircmoor, our new rural way of life. He assumed I loved it. That I was living the dream. He was so wrong. I accepted it because it was what fate had handed us. Dublin, the big house, the social life, the status, the generous income. That's what I had loved. Pointless regretting what was over and done with.

I started the car again and faced back towards Cowslip Cottage, intending to drop in and check with Mags that the children were still asleep and safe. Or maybe not. She would want to go as soon as she saw me.

I guessed by that stage that I should have driven in the other direction when I left the cottage. Towards the sea. I had read that upset people are attracted to water. To rivers, lakes or the ocean.

I pressed my foot on the accelerator and sped towards the coast road.

***

"Easy now! Easy! Lay him down gently," said Walter. "Vera, get me the big scissors."

It had been a slow and terrifying journey from the cave up to Cliff House, all the time stopping to check that the young man was still breathing.

Walter removed the drenched shoes and socks as soon as Tim Carey and his sons laid the makeshift stretcher near the kitchen stove. Vera handed him the scissors.

"Ring the emergency services again," Walter told Tim. "Find out how far away the ambulance is. Lads, turn on all the outside lights so that there's no delay finding us. Vera, get some dry blankets then fill a couple of hot-water bottles."

All the while he was talking, Walter was cutting away the sodden clothing and peeling it off. The feet and hands were white, the body having sent blood supply from the limbs to protect the vital organs. Walter remembered this from his classes and that he must get the wet clothes off and warm layers over the frozen body as quickly as possible. He also knew that if this young man did not get oxygen and a warm drip soon, it would be too late.

"ETA for ambulance ten minutes," Tim said. "They want to know if you have a name for the patient."

Vera picked up the now destroyed pair of jeans and searched the pockets. There was some loose change but no ID.

Just as Vera and Walter finished wrapping the young man in blankets, they heard the sound of a siren. They looked at each other and breathed a sigh of relief.

"I wonder if he meant for this to happen," Vera whispered.

Walter shrugged and then went to open the door for the ambulance crew.

CHAPTER TWELVE

I slowed down passing Cowslip Cottage. Peering through the trees on the avenue, I could see a light from the lounge window. The rest of the house was in darkness. A sign that the children were still asleep. No point in disturbing either them or Mags.

On the coast road I speeded up. One of the reasons we had chosen Paircmoor in the beginning was its proximity to the sea. When I say we, that really means me. Ben had been preoccupied at the time with applying for jobs. All day, every day, handing out his CV, posting it, emailing it. Even eventually applying for a job as a labourer. He didn't get it. He left me with all the packing while he dealt with the bank. He and Della together. Hammering out a deal so that we could pay off our mortgage and buy again. Downsized. Rural. A doer-upper. Buzz words to hide the fact that we bought Cowslip Cottage because it was what we could afford. Just about. With Della's help.

I came to the part of the road where the trees formed a tunnel. Beautiful when sunlight shone through the leaves and dappled the roadway. Threatening now as wind howled, rain lashed and branches lurched towards the car in the squalls. I looked ahead and saw no end in sight.

I was tempted to go back but the road was too narrow to turn. Besides, I was never comfortable reversing the car unless I really had to. That reluctance stemmed back to my provisional licence days when I had backed into a brand-new top-of-the-range BMW in a multi-storey car park in town. Unfortunately, the owner had been sitting in his car. When I heard the bang and saw the man clutching his neck, I knew there was only one way things were going to end up. He screwed my insurance company for every last halfpenny and made me very wary of reversing ever since. But I would have to find a place to do a U-turn soon. Ben would never have walked this far. Not without a coat. Not in this storm. Not in any weather.

I felt tears well. I don't know whether they were for Ben or for me. All I can say is that when I blinked the tears away, the tunnel was still stretching into the distance with no end in sight. That was until my vision was filled with the lights of an oncoming vehicle which had blue lights flashing. An ambulance, speeding, taking up the width of the narrow road, leaving no space for me to pass. No one can say for certain how they would react in an emergency, but I smiled. For some reason the irony of being killed by a speeding ambulance amused me. That didn't stop me from pressing with all my might on the brake. The car began to slow. But not enough. The ambulance was nearer now. My car aquaplaned on the wet road. I tried to remember what to do in these circumstances. Should I steer into the skid or was that on ice? I heard branches scrape against the passenger side of the car as it hugged the ditch. Time slowed as the car did a 180-degree turn, facing me back towards Paircmoor. I wondered who would look after the children if I died here and Ben was never found. Their grandmother. Della. And mould them to her liking. My engine had stopped running and my car had stopped moving. The wail of a siren was loud in my ears. I was right in the path of the ambulance bearing down on me with speed. I braced myself against my seat, squeezed my eyes shut, and waited for the collision. Nothing more to do except pray and I had long since forgotten how to do that.

I opened my eyes. I was bathed in the bright headlights and blue flashing light of the ambulance. No siren. No engine sound. I opened my door and got out, my legs shaking so badly I had to lean on the roof for support. The ambulance had come to a halt half a metre from the back of my car.

The driver got out and ran to me.

"Are you alright? Any injuries?"

I shook my head. I had no broken bones, no cuts or bruises. Just shock.

"Is your car drivable? We'll have to move it because we need to get our patient to the hospital as soon as possible."

"I don't know. The engine stalled. I'll try to move it now."

"If you're sure you're OK. It's a bad night to be out on the road."

"I'm looking for my husband. Tall, dark-haired, wearing a white T-shirt. You wouldn't have seen him along the road, would you? He went for a run, you see . . ."

I read shock, pity and a deep sympathy on his face and knew Ben was the patient needing urgent attention.

"I need to be with him," I said.

"Of course."

My car started straight away. I drove ahead, parked it in a gateway and put on the hazard warning lights.

Then the ambulance came and picked me up.

I held Ben's numb hand all the way into A&E. I learned what it was to stare death in the face.

The paramedics rushed Ben from the ambulance bay in through a separate entrance to the hospital. I was on autopilot as I trotted along beside the trolley, my mind numbed somewhat by shock, but mostly by the information the paramedics had given me. Ben, they said, had been seen heading down the cliff path to the strand at high tide and then, sometime later, he had been rescued from a cave. Figuring out what he thought he was doing was for later.

Someone took me by the arm. I turned to see a doctor.

"Mrs Parrish?"

I nodded, noticing that she looked very young. And tired. She had probably been saving lives non-stop for the past twelve hours.

"I'm Doctor Nyhan, I'll be looking after your husband. Does he have any allergies? It's important that we know."

I shook my head.

"Is he on any medication?"

"No."

In fact, Ben prided himself on never taking any pills. Not even for man flu. Ahead I saw him being wheeled through doors on the left.

"We're taking him to Resus – the resuscitation room – now," the doctor told me. "I'll have someone show you to the family room and I'll come see you as soon as we know the way things are going."

She left before I could ask any questions. I knew he was very cold. I'd felt that for myself. But what did she mean by saying *the way things are going*? Surely there was only one way now that he was here and being treated. Warmed up. Deathly cold being banished. Death itself being exiled to wherever it lurked in wait for all of us. But surely not Ben. Not now.

A nurse, not so young but also looking exhausted, appeared in front of me.

"Let me take you to the family room. The doctor will see you as soon as she can."

I allowed her to lead me along a corridor which was painted cream and had some lovely wall art. A colourful distraction from the smell of disinfectant overlaid with lingering aromas of hospital dinners. We passed signs for the X-ray department, Chemotherapy, Dialysis. The Morgue. I shivered.

"Is he going to be alright?" I asked the nurse. "It's just a matter of warming him up, isn't it?"

She stopped at a door and flicked a wall switch. Light flooded a small room which had several armchairs, a coffee table, a water dispenser and a television high up on the wall. She indicated for me to go ahead.

"The paramedics told me you were involved in a car accident, Mrs Parrish. I know you refused a check-up. How are you feeling?"

I was annoyed with her. I had asked about Ben and she had ignored my question.

"I'm fine, thank you. There wasn't any accident. Just a near miss. I don't need any treatment. But my husband. I want to know how he is."

"He's getting the best care now. Would you like a cup of tea or coffee?"

I shook my head. It was information I needed, not coffee. I understood that Ben was seriously ill when he was brought into the hospital, wrapped in the foil blanket the paramedics had used to keep life in him. But I had assumed once he was here, he would soon recover. I thought of all the hospital dramas I loved watching on TV. *Casualty*, *Holby City*, *Grey's Anatomy*. In those shows, phrases such as *the doctor is working on him* or *he's getting the best care,* were code for *prepare for tragedy*. I wished for *Doc Martin* type blunt honesty.

"Is my husband going to die?"

The nurse waved me to one of the armchairs and then sat herself opposite. She leaned towards me.

"His core temperature is low, Mrs Parrish. We're infusing him with warm saline now and oxygen to help his breathing. We will heat him up gradually and monitor his heart and other vital organs. Doctor Nyhan will talk to you when his condition is stabilised. In the meantime, is there someone you could ring to wait with you?"

Another catchphrase. *Someone to wait with you*. What it really meant was that I would need a friend or relation there to hold my hand when they told me Ben had not made it out of Resus.

"We're fairly new to the area," I said, in an attempt to explain away my isolated state. Doubtless, if I asked the nice smiley people of Paircmoor they would help. If I was close enough to them to have their phone numbers. Which I was not. After two years of spending our money locally, opening a business in the village, enrolling our children in the local school, we were still the outsiders. Ben knew that. It had taken a crisis for me to realise it. I began to shake with shock, fear and a profound loneliness.

"I'll have a coffee, please," I said, more for the nurse to go and leave me alone, than for any need of coffee. It might help to stop me shaking but nothing could fill the empty space I felt inside.

I longed to be with Ben, to warm his body with mine, to tell him what I should have told him a month ago.

Now he might never know.

CHAPTER THIRTEEN

Saturday 27th November 2010

Cowslip Cottage creaked and groaned and scared the living daylights out of Mags Hoey. She would have liked to turn up the sound on the TV but was afraid to wake the children. In fact, she was terrified here, remembering all the stories about the nearby workhouse and the ghosts of those wretched creatures.

It was after midnight and there was still no sign of either of the Parrishes. The baby monitor was silent. That should mean the children were sleeping peacefully. Mags wondered if she ought to go check on them. She had no faith in these baby-minding gadgets. There had been nothing like that when she was rearing her daughter. Yet, if she went to their rooms she might wake them, and how would she cope with three screaming children?

The phone on the coffee table rang again. That was the fifth time in the last hour. She had seen Leah take her phone with her, so she assumed the one here must belong to Ben Parrish.

Leah had said she would not be long. So where was she? Claire would soon be due her last dose of painkillers. Mags had given Leah time enough. She needed to get back to her own daughter.

She was about to contact Claire when her phone rang. It was Viv Henderson with some really interesting news.

"Mags, did you know Leah Parrish is out searching for her husband? She came into the bar but we hadn't seen him at all."

"I'm at her house, minding the children. She never told me he was missing. Just said he was out."

Viv's voice dropped to a whisper. Mags had to lower the volume on the TV to hear her.

"Well, a certain artistic lady has apparently packed up and is leaving Paircmoor. Rumour has it that her admirer might be going with her."

Mags said nothing. She could not because her thoughts had flown back twenty-four years to when her husband and his mistress had done a midnight flit, leaving her with a toddler and a broken heart that had never quite mended. Viv knew that too, so she could have tried to keep the gloating out of her voice. And, yes, Mags had heard the gossip about Ellen Riggs and Ben Parrish, always cosying up to each other at the school gates and on outings with the children. Poor Leah.

"I'd better go check on the children, Viv. Thanks for ringing."

She had no doubt that Viv was already on to the next person on her contact list. And, in a moment of honesty, Mags admitted that she herself was often the person to pass on the gossip. Unless it was about unfaithful husbands.

The phone on the coffee table rang for the sixth time. Annoyed, Mags left her armchair and went to the table. The ringing stopped as soon as she got there. She turned the screen towards her. *Six missed calls*. She swiped the screen. *Hmm!* The first call had been from Ellen Riggs. Maybe there was truth in the rumour after all. The name on the other five calls made Mags pick up Ben's phone. Without thinking she pressed the return-call icon. She understood this woman. After all, they were both mothers.

Her call was answered on the second ring.

"Ben! Thank goodness! I've been trying to reach you for ages. Everything OK?"

The line was a bit crackly and the woman's voice was soft. Her accent posh.

Mags cleared her throat.

"Hello. My name is Mags Hoey. I'm at Cowslip Cottage babysitting for Leah."

There was a pause before the woman spoke again.

"Oh! Hello, Mags. I'm Della Parrish, Ben's Mum. How come you're answering my son's phone?"

Mags also wondered why. She reasoned it had been a kind impulse to help an anxious mother. The missed calls had been from *Mum*. Mags was founder member of the Worried Mother Club. And yes, she was nosey. Defensive also now about being questioned.

"Ben left it behind when he went out. Leah's gone looking for him."

"What do you mean, she's gone looking for him? Does she not know where he is?"

"No, she doesn't."

"Do you mean he's missing? Since when?"

The accent was still cultured but the voice was no longer soft. In fact, it had gone up ten notches from calm to utterly panicked in seconds.

"Tell me what you know, Mags."

"Look, Della, all I know is that your daughter-in-law went out for Ben and said she wouldn't be long. Why don't you, ring Leah? And tell her I'm waiting to hear from her too."

The call was cut with an abrupt "Thank you".

Mags went back to her armchair and settled herself comfortably in front of the TV.

Instinct told her the wait would be long, and that the fallout from whatever was going on with Ben Parrish would last even longer.

When I looked at the time on my phone, it had been just twenty minutes since Ben had been wheeled away. It felt like twenty years. I paced the hospital Family Room. Ten steps from chair to television wall. Twelve from water dispenser to opposite wall. Up and down, forward and back. Every time I heard footsteps in the corridor outside I dashed to the door. It was never Doctor Nyhan or the nurse who had shown me to the room. I wondered what would happen if I walked into Resus. At least I would see him. Or would I? Maybe they had already pulled a sheet over his lifeless body. Called the time of death.

The functioning part of my brain told me I watched too many medical dramas on TV. Also that I should contact Mags and let her know where I was. I guessed she would be upset at having to stay longer but there was nothing I could do about it. Unable to cope with listening to Mags' objections, I texted her instead.

Sorry for keeping you so long. Ben in hospital. Will explain when I see you.

Almost instantly I had a reply back.

Don't worry about the children. Will take care of them. Hope Ben will be OK. Told his mother you were out looking for him. xx

Oh, shit! How had Mags been in contact with Della Parrish? I would not have called her until I had more definite news but I didn't have a choice now.

I dialled her number.

She answered immediately. "Leah? What's going on? Where's Ben?"

I should have planned how I was going to tell her what I then knew. That her son was critically ill.

I heard laughter in the background and imagined them all, Hugh and Piper and Della, the successful Parrishes, lounging around the swimming pool.

"*Leah! Talk to me!*"

"He's had an accident. He was rescued by the people in Cliff House and the paramedics wrapped him in a foil blanket but –"

"Cliff House? Am I right in assuming that's by the sea?

"Yes. The people there saw Ben going down onto the strand at high tide and –"

There was a sound. A guttural noise so primal I would never have associated it with Della. I was stunned into silence and apparently so was she. I heard someone talk to her and then take the phone from her.

Hugh's affected American drawl, laced with remnants of his native Irish accent, sounded in my ear.

"Leah? Hugh here. Could you repeat what you told Mum, please?"

"Ben went out for a run, a walk. I don't know. Anyway, he ended up being marooned in a cave at high tide. There's a big storm here. He had to be rescued."

"Where is he now?"

"In hospital. In Resus. He has hypothermia. They're warming him up but I don't know yet how it's going."

"Okay. Just give me the hospital number and I'll ring."

"There's no need for you to do that, Hugh. I'll let you know as soon as I have news."

"I'd prefer to talk to them myself, if you don't mind."

I did mind. Every time Hugh opened his mouth to speak down to me, I minded. I didn't have the energy to argue with him. I mumbled the number for him. He would look it up online anyway. It wouldn't do him much good. I was Ben's next-of-kin and the only person to whom they would give Ben's medical details.

"Thank you," he said. "Keep in touch, Leah. Mum will be home as soon as we can book her on a flight."

Then he was gone. So was all my courage and what energy I had left.

I sat on the armchair beside the water dispenser and cried.

CHAPTER FOURTEEN

There was a rumbling sound. The sea. And a steady whoosh. The wind. Ben was being carried along quickly. Smoothly. He opened his eyes and wondered why there were no waves and why intermittent lights flashed above his head. He felt a mask on his face, a needle in his arm. His eye lids closed. He remembered where he had been. He had left the decision to the sea. To take him and wash him clean of failure and despair.

"He's waking," someone said.

Hands touched him. Lifted him and lay him down on something soft and dry. Not water. The sea had spat him out.

"*Ben!*" a voice called. "*Ben, can you hear me?*"

His eyes flickered open. He did not recognise the face peering in to his. The girl was young, a stethoscope draped around her neck.

"You're in hospital," she said. "We're treating you for hypothermia."

So fate had decided. He would see the children again. And Leah. But not Ellen. Never again. He would collect Unemployment Benefit because Leah did not want him to go to California. He did not want to go either because he knew he would fail. It's what he did. His mum would be so disappointed in him. Again. For fuck's sake!

He felt his heart begin to beat very quickly. His pulse throbbed in his ears. A big weight, maybe a rock, hit him on the chest. The young girl with the stethoscope issued instructions while someone else pressed an alarm.

His eyes closed. It was difficult to get air into his lungs but he didn't struggle too hard. He was enjoying his journey towards the beautiful light that was drawing him forward. The essence of Ben, the inner perpetual child who cried and cowered in darkness, reached out to the light. Someone was trying to drag him back.

He fought for his place in the light while around him, the hospital staff fought for his life.

By the time the door to the Family Room opened, I was no longer expecting good news.

Doctor Nyhan walked in slowly, her head bowed. When she looked up her face reflected the ravages of the life-and-death battles she fought daily on behalf of her patients.

"I'm sorry you've been waiting so long, Mrs Parrish. Do you mind if I sit while we talk?"

I motioned to the chair opposite me. She slumped onto the seat. I got the impression she would have curled herself into a ball on the floor if the chair had not been there to support her. Is this how she had envisaged her career unfolding when she had been studying so hard to get her medical degree? Maybe she was seeing past the overcrowded, understaffed conditions of public hospitals in order to reach the goal of a consultancy ahead. And why was I in the least concerned about this stranger when I should be asking about Ben? The truth was I did not want hear the words I knew she was obliged to say.

She took a deep breath. I gripped the arms of my chair.

"Your husband's body temperature is no longer at a critical level. He responded well to the treatment."

I felt myself go weak as relief swept through me. He was still alive. I should have known he would battle through for the children. For me.

Doctor Nyhan was watching me closely. I sensed the *but* she had not spoken.

"Will he suffer after-effects from the cold? Permanent damage?"

"We'll be holding on to him for a little while yet, Mrs Parrish."

"Leah."

"Right. Leah, as we were moving him from Resus, your husband suffered a mild heart attack."

She held her hand up as I half rose from my seat.

"He's stable now. Luckily we were there to give him immediate attention. But of course we need to monitor him and follow up with more tests."

God! What had he done? Damaged his own heart and broken mine? Just because Ellen bloody Riggs had bruised his ego. I felt anger sweep my relief away.

"The incident, Leah. Do you know what happened?"

I noted that she had not said accident.

"All I know, Doctor Nyhan, is what the ambulance crew told me. Apparently Ben was rescued from a cave so I assume he was sheltering there waiting for the tide to turn."

"I see. We won't be able to talk to Ben himself for a while yet so it would be helpful if you could fill us in on a few details."

I nodded. That was what wives were for. Even angry ones.

"Your husband is not on any prescribed medication that you know of?"

What an odd question. Did she think he popped pills behind my back?

"He is not."

"What has his mood been like lately? Did you notice any change in his behaviour?"

Ben had been moody of late but that was nothing new.

"No. He's been the same as usual."

"Any change in his sleep pattern that you noticed? Or in his eating habits?"

I supposed that Ben sleeping on a chair in the twins' room could be regarded as a change. Going out in a violent storm and onto the beach in full tide was definitely novel. Probably because of Ellen Riggs. But that was between my husband and me.

"He's eating normally," I said. "While I'm there anyway. The past few years have not been easy for either of us. I'm the wage-earner now and he can find that difficult at times."

"*Hmm.*"

She made that sound as if she understood. How could she? What would she know about the sheer horror of losing a whole way of life?

"When can I see him"?

She stood up.

"I'll take you to him. We've moved him to the Intensive Care Unit. He's sedated so you probably won't be able to talk to him. Follow me."

Lights were dimmer and voices more hushed in the coronary care unit. Doctor Nyhan led me towards a corner bed where a nurse was checking a battery of instruments, wires and tubes. They were all attached to the man lying in the bed. Still as death.

The nurse and doctor were talking. I didn't hear them. I could not take my eyes off Ben's face. It was bloodless. More drawn than it had been when last I saw him. But he looked peaceful. Wiped clean of stress. Maybe it was still reflected in his closed eyes. They were so expressive, Ben's dark brown eyes. It was easy to read his mood in them. I longed for him to raise his eyelids and look at me. With love, like he used to do.

I leaned over him and kissed his forehead. His skin felt cold.

"I love you, Ben," I whispered.

I took his hand in mine. His fingers were limp and cold. I listened to the machines that were keeping him alive beep and click and willed him to bring himself back from wherever he was. From his place of peace. I put my mouth close to his ear.

"We need you," I said. "Rob and the twins and me. You must get better. We all love you."

I felt a tap on my shoulder. I straightened up to see Doctor Nyhan.

"I'm going off duty, Leah. I'd advise you to go home too and get some rest. Ben is doing well now."

"Really? He looks so ill."

"He's been through a big ordeal. So have you. We'll be monitoring him closely and will let you know immediately if there is any change."

"Thank you, Doctor Nyhan. Thank you so much."

She smiled a very tired smile and then walked away.

When I turned back to Ben, his eyelids were flickering. They opened and looked directly at me. I knew by the blankness in his eyes that he did not really see me at all. He seemed to be looking inwards. Maybe towards the people he loved most. His children. His mother. Perhaps Ellen Riggs. I had reached the point of pain saturation.

"Your mother," I said. "She's on her way. She'll be here as soon as she can."

I thought a saw a flicker of light in his eyes. The lids drooped again and he went back to wherever he had been hiding in his semi-conscious state.

I checked that the duty nurse had my phone number. Just in case. Then I walked out of the Intensive Care ward.

Outside I went to the taxi rank and got into the first car in line. I sat into the back seat and gave him directions to my hair salon. Then I realised that it would be a very expensive fare to Paircmoor. I checked my bag and saw that I had money from the salon there. I would use that and balance the books later.

As the lights of the town faded and the car headed out the rural roads, I laid my head against the back of the seat and closed my eyes. Maybe the taxi driver saw the tears trickle down my face. I no longer cared.

I dried my tears as the salon neared. I ran in and wrote a quick notice in black marker.

Closed due to illness.
Apologies for any inconvenience.

I stuck it inside the glass panel of the door. Let people make what they would of it. I jumped when the blasted cuckoo clock started squawking. Three o'clock in the morning. Bloody Della and her screechy clock. Bloody Della and her dependent son. I grabbed the appointments book, quickly locked up and got back into the taxi.

"The coast road, please. I must collect my car along the way," I told the driver who did not raise an eyebrow.

I was grateful for his silence. As I was for the help of the people who had called the emergency services for Ben. Likewise the paramedics and the medical team in the hospital. I was grateful also to Mags for minding the children. I was so overcome by gratitude at that point that I even appreciated his mother trying to get back to him as soon as possible.

As the taxi drove through the dark towards my scraped and possibly dented car, a horrible suspicion insinuated itself into my thinking. Ben would not be grateful. Surviving could not have been the outcome he had wanted when he had run off into the storm and onto the strand at full tide.

Because I could not allow any more pain into this already hellish night, I pushed the unacceptable thought aside, paid the taxi fare and drove my miraculously undamaged car back to Cowslip Cottage.

CHAPTER FIFTEEN

Traffic was heavy as Della and Hugh headed towards San Francisco airport. Hugh swerved from one lane to another and passed everything in sight. Della knew time was tight to catch the flight to Dublin she had been lucky enough to get. She also knew from experience that asking her eldest son to slow down would automatically result in him putting his foot more firmly on the accelerator. She noticed his knuckles were white as he gripped the steering wheel.

"Okay, Hugh. We need to talk. Of course you're worried about Ben. I understand that. What I don't know is why you're so angry. Or who you're angry with. Tell me."

He continued to stare straight ahead, as if he had not heard her.

She tried again.

"Why did you tell Piper that Ben had a car accident when you know that's not true?"

"That's rich coming from you, Mum. Don't pretend you wanted me to tell her the truth. You started this farce. Ben spent three months in boarding school, and then decided he didn't like it. Isn't that what you said so often that even the family came to believe it?"

Della leaned back against the headrest and closed her eyes. Yes, she had come up with the boarding-school idea. The alternative was to brand Ben, then teenaged, as a psychiatric patient. She had brought him to the Booly Clinic. A place where troubled people, with the financial resources, went to have their problems treated in privacy. She had been right, hadn't she? Until now. She opened her eyes as the car made yet another acceleration and swerve.

"I did what was best for Ben," she said. "He was only sixteen. He needed to be protected."

"He needed support, for Christ's sake! He needed his family to accept him as he was, depression, suicide attempts and all. And the same is true now."

"Isn't that what we did, Hugh? He got the best care. Look how he put it behind him and got on with his life."

"You think?"

What could she say? Ben had gone on to qualify as an architect, have a successful career until circumstances outside his control took it away from him. He was a husband and father. A wonderful dad. So yes, she did believe she had made the right decision for him all those years ago.

"You should have told Leah about his history," Hugh said. "His wife had a right to know."

Della made her ladylike version of a derisive snort.

"You think she would have understood? Or that she would have been able to keep the information private. You know what she's like, Hugh. Mouth Almighty."

"You've always been unfair to her, Mum. Nor have you ever let go your hold on Ben."

"Goodness, Hugh. I never would have guessed you held your sister-in-law in such high regard."

He was silent then, concentrating on turning off on to the airport access road and finding a space in the short-stay car park near the International Terminal.

In the terminal they headed towards gates 91-102.

On reaching it, Della turned to her son.

"Thank you, Hugh. I'll contact you as soon as I've seen Ben."

"You must tell the hospital," he said. "About Ben's previous suicide attempts. They need to know. So does Leah."

Della took her luggage from him. He looked at her and for the first time noticed signs of frailty in his mother. Her skin seemed thinner, her posture less assured.

"You don't know, Hugh. Maybe he really did have an accident this time. No point in dragging up the past unnecessarily."

"Come on! Why was he at the sea, in the dark, during a storm? A familiar pattern. At best his judgement was badly skewed. He needs help."

"He'll be better when he gets here to the States. When he's working again."

"Mum! You know that's only a very outside chance. I explained to you that there are no promises. Zach is a tough operator. He didn't make his billions by being a soft touch. Don't go giving Ben and Leah false hope."

"But he's a good architect. He'd be an asset to –"

Hugh caught her elbow and led her towards the gates.

"You'd better go, Mum. Time's pushing on. Let me know when you've seen Ben. The hospital wouldn't give me any details on the phone. Keep in touch. I'll be there if you need me."

She offered her cheek for a dutiful kiss.

Hugh watched her go, head held high, and wished that he had spoken more kindly to her. Told her he loved her. Heard her say she loved him. By moving to his right, he could see her walking down the long corridor. Elegant, proud, still beautiful.

He waited for her to turn around. To wave. To smile. To indicate that he meant as much to her as Ben did.

She turned a corner and went out of sight.

Hugh turned his back and tried to put her out of mind.

The wind had abated by the time I arrived back to Cowslip Cottage. I got out of my little car and was greeted by the fresh scent of rain-washed air and the bite of a November night.

As I started to walk towards the cottage, my phone rang. Was it the hospital? My fingers shook when I tried to prise my phone out of the front pocket of my bag. Just as I got a grip on it, the ringing stopped. By the time I had taken it out, it was ringing again. Blind with panic, I pressed the answer icon without seeing who the caller was.

"Leah, Della here. Any update on Ben's condition?"

For once, I was relieved to hear her voice.

"Oh! Della. Thank God. I thought it was the hospital ringing."

"I didn't think of the time difference. Sorry. You're early hours of the morning there, aren't you?"

"No problem. I've just left Ben. He's resting quite peacefully now."

I held my breath, waiting for her reaction and wondering if the San Francisco Parrishes had found out about Ben's heart attack. No sense in worrying Della even more at this stage if she did not know. Especially since that situation was under control. Or so the doctor had told me.

"I've got to go because my flight is boarding here in San Francisco," she said. "I'm due to land in Dublin around one thirty in the afternoon, your time. I must call out to Howth, to my house. Hopefully I'll be at the hospital four hours or so after that."

She sounded stressed. Even a bit panicky. A flash of empathy took me by surprise. She was a mother needing to be by her son's sickbed. I understood that instinctive drive to protect your child. Even if he was in his thirties.

"He'll be so happy to see you, Della. So will I. Safe journey."

We were both silent, me with shock at meaning what I said to her, she with shock that I had spoken those words at all. She cleared her throat.

"I'll see you later. Try to get some rest."

Then she was gone, leaving me standing in the dark, feeling very much alone. I shivered at the sudden sense that the cottage was watching me. Judging. Finding me wanting as a wife, a mother. I shrugged off the silly thought and opened up the front door as quietly as possible.

Mags was asleep on the couch, her mouth open, the remote control on her lap. The television was still on, playing a repeat afternoon show. I tiptoed down the hall to the children's rooms, and looked in on them – first Rob, then the twins. They were tucked up and sleeping soundly. I wondered what I would tell them in the morning. How would I explain their father's absence? Doubtless I would think of a story to satisfy them but where did that leave me and all my unanswered questions?

I jumped as I heard footsteps behind me. Mags stood in the doorway, a finger to her lips. She waved me to follow her. In the kitchen she took charge, seating me at the table, making hot sweet tea.

"For shock," she said. "Drink it. By the way, I'm sorry if I interfered when I answered the call I saw on Ben's phone tonight. It's just that his mum had rung so often, I thought I should."

"That's alright. I had been just about to ring her anyway."

"Good. Tell me, how *is* Ben? What happened to him? Why is he in hospital?"

Why, why, why, indeed. I didn't know, did I? Why had he smashed Ellen's vase, why had he gone out in a storm, why had he been on the beach in high tide? Time to start the fairy tale, laced with a smidgeon of truth.

"He's had a heart attack, Mags."

"*Jesus mercy!* A fit young man like him! How did that happen?"

"He'd been out jogging and unfortunately took a fall. By the time he was found he was suffering from hypothermia. He's warmer now but the low body temperature took a toll on his heart."

Just as I was really getting into my story I decided to stop and think about what I was saying. I didn't want the truth to come back and bite me. Other than the fall, the sequence of events was factual. As far as I knew.

"Oh my God!" Mags said. "Where did he fall? Who found him?"

I remembered what the ambulance crew had told me about the people who had rescued Ben.

"The Sanquests. They're the people who found him. They saved his life. I'll be forever grateful to them."

"Vera and Walter? But they're on the coast. What was Ben doing there on a stormy night?"

"Running away," I said and then began to both laugh and cry at the twists and turns of fate which had led me to this surreal moment in time when I heard the truth, the bitter, incontrovertible truth in my own glibly spoken words.

Of course Ben had been running away. Escaping. Just as he had escaped to work when he was employed. Just as he slipped into his fantasy of a liaison with Ellen Riggs when he thought that an option. Just as he ran away into the arms of the elements tonight. He was a runner-away. A serial escape artist. And I, Leah Parrish, the practical one, the manager, the glue that held the family together, was the person from whom he was running.

My tears were falling fast. I felt warm arms around me as Mags came to me and held me close. She stroked my hair and soothed me as sobs racked my body. The dam had burst and years upon years of suppressed or ignored hurts and rejections burst out of their hiding places, each making a mockery of my self-appointed position as perfect wife and mother. Each confirming the fact I had never wanted to acknowledge. Ben would not have married me had I not fallen pregnant with Rob when we were going out together. He had stood by me. Done the decent thing. For me and for his son. He had defied his mother and destroyed himself.

"It's all my fault," I sobbed into Mags' shoulder.

"Hush, now. Don't say that. Of course it's not. That pottery woman had some part to play in this too."

Mags' words made me cry even harder. So, she knew about Ellen Riggs and Ben. The whole village must know.

Mags walked away from me and left the kitchen. I felt even more guilty then and added selfishness to my list of self-loathing. She must be exhausted and anxious to get home to her daughter and yet I was keeping her here to comfort me. No wonder she too was running away.

Just as I stood up to follow her she came in the kitchen door, a brandy snifter in her hand.

"Here," she said, placing the glass in front of me. "I found a bottle of brandy in your sitting room. Drink up. You need it. And then you must get some sleep."

"Mags, I'm so sorry. You must be exhausted and anxious to get back to Claire. Apologies for delaying you and many, many thanks for your help. I don't know what I would have done without you."

"Go to bed, Leah. I'm not leaving until I know you're alright. I'll stay and look after the children's breakfast in the morning."

"What about Claire? She needs you."

Mags laughed. A roguish sound I had not heard from her before.

"No, Leah. The truth is that *I* need to be needed. She needs independence. She and I know the score and we'll deal with it when we're ready. I'll get myself a blanket from the hot press and curl up on the couch."

"But, Mags, at least let me get –"

"Off to bed with you now, Leah. This minute."

Too traumatised to argue, I hugged her and shuffled to the bedroom. Not bothering to undress, I threw myself on the bed, my head on Ben's pillow. I buried my face in the scent of him and breathed him in.

In seconds I passed from consciousness into deep sleep.

CHAPTER SIXTEEN

I spent the first few seconds of waking wondering what day it was and why I was lying here when there were chinks of light seeping through the curtains. I could hear the children in the kitchen. They were laughing – even solemn little Rob. Images began to emerge. Horrific scenes. Ben in the ambulance, ashen-faced, ice-cold, wet. Ben lying in a hospital bed, still ashen-faced, monitored by a bank of machines, his every heartbeat echoed in an electronic beep.

I jumped out of bed and grabbed my phone from the bedside locker. It was quarter to nine. There were no missed calls. I rang the hospital and asked to be put through to Intensive Care. While I waited I found my dressing gown and wrapped myself in its warmth. I shivered. The cold I felt came from inside, stoked by fear and my insidious guilt.

"Good morning. Intensive Care. How may I help?"

"Good morning. My name is Leah Parrish. I'm enquiring about my husband, Ben. He was admitted last night."

"Oh yes. Mr Parrish. He had a comfortable night. His condition is stable. The doctors will be with him shortly so we will have a more detailed report for you then."

"I'll be in to see him soon. Is he awake?"

"Not at the moment."

"I see. When he does wake, would you tell him, please, that I'll be in.

"Of course."

"Thank you."

He was comfortable. Stable. Half dead, yes. But also half alive. Thank God for half mercies.

Face washed, teeth and hair brushed, I stared at my reflection in the mirror and test-ran a smile for the children. Despite my best efforts it looked like a grimace of pain. Which it was. Bite-sized chunks of truth and a serious expression was all I had to offer them.

I stood behind the door jamb where I could see into the kitchen but not be seen. The table was cleared of breakfast ware. Anna and Josh sat either side of Mags Hoey and Rob sat across from her. In the centre was a little pile of playing cards.

Anna was closely examining the cards in her hand.

"Can you remember the game, Anna?" Mags asked. "If you have a card exactly like the one on top of the bundle in the middle of the table, then you must put your card on the bundle and shout '*SNAP!*'. Understand?"

Anna nodded and continued to examine her cards. I noticed Rob extend his leg underneath the table in order to give Anna a hurry-up. Mags saw him about to kick and silently wagged a finger at him. That was when Anna made her move. Quick as lightning she placed a card on top of the pile, then slammed her little hand on the bundle and shouted '*SHNAP!*' I didn't have to pretend a smile as I walked into the kitchen.

Mags turned to look at me, an eyebrow raised.

"I phoned," I said. "So far so good."

She stood as the children ran to me.

"That's great news. Coffee's made," she said. "I'll do toast for you before I go."

I didn't know what to say to her. How I could thank her enough? Even though she was turning my children into card sharks.

"I play bridge on Thursday evenings," she explained. "I always have a pack of cards in my bag. They came in handy this morning."

I had not known she played bridge. In fact, other than knowing that she fitted in her hairdressing job between sorting out emergencies, real or imagined, for her daughter, I knew very little about Mags Hoey.

"I the best at *Shnap!*, Mom." Anna said.

The mini-me hopping up and down with excitement brought the second smile of the day to my face.

"Me too," Josh said.

He was clinging to my leg. I put my hand down and touched his dark, silky hair, so like Ben's.

"Are you still tired?" Rob asked. "Mags told us she was minding us because you needed lots of sleep."

"I'm good, thanks," I told him as I smiled at Mags, only now realising how strange it must have been for the children to wake up to her this morning. They had met her before, but only briefly in the salon. She must have handled the situation well. And so, obviously, had the kids. I felt proud of them.

"Where's Dad?"

Rob stood directly in front of me as he asked the question. Calm. Still. Waiting for my answer.

I jumped as the toaster popped out the two slices Mags had done for me. She put them on a plate and walked over to me.

"You and the children need time together," she said. "I'm going now but I'll be back as soon as I've showered and organised a few bits and pieces for Claire."

"Mags, I can't ask you to come back again. I couldn't impose like that."

"You don't have to ask. I'm offering. There's somewhere you need to be today, isn't there? Not suitable for little people."

I nodded. I had intended taking the children to the hospital with me because I had no alternative. I was glad to accept Mags' very kind offer.

"What about the salon?" she asked. "Do you need me to do anything there?"

"I put up a notice on the door. I have the appointments book in the car. On the front seat. It's not locked. Would you mind very much calling the people booked in for today? Just a vague illness excuse. You know yourself."

"Are you sick?" Rob asked, more insistently this time. "Or is Dad?"

Mags closed the kitchen door quietly as she left.

Now the three children were looking at me. Waiting for an answer, their eyes shadowed with worry, Josh's bottom lip quivering with the sadness the child sensed. For me, nothing at that moment could justify what Ben had done. If only he could see his children now. How his running away was about to shatter their security.

"Listen, guys," I said as heartily as I could, "I've something very important to tell you. But first I think we should have a treat. How about I make hot chocolate and marshmallows? Then we can sit around the table and chat."

Anna jumped up and down. Josh let go his hold on my leg and sat up at the table. Rob stared at me, a wealth of understanding in his sad eyes. He knew. He knew the 'something' I needed to tell them was about Ben and was not good news.

By the time I had the four hot drinks made, I had decided to stick with my 'Ben fell' story. The children would understand that. It made more sense to me too than any other reason I would not allow myself to imagine at that stage.

The twins tucked into their drinks but Rob and I sat there without touching them. He stared at me, waiting for me to tell him the truth. To make everything in his world right again.

"Why was Mags here this morning?" he asked.

"Mags nice," Anna said.

"Nice," Josh agreed.

It must have been seconds before I spoke but it felt like a lifetime as doubts and guilt paralysed my vocal chords. I was about to lie to my children. No! I was protecting them. They were just babies. But I taught them to always tell the truth. Just like Mam had taught me. So why was I lying to myself now? Why could I not admit that the life in Paircmoor I so cherished was anathema to Ben? That maybe his unhappiness had tripped him up and laid him low.

"Mom! Why won't you answer me?"

There was an edge of panic in Rob's voice.

I reached across the table and touched his hand. "Sorry, Rob. I guess I'm still a bit tired. Okay. You all know Dad loves being out and about in the fresh air?"

They nodded.

"So he decided to go for a long walk last night."

"He was shouting," Rob said. "He scared me."

And me too, I thought, as I wondered what lasting impact all this upset would have on the children. Rob in particular.

"He was sorry, Rob. I told you it was just a silly game we were playing. Anyway, he decided to run for a while. It was very dark and windy and wet. The storm blew a big branch from a tree down on to the road. Daddy didn't see it in the dark and he tripped over it."

Josh put his hand up to his mouth, covering the frothy cocoa moustache along his top lip.

"Oh! Daddy sore!"

I nodded. Now the story was falling into place.

"That's right, Josh. He was sore in his chest so the ambulance came and took him into hospital. The nurses and doctors are looking after him now."

They were silent, each absorbing the details at their own pace.

"Us go to see him," Anna said.

I thought they probably would not be allowed into Intensive care. Besides, I would not want them to see their daddy all tubed up.

"Not for a day or two, Anna. They are busy fixing his chest so we won't want to get in their way. I'll go to the hospital later to ask the doctors when we can bring Daddy home."

"Phone them and ask them now," Rob said.

There was no fooling my eldest son. Not that I wanted to dupe him. Just to protect him until we knew exactly what situation his father had landed us in. He had inherited Ben's creativity and capacity to remove himself from the hurly-burly of daily life into a completely private space only he inhabited. But that didn't mean that Rob was not totally aware of what was going on around him. He was an extraordinarily clever, self-sufficient, observant child, who did not take kindly to being underestimated.

"I phoned the hospital when I got up, Rob. They said

he's sleeping now. He's getting better but it may be a few days before he's well enough to come home."

He nodded. Satisfied, I hoped.

"Are you going to work when Mags comes back?" he asked.

"No. Not for a few days."

Luckily, I would not have been working anyway for the next two days. Sunday and Monday were my days off. I just then thought of Tina and wondered if she had gone to the salon this morning. I'd have to ring her as soon as I got a chance. Another person I had let down along with the clients I had to cancel.

I looked at the three worried little faces around the table. "I have some good news too," I said. "Della is on her way back from America. She will be here later today."

As I said that, I realised I was making an assumption. Maybe Della would just visit Ben in the hospital and go straight back to Dublin without coming to Cowslip Cottage.

Josh and Anna were clapping their hands, doubtless anticipating treats from their grandmother.

"She will be going to the hospital to see Dad. I'm not certain she will have time to come out here too," I explained. "Besides, she will be very tired from all the travelling."

"Us go see her and Daddy in the hospital," Anna decided.

I reached my hand across to her.

"You'll get to see Della. And Daddy too. But maybe not for a day or two yet. Is that alright?"

Head to one side, mouth pursed, Anna thought about it. If she agreed, the boys would too. She nodded her approval.

I smiled at them. "Now, do you want to have another game of Snap or will I turn on the TV for you? I know it's not TV time but I'll allow it for today."

They were off their chairs and racing towards the lounge in the blink of an eye.

As I watched them scamper ahead of me, I knew the children and I would somehow muddle through this mess.

What I dared not think about was whether it would be with or without my husband.

CHAPTER SEVENTEEN

Sunday 9th December 2012

She was leaning over him, her face lined by living. A good life, he thought, as he noted the laughter lines. He saw too the slight puckering around her lips as if she was holding in some very private sorrow. Something secret and dark that must be hidden. He met her eyes and knew she understood his pain.

"Good morning, Ben," she said. "How are you feeling?"

He looked beyond her, to the curtain that was pulled around his bed, to the drip stand beside him, the various tubes and machines, and wondered if he was already dead. He remembered the cave, the white crested waves angrily pushing towards where he sat, his fear of going back to Paircmoor far greater than the fate the sea might have in store for him.

"You're in hospital," she said. "You were brought to Intensive Care last night. My name is Marion. I'm Ward Sister here."

So, even the sea had rejected him. He had failed, yet again.

"Can you remember how you got here?" she asked.

He closed his eyes and looked through the darkness to last night. He remembered the cold, the wet, the despair.

Then he saw Ellen Riggs. Her back was turned to him, her head bent, her hand to her mouth as if she was trying to supress a laugh. Of course she was. His adolescent crush on her was as amusing as it was pathetic. He opened his eyes in order to escape the image.

"What day is it?" he asked.

"Saturday."

Leah's busiest day in the salon. She would be there now, colouring and cutting the old biddies' hair, asking them where they were going on holiday, being mistress of her little hairdressing empire.

"Your wife rang," Marion said. "She will be in to see you later."

Weary, he closed his eyes again and was back in the cave. He remembered someone warm and kind singing to him. A lullaby. There had been a siren and lights and pain. Massive pain.

And then he saw them. The three of them. Rob, Anna and Josh. Huddled together. Terrified. He wanted to ask the Marion person beside him to look after his children because their mother was at work and their father was trapped in a hell of his own making. He could neither open his eyes nor speak. He had let them down. He would always let them down. Their image faded, leaving behind a shame so deep it hit him with the force of physical pain.

He welcomed the agony as the punishment he deserved, and welcomed his lapse into unconsciousness as the escape he craved.

I grabbed my phone when it rang, terrified it was the hospital calling to say Ben had a relapse. That I was now a widow.

It was Tina offering to babysit, cook, shop or help me in any way she could.

"Thank you so much, Tina. I'm sorry I didn't get around to contacting you sooner. I hope you didn't go to the salon this morning."

"No, I didn't. Mags rang me early to tell me Mr Parrish is in hospital. Anyway, Lady Paircmoor, sorry, I mean Mrs Henderson, rang Mom last night to tell her that you were out looking for Mr Parrish. She asked us to search around our area for him."

So, Viv Henderson had taken it on herself to broadcast the fact that I had lost track of my husband. Truth was, I had. I should be grateful that she had also asked people to search. I was pretty sure that by the time she was finished spreading the news the whole village was searching. And tittering.

"I knew opening the salon today would be the last thing on your mind," Tina added.

She was right but at the same time I would have to make decisions about it over the weekend. It was, after all, our sole source of income. Plus Ben's unemployment payment, of course. That didn't go very far on groceries for our family of five.

"Yes, Tina, my priority now is to help Ben recover. I'll see how he's doing over the weekend and then decide. I'll let you know as soon as I can. I appreciate your offer of help. Thank you."

After the call ended, I knew there were chores I should be doing, lists I should be making, decisions I should be taking. Even though Mags had given me the opportunity to sleep on this morning, I felt weary. It was more than physical exhaustion. I was pinned to the chair by the weight of worry. From what I could piece together, Ben had gone onto the strand, knowing the tide was on the way in. Had he deliberately put his life at risk? Why would he do that when he was so enthusiastic about going to the States to work for Hugh's big-wig brother-in-law?

I remembered the A&E doctor asking me last night if I had noticed any changes in Ben's behaviour, in his mood. What she should have asked was if I had noticed him at all. I would have had to answer no. I had managed to lump him together with the children on my never-ending to-do list. Perhaps that was why he had shouted at me. His way of getting my attention. And smashing the vase? I had judged that to be a spoiled-brat tantrum. Now I wondered if I should have told Doctor Nyhan. How could I do that without admitting I had been too busy to give my husband any of my time or attention? My fault. All my fault.

"You look sad, Mom. Are you lonely for Dad?"

Rob had materialised in front of me. I had not heard him leave the lounge and come into the kitchen. Also my fault. More guilt.

He came to stand beside me, which was as close as Rob usually liked to be. But this morning he moved forward to sit on my knee and put his arms around my neck.

"I'm a little bit lonely, Rob, but I know the doctors and nurses will soon make him better. Then he'll be home to us."

"I went out and looked in the broken tin."

Shit! He was talking about an old biscuit tin I kept for disposal of broken glass and sharps. And hand-painted vases crafted by beautiful women.

"Why did you do that?"

"You said the big bang last night was a cup Dad dropped. I wanted to see it. But the flower thing Ellen made is in the broken box. Not a cup."

He wriggled a bit on my knee so that he was looking directly into my face. Challenging me.

"You said a lie."

So I had. Many lies. All about mommies and daddies playing silly games and daddies tripping over fallen branches in the dark of night. I looked into my son's eyes and saw the confusion there. The hurt. How could I explain to him that the knowing of unfiltered truth was too heavy a load for a five-year-old? As it was, at that moment, for me also. It was beginning to wash over me in waves. Icy splashes of truth. I saw now that since we had moved to Paircmoor, Ben had been quiet, uncommunicative, even sullen. While I had jumped on the work/home treadmill, I had forgotten to look behind me to see how Ben was doing. My fault. My fault.

I put my arms around Rob. He cuddled into me, his face cradled against my neck. I felt the wispy puffs of his warm breath and remembered the first moment I had held him in my arms. My new-born, skin to skin, heart to heart, soul to soul. A bond never to be broken. Not even by the lies I must now tell him.

"I made a mistake, Rob. That's different to telling a lie. But I'm sorry you're upset."

"Is Dad very sore?"

"Yes, his chest is but the doctors are giving him medicine to make it better."

"So who will mind us while Dad is in hospital?"

"*I* will," I said.

Rob gave me a tight squeeze and then ran off to join the twins, leaving me to contemplate the enormity of what I had just promised him. My 'suppose' line of thinking took over. Suppose Ben took a long time to recover.

Suppose he would never again be fit to either look after the children or to work. Suppose I could not get someone to run the salon for me. Suppose the salon had to close and Ben was an invalid and we had to subsist on social welfare.

The only thing I knew for certain was that I would always do the best for my children.

All of them.

And that was another decision made.

CHAPTER EIGHTEEN

By the time Mags returned to Cowslip Cottage, I had managed to get the children and myself washed, dressed and fed. That was the easy part. Keeping their minds off worrying about their father was the challenge. Just as I was about to put on their coats to take them for a walk, Mags arrived in the door, followed by her daughter.

"How are you feeling, Claire?" I asked, surprised to see her here. "How is your back?"

"Just a little uncomfortable," she said. "Nowhere near as serious an injury as my mom probably told you."

Both Mags and Claire laughed then. I watched mother and daughter exchange glances. Their deep understanding and acceptance of each other was apparent.

I looked at Anna, my mini-me, her tongue between her teeth as she sat on the kitchen floor, concentrating on pulling on her wellington boots. I had a surreal moment. A speeding by of twenty, twenty-five years. All the problems of today, unemployment, illness, smashed vases, money difficulties, would be over. Anna would be settled into her career, the boys off living the lives they had chosen for themselves, Ben and me moving towards comfortable old age. And then, in one magic moment, Anna and I would laugh and exchange glances of complete acceptance and understanding.

"I'm so sorry to hear about Ben's accident," Claire said. "How is he today?"

I smiled at her, comforted by my glimpse into the future. Ben would be fine. He would recover and flourish. With my help. He must. How else could I ever have my precious moment of understanding between grown-up Anna and ageing me?

"He's through the worst now, Claire."

"Him fell over a tree and hurted his chest," Anna piped up without lifting her head from her boot task.

"He did," Mags said. "But he's getting better now."

It was my turn to look at Mags. I saw the same doubt in her eyes as I felt in my heart. And then the questions began to whirl around in my head again. *Why, why, why* had Ben climbed down onto the strand when the tide was rushing in?

"I hope you don't mind Claire coming along," Mags said. "I thought I would bring the little ones out for a walk to get a bit of fresh air. I'd need help to keep a proper eye on them."

"And on me!" Claire added.

I left quickly, knowing the children were in safe hands. I needed so desperately to see Ben, to touch him, to let him know I loved him enough to fix whatever was so wrong in our lives.

The four-bed Intensive Care unit was an oasis of calm. Silent except for the rhythmic sounds of the monitors. The cyber nurses. Ben's colour was better, his sleep more natural in comparison to his comatose state last night. He was still on oxygen but most of the tangle of wires and tubes had been removed. The raised back of his bed supported him in a half lying, half sitting position. I wanted to hold his hand, but he seemed so peaceful I didn't want to disturb him. Instead, I sat beside him, realising I had not really looked at him for a long time, finding new lines on the familiar face. There were a few white hairs too that I, a hairdresser, had not noticed. That I, a wife, had failed to see.

I started as someone softly called my name. I turned to see Doctor Nyhan standing behind me. I wondered for a moment if she had gone home at all.

"Good afternoon, Mrs Parrish. I hope you got some rest."

I nodded and smiled at her.

"How is he doing?"

"Ben's condition is much improved today, as you can see. His tests are going well so far. I'm just waiting on a few more results. If they are as I expect, then we'll move him from Intensive Care into a general ward."

"His heart," I asked. "Will it be permanently damaged?"

"As I told you, results are looking good but it's early days. He'll need follow-up with a cardiologist. I'm referring him on."

"So when can we expect to have him home?"

She hesitated. One second, two, three. She glanced from me to Ben and back again. "Depends," she said.

"Depends on what?"

I saw conflict in her eyes. In her hesitation to answer.

I heard a murmur and turned back towards Ben. He was staring at me, his forehead wrinkled in a deep frown, his eyes narrowed. It was as if he didn't recognise me. I moved closer, leaned over him.

"It's Leah," I said, reaching for his hand. "How are you, sleepy-head?"

He pulled his hand abruptly away from me and turned his head. As if he was afraid of me. Or hated me. I sat back, devastated by the rejection.

"What's going on?" I asked. "Is his memory affected? Is he brain damaged?"

When Dr Nyhan didn't answer, I turned to see that she had left, as silently as she had come, taking with her the answers to my questions.

Even though her flight from San Francisco landed twenty minutes early in Dublin, Della Parrish felt time had slowed down to an unbearable crawl. She needed to be with her son now, this very instant, but she had yet to travel from Dublin to Paircmoor.

She got a taxi from the airport to her home in Howth, taking just minutes to find her car keys and load her unpacked cases into the boot. She ran back to turn on the alarm and lock up. As she gave a last glance around the house, her eyes fell on the family portrait which took pride of place in the hall. It had been taken just a month before Gavin died. Five years ago. In it he looked handsome, strong, healthy, standing beside her and their two sons. No hint that a rogue artery was about to burst and that she was soon to become a widow. He had died on the floor of the office he loved more than anything or anyone else. Without saying goodbye. Without resolving his issues with Ben.

Della quickly keyed in the code and closed the door.

Nothing mattered now more than reaching Ben. To protect him from himself. And from his past.

"Your husband will sleep for a while yet, Leah," the nurse said. "Why don't you take a break for yourself?"

I was not sure he was really sleeping. His head was still turned away from me. So I continued to sit by his bedside as nurses came and went, checking monitors and making notes in his charts. I whispered to him occasionally. Things, like how much I loved him and that the children missed him. There was no response. I sat so long listening to the busy sounds of medical equipment and watching the rise and fall of his chest that I began to feel sleepy. What I most wanted was for Ben to turn towards me and tell me what had happened. And why.

I stood. I needed coffee, fresh air and to phone about the children. I told Ben I would be back soon. He either didn't hear or didn't care.

As I pushed open the exit door of Intensive Care to leave, I spotted Della coming down the corridor. A young nurse was scurrying to keep up with her.

"Leah! How is he? I've just learned he had a heart attack. Why didn't you tell me?"

She was level with me, the nurse breathless in her wake.

"He's good, Della. I didn't want to worry you more than necessary. Who told you?"

"Never mind. I just want to see him now."

I saw the distressed look on the young nurse's face and knew Della had somehow got the information from her. She was good at that.

"Just one visitor at a time," the nurse said. "And, Mrs Parrish, Mrs Leah Parrish is the next of kin. So . . ."

She let the 'so' hang in the air. As if I had a choice.

"I was just about to go for a cup of coffee," I said. "You go ahead, Della. But be warned, he's not himself. He may not talk to you."

She had gone inside before I had even finished the sentence. She made a beeline for Ben's bed. I watched as she sat in the chair still warm from me, as she gently laid a hand on his forehead, as he turned towards her, as she wrapped her arms around him.

His body shook with sobs while she cradled him. They looked like an animated version of Michelangelo's Pietà, where the suffering and grief of mother and son were released from the confines of marble, to live and breathe and cry in the Intensive Care Ward. They were a unit. Complete in their sharing of a very private moment.

I turned and walked away.

CHAPTER NINETEEN

I had smoked in my late teens. It had been the cool thing to do at that time, and Leah Scally, as I was then, was always one of the cool people. I soon gave up because I could not afford cigarettes on my trainee stylist pay. I had never since regretted my decision. That is until I found myself standing outside the hospital where my husband lay recovering – or not – from his pelting by wind and wave. I watched a group of smokers huddled beside the *No Smoking on Campus* sign. I envied their camaraderie, their cosiness inside the protective cloud of smoke. My yearning for a nicotine hit was so strong I had to rush past in case I found myself begging for a cigarette.

I walked through the car park and onto the main street. I did my weekly grocery shop in the mall on the outskirts and rarely came into the centre, so the area was not familiar to me. As I looked up and down, I saw that a right turn would bring me towards a park. I headed in that direction. It would have been a beautiful space had it not been strewn with litter. A bugbear of mine. Sweet wrappers, plastic bottles, even a disposable nappy beside a laurel hedge. I saw a wooden seat at the far end. It was under the branches of an oak, bare now. I sat and imagined for a moment how beautiful it would be in spring, resplendent in fresh foliage.

My call to Mags was short and sweet. Yes, the children were fine. They were having fun. I heard them laughing. A carefree, happy sound. I realised this was something I had not heard for a while. But then, how would I know how often they laughed?

"Ben's mother is with him now," I told her. "I'll hop back in to see him again and then I'll be home."

"No rush, Leah. Take as much time as you need."

The thanks I gave her before I cut the call seemed so inadequate. How could I ever have thought her to be disobliging and unreliable? I squirmed on the seat, feeling now that the laths were damp and cold. Or maybe my discomfort had far more to do with the level of my misjudgement about everything. And everyone. Even Ben. Especially Ben. There had been real anger in his eyes when he had looked at me. And real rejection as he had turned his face away. Why? Yes, it was very difficult for him to be unemployed. He had fallen far from the heady Dublin days. But then, goddamn it, so had I. Except I did not have the time or energy for self-pity. And Della, making everything worse by pandering to him.

There I went again. Judging. Misjudging.

I got up and walked onto the street. I was conscious of a wet patch from the seat on the back of my coat. Anyone walking behind me would probably think I peed my pants. A very minor humiliation after what I had been through in the past few days.

As I approached the hospital gates, I had to wait at the pedestrian crossing for the lights to change. The last in the string of cars to pass looked familiar. When it came level with me I saw that Viv Henderson was behind the wheel. Sitting beside her in the passenger seat was Minnie Curran, wearing a scarf over her hair and a frown on her face. Either they did not see me or else decided to ignore me. They headed for the Accident and Emergency Department. Of course. Why not? Minnie would need all the evidence she could get in order to maximise her claim against me. Viv would advise her well.

I followed in the direction Viv had taken, wondering if I should go into A&E and ask Minnie how she was. Or should I stay away? Not admit liability for her scalded scalp. Hadn't Tina said it was not my fault? My legs were shaking. I looked ahead to A&E and saw Viv and Minnie go in the door. I could imagine the triage nurse taking notes as Minnie told her in graphic detail how her local hairdresser had burned her scalp through negligence and incompetence. Tears of frustration sprang to my eyes. What had I done to deserve all this shit? I worked hard, looked after my family, I didn't steal or deal drugs. I had never broken the law or been deliberately unkind to anybody. So why was fate being so cruel to me?

I turned and walked towards the main reception area. I could access Intensive Care from there without having to risk meeting Viv Henderson and Minnie. I was reaching the limits of my strength and confidence. I must, somehow, get through all this. Get Ben home and fit again, deal with the salon and Minnie Curran's accident, or injury, or attempted murder. Whatever charge she and Viv Henderson cooked up. Look after the children. Cope with Della. Pay for the groceries, the heating and electricity, clothing, shoes, toys. No time at all for shaking legs and teary eyes.

I took a deep breath and then headed in to see Ben.

When I got back to Intensive Care, it was as if I had never been away. Della was still leaning over her son and Ben was turned towards her. As I got nearer I could see that his shoulders were no longer shaking. At least the crying had stopped. Their heads were close. They were whispering. I felt as if I should apologise for intruding. I sat on the side of the bed.

"You must be exhausted from travelling, Della," I said. "Why don't you take a break?"

"Oh no! I came here to be of some help to you both. You go home to the children, Leah. I'll stay with Ben."

I looked to Ben for support. He was turned towards me now, but not meeting my gaze. It obviously suited him well to have his mother fawning all over him. Being a child. And that was exactly what I longed for at that moment. To be four years old, sitting on Mam's knee, breathing in the scent of her Eau de Cologne, basking in her warmth, and the sense of security and belonging I had been too young at that age to recognise as love. I understood Ben's need for his mother. However, I wished he could find a little of the same need for me.

The nurse assigned to Ben's care approached.

"I'm sorry," she said. "One visitor at a time in ICU, please."

"My daughter-in-law is just leaving," Della said. "Isn't that right, Leah?"

I debated about having a stand-up fight with her. Grabbing her by the scruff of the neck and frogmarching her out the door. My sympathy of last night had been wasted on her.

"I need to speak with the doctor," I said. "I'll wait."

"Doctor Nyhan? I've already spoken with her," Della said.

I stood, kissed Ben on the forehead without saying a word. I did not trust myself to speak without crying or cursing. His lips moved as if to say something but then he just shook his head.

"Tell the children I'll be out to Paircmoor to see them some time tomorrow, "Della said.

I waved wordlessly in her direction. I had assumed she would be staying in Cowslip Cottage. I had no idea now what her plans were. Probably booked into the best hotel this town had to offer. Or maybe she would spend the night by Ben's bedside. Whatever their plans, Della and Ben, it was clear I was not part of them.

On the way out I left instructions at the nurses' station that Ben's medical condition must not be discussed with anyone but me. His wife. His next of kin. The mother of his children. The woman who apparently had driven him to clamber down a cliff path, in a storm, onto a tide-lashed beach.

I drove home quickly. I needed to know I still had a place in my children's lives.

The trees on the avenue to Cowslip Cottage dipped and swayed in the rising wind. I parked beside Ben's jeep, thankful that at least I knew where he now was. Rain started as soon as I put my foot on the ground. I made a dash to the front door. It opened before I had a chance to put my key in the lock. Claire Hoey stood there, the little troupe of children around her. My children. I stooped down and opened my arms to them.

"I hope you were all good for Claire and Mags."

"They're the best," Claire said, as the twins ran into my arms and Rob came to stand beside me.

"We had good fun, Mom," he said. "We played football and had races."

His face was more animated than I had seen it for some time. The smile on his mouth was touching his eyes, making them sparkle in an un-Rob-like way.

"I won," Anna announced. "At everything."

"Me too," Josh said.

Anna began to tug on my hand. As I stood to follow her lead into the kitchen, I got the most wonderful aroma. I suddenly realised I was hungry.

"We make surprises for you," Anna said as she dragged me over to the counter where a batch of muffins was cooling on a wire tray.

Mags was standing at the hob, wooden spoon in hand. Pots were bubbling and boiling. She turned towards me and smiled.

"You have three great little bakers," she said. "But you must eat your dinner before you get any cake. Isn't that right, guys?"

It was a relief to give in. To allow myself to be managed by Mags. To have her send the children to watch TV with Claire, to see a plate of delicious spaghetti bolognese placed in front of me. To feel cared for. Understood.

"Eat up," she ordered.

I did as told, realising now why Claire was still living at home with her mother. It was a safe place to be. And Mags was a very talented cook.

"How is he?" she asked.

How did I answer that question? That I didn't know

because he would not talk to me? That it was clear he wanted his mother, not me, beside him?

"He's improved," I said. "He'll probably be moved out of Intensive Care soon. Having his mother with him now seems to be a comfort to him."

Mags was looking at me, her eyes narrowed. She knew. She had heard the hurt, the pain of rejection, in my voice.

"He's been through a lot. So have you," she said.

She turned away and began to move quietly around the kitchen, cleaning and tidying things away while I ate.

Then she brought me a mug of coffee.

"Let me call your little scallywags so that they can give you your muffin," she said.

They crowded around me, my precious children, presenting a muffin as if it were decorated with the crown jewels. It was so much better than that. They watched, wide-eyed, as I bit into the cake, clapped their hands as I made *yum-yum* sounds, laughed as I licked my lips. They cuddled into me as I put my arms around them. I closed my eyes and gloried in the warm weight of the twins on my knees, the soft touch of Rob's silky hair against my face.

By the time I opened my eyes again, Mags and Claire had gone. I would ring them later to thank them. I could cope now. With whatever lay ahead. Nothing mattered more than my children. I would always be there for them. All of them.

CHAPTER TWENTY

Ben was sleeping. Della could still discern the child in his features. The straight nose and high forehead. Very like his dad. In appearance only. Gavin had been strong. Dominant. In charge. The vulnerability showed in Ben's mouth and the shadows in his eyes when he was unguarded.

He muttered in his sleep. Della reached across and stroked his hair, realising only now that there were quite a few white hairs amongst the dark ones.

His eyes opened.

"What time is it?" he asked.

"Almost nine o'clock at night. You've been asleep for a while."

"Why are you still here, Mom? You must be exhausted after your flight."

"I'm fine. Don't you worry about me. Your only concern now is to get yourself better."

He shook his head. "It's too late for me."

She caught his hand and held it tight. "I won't hear any of that defeatist talk, Ben. You have the children to think of. And Leah."

"Leah? Jesus! I can't even look her in the eye. She'd be

better off without me."

Della sat back in her chair. She had suspected of course that history was repeating itself. That was why she had needed so desperately to be by his side. But she had hoped. Until now. She leaned towards him.

"Why now, Ben? You've such a brilliant opportunity waiting for you in the States. All you have to do is meet Zack Milburg and –"

"*Mom! Stop!* Face facts. That man would have no interest in employing an out-of-work, second-rate architect from Ireland. Even if I'm an in-law of his sister. You must admit my portfolio is far from impressive. He only employs the best. I don't know why I let you persuade me that he was the answer to my prayers."

"You designed that block of apartments on the quay in Dublin. Your father invested in one. We still own it. Surely you're proud of that?"

"I'm tired, Mom. I need to rest and so do you. Just go now. Tell Leah I'll see her tomorrow."

"I won't be seeing Leah tonight. I'm staying in town."

"Oh! I bet you're booked into the hotel across the street from the hospital. You're camping out here just in case I let the family secret slip."

Della sat still, hands clasped together in her lap. She had heard it all before. Had felt the lash of his anger and self-hatred. She had absorbed the poison then. Been strong enough for them both. She closed her eyes for a moment, praying for the energy to be his strength this time around also. Leah would not understand. She had not been there when he had been pulled from the river. Lifeless. Vomiting water as the paramedics worked on him. Later, vomiting toxins when he overdosed. Pumping fountains of blood when he slashed his wrist. Crying bitter, bitter tears each time he realised he was still alive.

She opened her eyes and smiled at him.

"It's not a secret, Ben. It's just not anyone else's business."

"Not even my wife's business? For fuck's sake, Mom, I spent three months in the psychiatric unit of the Booly Clinic. I was utterly insane with sadness. That's what it was, insanity, even if the rip-off clinic dressed it up as hormone imbalance. What if my children have my manic-depressive gene?"

"Language! Don't be vulgar, please, Ben. You had an episode when you were sixteen. That's twenty years ago and there's never been a recurrence. What happened last night was an accident. Wasn't it?"

Ben pulled himself up to a sitting position. He leaned forward and stared into his mother's face. She had been treated kindly by time. It would never have been Della's style to have her life story written on her face for all the world to see. She should have several lines for her husband's affairs, another for his sudden death, and a great big gouge across her forehead for her youngest son's weakness and failures. His madness. Instead she had tolerated her husband's indiscretions, bore his death with fortitude, referred to her son's suicide attempts as 'an episode' and kept her face unlined by life.

He flopped back against his pillows. He was too exhausted to marshal the confused thoughts in his mind. Had he stumbled thoughtlessly down the cliff and been trapped by the high tide, or had he deliberately sat and waited for death to wash over him in the dark and freezing cave? Did he love and admire his mother or did he hate her? And his wife, the one he had, not the one he had wished he had. Ellen Riggs had been a distraction. A humiliating self-delusion. What about Leah? The disappointment she tried to hide. The way she never complained about having to be the breadwinner, but yet he felt her resentment. Every order she issued, every list she wrote, every detail of childcare she organised, was an indictment of his failure.

"They suggested that I talk to a member of the psychiatric team," he said.

"And?"

He stared at her, his eyes now so dark she could not read any expression in them.

"You think I would volunteer to put myself through all that shit again? As you already said, what happened at the beach was an accident. I confirmed that. They agreed there was no need for psychiatric assessment."

Before Della could react, a nurse came to the bedside and began checking monitors.

"You need to rest, Ben," she said. "And Mrs. Parrish, I'm sure you need some rest too."

"No. I'm good, thank you."

"Your son must have quiet now. He's been through a serious trauma. Goodnight, Mrs Parrish."

Della's expression flashed from shock to disapproval. She stood, put on her coat and picked her handbag up from the floor.

Ben would have laughed if he had the energy. It was the first time he had seen anyone getting the better of Della Parrish.

"I'll see you tomorrow, Ben. Sleep tight."

Then she was gone. Head in the air, back ramrod straight. With her went any chance he had of making sense of what had happened. Any chance he had of finding a way through the maze of unanswered questions. Through the weight of sadness pressing on his chest.

He turned his head so that the nurse would not see this grown man cry for his mother.

Get up, Leah, I told myself. Make decisions. Organise groceries, laundry, house-cleaning.

Instead, I continued to sit and watch my children sleeping. I saw myself in Anna, Ben in the boys. I tried to see the people they would become. Anna could be anything from a teacher to the Taoiseach. She probably already knew where her life was headed and was steering towards her goal. Josh was quiet and caring. He might be an environmentalist or a social worker. Though he had a lovely sense of fun that might tempt him into a less intense career path. He would be a good husband and father. And then there was Rob. I sat longer beside his bed than the twins. His future was harder to imagine. He could be an architect like his father. He was artistically as well as intellectually gifted. But as I watched him sleep I imagined him as an astronomer. Or an astrophysicist, not that I was sure what that entailed, but it sounded like something he would love. Studying the Universe. Discovering new planets. Observing. Being alone, his intellect roaming the galaxies, solving the mysteries of life. I kissed him softly on the forehead and crept out of his room.

Back in the kitchen, I sat at the table, sipping my hot milk, even though my aching limbs told me I would sleep tonight even if I drank coffee before bed. Mags had rung earlier and offered to babysit the children tomorrow afternoon while I went to the hospital. An offer I gladly accepted.

That thought reminded me that Ben's phone was still in the lounge. I should put it on charge overnight and take it in to him. At least I would be able to say good morning and goodnight to him without putting him through the obvious pain of having to look me in the eye. I brought his phone back to the kitchen and plugged it into the charger. Finished my milk, I rinsed my mug and put it in the dishwasher, then went around the house ensuring doors and windows were locked, taking comfort from the mundane routine.

Last check was on Ben's phone to make sure it was charging. It was up to ten per cent already. I wondered if it was password protected. Mine was. My head was still debating whether I should try or not when my hand reached out and switched on his phone. Then I knew. He did not have a password. But he certainly had a lot of messages waiting to be read. They were mostly from his mother. One from Ellen Riggs. The last message was from Hugh. His brother. Hugh, the perfect. Hugh, the high achiever. Hugh of the seven bedrooms and swimming pool. My hand overruled my head again. I opened the message.

You've got to tell Leah. She has a right to know the truth. Especially now.

I dropped the phone as if it was burning me. It was. Hugh's words were searing into my brain. What had I a right to know? Had Ben, after all, had an affair with Ellen Riggs? Did he intend to go and live alone in the States, leaving me and the children behind in Paircmoor? No! I knew without a trace of doubt that he loved the children too much to abandon them. So, did he intend to take the children and leave me behind?

I flopped onto a chair by the table. I was finding it hard to breathe. Ben had a secret. His brother knew what it was. It was a given his mother would know too. Probably what they were whispering about in the hospital. Could it be that this secret was so big and so dark it had almost cost Ben his life? I remembered now moments when his eyes seemed haunted. Times I spoke to him and he didn't even hear because his thoughts were so far away. Things I should have been concerned about if I had not been so busy organising.

If I had not been so busy keeping a secret of my own.

CHAPTER TWENTY-ONE

Sunday 28th November 2010

Ben woke to the sound of two nurses whispering as they stood at the end of his bed. They were the night-shift staff and would soon be going off duty. He gathered from their conversation that they had received notification of cutbacks in staff numbers. They were outraged, their whispers becoming louder as their anger grew. No consultation, they said. No consideration for the patients, for the standard of care. For their right to work after all their years of studying and training. He could empathise. They would have a hard road to travel, from rage to accepting their own powerlessness. Emigration might be their only option. He should tell them to go now. While they still had the courage. Before they were destroyed by self-doubt. He would have told them, except that he was reliving the day the redundancy memo had been circulated in his office.

Yes, he too had felt the outrage, ranted at the unfairness of protecting profits and sacrificing employees. His anger had been on behalf of the unfortunate people who would receive notice. Not himself. He knew he was an essential cog in the Walton, Walton & Meade firm. One of their best architects. The main driving force behind the acclaimed waterside apartment block. Innovative, yet sympathetic to the surrounding environment. A triumph of design, the press reports had said.

It is with deep regret we must inform you . . .

The letter had been hand-delivered to his desk. He had read it three times before he got past that opening line and three more times before he believed that he, Ben Parrish, was being thrown on the scrapheap. There had been redundancy pay, soon dwindled away on paying the huge mortgage on his devalued Dublin home. If it hadn't been for his mother, they could have become homeless. In his blacker moments since, he felt that would have been a better option than being buried alive in Paircmoor. Della was to blame for financing Leah's fantasy of living happily ever after in the arsehole of the country. She also was to blame for the fact that his teenage problems had to be kept secret. Especially from Leah. His darkness. His despair. He remembered the bite of the knife as it had sliced into his wrist, the spurt of blood, the drifting off into blessed oblivion, then waking up in hospital, hooked up to a blood transfusion. He remembered the times he had stashed his pills, then swallowed them when he had an overwhelming will to die and none to live, only to wake up to stomach-pumps in Intensive Care. And there had been the peace of drifting away in the embrace of the icy cold river, only to wake to the ubiquitous beeps of the monitors. Just like now. So many secrets.

The nurses had stopped whispering. One stood beside him and the other checked the screens. Ben didn't need to see any readouts. He heard his quickened heartbeat thump in his ears. Felt how thready and erratic his pulse was. Fear, his constant companion, was coursing through his veins. The sadness, the deep, deep, despair, was oozing from its dark hiding place. From the past. From his gut. From his cells. From the DNA he had passed on to his children.

"Ben! Take deep breaths," the nurse beside him ordered. "Stay calm."

"Leah!" he gasped. "My wife! I need to talk to my wife!"

He saw his mother approach just before the effort to breathe became too much.

The second Della opened the door to Intensive Care, she knew Ben was in trouble. One nurse was leaning over him and another was managing the numerous instruments attached to him. Della rushed to his bedside. He had an oxygen mask on and the nurse was urging him to slow his breathing.

"The doctor," Della said. "Have you called the doctor?"

The nurse glanced at her. Then she nodded to her colleague who came and caught Della by the arm.

"It would be better if you waited outside, please. The waiting room is first door on your right down the corridor."

"I know that! I'm Della Parrish. Ben's mother. What's going on with him? Why isn't there a doctor with him?"

All the time Della was asking questions, the nurse was leading her firmly towards the door.

"He needs rest and quiet now. The doctor will check on him later."

"I *demand* the consultant sees him now! He has private health care, you know."

They were at the door of the waiting room by now. The nurse opened the door and led Della to a chair inside.

Della opened her mouth to speak but the nurse got there first.

"Let me assure you, Mrs Parrish," she said. "It doesn't matter to us whether patients have private or public healthcare cover. Everyone gets the attention they need. There's a tea and coffee dispenser up the corridor if you want a drink. Make yourself comfortable."

The nurse went out, closed the door and disappeared in a haze of self-righteousness. Della sat there fuming. That snotty girl was just a whippersnapper. Very unlikely that she was a mother. Or that she had any understanding of what that meant. The all-consuming love, more intense than any other. The instinctive urge to protect your child, to shelter him from danger. From life. And, yes, there comes a letting-go time when the child becomes an adult and the mother becomes dispensable. Unless the child has a vulnerability. A need to be protected from himself. Unless that man-child is Ben. She knew from past experience that Ben was having a panic attack. He needed to hear her voice. Those nurses had no right to deny her access to her son. To deny Ben the support only his mother could give.

Della's hands began to shake. The trembling unsettled her. Overwhelmed her with unfamiliar feelings of doubt, and a coldness in the pit of her stomach she identified as fear. She could no longer deny it was happening again – a replay of Ben's nightmarish sixteenth year. Panic attacks and self-harm attempts. Rants followed by long silences. A palpable sadness. Had the idea of going to the States been the trigger? Had it been too much of a challenge for him? But why, why? It would have been a way out for him and his family. He hated Paircmoor, didn't he? So, as his mother, she had to help. Had to plan an escape route. She could have talked Zach Milburg into giving Ben a job, no matter what Hugh said to the contrary. She had done what she had thought was right. Hadn't she?

Her legs began to tremble. The room blurred as tears welled. Her body was telling her she was too old, too tired, to answer her own questions, to cope with her newfound doubts, to help Ben again. It had all been for nothing, the blind eye she had turned to her husband's affairs as she sat by Ben's bed in the hospital, the things they had sacrificed as a family to pay the exorbitant cost of the private treatment in the Booly Clinic, the carefully guarded secret. Now, she was under a compliment to Piper's very wealthy brother. She had gladly swallowed her pride for the sake of getting Ben a job. A new start. And this was her thanks. She started. Where had that vile thought come from? She had never looked after Ben for thanks. She did it because she loved him. Because he deserved success as much as Hugh. To see him get on with his life was all the thanks she needed.

The door opened and the whippersnapper nurse came in. Della had not realised the tears had tracked down her face until she saw the girl's expression soften.

"Don't be upset, Mrs Parrish. Ben is resting comfortably. He won't have visitors for a while though."

"I'm not a visitor. I'm his mother."

"I know. But he needs rest now."

"I won't disturb him. I just want to see for myself that he's alright."

The nurse shuffled from one foot to the other. She cleared her throat. She was obviously uncomfortable for some reason. Had they somehow injured Ben and were trying to cover up?

"Is there a problem with me seeing my son?"

"I'm sorry, Mrs Parrish. I think it would be better if you waited a while. Take some time to have lunch and maybe a walk in the fresh air. Ring later."

Della stood, hoping the shake in her legs was not noticeable.

"I want to see my son."

The nurse shook her head.

"I'm afraid you can't. Ben has said the only person he wants to see is his wife. We have to put his wishes first, Mrs Parrish."

Della stood there, willing herself not to cry. What else had she ever done except put Ben's wishes first? Leah, she didn't even know him, yet it was his wife he wanted. Nothing she could do now short of barging into Intensive Care. She nodded to the nurse.

"I'll be on my way. Thank you."

The girl laid her hand on Della's arm.

"I *am* sorry, Mrs Parrish. Ben has been through a lot. He'll come round."

Della lifted her chin, gave a tight smile, and left the room with whatever dignity she could muster. It felt like that was all she had left.

CHAPTER TWENTY-TWO

I must have been dreaming of my mother because when I woke in the morning, her words were echoing in my ears.

"You don't have to fight the world single-handed, Leah," she would always say. "Allow Lady Luck the space to help you."

She would have been wrong this time. A single-handed battle was my only option. I felt totally alone. Even more so as I remembered the message I saw on Ben's phone last night. The fact that Hugh knew something Ben had obviously been keeping from me made it even more humiliating. Della would know of course. In fact, she had probably ordered him to keep whatever it was secret from his wife.

The children were awake. I could hear Rob reading the twins a story. Anna was interrupting him every few sentences with questions. As I listened, I knew no matter what was wrong in my life, I had been blessed with my children. Our children. I jumped out of bed and threw on my dressing gown. I needed to see them. To put my arms around them and let them know how loved they were.

The three of them were in Anna's bed, she and Josh

snuggled underneath the duvet, and Rob sitting cross-legged on the end of the bed, facing them. They were so wrapped up in the story that they did not see me standing at the door. I soaked in the sight of Anna's head of blonde curls right next to Josh's dark hair. Side by side. And they always would be. They would grow up but never grow apart. I watched them mirror each other's expressions. Yes, Anna was more vocal, but Josh had the quiet strength to temper her impulsiveness. Two halves of a whole.

I marvelled, as I always did, at how beautiful our eldest son was. There was a depth to Rob's brown eyes, a translucence to his pale skin, an other-worldliness about him. And yet he was grounded in reality. He observed quietly. Everyone and everything. Just as I was now observing him. He knew I needed a lie-in this morning, so he had taken it on himself to entertain the twins. I felt a twinge of guilt. He was only five. He should not be burdened by that sense of responsibility. There were times when Rob was wise beyond his years and times when he was just a frightened little boy. Like two nights ago when he heard Ben and me arguing. I pushed those memories away. They had no place here with me and my children.

As I walked across the room to them, the treacherous idea crossed my mind that maybe Ben no longer had a place here either. The thought shocked me. Racked me with guilt. But then I remembered his irrational behaviour, running out into the storm in the pitch dark, putting his life at risk. Would it even be safe to allow him near the children?

Rob saw me first. He turned his dark, serious gaze on me.

"Mom! How is Dad this morning? When will he be home?"

"I made pictures for Dad," Anna said.

"Me too," Josh said.

"I made him a card," Rob added.

And then I was hit by how devastated I had been when I thought Ben might not survive the hypothermia. How bleak and empty a life without him had seemed then. I looked at the three anxious little faces turned towards me and knew one thing for certain. Ben Parrish might not love me. Perhaps he never did. But there was no doubt in my mind that he loved the children. And they, with all their hearts and childish drawings, loved their daddy.

"Tell you what, guys. We'll have a cuddle. Then we'll have breakfast and after that we'll ring the hospital to find out how Daddy is doing. How's that for a plan?"

Anna and Josh raised their tiny hands for high fives and Rob nodded his approval. Then we cuddled in together. All of us. Me and these precious little people Ben and I had created.

Rob cleared off the table after breakfast. He methodically scraped the residue off the cereal bowls into the scrap food bin, rinsed them under the cold tap and then put them in the dishwasher. When I squinted my eyes and held my head to one side, I could picture him as an adult. Caring, responsible. Maybe as a husband. A father. Maybe not.

"What you do, Mom?" Anna asked, mimicking my half-closed eyes and tilted head.

"Thinking about when you are all grown up," I said. "Are we ready to ring the hospital now?"

There was a chorus of yeses. I picked up my phone but, before I could key in the hospital number, the doorbell rang. I frowned. Mags was not due to call until afternoon so I had no idea who it could be. Anna was already as far as the door, Josh trotting behind her. Before I had even got up from my chair, I heard her squeal in excitement. She was talking to someone through the letterbox. That someone could only be Della. No one else caused Anna to squeal at such a high pitch. Even Rob showed signs of excitement as he preceded me out to the hall door.

So, Della had deigned to visit Cowslip Cottage.

"How are you?" I asked as I opened the door to her.

The children swamped their grandmother, not giving her time to answer. She was, as always, perfectly groomed but her face was pale and her eyes red-rimmed. Della had been crying.

I stood there, paralysed with fear.

"Have you been to the hospital this morning, Della? How is Ben?"

She looked at me and shook her head.

"What does that mean? Is he worse? Has he had another attack?"

I realised that my voice was shrill and I was frightening the children. Della obviously couldn't or wouldn't answer me. I rushed into the kitchen and phoned the hospital, knowing this is what I should have done as soon as I had woken.

"Leah Parrish," I said, when I had been connected to Intensive Care. "I'm enquiring about my husband, Ben."

"Could you hold on, please, Leah? Doctor Nyhan wants to talk to you."

As I waited, I began to shake. There had to be bad news. Why else would the doctor want to talk to me? And why else would Della arrive to our door looking like death warmed up? Death. It seemed to be lurking everywhere. In the ghosts of the poorhouse, in the violence of the storm, in the power of the ocean, in the ice-cold touch of Ben's skin and the erratic pumping of his heart. The hospital should have called me. I would have –

"Leah? Sorry for keeping you waiting. Kate Nyhan here. I believe you left a message at the desk that any discussions of your husband's medical condition were to be only with you. Is that right?"

"Yes," I said, more sharply than I intended. I just wanted her to get on with telling me the bad news.

"Well, I'd like to assure you, that I consult only with the patient. I speak to the next of kin, in this case, you, if I have the patient's permission. I have not given medical information to anyone else, either on the phone or in person. Nor would I ever do that."

"Oh, I see. I'm sorry – I –"

"Now, about your husband. He has improved enough physically to be moved to a general ward today."

"That sounds like very good news."

"Yes, he's recovering physically more quickly than we had anticipated. We have further tests to do before we can say anything definitive about long-term effects. But the trend is positive so far."

And then I heard it. The hint. The twice-repeated clue. Physically. Ben, because he was young and fit, was recovering well. *Physically.*

"Thank you, Doctor Nyhan. Goodbye."

On that note I cut the call. If I didn't ask the question, I wouldn't have to hear the answer.

I wondered, as I watched the children bring Della into the kitchen, what was behind her white-faced, red-eyed appearance. It could be age finally catching up with her. Even a much younger person would be jet-lagged after criss-crossing the Atlantic under such tragic circumstances. Maybe she had approached Doctor Nyhan in her arrogant way and demanded information about Ben's condition. She would have been told, politely, to keep her nose out. Or it could be the weight of the secrets she was hiding from me. The things, according to Hugh, that I '*had a right to know*'. It was so tempting to ask her now. To demand an explanation. But that would give her the satisfaction of refusing to tell me. Besides the message was on Ben's phone so it was up to him to explain. The children were gathered around their grandmother, looking for her attention.

"Guys, Della is very tired now. We must let her have a rest. You can watch your morning programme while I make coffee for her. Is that alright?"

I drew out a chair for Della and, without saying a word, she sat. Not one sarcastic comment. Not even a look down her nose at me. The children hugged her and then ran off to the lounge. I put on the kettle, then sat opposite my mother-in-law.

"You look tired, Della. How is your hotel?"

"It's good, thank you."

"You're welcome to stay here. You know that."

She nodded. A weary little bob of her head.

"Dr Nyhan has just told me that Ben is doing so well he will be moved from Intensive Care today. That's good news, isn't it?"

The kettle boiled so I went about making coffee, but not before I saw tears well in Della's eyes.

I was having difficulty adjusting to the idea of her showing any sign of vulnerability.

"You haven't told me if you've seen Ben today," I said. "Were you at the hospital?"

My back was turned to her as I got out mugs, milk and sugar.

"He won't allow me to see him."

Della had spoken so quietly I wasn't sure I had heard properly. I turned to face her. She looked old. Weary. Beaten down by sadness.

"What do you mean, Della? Surely he wants to see *you*, of all people."

She shook her head and then bowed it, as if ashamed of admitting her rejection by her son. Why? If there was anyone in the world Ben was close to, it was his mother. He idolised her. It was only a few days ago they were both hatching a plot to move our whole family over to America. Or at least I assumed it was the whole family. I still wasn't sure where I fitted into their great American dream. And now, when he needed all the support he could get, why would he be pushing her away?

"He told the staff not to let me in."

How cruel! I imagined one of my children refusing to see me under the same circumstances. How utterly heartbreaking that rejection would be. I reached across and took her hand. It was cold to the touch and shaking. It seemed Ben was adept at spreading the hurt around.

"He can't mean it, Della. He's been through so much and been so medicated, he doesn't realise what he is saying."

"Yes, he does. He wants to talk to you. That's why I came out here now. I'll mind the children while you go to see him. At least I can be useful that way."

She clung onto my hand. And I to hers. It was a fragile moment of mutual respect in a relationship which had been fraught with disrespect. I wanted to ask her about the text Hugh had sent. About the truth Ben was withholding. About Ben as a child. About the American job. But I felt words would break the tentative bond.

Then Della started to speak.

"Leah. There's something I should tell you –"

She suddenly stopped and withdrew her hand.

"Yes?" I prompted.

"Nothing. Nothing at all."

It was over. That moment of mutual respect. That moment which could have changed our relationship forever.

CHAPTER TWENTY-THREE

I rang Mags Hoey before I left the cottage. Just to let her know there would be no need for her to give up her Sunday to look after my little brood, as my mother-in-law would be babysitting today.

"That's fine, Leah," she said. "How about you call to me on your way back from the hospital. We can have a coffee and maybe a chat about the salon if you're up to it."

I agreed. I would have to face the salon situation sooner or later. Sooner was probably better.

Today, with Della looking after the children, was as good a time as any.

"Great, Mags. I'll give you a ring when I'm leaving the hospital. See you later."

"Tell Ben I was asking for him, won't you?"

I told her I would, but at that stage I had no idea if Ben would be interested in anything I had to say.

The Sunday visitors were out in force so it was difficult to get a parking space. I finally found one at the very back of the car park. That suited me because the nearer I got to the hospital, the more reluctant I was to go in there. I walked slowly away from the car, stopped every few steps, but yet the entry doors loomed. I wasn't sure what I was so afraid of. It could be that I knew Doctor Nyhan was not telling me the full story about Ben's condition. I had not allowed her to. Or it could be that I feared what Ben had to say to me. Or maybe my biggest dread was what *I* had to say to Ben.

I stopped at Reception to enquire. Just as well I did as I was told Ben was now in St Joseph's Ward on the first floor. So much for having a private chat with him. The ward would be lined with closely packed rows of beds, every word spoken within hearing range of the other patients. The lift up was crowded, everyone trying to avoid eye contact. It emptied onto the first floor, people scurrying off in different directions. I had to follow signposts to find St Joseph's. It turned out to be in the Coronary Care Unit. It was a four-bedded ward and nothing as bleak as I had anticipated.

Ben was in a corner bed near the window, giving him a view out over the town. He was sleeping. A more natural-looking sleep now that he no longer had the battery of monitors he had in Intensive Care. I put the clean pyjamas and shaving gear I had brought for him into his bedside locker. The children's drawings I put on top.

The elderly man in the adjacent bed nodded and smiled.

"He's asleep since they brought him in," he said. "I see he has a little fan club. His children, is it?"

I nodded and smiled back at him but silently cursed. I had intended pulling the curtain around the bed for privacy but that would seem churlish now. Besides, I knew instinctively this man was adept at finding out whatever he wanted to know.

"He's very young to have heart trouble, isn't he? I'm assuming you're his wife. Is that right?"

"Yes, Leah Parrish," I said, offering him my hand.

He manoeuvred himself across the bed to get closer to me. As he did so, the door opened and a smartly dressed, white-haired woman walked in. He dropped my hand as if it had burned him.

"My wife," he said, throwing back his bedspread and grabbing his dressing gown from the end of the bed. "We'll be going for a walk as far as the café. You can't say a word in here, you know. Someone's always poking their nose in."

"Really?" I said and managed not to laugh.

His wife offered him her cheek for a kiss. They smiled at each other before walking off arm in arm.

The three remaining patients were sleeping soundly. Including my husband. I regretted not bringing my book with me. Though with so many ifs and buts tumbling around in my head it would be difficult to concentrate on a novel. Instead, I took the time to watch Ben as he slept. He seemed restless, his eyes moving behind his closed lids. As if he sensed danger.

His eyes opened. He looked at me. I said nothing. I barely breathed, afraid that he would turn away from me again. He reached his hand towards me. I laced my fingers through his. His skin felt warm. He was alert. Alive.

"I'm sorry," he whispered. "I'm so, so, sorry."

I felt tears well up. This apology told me, without doubt, that Ben's foray onto the storm-swept strand had not been an accident. He had deliberately put his life at risk. This life we had carved out for ourselves in Paircmoor. For us and the children.

"Why, Ben?"

"Look. This is why."

He was holding his left hand towards me, palm up. I frowned, not knowing if I was supposed to take his hand or just stare at it. He pulled up the sleeve of his pyjamas.

"My wrist. Look at it."

I nodded, barely glancing at the scar I knew so well.

"The scar from way back when you were a kid. You had an accident with an electric saw. What about it?"

"It wasn't an accident. And it didn't involve a saw. I cut it with my Swiss Army knife. On purpose."

I glanced over my shoulder. The other patients were still sleeping.

"Don't worry," Ben said. "They're too out of it to hear. Or to judge."

I brought my attention back to the upturned palm in front of me and examined the scar in a new light. I traced its jagged course with my finger. It was a bumpy scar, as if the broken flesh had been gathered in clumps to stitch it back together. The accident with the saw had always made sense to me. Why would I have questioned it?

He was focused on me, his stare so intense it was as if he was trying to read my mind. So was I. My brain was reviewing every event, from the day we met to this very moment. I was desperate to decipher what was true and what was fabrication. I could see us, in what now felt like another lifetime, in our Dublin home, laughing, happy. Smug. And yet there had been times when I had wondered about the dark shadows in Ben's eyes. Shadows that had appeared a lot more frequently since our move to Paircmoor. Shadows I had been too busy to worry about.

I turned his hand over so that I would not be distracted by the scar.

"So, tell me," I said, "what really happened. The truth this time."

He flinched as if I had hit him. I knew, in my heart, that every word I said now would have a consequence. For Ben and for our future. He needed sympathy and understanding. But I needed the truth. God damn it, I deserved nothing less.

I touched his face, his hair. Felt the stubble on his chin, the softness of his lips. Grounded myself in the familiarity of the features I knew and loved. I stood and drew the curtains around the bed. We were enclosed in a warm glow as the wintery sunlight shone through the lemon fabric. An illusion of privacy on this day of broken illusions.

"Tell me about cutting your wrist, Ben. Why you did it. I'm listening."

He squeezed my fingers so tightly it hurt.

He leaned towards me and whispered. "When I was fifteen, my world began to change. I got so tired, Leah. Getting up in the morning was a huge effort. I would lie in bed and try to think of one good reason to go in to school. I never could. I had this overwhelming feeling of – of – outsidedness. I had family and friends, attended a good school, had hobbies. And yet I had nothing. I was empty inside. I was alone. At fifteen I did not have a future or the words to explain how I felt."

I stayed quiet but I was struggling to understand because at fifteen years of age I had not had the opportunity to lie in bed and wonder about a reason to get up. But I could see what an effort Ben was making to explain. I also knew this was just the start of the story. I nodded to encourage him.

"You don't understand, do you?" he said.

I couldn't deny that. "Your wrist, Ben. What happened?"

He shrugged. A careless gesture, as if hacking your wrist was nothing of note.

"Hugh gave me a Swiss Army knife for my sixteenth birthday. I had asked him for it. I needed it for scouting. Or so I thought. As soon as I had it in my hand, I realised it could be the answer to the suffocating, non-existence that passed for my life. The lethargy, the feelings of isolation, hopelessness and loneliness that were growing every day. I went into the bathroom, locked the door and cut my wrist with the sharpest blade. Just a nick. The pain reached through the fog in my brain. Brought me to life. It was all-consuming. It banished the sadness. The nothingness. It felt like the supportive friend I needed. But that initial relief did not last. So I had to cut again. And again. I managed to keep the small cuts hidden. I was the kind of kid who went unnoticed anyway."

How had Della not seen? I was sure I would be aware if one of my kids was cutting themselves. And what about Hugh? Or Ben's dad? Were they all so busy with their own lives they had not seen Ben struggle? That thought brought me back from the brink of blaming his family. I had not seen his struggle for the past – what – the past few weeks, months, years? Ever since he had been made redundant? Ever since he had done the right thing by marrying me?

"The scar, Ben. It's not a lot of little ones. It's a long, deep cut."

"That was when I knew I could no longer cope. Hugh had university, Dad had work and Mom had Dad. I had my Swiss knife. I drank a few swigs from the bottle of vodka I had taken from the drinks cabinet, sat on the side of the bath, and cut. Deep and straight."

I instinctively reached for his wrist and touched the

scar. I closed my eyes and shuddered. Not at the feel of the physical scar. I was used to that. It was the thought of Ben, so young, so desperate.

"Mom found me before I bled to death. I don't know how because she was meant to be out for the night. I have often since cursed her for –"

The curtain drew back with a swishing sound. A nurse stood there, a tray of instruments in hand.

"Mr Parrish, I must take blood samples from you." She turned to me. "Excuse us, please. We won't be long."

I stood up and immediately had to put my hand on the bedside locker to steady myself.

"I'll grab some lunch, Ben," I said. "I'll be back soon."

He looked at me and in his eyes I saw his plea for understanding. For compassion. For forgiveness.

I know he must have seen the hurt, the anger and the utter confusion in mine.

I left the hospital, and walked to the park with the bench under the oak tree and the litter under the hedge. It was becoming my place of refuge.

CHAPTER TWENTY-FOUR

"Still think this was a good idea to come up here, Mom?" Claire Hoey asked.

Mags glanced at her daughter, then immediately turned back to the road again.

They had left Paircmoor village behind and were driving towards the Conicmoor Hills. The road narrowed as it climbed. The higher you climbed the more spectacular the view of the surrounding countryside. If you could see, that is. A thick fog blanketed the area. The ditches seemed to be closing in on them, and the line of grass that grew in the centre of the pot-holed tarmacadam was getting more difficult to discern.

"We're nearly here now," Mags said. "Her house is very close to the signpost for St Brigid's Holy Well. That's on the left there. See it?"

Claire saw the sign. She remembered a time when all the villagers, or most of them, had trooped up here on the first of February every year, to honour Saint Brigid on her feast day. She smiled as she recalled her childish devotion to Brigid. She had long since left it behind, along with her belief in fairy tales.

"Ah! Here we are," Mags said, as she brought the car to a stop beside a gate.

"I hope she's home after traipsing all the way up here."

"Of course she is, because today is Sunday. Thursday is the only day she leaves here to collect her pension and groceries in the village."

Claire laughed. Paircmoor did not need a local newspaper while they had Mags Hoey to keep tabs on everyone. Claire was nervous about this visit. She had always been afraid of Gobnait Slevin.

"Be careful what you say to her, Mom. You know she can be nasty."

"She's alright. Just doesn't suffer fools gladly."

Claire shrugged. Her mother was on a mission and there would be no stopping her. She followed her through the gate and along a path leading to the long, low cottage. The building was so smothered in ivy, it appeared to be growing out of the soil. Even though it was November, the surrounding garden was lush with greenery – at least what could be seen of it in between the many pots and raised beds. There were several glasshouses, and the outline of a polytunnel peeped out from behind the house.

"Bloody hell! Are you sure Gobnait is not running a grow-house, Mom? She certainly has stepped up production since I was here last."

"Don't mock. Some swear by her herbs and potions for pains and aches and the like."

Mags was just about to knock on the door when it suddenly opened. Gobnait was much as Claire remembered her. A tiny woman with sleek auburn hair pulled into a bun, piercing blue eyes and exquisite, unlined skin. It seemed she had discovered the secret of eternal youth, as she looked no older now than she had twenty years ago.

"So, Mags Hoey," she said. "What are you doing up here?"

"I need to talk to you, Gobnait. Can I come in?"

Gobnait turned and led the way into her kitchen. It was mostly like herself, neat and timeless, except that the blazing log fire and gleaming ware on the dresser gave it a very welcoming air. She stared at Claire.

"You're the daughter," she said as she pulled out chairs at the table for them both to sit.

Claire nodded.

"You look very like your father. Is he dead or alive?"

Claire was just about to answer when Mags gave her a warning look.

"We don't know anything about him," Mags said. "We came here to talk to you about hair. To be exact, your sister's hair."

Gobnait pulled out a chair and sat opposite Mags. She placed her hands on the table and joined them together. The picture of calmness, unless you noticed the nervous tic beneath her right eye. She sighed.

"What has Minnie Curran been up to now?"

"That, Gobnait, is what we're here to find out," Mags said.

Mags sat in her chair, back straight, chin held high. She looked as threatening as it was possible for her to be.

"*The truth, Gobnait. Talk.*"

Claire smiled. She knew from experience that in this mood her mother would get her way, no matter how long it took.

Gobnait Slevin obviously knew too. She took a deep breath, then began to talk about her sister, Minnie Curran, and what she had been up to.

***

I finally got myself together enough to leave my park bench under the oak tree and make my way back to my husband in the hospital. When I reached the ward, it was packed with visitors. The bed beside Ben was empty so the elderly man and his white-haired wife must still be having their private conversation in the café. I could not see the other two patients in their beds because they were so swamped by visitors.

The curtains were pulled around Ben's bed. As I parted them to go in, I had a moment's dread that he might not be there. He was. And he was sleeping, turned towards the window, back to me. I leaned over to get a proper look at his face. He seemed peaceful. Relaxed. His mouth slightly open, dark eyelashes stark against his pale skin. I was shocked to see his shoulder blades protrude underneath his pyjama jacket. Gently, so as not to wake him, I put my hand on his back and felt the sharpness of the bones. He had been on a drip for the past few days, but I wondered if he could have lost so much weight that quickly, or had he been losing it ounce by ounce without me noticing. Yet another stick to beat myself up with.

All the available chairs were in use, so I sat on the side of his bed. The other patients' visitors were a noisy lot. It sounded like they had joined forces to swap jokes and anecdotes. I didn't know how Ben was sleeping through the din.

I noticed that the children's drawings had been rearranged on top of the locker. I hoped they had been moved by Ben. That he had seen them and knew how much the children missed him. I should have handed them to him when I came in earlier. Pointed out that each wriggly line and crayon mark, each painstaking drawing, was a labour of love. If he had known how much he meant to us, he would not have put his life at risk by going down to the storm-whipped sea. Or had he? Had that just been bravado, carelessness, a tantrum because Ellen Riggs had gone away?

As I watched him sleep peacefully, my frustration and confusion rose to such an extent that I wanted to shake him awake. Have him take up his story where he had left off. At his wrist-slashing, teenage years. Why had he lied about it? And, more to the point, what else had he hidden from me? He and his enabler, Della.

I had my hand raised to shake him awake when the curtain opened. A nurse, dark-haired and dark-skinned, nodded to me. She picked up his chart from the end of the bed, read it and then wrote something on it. There was a particularly loud roar of laughter from the gaggle of visitors. The nurse frowned.

"Are they disturbing you?" she asked.

I shook my head. "I'm fine with it but I don't know how my husband is sleeping through it."

"Oh! You're Mrs Parrish? The noise won't disturb your husband. He's had a sedative. He needed it after this morning."

"What do you mean? What happened this morning?"

I saw an initial look of puzzlement, closely followed by embarrassment, cross her face as she realised I didn't know what she was talking about. She hesitated for a moment, as if weighing every word before it left her mouth.

"Sorry, I assumed you knew. Mr Parrish had a panic attack. Nothing major but we're just being cautious because of the trauma he suffered in the past few days. He needs rest now."

"I see. Thank you for telling me."

But I didn't see at all. Della had been with him this morning. Why hadn't she told me what happened? Had he secretly been having panic attacks since I met him? And then I remembered Hugh's text.

You've got to tell Leah. She has a right to know the truth. Especially now.

They were liars, all of them. The snotty, deceitful Parrish clan.

"I'll get a chair for you," the nurse offered.

I stood and picked up my bag from the floor where I had left it.

"No need, thank you. I'd better get home to the children."

I opened my bag and took out Ben's phone and charger. I put them in his locker drawer. I could ring him later. Maybe.

"Would you see that my husband gets these, please?" I asked the nurse.

She nodded, then glanced at the drawings on the locker top. She smiled with such sympathy reflected in her eyes that I wondered if she also knew Ben's secrets. She probably did.

As I walked past the partying visitors and down the corridor from St Joseph's Ward, I was pretty certain that I, Ben's wife, was probably the only person in the world who knew nothing at all about him.

CHAPTER TWENTY-FIVE

I stood in the car park and looked back at the hospital. My eyes were drawn up to the first-floor windows. I wondered if Ben was still in his sedated sleep or if he was, at that very moment, looking down at me and wondering if I had forgiven him for hiding the truth from me. A hard thing to do since I didn't really know what the whole truth was, did I?

When I sat into the car, my first priority was to find out how my children were. That meant talking to Della. My instinct was to go on the offensive. Demand to know why my mother-in-law had not told me about Ben's panic attack this morning. She had been there in the hospital. She must have known. She had been there too all those years ago, when he had cut his wrist. Deliberately. A suicide attempt at sixteen years of age. No. That conversation with Della would have to be face to face. All I really needed to know was that my children were safe. I keyed in her mobile number. She must have had her phone in her hand as she answered after one ring.

"Leah! How is he? Is he alright?"

I paused, giving her a chance to mention the morning's panic attack I assumed she had witnessed. She was silent.

Maybe I was being unfair. And maybe she was being a bitch. I had to bury my base instincts. Nasty, vengeful instincts. For now, Della was a mother, concerned for her son.

"He's sleeping," I said. "He's been sedated. How are the children?"

It turned out they were a contented little crew. The twins were occupied building a hospital with their wooden blocks and Rob a space station with his Lego.

"I need to do some grocery shopping, so I'll hop into town now."

"Are you going back to see Ben again?"

"No. I won't disturb him. He needs to rest. And I have to make some arrangements with Mags Hoey about cover for the salon. She's the stylist I employ. She lives in the village. I could call to her on the way home. If that's alright with you."

"No problem. The children are as good as gold. I can give them their dinner. Just a matter of heating up the casserole you left for us. Take as long as you like."

"Thank you, Della. I'll see you later."

I rang Mags then and told her I would be with her in an hour's time. Immediately all the salon worries began to crowd in on me. Minnie Curran and her inflamed scalp. My fault or not? Viv Henderson and her championing of the injured Minnie. Insurance claim or not? Would I be able to keep the place open? Or not?

All I could do for now was the grocery shopping. I swept everything out of my mind, except my shopping list and how to pay for it. That was my forte. Leah Parrish, the sweeper-upper of life's detritus.

Mags' house was at the top of Paircmoor village, just before the road headed back towards Cowslip Cottage. It stood out in the terraced row for its bright yellow door, colourful blinds and flower baskets in bloom, even in November. It was the type of house that brought a smile to your face and made you feel welcome. Mags opened the door before I had a chance to ring the bell.

"I was watching out for you, Leah. Come on in."

She led the way towards the kitchen. I followed on, my mouth watering as I got the aroma of cooking.

"I'll take your coat and you sit down at the table," Mags ordered.

She pointed to where a place had been set for dinner.

"How is Ben?"

"Much improved. He's been moved to a ward. And Claire, how is she?"

"Claire is on the mend too. She's gone off to town with her cousin to do a spot of shopping. The only therapy that works for her. That's great news about Ben. He'll be back on his feet in no time."

As she was talking, she was heaping a plate with roast chicken, roast potatoes, veg and stuffing. Proper Sunday dinner, gravy included. I was hungry, yes, but the attention Mags was lavishing on me was even more welcome than the food. She put the plate in front of me.

"Eat up, Leah. When you're finished, I have something to tell you."

Given my recent history, I had to assume that whatever Mags had to say would not be good news. I was glad she was holding back until I had finished eating. I had not realised just how hungry I was, or how long it had been since I had sat down and enjoyed a meal.

"That was delicious, Mags. Thank you. Now I'm ready to hear whatever you have to tell me."

She poured two coffees and sat opposite me at the table. I heard her take a deep breath. So did I.

"This is a long story," she said. "It started when I met Minnie Curran's niece in the supermarket. I don't think you know her. She and Minnie aren't the best of friends. There was a row years ago involving Minnie's daughter and this niece. Minnie is not one to forgive easily. Anyway, we got to talking about Minnie's drama with her inflamed scalp."

I felt the dinner I had just eaten turn sour in my stomach. I braced myself to be strong. Mature. To appreciate that Minnie Curran's suing me was a small problem in the grand scheme of things.

"Go on," I urged Mags.

"Look, I know I waffle on, so I'll cut to the chase. Have you heard of Gobnait Slevin?"

I nodded. I had heard people talk of her in reverent tones. From what I gathered, people credited her with the gift of healing.

"Is she the healer who lives up Conicmoor Hills?"

"Yes. And she's Minnie Curran's sister."

Everybody was interrelated here. Mags let that nugget of information sink in before continuing.

"She's a healer for those who believe in that sort of thing. Gobnait grows herbs, mixes them up into creams and lotions. She has people who swear her brews have cured them of everything from acne to baldness. Which brings me to Minnie."

"Is she involved in the business too?"

Mags laughed.

"Minnie Curran never did a day's work in her life. Pure spoiled she is. The reason she went to Gobnait was about her thinning hair. You know how obsessed she is about it. In fact, she mentions it every single visit to the salon. Including her last one."

"So what are you saying, Mags? That Gobnait was getting treatment from her sister for alopecia?"

Mags nodded. "In fact, she went straight from the salon to Gobnait last Thursday, to collect her new custom-made brew. A distillation of nettles, peppermint plant and god knows what else."

As Mags stopped to draw breath, I began to pull pieces of the story together.

"Had she ever used it before? Do you know?"

"No, she couldn't have. Gobnait said it's a new recipe. An experiment. A combination of essential oils and herbs she had just distilled. She warned Minnie to allow it to mature for three weeks before using it. And then just to use it very sparingly. Minnie promised she would."

"Gobnait said? You've been talking to her about this?"

Mags looked a bit uncomfortable. She took a sip from her coffee before answering me.

"Well, yes. I went to see her this morning. Claire came too. I hope you don't think I'm interfering, but Minnie Curran was badmouthing the salon. I feel responsible because I was the one who put the colour in her miserable bit of hair in the first place. And I know you have more important things on your mind. I wanted to help and I –"

Mags was talking herself into a panic. I reached across the table and caught her hand.

"Mags! Don't think for one minute your bear any responsibility in this. You did your job perfectly well, including doing a patch test. You're not to worry about it anymore."

She surprised me then by laughing. I thought for a moment that she was edging towards hysteria.

"What's so funny, Mags?"

"It turns out Minnie went against Gobnait's advice and plastered her scalp straight away with the newly brewed concoction. When it began to burn and itch, she blamed our colour treatment. I believe she paid you a visit at the salon the next day."

"She certainly did. That was the day Claire had her accident. And Ben – he had his accident too."

I shivered, remembering last Friday and how I had thought then that things could not get any worse. It was only two days ago but it seemed like a lifetime.

"Yes," Mags said. "That awful day. But we all survived, didn't we?"

We sure did. Some better than others. I was still waiting for the funny bit of Mags' story. So far it was more tragedy than comedy, even though she was grinning. I nodded to her to continue.

"So Minnie, convinced it was the colour affecting her scalp, kept rubbing in Gobnait's brew. Eventually it got so uncomfortable she had to go to the doctor, who sent her to A&E with a sample of Gobnait's hair-thickening brew. It turns out that Minnie Curran owes us an apology. Especially you, Leah."

I had to sit back to absorb this news. Had the hospital confirmed that Minnie's scalp had not been affected by the colour treatment? Had she agreed to keep her damaging allegations to herself in future? Was her mentor, the manipulative Viv Henderson, willing to spread this news as willingly as she had the accusations against my salon?

"You can take that scared look off your face, Leah. The hospital confirmed the reaction was caused by Gobnait's mixture. In order to protect her sister, Minnie told them she brewed it up herself. But I put Gobnait straight on that one."

"How do you mean?"

"I have often felt, long before now, that what Gobnait was doing up there in her mountain cottage had the potential to be dangerous. It's not the Paircmoor way to snitch on anyone so I kept my counsel. Now, I felt it was time to talk up. I warned her that if she handed out any more hair treatments, I would report her for running a pharmacy without a licence. I . . . *uumm* . . . I told Minnie also that you would sue for defamation of character if there were any more false allegations. I hope you don't think I overstepped the mark."

Then Mags and I laughed together. The sweetest, last laugh.

I laughed until the tears of laughter turned to tears of relief. Then tears of relief turned to tears of fear. Dread of not knowing the truth, of facing the truth, of finding the strength to be mother and father to my children until Ben, my Ben, came back from the dark place his mind had taken him.

CHAPTER TWENTY-SIX

When I had no more tears to shed, Mags made fresh coffee. We sat at the table and discussed the salon. I had no idea when Ben would be out of hospital, or of how much care he would need when he came home. Looking after the children and getting Ben well again were my priorities.

But, but, but. The salon was our main source of income. I could not be at home and in the salon at the same time. There could only be one answer.

"Mags, would you consider running the salon on a temporary basis? Just until Ben is back on his feet again."

She was silent. Head bowed. I tried to give her time to think. Tried to be calm, but all I could see was my business failing, while at home bills built up.

"You would, of course, have an increased salary," I offered.

Mags raised her head. She was smiling.

"I am so flattered that you would trust me to do it. And no more silly talk about money, please."

That was one problem solved. Temporarily. Tina had three weeks left in her work experience. Both Mags and Tina together would be able to keep the place ticking over.

Assuming we still had customers after the Minnie Curran saga.

It was a lucky break that the next day was Monday. The day the salon always closed in keeping with hairdressing tradition. That would give me time to contact Tina. I would have to, tactfully, talk to Mags about giving Tina the chance to show initiative. Then I realised that Tina was more than capable of looking out for herself, and Mags, I knew now, would never deliberately upset anyone. They would settle that situation between themselves. We should, with a little luck, be ready to open for business on Tuesday.

"I'll ring Tina later, to see if she'll be willing to come in to help you until I get back."

"Do that," Mags said. "But don't worry about it. I sort of mentioned it to her. She said she would be delighted to do it. I hope you don't think –"

"*Don't!* Don't say it again!" I warned her. "I do *not* think you're interfering. What would I do without you?"

I smiled at her and then impulsively got up and threw my arms around her. I wished at that minute I could tell her about Ben and his scarred wrist, about his panic attack and the text from Hugh hinting at secrets and lies. About Della and her constant, draining disapproval of me. And about my own secret. Instead I stayed on the safe subject of the salon.

"I'll do a stocktake tomorrow," I told her. "And I'll order in whatever has run low. I'll drop the keys in to you on the way back."

"Tomorrow will look after itself, Leah. Go home to your children. They need you."

Wise words. And I, with all my heart, needed to see my

children, to hold them in my arms and tell them everything in their shattered little world would soon be put together again. Just like Humpty Dumpty.

The children were ready for bed by the time I got back to Cowslip Cottage. They crowded around me, all with their stories to tell. It was a stream of what Della did and what Della did next.

"Mine hair – Della fixed it," Anna said, tossing her head so that her two curly, blonde pigtails, tied with sparkly clips and ribbons, shimmered. "Do you like it, Mom?"

"Gorgeous," I said as she twirled around in front of me.

"And mine nails," she said, holding out her hands to show me the sparkly nails.

As I admired the tiny nails, so carefully varnished, I wished it had been me painting my daughter's fingernails and not her grandmother.

Josh showed me the hospital he had built from his wooden blocks. It had a sign on top, written on fluorescent green card, saying *Daddy's Hospital.* It was of course, in Della's copperplate writing. Calligraphy was one of her interests, which she apparently was passing on to Rob. He had another piece of the green card in his hand.

"For you, Mom," he said.

I took the card from him and immediately felt tears in my eyes. Happy ones, this time.

For the best Mom in the world. Love from Rob, Josh and Anna.

"Della showed me how to do the squiggly writing with the funny pen," he said. "Do you like it?"

"I think it's very beautiful, Rob. Thank you."

I stooped down and gathered the three of them

together in a hug. They smelled of shampoo and baby bath oil. They were safe, clean, fed and happy.

I looked over their heads at Della. She was smiling as she watched the children, her expression for once unguarded. I knew, without doubt, she loved them almost as much as I did. Maybe, just maybe, our mutual love for Ben and the children would eventually bridge the gap which yawned between us.

"Thank you so much, Della." I said. "I really appreciate what you've done for us today."

She raised her head and looked directly at me. It was there again, that coldness. The disapproval.

"Glad to help," she said. "And by the way, I had a headache when I came here and needed something for it. I found Paracetamol in your medicine cabinet. I hope you don't mind."

I did mind. A lot. There was something very private about a medicine cabinet. It exposed your vulnerabilities and held information that rightly belonged to the owner of the cabinet and nobody else. That is why it was always locked. I remembered the Paracetamol was on the bottom shelf. Della would have had no reason to search the top shelf where the most personal of my things were safely stowed. Or would she? I couldn't imagine her poking around in our medicine cabinet. That kind of behaviour would be beneath her. Hopefully. And yet she would have had to reach up to the very top of the cabinet to find the key. Maybe she was not above poking around after all. Her expression was giving nothing away.

"You locked it again?" I asked, worried also about the children's safety as well as my privacy.

"Of course. I left the key back where I found it."

She turned and walked out into the hall. I heard the closet door open and the rattle of a hanger on the rail as she got her coat. When she came back into the kitchen, the children ran to her.

"I'm going to my hotel in town now," she told them. "But I'll be back soon."

"You're welcome to stay here," I said.

She gave me one of her cold smiles.

"I know that, but for the time being I prefer to be nearer Ben. I'll go in to see him in the morning. After that I'm available to babysit again, if you want. I thought I might use Ben's jeep to take the children for a spin somewhere. It's all set up with their car seats so I may as well use it."

The children were whooping and hollering so the trip would have to be on, whether I approved or not. Besides, it would be good for them to get away from here for a break. I wondered though, about Rob and school. I didn't like him missing any class time. I also knew that the story of Ben going missing and then being found in a cave on the strand would be the talk of Paircmoor. There was a chance Rob would hear a very frightening version of what happened. In other words, he might learn the truth, whatever that was, and not the edited version of tripping over a fallen branch I had given him. Ben's drama would be old news in a few days. I decided that would be time enough for Rob to go back to school. I would ring his teacher in the morning and give her an adult spin on Ben tripping over a fallen branch.

"Thank you, Della. It would be a great help if you could come here tomorrow afternoon. I'll hop in to see Ben then."

She hugged the children and turned her back to me. The raised shoulders, the head held high, the assertive tap of her heels on the tiled floor, all spoke louder than words of her disapproval. And blame. It was very obvious that she believed me responsible for what had happened to Ben two nights ago. For whatever had driven him out into the storm, down the cliff and into a black cave to almost freeze to death.

I wondered then who she had blamed when, as a sixteen-year-old, he had cut his wrist. Not Hugh, the golden-haired boy, for sure. Perhaps she had blamed her husband. The renowned architect, Gavin Parrish. The icon Ben always tried to emulate.

As I stood at the front door, watching the children wave Della off, I realised that someday I would have to break down the wall she had built between us. With a sledgehammer if necessary. There was so much I didn't know about Ben. So much, I now believed, that his mother did not want him to tell me. But they both must, if there was to be healing, share the past with me so that we could share the future together.

The children scampered ahead of me into the kitchen. Inside I felt a tidal wave of fear. Who was their father really? Not the Ben I thought I had known. Why had he hacked at his wrist when he had been little more than a child himself? And most of all, what other revelations were yet to come?

CHAPTER TWENTY-SEVEN

Monday 29th November 2010

I didn't feel well on Monday morning. A combination of exhaustion and eating too many roast potatoes in Mags' house the previous evening.

I sat at the table, sipping hot water, as the children ate breakfast. While they were occupied, I rang the school to explain Rob's absence for the next few days. They were very understanding. Next I gave Tina a quick call about the salon. As Mags had said, they had it all organised between the two of them.

I called Ben. No ring. The battery could not be down already. He must have switched his phone off. Obviously not in a talking mood. The hospital was next call. The nurse who answered told me Ben had a comfortable night and was now being transferred to a private room. I knew then that Della was already pulling strings. Organising her son. My husband. The interfering old biddy had a right, I supposed. Not just because she was his mother, but by virtue of the fact that, since Ben's redundancy, she had taken over the payment of the private health care he could no longer afford. The coverage was for him and the children. I had refused to have her pay for me. She had not pushed too hard to change my mind. I depended on the public healthcare system, just as I had always done before I became Mrs Ben Parrish. It was true Ben would probably feel more comfortable in his own room, but I was not sure that isolation was the right thing for him now.

"How's Dad?" Rob asked.

"Much improved. He's getting better every day."

"Can we go to see him so?"

I had been considering that. Whether it would be good for the children to see him. And for him to see them. They had never been separated before. But then I did not want them in the hospital environment where they might be exposed to infections. And instinct told me I should ask Ben first. He might find seeing them too emotional at the moment.

"Tell you what," I said. "I'll ask him to phone you. Or write you all a message."

"Why can't we get one of those iPhones?" Rob asked. "Like Uncle Hugh has. Then we could see Dad and he could see us."

"IPhone!" Anna and Josh echoed.

I smiled at my tech-aware tots. Hugh was introducing them to the wonders of modern technology. Unfortunately it was my job to introduce them to the reality of life in Cowslip Cottage.

"We will have to save our money for a long time to buy one," I explained. "They cost a lot."

"When are you going?" Rob asked. "What time will Della be here?"

I felt a little bit hurt by his question but also relieved. He obviously had forgotten about his lack of an iPhone and also was happy to have Della here. If he was happy, the twins would follow suit. I could leave them without guilt.

"She will probably be here around lunchtime. Okay?"

The twins clapped their hands and began making the strangest sounds. They mooed and baaed and giggled. Rob was smiling at them. An indulgent smile, as if he was their doting grandfather. I often suspected Rob had lived many lives before and that he was a very old soul.

"Della's taking us to the pet farm," he said. "Alpacas live there too. They're from South America and they have three tummies and woolly coats."

This sent the twins into another fit of laughter and me into a mini-tantrum. Della had told the children about the farm before checking with me if I wanted them to go there. And I did, but not with her. Like painting Anna's nails, it was one of the things I had planned on doing later. When I had time. When Ben had a job. When the salon was making a profit. When the moon was blue.

"It's a long way away," Rob said.

It was 15 kilometres. Definitely a long way with three small children in tow. Della would cope though. I had no worry on that front.

"It's not that far, Rob. Just a small spin. And you will all have a wonderful time. Ask Della to take pictures so that I can see the animals too."

But I promised myself that I would talk to Della. Ask her to check with me first before organising anything for the children. No! I would tell her, not ask.

I sighed as I stood up from the table. I was fooling myself. I had no space in my head now for analysing my relationship with my mother-in-law. I had too much to do, was too afraid of upsetting Ben, was too beholden to Della for all she had done for us. I was, I supposed, too much of a coward.

* * *

Della went to Reception before going up to the first floor of the hospital. She never again wanted to set foot in St Joseph's Ward unless she absolutely had to.

"I'm visiting my son," she told the bored-looking girl behind the desk. "Ben Parrish. Could you tell me where he is, please?"

The girl scrolled through her monitor.

"Take the lift. First floor, Turn right. Room 5."

This was conveyed without lifting her head. Della didn't care. Obviously her stream of phone calls and complaints had worked. Ben was in a private room.

"Thank you so much," she said to the girl, who had already turned her attention to paperwork on her desk.

The lift was crowded. It was a relief to arrive at the first floor. Della turned right, as instructed by the grumpy girl at Reception. She tapped on the door of Room 5 and tiptoed in.

Ben's breakfast tray was pushed down to the end of the bed, the food untouched. He was asleep. She stood there, looking at the plate of congealed scrambled egg, and she fumed. Why had they not woken him? Made sure he had some nourishment. He needed it. He had the gaunt appearance of someone who had been suffering a long-term illness, despite the fact that he had been here just a few days. This was totally unacceptable. First she would find whoever was in charge of this section and then she would insist on seeing a member of the administrative staff. Make sure her complaint reached the highest possible echelon of hospital bureaucracy. They had better know they were dealing with Della Parrish, and she would not allow her son to be so disgracefully treated. Mistreated.

Fired up by her mission, she turned on her heel and walked towards the door, forgetting to tiptoe. She put her hand on the door handle.

"Mum."

When she turned, he was sitting up in the bed. He had the haunted look she had seen so many times in the past and had hoped she would never see again. She walked towards him, quelling the urge to run to him and hold him in her arms. He had sent her away yesterday. She knew she would have to tread very carefully.

She took off her coat and sat on the chair beside the bed.

"Good morning, Ben. I was just about to order some fresh breakfast for you. Pity they didn't wake you."

"They did. I'm not hungry."

"But you must eat. You –"

She stopped talking as he leaned towards her. She was mesmerised by his eyes. Deep, deep brown. They sparkled when he laughed or was angry, but they became clouded and dull when he was sad. Like now.

"Get this," he said. "I'm thirty-six years of age. I have a wife and three children. While I'm very grateful for all you've done for me, it's long past time I stood on my own two feet."

Della barely allowed herself to breathe in case he dismissed her again. There seemed to be a new determination about him. She nodded for him to continue.

"I know I've messed up, Mum. And I appreciate that you've always been there for me. But I must handle things my way from now on. For a start, I should never have kept secrets from Leah. I told her yesterday about cutting my wrist with the Swiss knife. I should have told her before we married. Given her the choice whether to accept me as I am, or not. I can change that now by telling her the rest of my sorry history. Being honest with her."

Della was shocked. Leah had not given any hint last night about Ben's confession. She would not have credited her daughter-in-law with discretion. Nor did she now. Leah was obviously waiting for the right moment to use her new-found knowledge to her advantage. Despite her earlier caution, Della could not stay quiet while Ben destroyed all the work that had gone into allowing him to lead a normal life.

"Have you thought through the consequences of dragging all that history into the daylight now?"

"The consequences for whom? You? Mother to a suicidal son? How shameful is that! What about the consequences for me? Carrying all that shit inside my head and believing I would disgrace the family if I ever spoke about it. Do you know how fucking heavy that burden has been? I breathe in sadness every minute of every day and I never breathe it out. It stays inside, choking me, draining every ounce of energy from my body. It's a parasite, Mom, feeding on my life. I can't cope with it anymore."

Della sat back, subconsciously distancing herself from the anger being directed at her. It was best to allow him vent. It was right that she should bear the brunt of the curse she had passed on to him through her genes. Her brother, George, had lived, and died, under the same cloud as Ben. Not even Gavin knew about George. Perhaps he should have. Then he might have understood his youngest son.

"Are you listening to me, Mom? Being honest with my wife can only be positive. I know Leah. She won't judge me. Or be ashamed of me. Or try to pretend I'm something I'm not."

Della knew he needed to purge himself of all that angst. The bile. The resentment. But certainly not by telling Leah. For at least two reasons. One, it was likely that she would talk outside the family. To her employees maybe, or friends. Not the Parrish way and ultimately detrimental to Ben's employment prospects. Not that any employer would admit discrimination but, the fact was, they would not give him a job. Two, there was a risk that Leah might reject Ben once she knew his full history. He would get over separation from Leah. He would have to. But not from the children.

"Ben, about the position with Zach Milburg in the US –"

"Mom! That was a pipe dream. Yours more than mine. And I'm really, really sorry I've disappointed you again. I'm tired now. I need to sleep."

He was exhausted. She could see that. She stood and put on her coat. She reached out her hand and brushed his hair back from his forehead. Her baby! Where, oh, where had that happy little toddler gone?

"I'll leave you to rest, Ben. I'm taking the children to the pet farm this afternoon."

"They'll love that. Especially Rob. He has a thing about alpacas."

"I'll see you tomorrow."

He didn't answer. Della walked to the door. She stood there, her back to him, thinking about the things he had said. Knowing that he was putting all his trust in Leah. She was sure that he must not. As his mother, she would protect him to her last breath, no matter what he said.

She remembered the medicine cabinet in Cowslip Cottage. How reluctant she had been yesterday to open it, feeling she was intruding, but her headache had been severe. When she was putting back the Paracetamol packet, she noticed something protruding from the top shelf. Enough so that she suspected what it was. She checked it to be sure and confirmed her suspicion before putting it back exactly as she had found it. The box was unopened but obviously Leah had use for it. Just as obviously Ben did not know. He would definitely have told her. And he should know.

She turned back to look directly at him.

"Do you really believe, Ben, that Leah has no secrets from you? Are you one hundred per cent sure about that?"

"What are you hinting at now?" he asked "Leah never hides anything. She is the most open, honest person I know. Just go, Mom, please!"

She heard it in his voice, not in his words. The suspicion that what she had said might have substance.

Satisfied that she had planted the seed of doubt, Della opened the door and left.

CHAPTER TWENTY-EIGHT

From the instant Della arrived at Cowslip Cottage on Monday afternoon, I could see she was in a snooty mood. I assumed her hospital visit to Ben that morning had not gone too well. The children were giddy with anticipation of visiting the animal farm. Knowing that she would calm them down, and they would cheer her up, I left them to find their balance.

I had intended going straight to the hospital but, as I approached the salon, I decided it would be just as well to get the stocktaking done. The first thing I did when I opened up was to take down the note I had so hastily pinned up in the early hours of Saturday morning. I shivered as I read it.

Closed due to illness

Apologies for any inconvenience

I scrunched it up and threw it in the bin. At least I now knew that Ben had survived hypothermia and a heart attack. After that, we could probably cope with anything.

I did a quick stocktake. Thankfully the order was small as we had been closed on Saturday, which would have been our busiest day. I ordered what was needed and then sat in one of the swivel chairs and looked around my little empire. I thought how strange it was that, up to Friday night, the salon was the focus of my days. Running it, building up a clientele, every day trying to improve the service and keep the bills paid. Today, its only importance for me was as a source of income for my family. At least until Ben was back on his feet. Until he was mentally, as well as physically, fit. Until he could get back to work. If the economy ever picked up again. Realising I was thinking myself into despair, I locked up and headed into town.

It was only as I headed towards Room 5 that I allowed myself to consider what he might tell me today. There was more than the Swiss knife incident. Hugh's message on Ben's phone implied that. I also suspected that Della's very subdued mood earlier was connected to Ben confiding in me. Tough luck, Della, I thought. Ben would tell me his secrets and I would tell him mine.

I was smiling as I tapped on the door and pushed it open. It was a nice room. Airy. Bright. Ensuite. TV on the wall. But no Ben. I had to be in the right room because the children's drawings were on the bedside locker. I checked the bathroom. He wasn't there. My pulse raced. Had he had another heart attack? Been wheeled off to Intensive Care again. I rushed down the corridor to the nurses' desk. It was unattended. I saw a nurse in the nearby ward. She was writing in a chart at the end of an elderly lady's bed. I went over to her.

"Excuse me. Ben Parrish. Room 5. He's my husband. He's not in his room. Do you know where he is? Is he alright?"

She attempted a smile but I could see I was annoying her.

"Just give me a moment, please, and I'll be with you."

I stood outside the ward, heart thumping, wondering just how many more things could go wrong. And then I saw him. Being pushed on a wheelchair down the corridor by a porter, a nurse walking alongside. They were chatting, the three of them. Ben seemed more animated than I had seen him for a long time. I walked towards them. He saw me and smiled. Time rolled back eight years, to when we had first met. It was a cliché. Our eyes met across a crowded bar. I had gone there with friends from work, celebrating an engagement. I had left with the man I would marry eighteen months later.

"Ben Parrish!" I said. "You gave me such a fright."

"Don't worry, Leah. No more drama. I was just having a scan."

With Ben safely back in his room, the porter trundled off with the wheelchair and the nurse settled him into bed. When we were alone, Ben patted the bed.

"Sit beside me, Leah. How are you?"

Scared, confused, disappointed, angry. All of those answers would have been true. But I was hopeful too. And grateful that we could be sitting here talking just a few days after Ben had been fished out of the cave.

"I'm good, Ben. Missing you, of course. What was this scan about?"

"CT on my lungs. And before you start worrying, the results are good. So was the ECG on my heart this morning. I think I might be ready for home soon. How are the children?"

"Good. Very excited today because your mother is taking them to the pet farm."

"She told me."

"Rob is over the moon. He can't wait to see a real live alpaca. I wonder why he is so fascinated by them? Apart from the fact that they're cute and furry."

Ben laughed and then he got a faraway look in his eyes. "I was obsessed with hummingbirds when I was his age. I gathered facts about them, like Rob is doing with alpacas now. Did you know their wings flap at fifty to two hundred times per second and they must eat every ten minutes? That's the equivalent of a human being eating a fridgeful of food every day. I saw one, a real live hummingbird that is, in San Francisco. I was grown up by that time but it was a thrill anyway."

It wasn't hard to imagine Ben as a little boy. From photos he looked exactly like Rob did now. When had the contented child become a troubled man? What had happened when he was sixteen? I didn't want to bring his mood down but I knew we must continue the conversation we had yesterday.

"So how did you get from hummingbirds to Swiss Army knives, Ben?"

Even as the words left my mouth I knew they sounded glib. Ben obviously thought so too, judging by his change in expression.

"If I knew the answer to that, Leah, I probably wouldn't be in the mess I'm in now."

I reached for his hand and held it in mine.

"I'm sorry. That came out all wrong. I'm just trying to understand. Maybe we should work backwards. Friday night. I need to know what happened then and you need to talk about it. Agreed?"

He squeezed my hand. I took that for assent. So I waited. And waited. He was remembering. I saw his eyes grow darker, sadder. I was out of my depth. What if he really had just gone for a run on Friday and accidently been cut off by the tide? He would be angry at me then for thinking he . . . He what? That he had been devastated by Ellen Riggs' departure for London? That he had meant to go into that cave and not leave it until the tide had swept him out to sea? That he had thought of nobody but her and had forgotten about the children and me?

"Ellen Riggs," I said.

Her name shimmered in the air between us, just like the beautiful woman herself.

Ben nodded. "She was the trigger. I thought we were friends. It turned out that we were not. I didn't even know she was married. To a very successful plastic surgeon."

I had wanted the truth but I was finding it hard to hear now. If I questioned him about the depth and breadth of their friendship, he could lapse back into silence. The need to know and the jealousy were bitter in my gut but I manged to stay quiet.

Ben must have read my thoughts.

"It was just companionship, Leah. An adult to talk to at the school gates. The children also liked her and Finn. And I suppose I felt she was, exotic, different. A glimpse of the world we had left behind when we came to Paircmoor. Or, should I say, the world that left us behind. That's all there was to it."

It was enough. He had told me a lot already. He had thought Ellen exotic, the children liked her, and Paircmoor was only tolerable when she was there. So while I had been cutting, shampooing, conditioning, doing free French plaits for Viv Henderson, and working my fingers to the bone, he had been weaving fantasies around the beautiful Ellen. Even as I burned up with jealousy, I realised that she had been nothing more than an escape from reality for him. An adolescent crush.

"I understand that you would be disappointed about a friend leaving, Ben, but smashing the vase she had given us? Running out the door into a storm without even a coat? There had to be more going on."

"There was, Leah. So much more. And it all crowded on top of me that night. I had just admitted to myself that my big plan, to manufacture and market scale models of historic Irish buildings, was a farce. A failure. A stupid, useless idea that I had pinned my hopes and dreams on. It was to be our future. I would export to the US where a Ben Parrish scale model of Blarney Castle would become a must have for the rich and famous. How fucking pathetic!"

Guilt took over and gave me a painful shove. I had known little and cared less about the project he had been working on since we had come here. That wasn't exactly true either. I didn't have the time to worry about it, but I could have shown some interest.

"It *is* a good idea, Ben, and I'm sure your work is superb. It's just that the time is wrong. Maybe when –"

"Don't say it! If I had a euro for every time someone says, 'when the economy picks up', I'd be rich. Anyway, Mom had kind of boxed me into a corner about this interview she was trying to set up with Hugh's mega-rich brother-in-law. I had tried to go along with her enthusiasm, but last Friday night, that awful night, I knew I would be setting myself up for another failure. A very humiliating one."

I nodded. Not that I knew too much about the job in the US, or anything about Hugh's brother-in-law, but I did believe Ben was not ready for such a big challenge, and our family belonged here in Paircmoor for the time being.

"Maybe that's for the best, Ben. I was reading about

the bureaucracy involved in getting a work visa, let alone residency. It's mindboggling. And the business environment is so cutthroat."

He pulled his hand away from mine and glared at me. "You mean I wouldn't be up to it. Isn't that right? Just say it straight out, Leah. I'm better off hidden away in Cowshit Cottage."

I'm not sure which was most shattering – his sudden anger or the fact that he was calling our home Cowshit Cottage. I did see a funny side to it and had an urge to laugh. And laugh. But I knew that release would open the floodgates to all the mixed-up emotions churning around inside me.

"You know that's not true, Ben. I realise how good you are at your job. It's just that it's not the right time for our family to emigrate."

I stopped talking, trying to frame the right words, the right approach, the best way to tell him that our place, for now, was here in Paircmoor.

"The children, Leah. I've let them down so badly. And you too. I'm sorry. So sorry."

He laid his head back on the pillow and closed his eyes. When I saw tears seep from underneath his eyelids, I leaned over him and kissed the tears away.

"It's okay, Ben. It will all be okay."

He opened his eyes and I had a glimpse into the torment in his soul. His eyes, his beautiful brown eyes, swam with tears and the deepest, darkest sadness.

"I frightened Rob," he said. "I shouted and terrified my son. I saw his face. How afraid he is of me now. He will always fear me. I will never forgive myself and he will never forgive me."

"Yes, he will! He has. He is asking for you all the time."

"That's because he thinks it's all his fault. I know."

As I was about to ask him what he meant by that, I heard the rattle of the tea trolley coming down the corridor. It stopped outside the door. Ben rubbed his eyes with the heels of his hands and sat up straight in the bed. He smiled at the lady who brought in his tea. He looked happy. I wondered how many times over the years I had taken it for granted that happy face meant happy Ben. How wrong I had been, about so many things.

The walls of the room, the sounds from the corridor, the smell of disinfectant, the sight of Ben, so vulnerable sitting in a hospital bed with his despair hidden behind a false smile, all crowded in on top of me. I needed fresh air. Bile burned my throat. I knew Ben had reached the limit of his revelations for today. I also knew I must get out of Room 5 or else I would be sick.

"I'll leave you to enjoy your tea, Ben. I'd better get back home. Your mother will be tired after taking our three ragamuffins out today."

I thought he looked relieved. I couldn't blame him. So was I. Our conversation had been intense. Draining.

"Just before I go, I promised the children you would write them a message. Or would you text or phone later before they go to bed?"

"No, I can't. I don't feel up to contacting them. Just tell them I miss them and I'll see them soon."

I nodded. It would have to do.

"Thanks for bringing in my phone," he said, "but I don't want to make or take calls now. Take it home, please."

No, I could not. Let him keep his phone and read that

message from Hugh over and over until he saw fit to tell me what it was about.

"Keep it," I said. "You might need it. See you tomorrow."

I blew him a kiss from the doorway. Just as I was about to close the door, he called me back.

"I've bared my soul to you, Leah. How about you? Do you have secrets I should know about? Are you keeping something from me?"

I stood there, stunned. He looked so vulnerable in the bed, his eyes so dark in his pale face. I felt like a traitor.

"What makes you ask that, Ben?"

"Just something Mum said. Well, do you have something to tell me?"

So Della had poked in the medicine cabinet. I wondered how much she had told Ben. If I knew her, she would just have hinted. Anyway, she couldn't know for sure nor could she admit to common snooping.

"All I want to tell you is that I love you, Ben. Hope you'll be home soon."

I closed the door and rushed down the corridor, used the stairs so that I didn't have to wait for the lift, and fled as quickly as I could out into the fresh air. I kept walking, past my car, out of the hospital grounds, and into the town park. At that stage, the wooden seat underneath the bare branches of the oak tree represented the only peaceful spot in my turbulent life.

CHAPTER TWENTY-NINE

While I was sitting under the oak tree in the litter-strewn park, the idea struck me that I should have a little plaque engraved and stuck onto my bench. *Leah Parrish was 'ere* kind of inscription. I smiled at the thought. Then I stood up and brushed myself down. I needed to get home as quickly as possible. Della was a healthy woman but minding three young children for longer than a few hours might be a bit much for her. She must be exhausted by now.

Mags was not at home but I dropped the keys in through her letterbox with a note telling her about the stock I had ordered and the float I had left in the till.

As I drove out the road towards Cowslip Cottage, an idea hatched in the town park would not leave me. It was what I needed to do to get another perspective on the events of Friday night. I pulled the car in to the side of the road just before the bendy bridge. I keyed in Della's number. When she answered, I heard music and chatter in the background and the unmistakable sound of Anna's laugh.

"Hi, Della. Seems like you're all having a good time."

"We are indeed. Are you back from the hospital already? I thought you would be later."

"Ben was tired. He needs lots of rest to get back his strength."

"Yes. That's true. I've taken the children out for tea. Is that alright with you?"

That was so Della. Leaving me with no choice. But it was good for the children to be out.

"Of course. Thank you, Della. Actually, now that you're still out, I need to see someone before I go home. I shouldn't be long."

"Take your time. Bye."

Then she was gone, without giving me the opportunity to talk to the children. They were probably overexcited at this stage between the farm and tea out. I would see them soon and would have the job of calming them down for bedtime.

I started the car again and went on my way. Past the bendy bridge, Cowslip Cottage, the treelined road where branches twined together overhead to form a tunnel. It had seemed threatening on Friday night as wind howled and rain lashed. It was less so now with flashes of fading daylight breaking through the overhead growth. Images and sounds played out in my head as I retraced my nightmare journey. The lights of the approaching ambulance, my car out of my control, screeching brakes, howling wind, and Ben, ashen-faced and frozen, barely breathing, strapped to a stretcher in the ambulance. I was shaking now, veering towards the ditch. There was no space for me to pull in safely so I breathed deeply, swallowed my fear and drove on.

I smelled the sea in the air. I knew there should soon be a turn-off for the beach. To drive straight on would bring me to Pouldubh Head. I had only been there once, but the dizzying height of the cliff above, and the churning sea beneath had made me shiver. I veered left at the beach turn-off. There was a car park where the tarmacadam road ended and the grassy approach to the cliffs began. A silver saloon car was fitted snugly against the back wall, looking as if it grew there. Maybe someone fishing, though that was unlikely. I parked beside the silver car, conscious that the light was now very quickly fading. The cliff path was narrow, smoothed by centuries of people making their way down to the shore. Including Ben on Friday night. The tide was out. I could see the waves in the distance, restless, throwing off glints as the last of the day's light shone on the western horizon. To my right, I saw lights being switched on in the house that clung to the cliff edge. I guessed that the other car in the park was probably belonging to the occupants, as it would be impossible to drive right up to the house. It had to be Cliff House, where the Sanquests lived. Vera and Walter. The people who had saved Ben's life. The people I had come here to see.

I walked the cliff path until it forked, one section heading straight for the strand, and the other right, towards Cliff House. I had wanted to follow exactly in Ben's footsteps, to go on the strand, to find the cave that had almost become a tomb. But I was afraid I would fall in the dim light, hit my head on a rock, be knocked unconscious and then swept away by the tide when it discovered me lying prone, at the foot of the cliff. I quickly shook my head to rid myself of that thought and turned right towards the Sanquests' house.

There was a low wall around the garden. The gate was closed but not locked. I opened it and walked in. The lights were coming from the front of the house, so I followed the path to the front door. Before I knocked, I stood spellbound, watching the last rays of light bleed from the horizon into the sea. I imagined the Sanquests must spend a lot of their time mesmerised by the power and beauty of their view. And then I noticed how near their front-garden wall was to the cliff edge. No more, I estimated, than fifty metres. How terrifying it must be to stand here when the sea lashed giant waves against the ever-eroding cliff face. Just as it had done last Friday night. I wondered, as they must do, how long it would be before Cliff House was claimed by the sea.

I turned and was about to knock when a dog started barking. Furiously. I took a few steps back from the door. I liked dogs, but I was wary of them. Particularly ones with terrifying, savage barks. I jumped when the door suddenly opened. A woman stood there, a tiny little dog in her arms.

"Quiet, Pilot. No more barking."

And with that gently spoken command, the threatening barking stopped, and Pilot became a cute little dog with a ribbon in his hair.

"Don't be afraid," the woman said. "As you can see, he's all bark. How can I help you?"

"Mrs Sanquest?"

She nodded.

"I'm Leah Parrish. You helped my husband on Friday night last. I wanted to thank you and your husband."

She stooped down and put the dog on the floor, then reached out her hand to me.

"Mrs Parrish, come in, please. Don't worry about Pilot. He won't touch you."

She led me along a passageway and took me into a room that was combined kitchen and living area. A log-burning stove threw out heat and light and gave the room a cosy glow. So cosy that the elderly man sitting in an armchair in front of the stove had fallen asleep, a newspaper on his lap and glasses halfway down his nose.

"*Walter! Wake up!*" Mrs Sanquest said, a lot more stridently than she had spoken to the dog.

I was just about to tell her not disturb him on my behalf when Walter opened his eyes. He had a very direct, but kind, gaze.

"Would I be right in thinking you're Ben Parrish's wife?" he asked.

"Leah Parrish," I said, walking towards him and offering him my hand.

He took it in a warm grip.

Everything about Vera and Walter and their home was warm and welcoming.

I opened my mouth to say my words of thanks, but nothing came out except a sort of strangled gulp.

Vera pulled another armchair in front of the stove.

"Sit yourself down, Mrs Parrish. Tea or coffee?"

I sat, feeling the heat from the blazing logs warm me, even through to the coldness that had lodged itself in my body on Friday night and had not shifted since.

"Coffee, please," I muttered, still trying to find my voice.

"How is your husband doing now?" Walter asked. "I assume he is still in hospital."

"He's improving. He had hypothermia. But you must know that because . . ."

I struggled to voice the thanks I owed these two people. I must find something to say so that they knew how very grateful I was, but yet I could not find words to adequately thank them for what they had done.

"They told me," I said. "The ambulance people. They said that you risked your own lives to save Ben's. I-I-don't know how to thank you. I –"

They both spoke together. As one.

"No need for thanks. We were glad to help."

They glanced at each other. I had never been a sentimental person, but what I saw Vera and Walter exchange was a look of pure love. They smiled at each other, obviously amused, but not surprised, by the fact that they had uttered exactly the same words, at the same instant. It was as if they had genuinely become one through sharing a lifetime of experiences. That was what I had hoped for Ben and me. An easing into old age together, bonded by a lifetime of memories.

"Do you have children?" I asked.

"A son and a daughter," Vera answered. "Our son is in Australia and our daughter in Brussels. Sad to have them so far away but they get home whenever they can. And more importantly, they're happy where they are."

As she was talking, she was putting a side table beside my chair and placing a mug of coffee and a plate of cake on it.

"Drink up," she said. "And have a slice of carrot cake. I always say it's one of my healthy five a day! Tell me, how many children do you and Ben have?"

"We have a five-year-old son and twins aged two and a half. And . . . we have a baby due next summer."

I stopped, shocked that I had told strangers what I had been unable to tell my husband. Or anybody. Maybe it was because they *were* strangers. But how could that be true? They had saved Ben's life. That connection made them closer to me than people I had known all my life.

Vera was smiling at me.

"Twins! How lovely. Boys? Girls? One of each?

"A boy and girl. Rob is their big brother. He has started school."

"You'll have your hands full so when the new baby arrives."

I could have just nodded and agreed but I felt I owed them the truth.

"Actually, Ben is the carer. He was, is, an architect but he was made redundant. You know what the building industry is like at the moment. Not much chance for him to get a job now."

"Not in Paircmoor anyway," Walter said.

I nodded, though the fact was, at that stage in Ireland's economic history, the building industry was in a total state of collapse. There was as little chance of employment for Ben in the capital as there was in Paircmoor.

"That must be very difficult for him," Vera said. "I don't mean minding his children. I know modern men are far more involved in the caring than they used to be. More 'hands on', isn't that the saying? But it takes a long time to train to be an architect. He must miss that creative outlet."

Of course she was right. Ben had loved his work and the lifestyle it provided for the family. I missed my old way of life too but I didn't go racing down cliff paths in storms. It was time now for me to put the questions I had come here to ask.

"Did either of you get a chance to talk to Ben on Friday night? Did he say anything?"

"We both did," Walter said. "I saw him on the road when I was driving into Paircmoor. It was, as you know, a bad night. He was running but I thought he looked under pressure. I stopped to ask if he was okay. He said he was and ran off towards here. I did wonder though about anyone out running in the atrocious conditions of Friday night."

It figured that Ben was uncomfortable running a distance. He was not as fit as he used to be. No more expensive gym. Paircmoor did not have a gym anyway.

"I took Pilot for a walk while Walter was in Paircmoor," Vera said.

When the dog heard the word '*walk*' he began barking and running around in circles. I had to wait until Vera had calmed him down again to hear the rest of what she had to say.

"Sorry about that," she said, as soon as Pilot had been appeased with a handful of treats.

"When I met Ben, I thought he was on his way down towards the cliffs. I asked if he was alright and invited him to come and have a cup of tea. He said no, he was fine and turned back towards the Paircmoor road. I felt a bit uneasy about him and when I got back inside the house I kept a lookout. Sure enough, I saw him come back and head down the cliff path that leads to the strand. That worried me as the tide was almost full in and it was very angry. I waited and waited but there was no sign of him coming back up."

"Deadly that strand is in a storm," Walter said. "Especially for people not familiar with it. I think you know the rest of the story, Mrs Parrish."

"Leah, please."

"Leah. When I came back, we went down and found Ben in the cave and alerted the emergency services. I believe you met the ambulance on the road and accompanied Ben to hospital."

I shivered. That pale, deathly cold person in the ambulance had been Ben, but at the same time, he had not been. He was just the framework within which the real Ben had lived. The one I obviously had not known at all.

"Was he conscious when you found him?"

"No. He was barely alive," Walter said. "We did our best to warm him until the paramedics arrived."

Vera Sanquest, wise woman that she was, zoned in on the fact that I had come here for answers. She pulled a chair next to mine and looked directly at me.

"I understand that you need to know why your husband took such a terrible risk. Only Ben can answer that. Only he knows."

I nodded. Of course. It was not fair of me to make these two wonderful people uncomfortable.

"I'm sorry," I said. "I came to thank you both and to let you know how very grateful I am. The children and Ben's mother and brother also. We will never able to thank you enough."

"The only thanks we need," Vera said, "is for you and Ben to live long, healthy, happy lives. And, just so you know, we found Ben in the cave. Towards the back of it. We don't know why he went on the strand, but it would appear he went into the cave to escape the rising tide."

And there it was, the answer I had been hoping for. Ben had been driven out into the violent night by disappointment and anger. He had run towards the turbulent sea to have his fears washed away. And in the cave he had faced his fears and chosen to live.

I stood and hugged the two strangers. Odd that I now felt closer to them than to anyone else. Vera walked me to the door. As I was about to leave she took my hand.

"Try to get some rest. Think of your baby."

I thought about what she had said all the way home. About the baby. By the time I reached Cowslip Cottage I realised I still had a lot more thinking to do before I reached any decision.

CHAPTER THIRTY

Tuesday 30th November 2010

It felt strange not to be going to work on Tuesday morning. While I knew Mags and Tina would look after Leah's Salon, I was uneasy about not being there. I had never seen myself as controlling, but my degree of discomfort about letting go the reins of the salon gave me pause for thought. I rang them, thanking them both and reminding them to make sure they left the used towels there for me to collect later. If they used any. From what I remembered of the appointment book, they would have ample time for putting their feet up.

Life in Cowslip Cottage seemed to be quickly falling into a pattern. I looked after the children in the morning, while Della visited Ben in the hospital. Then we would switch roles in the afternoon. Even though it was only days, it felt like we had been working this rota for a long time. I had spoken to the sister in charge of his unit this morning and she said Ben was making very good progress. I would have to ask later exactly what that meant.

The children had had breakfast, were washed and dressed, and were playing in the kitchen. Anna was occupied with colouring book and crayons, Josh with his blocks, and Rob with his wildlife sticker book. I stood at the kitchen door, watching them, thinking how touching their innocence, how brave they were being about their Daddy's accident, and how much I loved them.

I knew then it was time. Time to make sure. To confirm what I already knew instinctively. In the bathroom I unwrapped the digital pregnancy testing kit I had bought three weeks ago. The one I was now sure Della had seen. I closed my eyes as I waited for the result to show, wishing with all my heart that things could be different, that Ben was there to share this moment. That it could be a celebration. I opened my eyes. The result was positive.

Instinct led me to cradle the child I was carrying. I quickly dropped my hand to my side. It was not a Rob or Josh or Anna. It was an eight-week embryo. It was a mistake. The result of a passionate reconciliation after an equally passionate argument. Also the result of my carelessness about taking the contraceptive pill. My fault. Ben's fault. I should not be blaming the embryo. But how could I not? We were struggling to survive now. How could we cope with another mouth to feed, more clothes, shoes, more work, less space? It was obvious that Ben's mental state was as fragile as his physical health. He was going to need a lot of help to recover his confidence. To be Ben again. How could he look after a baby as well as the other children? He would not be able to cope or recover.

I regretted now telling the Sanquests about the pregnancy. Speaking aloud about it had betrayed my secret. And that in turn narrowed my options. Despite not wanting to, my hand crept to my belly again and curved protectively over where our fourth child lay, tiny heart beating. I had been so sure. So certain that this, this mistake, should never become part of our family. Maybe that was why I hadn't yet told Ben. Not maybe. It was. I knew that Ben could not cope with the added responsibility of another child, even before he did something as irrational as daring the tide to sweep him away. I was not putting the onus just on Ben. *I* absolutely could not see how, in our present circumstances, which were getting worse instead of better, we could financially support and care for a new baby. Or two, if I was carrying twins again.

As I had not seen my GP or booked a scan . . . or made an appointment with an abortion clinic, the only proof of the embryo's existence was the positive pregnancy test which I now held in my hand. And the fact I had told the Sanquests.

My legs began to shake. This was the first time I had allowed myself to seriously examine the abortion thought. Ever since I first suspected that I might be pregnant, I had gone between denial and rejection of the growing baby. I had even hoped that I would have an early miscarriage, prayed that I was wrong and not pregnant at all. I glared at the positive test. Proof that my fears were being realised. And yet, treacherous tears spilled onto the kit. I moved to throw it in the bin, but then was struck by the thought that it might be all I would ever have of this baby. I decided then to keep it for as long as the result was showing. I laid it carefully on the top shelf of the cabinet and locked it away.

Back in the kitchen, I stood at the door, watching our children play. I thought of my mother. How she had battled single-handedly to raise me. To love me and make me feel secure. I wondered if she had considered having an abortion. She must have. Especially since the ethos of the time made her a social outcast for being pregnant and unmarried. This baby would be her grandchild. She would have loved it with the same passion she had loved Rob and the twins for the short time she had known them. And, to be fair, the same could be said of Della. She was a warm and loving grandmother. It, this inch-long collection of cells, had the potential to be child, grandchild, sibling. After next week, it would shed its embryo status and become a foetus. A baby. Our baby. The decision was too big for me to make alone.

Josh's trademark piercing cry made me almost jump out of my skin. I had seen a flash of Anna's hand as she had suddenly looked up from her colouring book and swiped at the tower of blocks Josh had painstakingly built. In an instant she was back colouring her picture again, a smile of satisfaction playing on her mouth. She was, I thought, a little minx, and Josh needed to toughen up. Rob got up from the table, looked at me, shrugged his shoulders, and walked away towards his bedroom. His actions had the hallmark of a well-practised escape plan for my eldest son.

With Josh still crying, Anna still smiling, I sat down at the table with them to talk to them in two-year-old terms about sharing and bullying and looking out for each other. All the while I spoke, with the twins nodding sincerely and pretending they would never again fight, I was conscious of the fact that I could no longer keep my pregnancy a secret from Ben.

We had made this embryo/mistake/baby together. Together we would have to decide its fate. But not yet.

It was midday when Della got to the hospital. She'd had a lot of organising to do this morning. And then there had been the call from Hugh, telling her what she must *not* do. Warning her. He got more like his father every day.

She had to circle around the car park several times

before getting a parking space. Annoying because she needed all the time she could get to explain things to Ben. To ease him past his stubborn, self-destructive streak that she had thought gone forever. When she finally reached the first floor, she took a moment to stand and breathe slowly. To calm herself. To reassure herself that she had everything under control. Satisfied, she walked down the corridor, tapped on the door of Room 5 and went in.

Ben was sitting on a chair by the window, his back to the door. He did not turn when she came in. She tiptoed across the room.

"No need to creep, Mom. I heard you walking up the corridor. You make a very distinctive sound with your high heels."

He still had not turned to look at her. She pulled the other chair over and sat beside him. He looked gaunt.

"Are you eating, Ben? I know hospital food isn't the greatest. I can bring you in whatever you want. What would you fancy?"

"The food is good here. I don't know why people complain. I'm just not very hungry at the moment."

"Well, I suppose they do their best, but there have to be shortcomings when you consider the number of patients they are trying to care for."

"They saved my life, Mom. I'm very grateful to them and I don't give a shit about the food."

Della sat back. She read his mood as belligerent. He would be downright angry if he had the strength.

"Have you seen a doctor yet today?" she asked. "How are you feeling?"

"How do you think I feel? I've had a heart attack. And no, I haven't seen any doctor yet."

"Oh! That's not satisfactory. I'll have a word with them."

"No, thank you. No need."

"But there's every need, Ben. You must have specialised care now so that you can recover your full health. Mentally and physically. You won't get that here. I've been in contact with the Booly –"

Ben made such a sudden move that Della started. He was on his feet, towering over her, the veins on his neck standing out, his eyes sparking anger.

"Don't say you've been in contact with the Booly Clinic! Tell me I'm wrong. Please tell me you have more respect for me than that!"

For the first time ever, Della was frightened of him. Since his early teens, he had turned his anger in on himself. It was apparent that the anger was so intense now he could no longer contain it. He was ready to lash out. Proof that she was definitely planning the right course of action for him.

"Yes, Ben. That's exactly what I did. The Booly Clinic set you back on your feet before, and it will do so again. Professor Giles has retired but his son is there now. I know that's where you'll get the peace and privacy to get well. Don't worry about the expense. Your insurance will cover it. I checked with them. If there's a shortfall, I'll pick it up."

Just as suddenly as he had jumped up, Ben sat. Sank back onto his chair, shoulders drooped, head in hands. He had gone in a flash from demented to defeated. Della was instantly planning to bring the date of his transfer to the Booly Clinic forward.

"You're quite entitled to sign yourself out of here, Ben. I'll organise an ambulance for the transfer. It will only be about a two-hour journey and I'll travel with you. Just you leave it to me."

He raised his head. His eyes shone black in the pale face. He was drawn, like he had aged since she had come into the room. His voice was soft when he spoke. His words were not.

"Because I know you believe you're helping me, I won't have you removed from my room. But you've got to understand, you have no right to interfere in my medical care. Try that again and I'll remove you, not just from this room, but entirely from my life."

Della stared at him. She would have said she was gobsmacked if only she could bring herself to use that type of language. Images of Ben flashed before her. As a small child, coming to her when his father had been impatient with him, taking her hand for comfort, smiling his slow, angelic smile. As a teenager, crying in her arms when his sadness broke through the defences he had built up. As a man, sharing his triumphs and tragedies, relying on her. Respecting her. Until now.

"Are you saying I'm interfering? I've always done what was right for you."

"What's right for me now, is for you to allow me make my own decisions. About my health and my future."

Della could not help but give a little smile. Her boy was starting to grow up. To go through the teenage defiance he had skipped during his traumatic teenage years. He would get over this tantrum and then she could sort everything out. She stood up.

"I'm going out to Cowslip Cottage now. I'll be minding the children so that Leah can come to see you."

His head was bowed again. She wasn't sure whether he

was awake or asleep. She put her hand on his shoulder. When there was no reaction, she walked out of the room and gently closed the door.

Then she went to the duty desk to complain that her son had not yet been seen by a doctor.

"It's most disturbing," she told the junior doctor she had managed to collar. "My son came from Intensive Care and now he's just left here unattended. Don't give me any excuses about under-staffing and under-funding. This is just plain bad practice."

The young doctor had waited patiently until Della stopped talking, then he calmly told her that he would be unable to discuss Ben's treatment with her.

"If you need to know anything, I suggest you ask your son."

Della turned and almost knocked sparks from the floor tiles as she walked towards the lifts. She vowed to herself that she would get Ben out of this hospital, out of Paircmoor, and out of the life-threatening depression only she seemed to see. If not the Booly Clinic, then somewhere else Ben would accept.

By the time the lift arrived to the ground floor, all the outline of the alternative plan she must now set in place for Ben and for his future had begun to form. A far superior plan to a few months' stay in the psychiatric wing of the Booly Clinic. A plan with which, she knew in her heart, he would agree.

I had turned on the television for the twins, to keep them occupied while I got ready for my trip to the hospital. Rob was in his room with his computer. He would spend all day long on it if he was allowed.

Della was late. It was already past two o'clock and she had been due in Cowslip Cottage at one. When my phone rang, I was certain it would be her to say she was on the way. I glanced at the screen on my phone but didn't recognise the number. The caller obviously wasn't on my contact list. Nor was it the hospital. I hesitated about answering. I had to work hard to get these few minutes to myself to put on make-up. Something I had not had a chance to do for the past few days. It was an overseas call. It could be one of the scams promising me a fortune if I gave them my bank details. Maybe I should and let them scrabble around there looking for non-existent wealth.

The phone stopped ringing just as it dawned on me that the number looked familiar. I had definitely seen it before. Curious, I wondered what the charge would be if I rang back. I was about to look up the international code when the ringing began again. I answered straight away.

"Hello. Leah Parrish here. Sorry I missed a call from you earlier."

"Hi, Leah. How are you?"

So, the international code was the US, the area code San Francisco. Just as well I had not rung back. That call would have eaten up my credit. I was taken aback that Hugh Parrish was in the least bothered about my welfare. He probably was trying to find out if Ben had told me whatever it was his message said I had a right to know. I couldn't ask him now without admitting I had read his private text to Ben.

"I'm fine, Hugh, thank you. I'm assuming Della is keeping you informed about Ben's progress."

"She is. Her version of it anyway. I want to know what you think. How he really is."

"I'm not sure how much Della has told you, but Ben has responded well to the hypothermia treatment and so far it appears he has escaped any permanent damage as a result of . . . of what happened."

"And the heart attack?"

"It was mild. He was lucky to be in hospital when it happened so he had immediate treatment. His doctors say they are very pleased with his rate of recovery. It's only been a few days and it looks like he may be home soon."

"*Hmmm.*"

Not sure how to respond, I said nothing. Neither did Hugh. The silence seemed as long as the physical distance between us.

Eventually he spoke.

"Has Mum said anything to you about her plans?"

"What plans? I think you know, Hugh, she would not be discussing her schedule with me. I'm not having a go. It's just fact. Having said that, I would have been lost without her the past few days. She's been marvellous with the children. They adore her, and she them."

"Yes, that's Della for you. She knows how to make herself indispensable. The trouble is, she sometimes doesn't know when to pull back. Especially with Ben."

He stopped talking, as if to let me absorb his critical remark about his mother. Of course her manipulation of Ben wasn't news to me, but the fact that Hugh had mentioned it made me think there was a lot afoot that I did not yet know.

"Is this about the potential job for Ben in California with your brother-in-law? Is Della thinking of kidnapping Ben from the hospital?"

I had tried to put a light note in my voice. An implied

ha-ha. It didn't work. I was trapped in a net of Parrish family half-truths and lies and I was struggling. What in the hell was Della up to? Why was Hugh suddenly concerned enough to ring me?

"I've been trying to contact Ben. Does he have his phone with him in hospital?"

"Yes, but he doesn't want to use it."

"I thought as much. Look, Leah, I'm on my way home. I'm at San Francisco airport as we speak. I want to see my brother and I need to see you too. Try to get Ben to talk. About when we were young."

"You mean about the Swiss Army knife you gave him for his sixteenth birthday?"

I heard his intake of breath from across the North Atlantic.

"So, you know," he said. "You have no idea how much I've regretted that present ever since."

I could just imagine. Successful student Hugh, gifting sad little brother Ben the weapon to cut his wrist. A tough burden to carry.

"Not your fault, Hugh. Not anybody's fault. Then or now."

I heard my own words echo in my ears. I had just admitted that Ben careening down a cliff path into the waiting arms of a vicious tide had been as much a suicide attempt as him hacking his wrist. I sat on the side of the bed. The huge sleigh bed we had brought with us from Dublin. The bed we had shared together for over six years, where we had created our twins. And the embryo. Now it was as if I had slept with a stranger for all those years. I probably would have cried had not the sound of Hugh's voice brought me back to the here and now.

"I know logically it wasn't my fault, Leah. I just have to learn to believe it. Thank you for saying it, anyway."

There was a sudden onslaught as Josh ran in the door, chased by Anna.

"Anna say a curse at me," Josh said.

"Not!" Anna insisted. "Josh say bum too."

"Sorry, Hugh," I said. "As you can hear, this pair need sorting. I'll be going to the hospital as soon as your mother arrives. I'll tell Ben you were asking for him."

"Tell him I'll see him soon. And, Leah, take care. It was nice talking to you."

"And you too," I said.

When the call was finished, I realised that we had spoken in riddles and hints. Della's plans. Ben's past. An urgent need for Hugh to travel from San Francisco to Paircmoor. I had also forgotten to ask him when he was due to arrive here. I assumed he would be staying in the hotel in town, like his mother.

A squeal from Anna told me her Della radar was on high alert. I was convinced she was capable of hearing her grandmother's car from as far away as the bendy bridge.

I closed my make-up drawer. It was time for me to go to my husband and for both of us to face the truth together.

CHAPTER THIRTY-ONE

While driving through town to the hospital, I noticed groups of people in high-vis jackets, clustered around ladders here and there. They were obviously volunteers, Tidy Towns' members, stringing up Christmas lights from poles and shop canopies. The sight made me shiver. I had been putting some Christmas money by whenever I could for the past few months. It came nowhere near what it would take to give the children, not just what they wanted in toys, but what they needed in clothes and shoes. I shrugged off those thoughts. Christmas was a month away. The situation with Ben was now.

I was in a determined frame of mind when I tapped on the door of Room 5. No more pussyfooting around the facts. No more hints and half- truths. Hugh had said ask Ben about his early years. That was exactly what I would do.

I strode into the room to find Ben asleep. He looked peaceful. Vulnerable. His features relaxed. He did seem thinner than I had ever seen him, but that would soon be sorted when he got home. I took off my coat, hung it in his wardrobe, and sat. I watched him sleep, his breath slow and even, his mouth slightly open. I had an urge to lie down beside him, cuddle into him and sleep. For a long time.

His phone was beside me on the locker top. I checked it. The screen was blank. He had let the battery run down, not caring about people wanting to contact him. His brother for instance. That was the thing about Ben. His life, his real, thinking, feeling life, was lived privately in his head. His interactions with the world around him and the people in it were superficial. I sighed, knowing I was being unfair to Ben. And I would soon be angry also, if I was forced to sit here and wait much longer.

I shook him gently by the shoulder. He woke slowly, rubbing his eyes, stretching and then turning towards me with the slow, gentle smile I loved so much.

"How long have you been here?" he asked. "I got tired waiting so I had a snooze."

He pulled himself up in the bed.

I leaned towards him and kissed him. His eyes were glazed. I assumed he was still being sedated.

"Not long," I said. "Your mother was a bit late coming out to Paircmoor. She must be tired at this stage from all her travelling around."

"*Hmm*. There's no need for her to be here. She could still be in Hugh's house if she wanted."

"Don't be nasty, Ben. She went to a lot of effort to be here for you."

He pushed back his bedcovers impatiently and swung his legs out. Sitting directly in front of me, he looked at me, all traces of sleep now gone.

"I think we should take up where we left off yesterday, Leah. There's a lot to tell."

"That's what Hugh said."

"Hugh? When were you talking to him?"

"He rang me today. Said he had been trying to get in

touch with you. You do realise your phone battery is flat, don't you? The charger is in your locker. You'll see Hugh soon anyway. He's coming home."

"Here?"

I was becoming annoyed. We were allowing ourselves to get side-tracked again.

"Yes, here. Forget about that now. Just talk. Tell me what you've been hiding from me. And why."

"I've been ashamed to tell you the truth, Leah. Terrified that you would reject me if you knew the real me."

He took my hands in his. His fingers felt bony. Cold. I was finding it difficult to control the trembling in my limbs. The longer it took Ben to tell me 'the truth' about himself, the more I anticipated unbearable news. A criminal conviction? A previous marriage? He squeezed my hands and I felt him tremble too.

"Imagine I'm sixteen," he said. "Trying to recover from cutting my wrist. Because my mother had given a plausible explanation to the hospital about me messing around with tools, there was no real follow-up. She tutored me so well on the electric-saw cover-up story that I had almost come to believe it myself. Shortly after, we went on a family holiday, an Easter break cruising on the Shannon."

He shivered. I heard his breathing quicken. I didn't want to say anything in case my words were the wrong ones and would stop him talking.

"Dad and Hugh always had a close bond. It was even more apparent than usual on that trip. They laughed together, shared the work of piloting the boat, played golf in one town we docked in. Mum just basked in the glow of their camaraderie. And me? I had never felt more alone, or more devastated that I had not bled to death from my cut wrist."

I winced, hearing an echo in his voice of what he had suffered.

"I waited until they were all asleep. Then I slipped overboard, into the black, cold water. It wrapped around me. Over my head. Into my lungs. Down. Down. But it spat me up to the surface again and my mouth opened to gasp for air. My mind did not want to fight for life, but my body did. My arms and legs flailed. Splashed. I spluttered, spitting out water. Lights went on in the cruiser. I saw Dad's face appear at the rail, shadowed by Hugh. The water closed over my head again. That's all I remember until I woke up on board. Mum was crying and Dad was shouting at her about having me sectioned. I wasn't sure what that meant until I heard him mention the mental hospital. Then I was doubly angry that I had neither bled to death nor drowned."

He let go my hand and lay back on the bed. Eyes closed, so that I could not see the pain in them. I lay down beside him, held him close, and felt his pain by osmosis. I was holding the boy. The sad and lonely teenager. Isolated in his difference.

"They reached a compromise," he said. My parents. They booked me into the Booly Clinic."

"I heard of that. It's where the rich and famous go for rehab, isn't it?"

He opened his eyes and smiled at me. "And where the not so rich and famous can go for discreet treatment for their son's mental health problems. Didn't stop me trying though. I stashed my medication and made two more suicide attempts. As you can see, I never managed to get it right. Typical. I've always gone along with Mum's need for cover-up. I felt I owed her that for being such a burden to her. So my stay in the Booly Clinic was always referred to as a three-month unsuccessful trial at boarding school. I even failed in that imaginary task."

His self-hatred was tangible. Eating him up, like caustic bile pumping through his veins. I moved away from him and sat on the side of the bed.

"So how long were you in the Clinic?"

"Three months. I had intensive counselling, medication, and eventually a pass back into the great big world. I was still sad, but no longer suicidal."

"Until last Friday. Am I right, Ben? Did you mean to end your life then? Is that why you went to the beach?"

He pulled himself up in the bed and sat beside me.

"No, Leah! No! I had no great plan on Friday night. All I wanted to do was run away from the pressure. My scale model business was a joke, the only friend I had in Paircmoor had turned out not be a friend at all, my mother was pimping me out to a rich developer in the US. Begging him to take me on. For fuck's sake! Who would employ a thirty-six-year-old man whose mother has to go touting for a job for him? Certainly not Zach Milburg. He has a reputation for being ruthless. And successful. Maybe they are the same thing. I just had to get away from it all."

I felt like distancing myself from his bitterness, but knew I could not. It was good that he was talking, even though it was hard to hear that Ellen Riggs was the only friend he had in Paircmoor. I would have named Ben as first on my list of friends, no matter where we were living. "The cave you were in. Is that the one the children told me about? Where Ellen Riggs taught them the names of the fish in the rock pool."

He nodded. "Yes, that's the one. I went there to think.

To sort my head out. I stayed too long. The tide blocked my exit. I wasn't suicidal, Leah. I'd have gone into the water if I was, wouldn't I?"

Would he? I didn't know. He seemed he didn't either. What I *did* know was that he had probably gone to that cave to relive that happy day with Ellen and the children.

"The worst thing, Leah, is that my mother is still trying to control me. I'm not blaming her. I'm just saying she'll have to work things out for herself, but I've reached the stage where I must take responsibility for my own life."

"No, Ben. Not just you. I'm with you every step of the way. And there is so much help available now. But no more lies and cover-up. You've nothing to be ashamed about. Have you seen a counsellor here? Or a psychiatrist."

"No. They offered the service but I refused it. I don't need it. Do you remember I went to the GP in Paircmoor about the pains in my neck and shoulders? Doctor Kelly. He knew straight away that I was suffering from stress. Unemployment, money worries, looking after the kids, Paircmoor. All that shit. I told him I had previously suffered from depression. He gave me the name of a counsellor and wrote a prescription for me."

I was stunned. "I didn't know you were taking medication."

"That's because I wasn't. I didn't fill the prescription. But I will. I'll go back to the GP, good old Doctor Kelly, and tell him I'm ready to listen to him now."

"I'll go with you."

"No, you won't. I must do this myself, Leah. Mum never let me take control of the situation, so I never took responsibility for it. I must do it now. For you and for the children."

"And for yourself."

"Exactly."

We were silent then. Each of us isolated in our separate pool of thought. Mine was about all the lies I had been told and the truths that had been withheld for so long. Was this it? Did I now know all the Parrish family secrets? While Della had manipulated her vulnerable son in his teens, he had been an adult when I met him. Confident, successful. It was unfair of him now to let his mother take all the blame for hiding the facts. Just as it was unfair of me to withhold my news. Our news.

"We'll get through this, Leah. I'll do the right thing for you and Rob and the twins. I love the four of you so much."

The four of us. Rob, Josh, Anna and Leah. How could I tell him about the embryo? About the soon-to-be foetus. About the baby that I had not planned and did not want. And yet, I yearned to grow and nurture and give birth to this baby. To hold it in my arms and love it. Protect it. I smiled at Ben.

"We love you too, Ben. The four of us. The Paircmoor Parrishes."

I left then. Quickly. Taking with me the fifth, unacknowledged, unwanted, member of the dysfunctional Paircmoor Parrishes.

CHAPTER THIRTY-TWO

Wednesday 1st December 2010

The sound of my phone ringing woke me at six o'clock in the morning. I panicked, sure it must be the hospital. It could only be bad news when they rang at that hour. I grabbed it after two rings, worried it would wake the children, afraid to hear what the caller had to say.

I was relieved but puzzled to hear Della's voice.

"Sorry to wake you so early," she said. "I want to let you know I won't be available to babysit for you this afternoon."

"Good. I-I don't mean good that you can't babysit. It's just that I thought there might be bad news about Ben when the phone rang. I mean an emergency. A new crisis. Or something . . ."

I winced as I listened to myself waffle.

"I've some business I need to attend to in Dublin. I'm not sure how long it will take but it will probably be late when I get back down here. It may even be tomorrow."

"That's no problem, Della. Thanks for letting me know. Have a safe journey."

Then she was gone before I could ask her if she was going to pick Hugh up at the airport. Swanning off to do her 'business'. Now I had to cope with the 'no problem' of minding the children. Mags and Tina were holding the fort at the salon, so they would not be available. Claire Hoey was probably gone back to work. Unless her back was still giving trouble after her car accident. One way or the other she would not be available to babysit. I considered asking Vera and Walter Sanquest but the children did not know them. Neither did I. Besides, they had already done enough for this family.

That left me with the option of bringing the brood to the hospital with me. I would have to quell my fear of them picking up all sorts of bugs. They would be delighted to see Ben. Or would they be upset at seeing him in hospital? He might be moody. Angry. Not something the children should see.

I threw back the duvet and got out of bed, suddenly struck by the thought that the children might already have been subjected to Ben's moods. The depression I had failed to note. The anger. The resentment. I shook my head in denial. They would have mentioned it to me. Not the twins of course. They would not have the vocabulary to describe such behaviour, but they would have shown signs of upset. Bed wetting maybe. Or aggression. I immediately thought of Anna. How she manipulated the two boys. Especially Josh. Occasionally making Josh cry. It had never dawned on me that she might be copying behaviour she had seen. I shrugged off that thought. Rob had been very upset on Friday when he had heard Ben shout and smash Ellen Riggs' vase. If he had previously seen aggressive behaviour like that, he would certainly have told me. Wouldn't he?

I put on my dressing gown and tiptoed along the corridor to the twins' room and checked on them. They were still asleep. Even Anna, unusually for her, was motionless. Rob, also, was sleeping peacefully when I checked on him. I continued on out to the kitchen, then to the lounge. I stood in the doorway and looked directly across the room at the door opposite. The one that led into Ben's office. That quaint little room which had once been a dairy, where butter was churned and cheese made for the family. Or so Mags Hoey had told me. It was obviously true, as we had found some beautifully carved wooden butter moulds and paddles on the shelf there. I displayed them on the dresser in the kitchen now.

I stood staring at the door of the ex-dairy as if I could discern from across the room if it was locked or not. Or if I had any right to go in there and poke through Ben's work. His computer. Anything else he might have in his private space. He kept it locked in case the children interfered with his work. He said. And why would I do that? What was I looking for? More secrets? The sad fact was that I did not really know Ben at all. As I stood there staring at the door of his office, I realised I did not trust him either. How could I? He had withheld the truth of his teenage years from me for as long as I had known him.

Suddenly making up my mind, I strode across the room and tried the door handle. It opened inwards. I shivered. I always found that room to be exceptionally cold, maybe because it was north-facing and had not yet been insulated. Another job for when our luck changed. By that standard, it would be cold for a long time. There was an electric radiator by the desk. I ignored it, conscious of the electricity bill. A filing cabinet, printer, a few shelves over the desk, chair, walls still whitewashed in respect for the dairy tradition. That was it. Ben's office. His escape space.

The filing cabinet was not locked. Feeling like a traitor, I opened the drawers and flicked through the files. Drawings, plans, proposals. Every single file work-related. Even though I was not sure what I was looking for, I knew it was not in the filing cabinet. Next I sat at his desk, staring at his laptop. This was where he spent his private hours. The times when he could stop pretending to be content with his lot. Mostly at night, after the children had gone to bed. The fact was, he could not have much time during the day to sit here soul-searching. Or working on his scale models. The children were a full-time job, at least until the twins went to kindergarten next year.

I began to think what it would have been like for me to look after the children at the same time as I was trying to establish my salon. I had never thought of it that way before. I imagined the conflict, the time pressure, the sheer frustration of catering full-time to the needs of three children while trying to manage a start-up business. I shivered again, but not from cold this time. Guilt put its icy fingers around my heart and squeezed. In that moment of honesty, I knew I had not supported Ben as I should have. If nothing else, I could have shown interest in his scale models. Given him encouragement. Instead I had side-lined him. Put him at the bottom of my long list of priorities. I saw my reflection in the laptop screen. My face looked mean and pinched. That is exactly how I felt.

Now that I felt so bad about myself, I decided to go ahead with turning on his laptop and snooping there. It flickered into life. The start screen image flooded the dreary room with sunshine and light. I gazed at the photo of the children, the three little Parrishes. Plus Finn Riggs. They were on the beach, in swimwear. All happy and smiling. In front of them was a little pile of sandcastles, one with a bunch of sea thrift stuck on top, and another decorated with cockleshells. Behind them stood Ellen Riggs. In a bikini. Her body was perfect in every curve. No stretch marks. She was smiling at the photographer. At my husband. I leaned forward and peered more closely at the background. It was as I suspected. They were standing in front of a cave, the dark slash of the mouth sinister in the otherwise happy picture. A family photo. Now I knew for certain what had drawn Ben to that cave.

The cursor was blinking at me, asking for a password. Of course he would have had his work protected. Or whatever else he had stored there. I turned off the computer and stood up. As I was pushing the chair back under the desk, I noticed the drawers. I opened the righthand one. Pens, pencils, printer paper. All the paraphernalia of a working office. I tried to open the left-hand drawer but it was locked. I searched the desktop but no sign of a key. I glanced up at the bookshelves over the desk. They were high. By standing on the chair I was able to reach up to the top shelf. I found the key, obviously put there out of reach of the children. And me. My hands were shaking as I inserted it in the drawer lock and turned it. I pulled the drawer towards me and gasped when I saw three pill bottles. Full. I picked one up and read the label. It had been prescribed by the local GP, Doctor Kelly. For Ben. I knew they were an anti-depressant, because I had read an article about that particular drug. A controversial article about side-effects. These were the pills Ben had told me he had not got. I remembered his words exactly. "*I didn't fill the prescription. But I will. I'll go back to the GP, good old Doctor Kelly, and tell him I'm ready to listen to him now.*"

This was another half-truth. True, he had not taken the pills. But he *had* gone and bought them. According to the dates on the labels, he had filled the prescription every month for the past three months. Stashed them. I didn't have to ask why. Had he not admitted to me that he had overdosed twice in the Booly Clinic using the same technique? A sort of stash-and-slash policy. An insurance against life being too unbearable. What was I to do now? Confront him? Take the pills away? Go talk to the GP? I was shaking so much I felt dizzy and had to lean on the desk for support.

A shout that was unmistakably Anna's reached me. I quickly put the pills back in the drawer, locked it and returned the key to where I had found it. I rushed back and met the children, all three of them, in the kitchen. Rob had Anna on one side of him and Josh on the other, holding their hands. Their faces looked terrified. Anna rushed towards me.

"Mom! I think you were gone too."

"We went to your room, Mom," Rob said. "It was scary when you weren't there cos neither was Dad. And we miss him."

"Miss, Dad," Josh said.

I knelt down and opened my arms to the three of them. My life. My love. My sanity. I kissed their faces and held them close to me, conscious that the embryo, their sibling, my fourth child, was also in that circle with us. I felt devastated that I could not welcome it with the same joy as I had Rob and the twins. Or with any joy at all.

I made the children pancakes for breakfast. Leaving the tidy-up and washing to one side, I sat with them reading stories and drew strength from their innocence and honesty. From their love for their father. And despite Ellen Riggs, half-truths and pill stashes, I knew I loved Ben with all my heart.

I vowed then that I would do whatever it took to get Ben back to full health.

CHAPTER THIRTY-THREE

The usual background hospital noises were missing. Ben knew that was because the change-over was happening. The exhausted night shift would be at the nurses' desk, handing over charts, observations and patients, to the day staff. He had heard a lot of activity in the small hours. Hurried footsteps along the corridor, a trolley, wheels rattling as it was pushed at speed. He had lain there in the dark, wondering if somebody had died, or if, like him, the patient had been pulled back from the brink. Whether they wanted to or not. He thought about it again last night. About dying. About that very last breath, the one he had almost drawn several times. How it would feel. Painful. Terrifying. Liberating. And what then? Harps and angels? Judgement? Ben Parrish found wanting in death, as in life. Condemned to the hell of reincarnating as himself in a different guise, again and again. Or maybe, just maybe, that last breath would shudder into nothingness. Blissful annihilation of shame and despair. That comforting thought had lulled him to sleep.

The hospital silence was broken by a very distinctive tap-tap sound coming along the corridor. Ben sat up, wondering what his mother was doing here at quarter to eight in the morning.

"Do you sleep at all?" he asked, as Della opened the door.

"Not much last night," she answered. "A lot on my mind."

Ben cringed. His fault again. He remembered being cruel to her. Threatening to remove her entirely from his life. He knew he had hurt her. Perhaps he had meant to then, but not now, seeing how tired and frail she looked.

She pulled a chair over to the bed, then took off her coat and hung it up. She smoothed her hair and straightened her already perfect skirt before sitting down.

"Thinking about my future kept me awake last night, Ben."

He leaned back against his pillows, waiting for her to continue. She was silent.

"And?" he prompted. "What conclusions did you reach?"

She clasped and unclasped her hands. It was not like Della to be nervous. Ben began to feel anxious. Worried that maybe she was not well. Terminally ill. Because of all the worry he had caused her.

"Are you alright, Mum?"

She stopped fiddling with her hands and looked him straight in the eye.

"The answer to that, Ben, is yes and no. I am reasonably fit and healthy for a woman of my age but I don't have the energy I once had. I'm finding the house and garden in Howth too much for me now."

"How? You have a cleaner for the house and Tom Dempsey still looks after the garden."

"Yes, I have help, but that house is too big for me. It's

a family home. A lonely place for me to be these days. When I'm in San Francisco with Hugh and Piper, I stay in their guest house. It's a two-bed bungalow. I really like the more compact space. It's cosier."

Ben shook his head in puzzlement. The last thing he ever thought he would hear his mother say was that she wanted to leave the family home. Yet that appeared to be where this conversation was leading.

"Mum, is this because of what I said to you yesterday? I'm sorry. Really I am. Not about what I said. It *is* important that I take responsibility for myself and stop leaning on you so much. But I do regret the way I said it."

She smiled at him. A patient, longsuffering smile, practised on her husband and perfected on her son. A martyr to the cause of domestic harmony.

"You were right, Ben. In fact, I'm glad. It's a very healthy sign that you're ready to strike off on your own. Serendipitous in fact, since I find myself in exactly the same position. I want to live the life that suits me now, not a shadow of the life I used to live when we were all together. Do you understand?"

No, Ben did not understand. Della was defined by that house in Howth. She had chosen the furniture, the décor, planted the willows in the garden when she had been young, reared her babies there. She was the very spirit of that house. His childhood home.

"But where would you live, Mum? With Hugh and Piper?"

"Goodness, no! I love going there for a holiday but never to live. Besides, I would quickly wear out my welcome. What I'm thinking is that I need to be nearer the town and all the amenities at this stage of my life. Less travelling."

"But you love Howth, the village, the sea, the walks, the views. Your friends. You can't move into the hustle and bustle of the city. You'd hate it."

Della sat back in her chair and laughed. Ben raised an eyebrow.

"Who was lecturing me about being allowed to make his own decisions?" she asked.

Ben grinned. She was right. She was taking responsibility for her own future. Just like he said he wanted to do.

"Touché. So tell me, where are you planning on living?"

"The quay apartments you designed. Remember your father invested in one? We still own it. It's let out at the moment but my solicitor will deal with finishing up that contract. Once it's refurbished, I'll be happy to move in there."

It would all make perfect sense to Ben if the woman involved had not been Della. It was impossible to see her living happily in the busy surrounds of the apartment block.

"Mum, is this about money? I know I've been a drain on your resources for the past few years. Do you have to sell The Parrish House because you can't afford the upkeep?"

"Who said I was selling The Parrish House?"

"Oh! You'll be letting it out so. But maybe you should change the name first!"

Della laughed, making her look years younger.

"I don't know about that," she said. "Your father named it the day we moved in. He had a wry sense of humour, hadn't he?"

Ben shrugged. He had never seen too much of his father's humour, wry or otherwise.

Della began clasping and unclasping her hands again.

So here it comes, Ben thought, the thing that's making her so agitated.

"I want you to listen to me, Ben. Don't interrupt and don't say anything when I've finished. Just think about what I'm going to tell you for a while. Then we'll talk. Agreed?"

Ben nodded. He had to if he wanted to know what was making his mother behave in such an un-Della-like way.

"Firstly, I have no money worries. You know your father was a wonderful architect. What you may not realise, is that he was an even better financial investor. A wizard, in fact. He left me very well provided for. I'm free to make the decision to move because I want to, not because I have to."

"I'm glad to hear –"

She raised her hand to stop him mid-sentence.

"No talking. You agreed. Now it's my turn to apologise. I had no right to contact the Booly Clinic on your behalf. It was disrespectful and I'm very sorry. I suppose I just panicked, thinking all this was a replay of what – what happened when you were sixteen."

Reaching across to her, Ben took her restless hands in his and smiled at her. She returned the smile.

"I believe now that what happened on Friday night was an accident," she told him. "But I also know if you stay in Paircmoor any longer you will definitely struggle to maintain balance. That is why I intend signing the Howth house over to you. On condition that you and the children move in there as soon as the paperwork is done and dusted."

Ben's gasp was one of shock, and anger too. Della put her fingers to her lips.

"You can't do that! How do you think Hugh would –"

"*Shhh!* No talking. Not until you have thought it all through. It would mean a lot to me to have family in the house again. I've run it by Hugh and he says he won't be back here. He's settled in California for good. Paircmoor is dragging you down, Ben. The city is already showing tentative signs of recovery. You'll get work there eventually. It will be better for the children too. You would have more space, should you need it in the future. Come back home."

She stood, got her coat, then turned on her heel and walked out the door.

Ben sat still, eyes closed, for a long time after his mother left, furious with himself for allowing her to silence him. He should have demanded to know why she had not mentioned Leah. Did she really think he would move back to Dublin with the children and leave his wife here? No. Obviously she had assumed that Leah would be coming too. Hadn't she? A wrong assumption, since Leah was rooted in Paircmoor. So tied to her blasted little hair salon that nothing would prise her away. Why did Della say she recognised his need for independence, while at the same time demeaning him by continuing to make decisions for him? And what did she think he would need more space for?

He punched his pillow, then texted Leah to tell her he needed to talk to her. Urgently.

After pancakes and stories, I asked the children what they would like to do. They all voted for making muffins. I was looking forward to, for once, being the mom who joined in the fun with them. I sent them to the bathroom to wash their hands while I finally cleared up after breakfast.

When the text alert beeped on my phone, I glanced at it to see who it was from. Then I kept staring at the text message from Ben, as if I could read the answers to all the questions it raised by gazing long enough.

When will you be in to see me, Leah? Important that we talk. Ben

I had decided not to visit Ben in hospital that day. Not because I didn't want to see him, but I felt it would not be right for either him or the children. Now, I might not have an option. There was an urgency in the text message, but I had no babysitter. I wondered if his text was about the hidden pill stash. A confession. An admission that he was sorry he lied about the prescription. And I would confess that I had invaded his private space. He was right. We really needed to talk.

I rang Ben. The call went to voicemail. Typical. He could be gone for some tests or procedures. He might be asleep. Or he might well be sitting there, listening to the ring. Whatever the reason, he was not answering his phone. Sending me this worrying, cryptic message then making himself unavailable to talk, was so very Ben.

I heard Anna demanding that the boys show her their hands. I tiptoed to the bathroom door and watched as they obediently held them out for her inspection, front and back. She nodded and her blonde curls bounced with the movement. Obviously she was the appointed hygiene inspector for baking sessions. I could see that Josh was anxiously waiting for her approval, while a tolerant smile lit Rob's usually solemn face. They were such a tight little unit. Not needing the embryo for completeness. I pushed that thought away, but not before I put my hands on my stomach. On baby Number 4. It took all the strength I had not to cry out at the treachery of the decision circumstances were forcing on me. I stepped back into the passageway and leaned against the wall.

"You pain in tummy, Mom?"

I had not noticed Anna come out, the boys trailing behind her. I levered myself from against the wall and forced a smile on my face.

"No, Anna. I'm good. Are we all ready for muffin-making now?"

The log stove, which I had lit earlier, was glowing. I switched on the oven, then supervised while ingredients were weighed, muffin tins lined with paper cases, and eggs cracked. All the while the kitchen was filled with the sound of laughter, mine as well as the children's. I wallowed in that precious oasis of happiness. We high-fived when the filled muffin tins were finally in the oven. That was when Josh went into listening mode, head cocked to one side. His hearing was as acute as a bat's. He ran to the lounge where he had a view out to the avenue.

"*Red car, Mom!*" he called.

I was just setting the timer for the muffins, so I did not take too much notice of what he said. That was until Anna came racing into the kitchen and grabbed my hand.

"*Uncle Hugh!*" she said. "*C'mon! Open door for him!*"

I allowed her to lead me out to the hall, wondering if it really was Hugh. Even though Anna had seen him several times, it was a few months since last she had met him. I should not have doubted her. Sure enough, when I opened the front door, Hugh Parrish stood there in all his tanned glory.

"Hope you don't mind me calling unannounced," he said. "I thought it better to come here before going to see Ben."

I held my hand out to him. "You're very welcome, Hugh. Come in."

I wasn't sure about how welcome he really was. That depended on why he called and what he had to say. The twins escorted him into the kitchen, with Rob, ever watchful, behind him. Anna and Josh were giving him the two-and-a-half-year-old version of our muffin-making adventure. I was surprised that such a high-powered techie person seemed so at ease with their chatter.

"Do you mind if I give them these?" he asked, pointing to the bag he was carrying. "A few little things I picked up in Duty Free."

Anna and Josh were peering into the bag in the blink of an eye. I was cross with them for letting me down.

"Guys! That's rude," I said.

Hugh laughed. "No! Just healthy curiosity."

He handed Rob a camera and the twins a soft toy each. Anna's was a donkey, and Josh's a dog. Josh discovered straight away that the soft toys had an on/off switch. They were super-excited, flicking the switch through different levels of toy activity like tail-wagging, ear-twitching, noisy braying and barking, while Rob snapped pictures of them.

Time to herd them into the lounge once they had said their thanks.

Another ten minutes of small talk passed while I made coffee and took the muffins out of the oven. Distracted by the toys, the children had forgotten all about them, so I just put them on a wire tray to cool. I poured coffee, then sat down across from Hugh at the table.

"How is Ben?" he asked. "And I don't mean just physically."

I shrugged. Truth was I didn't know anymore. The discovery of the bottles of pills had called everything into question.

"Hard to tell, Hugh. Physically he seems to have coped

well." I sat back and looked him straight in the eye. "I happened to see a text you sent to Ben. You were urging him to tell me the truth. I'm sure that didn't just refer to the Swiss Army knife. So now that you're here, why don't you do the honours?"

He looked back at me steadily. None of the down-the-nose stares of his mother. I suddenly realised that was the first time Hugh and I had ever had a direct one-to-one conversation, despite the fact that I had been married to his brother for over six years. Also surprising was how comfortable I felt in his company. I had judged, no, misjudged him, to be a pompous arsehole with an affected, quasi-American accent. Wrong again, Leah Parrish. More guilt. Though the accent *was* grating.

"He told you about the Swiss knife. The cutting."

"Yes, he did."

"About the cruise and his leap overboard?"

I nodded.

"The Booly Clinic? The drug overdoses?"

"Yes, he's told me all that, Hugh. But that doesn't mean I understand it. And I'm baffled and hurt by the secrecy. I can understand, maybe, that twenty years ago mental-health problems were a stigma. At least that's an explanation for the boarding school cover-up story. But why did he feel he had to keep it secret from me? He should have been able to trust me. I suppose I should be grateful that he has told me now."

I stopped and stared directly at him.

"But do I know the full story, Hugh? Is that all there is?"

He hesitated just long enough to make me nervous.

"It is. And it isn't. The elephant in the room is Mother. Della Parrish, matriarch supreme. Though if she knew she had been referred to as an elephant she would not be amused."

Now that, I thought would be perfectly true, and I was highly amused at the idea. I don't know whether it was nervousness or a touch of hysteria that made me laugh then. Heartily. Hugh joined in.

Rob came to the door, took a photo of us, gave us a puzzled look, and went back to the lounge. It seemed that Hugh had also needed the release of a good belly laugh. At nothing.

When I got my breath back, I continued. "You know well that Della has as little as possible to do with me. From what I can see she is a wonderful grandmother, a caring if controlling mother, and a disapproving mother-in-law. Other than that, I really don't know her."

"You're being very generous in your assessment, Leah. It's the controlling part is the problem. Have you been told that Ben was discharged from the Booly Clinic on condition that he continued on with medication and counselling? Della decided otherwise. She felt he would be 'labelled' if he had ongoing treatment and that it would adversely affect his future education and employment opportunities. She defied everyone to get her way. That made a bad situation between herself and Dad worse."

I could not hide my shock. I wasn't sure if Ben had painted a rosy picture of perfect harmony in his childhood home, or if I had assumed it. Because I had come from a single-parent family, I sometimes thought that having two parents to raise you would automatically be twice as good.

"I can see you're surprised," Hugh said. "Dad, the renowned Gavin Parrish, was, to put it mildly, a bit of a lad. That wasn't always true. Not when we were children.

But in teen years, the more involved Mum became with Ben and his problems, the more Dad strayed."

"Sure I'm surprised! On two fronts. One, that Della's marriage was less than perfect. Two, that she did not allow Ben to have the treatment he needed. Although in the years between his stay in the Booly Clinic and now, it would have appeared she had made the right decision."

I saw that Hugh's cup was empty. As I got up to pour him another, I noticed a faraway look in his eyes. Obviously our chat was bringing him back to childhood times in that great big house in Howth. I had always felt it was more a mausoleum than a home. He looked up at me when I placed the cup of fresh coffee in front of him. I was struck by how different Hugh's appearance was to Ben's. His eyes were as blue as Ben's were brown. His hair as fair and thinning, as Ben's was dark and thick. But at that moment I recognised the same shadow of sadness in Hugh's eyes, as in Ben's. A lost look.

I sat again, opposite him.

"So, Hugh, if Della was so preoccupied with Ben, does that mean she did not have the time to give to you?"

"No. She had plenty of time. Just not the will. Ben was her boy. Dad and I were close. I lacked for nothing, Leah. Except that most precious of things, a mother's love."

He bowed his head. I wondered if he'd had counselling. It was not often that Irishmen could be so comfortable discussing their emotions. He looked up at me and smiled.

"I've picked up more than just an accent in the States. I've adopted their frank and open attitude as well. Talking is good for the soul. Or whatever it is inside us that makes us who we are. Which brings me to the real reason I wanted to talk to you now."

"Is this about the job for Ben in the US? I think it's very nice of your brother-in-law to consider employing Ben, but honestly, Hugh, he's not ready for that. And apart from his near brush with death, accidental or not, he's had a heart attack and –"

He reached across the table and caught my hand. His grip was warm and firm. Comforting.

"I know, Leah. I agree. But Mother, as usual, is pulling the strings. Zach Milburg is a man I admire. As a businessman and brother-in-law. But to have him as a boss would be a challenge. He's demanding and not what Ben needs now. Besides, he doesn't do favours. I don't think he would have taken Ben on. That doesn't mean Ben's not good enough. Ben's very talented. His lack of experience would be a deal-breaker, though. And I think Della has finally realised this. It's her new plan I needed to talk to you about."

"Oh? I didn't know she had one. Would it have something to do with her needing to go to Dublin on business today?"

He nodded. "She's setting up the legal framework so that she can move into a city-centre apartment and sign the Howth house over to Ben."

"What!"

"On condition that he moves in there immediately."

That was when the children came into the kitchen, crowding around Uncle Hugh, demanding his attention. He played with them, showed Rob how to edit photos on his new camera, kept them occupied while I tried to absorb the information he had just given me.

I knew this was why Ben needed to talk to me urgently. What I did not yet know was if he intended to live in the Howth mausoleum alone.

I agreed with Ben. We urgently needed to talk.

CHAPTER THIRTY-FOUR

The satnav brought Hugh directly to the hospital grounds, but once there he had to depend on the sporadic and often confusing signage to get to Room 5 on the first floor. Ben was sitting out on a chair beside his bed. He was so still that Hugh was not sure at first whether he was awake or asleep. As he walked across the room, Ben turned to face him.

Hugh tried to keep his expression neutral but he was so shocked by Ben's gaunt appearance, it must have shown.

"Hi, bro," Hugh said as cheerfully as possible. "How are you doing?"

Just like a child needing to be picked up and cuddled, Ben held out his two arms to his big brother. They hugged and slapped each other on the back in an accepted manly way, but there was no disguising the depth of their emotions.

"I'm still alive, just about, so I suppose that's good," Ben said.

To Hugh's ears, Ben sounded anything but glad to have survived.

"Of course it's good, Ben. You have so much to live for. I've been out to the cottage with Leah and the children.

You have a beautiful family. They miss you."

"*Hmm*. Sometimes I think . . ." He stopped speaking and took a deep breath. "Never mind that. Tell me about you. And why are you here, you daft beggar? I know how busy you are."

Hugh went to the other side of the room and brought over the chair obviously meant for visitors. He placed it across from Ben, where they were obliged to look at each other, to make eye contact. To be honest.

"I'm here, Ben, because you're my brother and because I care. You've been avoiding my phone calls. Why?"

Ben opened his mouth to deny the accusation but stopped when he saw Hugh glance at the switched-off phone on top of the locker. His brother had travelled all that distance for the truth so nothing else would do. A band of tension tightened around Ben's head. What the fuck was the truth? He didn't know, did he? Had he meant to die on the beach? To never again have to live in Cowshit Cottage or suffocate in Paircmoor? To never again suffer the humiliation of endless unemployment? To never again see Leah? Or Rob. Or Josh. Or Anna. Or Mom. Or Hugh. No! Not all never-agains were bearable.

"I'm waiting, Ben. Why don't you want to talk to me?"

Ben's face suddenly became animated. Flushed. Eyes sparking anger. The change was so sudden, Hugh was taken aback.

"Why should I talk to you? You wouldn't understand. How could you? You and your perfect life. Your perfect wife. Your fucking swimming pool and billionaire brother-in-law. I have no future, Hugh. No job, no money, no prospects. We have nothing in common."

Hugh nodded. He had been here before. A very angry

teenaged Ben, lashing out, blaming everyone and everything for his depression. Protecting his inner core of sadness from any attempt to bring it into the light of day. He knew he must be calm now, even though he felt like shaking some sense into his younger brother.

"Who told you my life was perfect, Ben? I've just spent the morning playing with your wonderful children. I would give all the material things I own just to have a family like yours."

"Go and make your own family then."

Hugh flinched. He had to make allowances for Ben now. Otherwise he would have been tempted to give him a thump. But Ben didn't know, did he? How unfair to expect all the truth-telling to be one way only. He took a deep breath.

"The fact is, Ben, Piper is very career-focused at the moment. I'm not sure when, or if, she'll decide to start a family. I keep hoping though."

Ben's expression changed again, to one of sympathy. Hugh had never noticed before how clearly emotions were reflected on his brother's face. Or how often they changed.

"I'm sorry, Hugh," he said. "I didn't know. But to be fair, she's a lot younger than you. She has time on her side."

"But I don't. And that makes my point for me, Ben. From your perspective everyone's life seems better than yours. That's just not true. You've no idea what's really going on with other people."

"And you've no idea what it's like being me, so hold the lecture."

Hugh nodded. Fair point. He had wanted to tell Ben also how lucky he was to have Leah. It was easy to see she had his back, no matter what. He wished he could say the same about Piper.

The wife conversation would have been a sharing too far for both of them. Instead they were silent for a moment.

Hugh broke the silence.

"Mum has told me about the house in Howth. It's one of the reasons I'm here."

"I knew it! I tried to tell her she can't just sign it over to me. Dad would turn in his grave if he thought you had been denied your share of our family home."

"No! The house is not the problem, Ben. I don't want it. I'm settled in San Fran and it's where I'll stay. It's Mum I'm worried about."

"What are you saying? That I'm throwing her out of her home? I didn't ask her to –"

"Ben! For heaven's sake, we both know Mum will only do exactly what *she* wants. When has it ever been different? It's the way she was reared by Gran and Grandad Roache. Do you remember them?"

Ben couldn't help the shiver that ran through him. Yes, he remembered his Roache grandparents and the musty smell of the big old house they lived in. Curra Manor in Wexford. He had thought of them as austere before he understood the meaning of the word. He had felt disapproved of by his grandparents. Even by the house that seemed to ooze disapproval from the walls, drip it from the high ceilings.

"Well, she *was* an only child. I suppose they spoiled her."

Hugh nodded. Della Roache had been a spoiled child. Marriage, motherhood or time had not changed that fact. Her innate belief that only she knew best was a core part of her deceptively genteel character. She was steely from the inside out.

"Ben, if you and Leah want to move back to Dublin and to live in The Parrish House, then I think that's great.

But I need to hear it from you."

Ben shrugged. "I suppose it would mean I'm taking another handout. Ben the charity case."

"Stop! Stop feeling sorry for yourself and think of your family. Look, I love Mum. I know we both do. Doesn't change the fact that, especially where you are concerned, she is manipulative. Christ above! You're heading for forty but she's still making decisions for you."

"You're not being fair to her, Hugh. I don't know where I'd be without her. She paid our mortgage when we couldn't, paid the deposit on the cottage in Paircmoor, bought the jeep so that I could drive the children around. She even pays our health insurance. She does all that because I'm her son, not because she is manipulative."

"She can well afford to, Ben. Dad left her very comfortably off. And before you say it, yes, I agree she can be generous. But there's always a payback. I just want to be sure she's not forcing a decision on you."

Ben stood. He was stiff from sitting in the bedside chair. He felt the shadow of the thousands of other patients who must have sat there too, wondering if they would ever see home again. Or like him, if they even wanted to. Hugh had to pull his feet in to allow him pass. Standing over his brother, Ben noticed how thin Hugh's hair was getting, how lined his skin from the sun. No doubt about it, the Parrish brothers were aging. Even the fucking perfect Silicon Valley tycoon.

When he reached the door, Ben turned back and looked at Hugh.

"This job with your brother-in-law. Zach Milburg. I don't want it. I don't want to leave this country. Ireland is shagged. So am I. We're a good fit."

"Good decision, Ben. About the job, I mean. Mum may have promised more than she could deliver there."

Ben could see them now, Zach Milburg, Hugh and Piper, all sitting on sun loungers, laughing, pitying Ben Parrish, whose mother was trying to find a job for him.

"Fuck Milburg! I wouldn't work for him anyway."

Hugh walked over to Ben and put a hand on his arm.

"Sorry, bro, I didn't mean it that way. It's just that the time is not right for you now. It's more important that you recover your full health before you make any life-changing decisions"

"You're patronising me."

"I'm worried, Ben. Mum stopped you getting the medical help you needed when you were a teenager and I think she is doing the same now. You're obviously very upset."

Hugh knew he was handling this wrongly, but he had witnessed for himself how disturbed Ben was. The despair was bubbling just beneath the surface, erupting in anger every so often. He took a step back. Now at a safer distance, he posed the questions he had come here to ask.

"Has anyone spoken to you about last Friday night and what happened? Why it happened. Have you seen a psychiatrist? Have you had counselling? Or is Mum trying to cover it all up again by bringing you back to Dublin?"

Hugh watched a flush of anger spread up Ben's pale neck and face. There was something else too. Maybe hatred

"You think you know it all, Hugh, don't you? There's something you need to get straight. Friday night was an accident. I went on the beach, misjudged the tide and sheltered in a cave until I was rescued. Reckless, yes. Suicidal, no. I don't need any nosey fuckers prying into my private life. Poking and prodding. That includes you.

Now, I'm tired. I need to sleep. Thank you for coming to see me."

Ben offered his hand to Hugh. As if they were work colleagues. Hugh shook his hand.

"I'm going back to the cottage. I'll be babysitting so that Leah can come to see you later."

"Tell her not to bother. I'm tired."

"I'm not your messenger, Ben. Tell her yourself if you want to. I'll see you tomorrow."

By the time Hugh had put back his chair where he had found it, Ben was already in bed, blankets pulled up to his chin, eyes closed. He was not asleep though. Or resting. His eyes were moving behind the closed lids, a pulse beating rapidly underneath the left eye. It seemed to Hugh that it had been a long, long time since his brother last had a peaceful sleep.

CHAPTER THIRTY-FIVE

I listened to my children chatter amongst themselves as I drove along. It felt good to be leaving Cowslip Cottage for a little while, the children safely strapped into their seats in the back of the jeep. A normal Mom taking her kids for an afternoon spin. As we passed the school, Rob asked me when he could go back there.

"Just another few days at home," I said. "You can go next Monday. Okay?"

"Will Dad be home then?"

Good question. I assumed he would. With so much pressure on hospital beds, they would not be holding him there for no reason. Unless they were waiting for a psychiatric assessment. Waiting for him to admit he needed help.

"I think so, Rob. But that's up to the doctors. They must make sure he is better before they send him home."

"Ellen all gone," Anna piped up. Obviously seeing the school reminded her of the daily meeting place.

"And Finn," Josh added.

Good riddance, I thought. Not my finest moment. The mention of Ellen's name clouded what had been a more hopeful day than any other this week. Mainly thanks to

Hugh. It had been good to talk to him this morning. An open, unexpectedly honest, conversation. A bonus too that he had so kindly offered to babysit the children this evening while I went to visit Ben.

"You said we were going to the woods," Rob said. "You've just passed them."

I had forgotten to tell the children that I was calling to the salon first. I had, of course, been in phone contact with Mags and Tina over the past two days. They seemed to be working well together from what I could tell. They said the salon was busy. Maybe the customers were people wanting to find out the gory details of Ben's rescue from the cave. Or perhaps Minnie Curran had been scared into spreading a positive word about Leah's Hair Salon. Whatever the reason it all seemed to be good news. Which was why I needed to see for myself. I had experienced the flip side of good so often, I always expected bad to make an appearance.

"I must call to work first. See that everything is alright there."

"No!" Josh said. "No work, Mom!"

I glanced at him in the rear-view mirror and saw his eyes, Ben's dark, dark, brown eyes, glisten with tears. Anna put her arm around him and snuggled her blonde head close to his dark hair. Rob was looking away from me. Staring out the window. I could not see his face but knew it would echo the expression of the other two children. Disappointment. Betrayal. What was I to do? How could I explain to them that the salon was our main source of income now? That I needed to call to thank Mags and Tina in person for their help. I gripped the steering wheel tightly as the weight of so much responsibility and guilt made my hands shake.

"Of course I'm not going to work, Josh. You silly goose! I just want to have a small chat to Mags and Tina. How about you all come in with me? You can make sure I don't stay too long. Then we can go to the woods."

The chorus of yays from the back was the answer I had wanted to hear.

When I pulled in at the salon I was surprised to see the parking space in front of the building full. Admittedly that was just four spaces but if it meant four customers, that was good. I parked on the roadside and herded the children into the salon. They had rarely been in there before so they were curious. The boys stood quietly beside me but Anna took off, scampering around inspecting everything from clients to hair rollers, to containers of product. I waved at Mags and Tina. They both smiled and greeted me, but I could see they were busy, Tina shampooing and Mags setting up a perm for Mrs Gillis. The old lady caught my arm as I passed her.

"I'm so sorry about your husband, Leah. I hope he'll be better soon."

Aware that the boys were listening, I quickly thanked her and walked into the kitchenette. Everything was in order there. In fact the whole salon had an air of friendly efficiency. So much so that I wondered for a moment if I had even been missed. Just as quickly I realised that I was being silly when I should have been grateful. Mags appeared at the door.

"I think your daughter is going to follow in your footsteps," she said. "Anna is very interested in what we're doing."

It was on the tip of my tongue to say no! I want Anna to be educated, go to university, have a proper profession.

I stopped myself just in time from demeaning my own career, insulting Mags and deciding Anna's future for her.

"I'll take her out of your way now, Mags. I just called to say thank you. I'm so grateful to you and Tina."

"Don't worry about us or the salon, Leah. We're doing fine. How is Ben today?"

"I'm not seeing him until this evening. His brother is here so he's in with him now. Hopefully he'll be home soon."

She walked over to the press under the sink, took out her handbag and handed me an envelope. My heart sank. She couldn't be giving me her notice. Not now. She mustn't.

And, of course, she wasn't, because what I held in my hand was an envelope of cash.

"The takings," she said.

I started to hand it back to her. I wanted her to know I trusted her to pay herself and Tina a fair wage and to pass on what was left to me. If any. She had other ideas.

"I don't like the responsibility of holding cash," she said. "Please take this and pop in with our wages whenever you can."

"If you're sure. Where's the laundry bag? There must be a lot of towels to be washed at this stage."

"You've enough to do besides washing. I've looked after it. Don't worry about it. You're looking very tired and skinny. When can I cook dinner for you?"

I smiled at her, took the envelope, and hugged her.

"Soon, I hope, Mags. What would I do without you?"

And that reminded me of Mags' daughter and her dependence on her mother.

"How is Claire?" I asked.

"Not a bother on her."

Anna came running into the kitchenette, waving a five-euro note. I flushed with embarrassment, not sure whether my daughter had stolen it, or begged for it.

"The lady give it to me!" she said. "I fix her hair."

I realised then it had not been a good idea to bring the children in. I mouthed an apology to Mags and took Anna by the hand. A new customer, not someone I had seen before, was sitting on a chair inside the door, waiting her turn. She had a roller stuck on the side of her head. Just at Anna height. I had found the donor of the five euro. As I opened my mouth to thank her and return the money, the woman smiled at me.

"Your little girl has brightened up my day. She's going to buy herself and her two brothers a treat from the money I gave her. With your permission, of course. I hope you don't mind."

Before I could answer Anna had stood on tiptoe and given the woman a hug and the two boys thanked her politely. I was proud of them. They deserved their treat. I thanked the woman and shepherded my little brood out of the salon.

Later, in the woods, as I watched the three of them skip along the path in their wellingtons and raincoats, I smiled. They were munching the sweets I had allowed them buy in the shop, splashing in puddles, finding treasures of special stones and sticks, laughing, being carefree little children.

I looked up through the bare branches, into the greyness of the November sky, and I saw the tiniest of opening in the clouds, a hint of light in the gloom, the minutest spark of hope. Ben was alive, even if he had a way to go to wellness. The children were happy and healthy. The salon was surviving.

I hurried to catch up with the children. To skip along

the path with them, to join in the fun. To share these few magic hours in the winter-ravaged woods with my children. All four of them.

Hugh arrived back from the hospital as I was serving up dinner. He sat at the place I had set for him. The children greeted him as if he were a long-lost friend. In a way he was. Or more correctly, a new-found friend.

"How is Ben?" I asked.

He glanced at the children before answering, so I knew his reply would be censored for their protection.

"He's good. Getting better and looking forward to coming home. Mum rang. She's on her way back from Dublin."

We exchanged looks, both wondering if Ben was now in the process of becoming the owner of an imposing house in Howth. My appetite suddenly left me. I pushed the food around my plate as the children told Hugh all about our walk in the woods and trip to the shop. I had the idea that Della was about to spirit my husband away to live in her ivory tower in Dublin. Just as she had hidden him in the Booly Clinic all those years ago. That I might never see him again.

"Are you alright, Leah?" Hugh asked. "Don't know why you're not eating. This lasagne is delicious."

I smiled at him, appreciating his concern. I excused myself from the table and put on coffee for Hugh and me. Josh was rubbing his eyes. A sure sign he was exhausted. Anna was still talking, this time in deep conversation with her new toy donkey. For reasons best known to herself she had christened it Jenny. It looked like Jenny was set to become her new best friend.

"Jenny is tired now," I told her as soon as I had

finished my coffee. "How about we get her ready for bed. You and Josh say goodnight to Uncle Hugh. And don't forget to thank him."

The twins hugged Hugh then sped off towards the bathroom. I was thankful that the walk in the woods had tired them enough to make this bedtime routine painless and mercifully quick. They were both asleep before I had reached the end of their bedtime story. I kissed them on their foreheads, smiling as I saw Jenny clutched tightly in Anna's arms. I made up the camp bed for Rob, who had voluntarily offered his bedroom for Hugh's stay.

When I got back to the kitchen, the table had been cleared after dinner.

"Hugh, there was no need for you to do that. Thank you."

"We had to," Rob said. "Uncle Hugh is going to show me how to print out the photos from my camera with Dad's printer. Won't that be cool, Mom?"

"That will be great, Rob! I'm going to the hospital to see Dad. Go to bed when Uncle Hugh says so. Okay?"

He nodded his agreement and then immediately turned his attention back to his camera.

I gave Rob a hug before I left. Hugh and I exchanged looks, made a slight move towards each other, then stopped, neither wanting our new sense of camaraderie to be interpreted as anything else but friendship.

I smiled, waved goodbye, and tried to ignore the niggling disappointment at not enjoying the comfort of Hugh's hug.

CHAPTER THIRTY-SIX

The instant I saw Ben lying in the bed, blankets up to his chin, I knew he was in a grumpy mood. His defiant look threw out a challenge. My first thought was that he was behaving like a spoiled brat, my second was that I was hard-hearted. I kissed him on the forehead, then organised the clean pyjamas and clothes I had brought him and sat down on the bedside chair.

"How are you?" I asked.

"How do you think? I told you this morning I needed to talk to you urgently. I've been waiting for you all day."

"I got here as soon as I could. What's this mad idea your mother has of signing her home over to you?"

He sat up in the bed, no longer sulky, but downright furious.

"Don't, Leah! Don't start slagging my mother off. I won't have it anymore. Can't you, for once, appreciate what she has done for us?"

Needing to put distance between me and his rage, I sat back in my chair. The awful truth was that I was afraid of Ben at that moment. And in a blinding flash of honesty I admitted to other terrifying moments. Too many. I took a calming breath and tried to look him in the eye. I dropped my gaze when I saw anger spark there.

"I agree with you, Ben, of course. She's an extremely generous woman. And, yes, we are in her debt. But I worry about her making decisions for our family. That's our responsibility."

"Look what happens when the decisions are left up to us. We end up in Paircmoor. Jesus Christ! You call that good decision-making? You think we are responsible parents?"

I flinched. That was a question I often asked myself. One that only time would answer in full.

"I do think we're good parents, Ben. Look how the children are thriving in the clean air, how they love nature, how Rob is benefitting from the small numbers in his class. The twins will too."

"For heaven's sake, Leah, we don't belong there. It's a place with a past and no future."

"Why are you arguing about Paircmoor when we should be talking about the house in Howth? Hugh told me your mother is signing it over to you on condition you move up there immediately. Is this true?"

He sighed and leaned back into his pillows. Anger must have been puffing him up, because now that it seemed to have left him, he looked gaunt.

I was the angry one now. Even before he answered, I knew that Della had somehow pulled a masterstroke. She could have him back under her roof again, while at the same time covering up his need for . . . for what? Psychiatric care? Medication? Counselling? All of them.

He nodded. "Yes. Mom has decided that the house is too much for her now. She needs the convenience of city-centre living. Hugh said he doesn't want it. His home is in San

Francisco and he won't live in Ireland anymore. Since she doesn't want to either sell or let it, she wants us to live there."

I did not know what to say to this boy-man who seemed to need his childhood home and his mother's approval far more than he needed his wife and family. I wanted to tell him grow up. Take responsibility for himself and his family. To stop feeling so sorry for himself and realise he was only one of tens of thousands of unemployed people struggling to survive day to day. To tell him I loved him and so did the children and ask him was that not enough. Instead I just sat there by his bed, watching his expression change from conciliatory to exasperated.

"Are you going to say anything, Leah? What do you think?"

"Now you ask me. Anyway, I can't say until I know the details. I understand from Hugh that Della has already started the legal process of transferring ownership to you. Is this true?"

"Well, she's been to see her solicitor today, yes. But I've not agreed anything with her, if that's what you're being so bitchy about. She just asked me to think about me and the children moving back to Howth."

"You and the children! What about me?"

"You as well, of course. God! You just can't accept that Mum has our best interests at heart, can you?"

He was right there. I wanted to believe that Della wished the best for our family when she made the very generous gesture. But if so, why had she not spoken to me? Why was she already taking legal advice as if it was a done deal? It was clear to me that Ben wanted to accept his mother's offer. And maybe, just maybe, it would be the right move for him. Under different circumstances.

I braced myself before talking again, not sure if I should say anything, but at the same time needing to bring it out in the open.

"Ben, the prescription Dr Kelly wrote for you. The anti-depressants you did not want to take."

"Yes. What about them?"

"Why did you lie about filling the prescription? I found the three pill bottles in your desk drawer."

He sat bolt upright in the bed. What colour he had in his face drained from it.

"That drawer was locked," he said so softly I had to strain to hear him.

"Yes, it was. I apologise for invading your private space, Ben, but can't you see I'm worried about you? Particularly in view of your past history."

He threw back his blankets and leapt out of the bed, so furious that specks of spittle flew from his mouth when he spoke.

"I confide in you and then you throw it back in my face! I was only in my teens when I took those pills before. That doesn't give you the right to go poking in my desk. Everything in there is private. That's why it's locked. Jesus! Have you any respect for me at all?"

Everything in there? I didn't know what he was talking about. All I had found were the three bottles of pills. I stood and took a few steps back, afraid even though the bed was between us. The fact that the door was just a few feet behind my back gave me the confidence to stand my ground. To make an attempt to reach the man I used to know before this volatile person in front of me took over.

"Of course I respect you, Ben. I love you, for heaven's sake! That's why I want you to be well again. There's no shame in needing help. If I was depressed, you would want me to get treatment, wouldn't you?"

"I am not, do you hear me, *not* fucking mad! My problem is that I'm too sane."

"Your problem, Ben, is that your mother was too controlling and selfish to allow you have treatment when you needed it. And she's making the same mistake now. You're obviously grossly unhappy. I don't believe you anymore when you say that going to the flooded beach on Friday night was an accident. It was another botched suicide attempt. You need help. Running away is not going to solve any of your problems. And your mother is only making things worse for you. You call that caring?"

Ben was so still I regretted my rant. Yes, it was important to get the truth out in the open but I should have been more circumspect. He was silent, staring over my shoulder.

I turned to follow his gaze.

Della Parrish, mother, grandmother, mother-in-law, was standing in the doorway. She brushed past me, went to her son and put her arms around him. Words of apology formed in my head but I knew they would only add to the damage already done. I gathered my coat, bag, what remained of my composure, and gently closed the door of Room 5 as I left.

CHAPTER THIRTY-SEVEN

I don't remember travelling home that evening. All I was aware of was that I had driven yet another wedge between myself and Ben. I should never have called his mother controlling or selfish. Certainly not within her hearing. And Ben should have warned me when he saw her. It was as if he wanted to let Della hear exactly what I thought of her. To let her see for herself what a shrew I was. He had made his point without having to say a word himself.

Hugh was sitting at the kitchen table when I went in home, his laptop open in front of him.

"Any trouble getting Rob to bed?" I asked.

"No. He's a good kid. His photos are excellent. He's obviously inherited the artistic gene from you and Ben."

"Ben maybe. Not me."

"Why not? Hairdressing is a very creative profession."

I smiled at him as I thought of the conservative cuts and colours I did on a daily basis. Hardly an outlet for creativity.

"How is Ben?" he asked.

What was I to say? That I feared my husband was having a nervous breakdown. That I had wrecked whatever chance

I might have had of a good relationship with Della. That I did not know where our lives were headed from now on.

"Your mother is back from Dublin," I said, as if that answered his question about Ben.

Then much to my embarrassment, I felt tears fill my eyes. I walked towards the sink, needing to busy myself.

"Tea or coffee?" I asked, horrified to hear my voice quavering.

Hugh stood up, walked over to me and took my arm.

"Sit down," he said. "I'll get this."

I did as I was told. Took my place at the table and tried to control the vast wave of emotion threatening to engulf me. I was aware of Hugh opening cupboards, of the glow from the log stove, yet my mind was back in Room 5 in the hospital. I closed my eyes and replayed the scene over and over, trying to read Ben's expression as he stared towards his mother. Had he been shocked or glad to see her there? Satisfied that his mother could hear for herself what a bitch I was?

A gentle thud brought me back to the kitchen. Hugh had placed a mug of hot milk in front of me.

"How did you know about my comfort drink?" I asked.

"I remember from the time I stayed here. Just after you had moved down from Dublin. You never drank coffee at night. Neither do I."

My clearest memory of that time is of list after list of things to do. The logistics of shifting a family, plus furniture and all the necessary bric-a-brac of daily living, across the country were overwhelming. And then Hugh and Della had shown up in the cottage while we were knee-deep in unopened cases and boxes.

I smiled at him. "You got more than you had bargained for then, didn't you? Hours and hours of unpacking and finding places for things."

"I was glad to help. Do you mind me asking if you miss the city? Dublin and Paircmoor are chalk and cheese."

I didn't have to think long about that one. No, I did *not* miss the Dublin I left two years ago. Or the friends who had faded away when we hit a bad patch. Or in my case, the childhood friends who drifted away when I moved to the other side of the city. Their choice, not mine, but I'm sure they blamed me for it. In fact, I know they did, as I overheard one of them say I was so 'up myself' since I had met Ben.

I shook my head.

"No, Hugh, I don't miss the life we had there. Looking back, it was superficial. I do miss the convenience though. The shops and services at your fingertips. Although we can access what we actually need here, rather than what advertising tells us we should have. Maybe that's a better way to live."

"Yes, there's a lot to be said for pared-back living. It's not for everyone though. Ben, for instance. He's always been evasive when I've asked him about his move to the country. What do you think? Has he settled here?"

Hugh got up to get biscuits, giving me time to think about that question. The honest answer was that, for the most part, I had been too busy for the past two years to notice whether Ben was really happy here or not. He had seemed to be until very recently. There must have been hints. Clues that I missed. Or it could be that he only found Paircmoor bearable while Ellen Riggs was imbuing it with her particular brand of beauty and sophistication.

I took one of the chocolate biscuits Hugh offered but left it beside my mug on the table. My stomach had knotted tight at the recollection of Ellen Riggs and her hold over my gullible husband.

"I thought he was happy in Paircmoor," I told Hugh. "No matter what he says now, coming here was an agreed decision between the two of us. We didn't make it lightly. But he seems to have snapped all of a sudden. Well, since . . . He had a friend – a woman. She . . ."

Hugh put his elbows on the table and leaned towards me. "I'm not prying, Leah. You don't have to tell me anything you don't want to."

"Oh, but I do, Hugh! I must tell somebody. It's not that he had an affair. It was a platonic friendship because that is what she wanted. I believe Ben saw it differently. He was obsessed by Ellen Riggs. But she suddenly left and went back to the husband she had never mentioned until she was leaving. That was when Ben hurled himself onto the storm-flooded beach. So you tell me – is he depressed because of Paircmoor, unemployment, or Ellen Riggs? I sure as hell can't answer the question."

Hugh sat back in his chair, shaking his head. "Seems like he's more like my dad than I thought. Playing away from home, I mean."

"In a way I can understand that. Ellen is extremely beautiful. By far and away the most exotic flower in Paircmoor. I'm sure he wasn't the only man here to drool over her. He just took his fantasy to a different level."

"His overreaction shows that his problem lies deeper. Do you mind if I give you my spin on the situation?"

It was my turn to sit back. I nodded at Hugh, wondering what he meant by his 'spin'. Very Hollywood.

"I've been thinking about Mum and how determined she seems to be to prevent Ben being diagnosed with a mental illness. I thought at first her attitude was influenced by her age. Her generation was raised to see any mental vulnerability as shameful. But that doesn't wash. In other areas she is very broadminded. Also well-educated and well-read."

"So you *do* think Ben is mentally ill?"

"Depressed. Stressed. Put any label you like on it. He needs professional help, Leah. *You* know that. *I* know it. Have you spoken to Ben's medical team? Has he been offered counselling?"

"Yes, he has. And he's turned it down. When I was asked by his specialist in ICU if I had noticed any changes in his behaviour, I said no. As far as I was aware he was well and at least coping, if not happy. I haven't spoken to them since because he doesn't want me to. He said he needed to take responsibility for himself and that he would talk to his GP. He didn't want me controlling him like Della did. And does. I went along with that."

"Della." After uttering that one word, Hugh pointed to his laptop. "I've been doing a bit of research on my mother's home place. As you know it's in Wexford."

"I know very little about your mother's background."

"None of us know her really. She just won't talk about her childhood. Can't say I blame her. When, as children, we were brought to visit her parents we found them quite intimidating. Especially her father. Looking back, I can see he was very authoritarian. A bit of a bully. Might explain why she was so protective of Ben when Dad used to get annoyed with him."

I raised an eyebrow and looked at Hugh in surprise.

"No," he said instantly. "Dad never lifted his hand to Ben. He wasn't that type of person. But he did resent the attention Mum gave her youngest son. In fact, Ben was, and still is her priority."

I heard it. The note of hurt in Hugh's voice. I understood how he felt. I, too, had been cut to the quick by the cold edge of Della's rejection.

"I'm going there tomorrow," Hugh said.

"To Wexford?"

He nodded. "Mum, as you probably know was an only child – so she sold the house when her parents died. Curra Manor was bought by a German family. I don't know if they are still there or not. But what I *did* discover online is that the Cosgraves have stayed in the area."

Cosgraves? I had never heard Ben mention that name. "Are they relations of your mother?"

"No. James Cosgrave and his wife Breeda worked for Gran and Grandad Roache as cook and gardener. In fact, they were more than that because James did all the maintenance work and Breeda did all the housekeeping. They had a daughter, Maria, who was around the same age as my mother. Maybe a little older by a year or two. If anyone can give me information about the young Della Roache, it's Maria Cosgrave. They were friends until Mum went to boarding school in Dublin."

"All sounds very Victorian to me, Hugh. But, from what I read, I don't see that your mother and the cook's child would have been allowed to have a friendship."

Hugh laughed. "They were not royalty, Leah! Though Grandad Roache held himself like he had a poker up his bum and Gran certainly had airs and graces."

I frowned as I tried to figure out where Hugh was

going with his research. It seemed very odd that he chose this traumatic time to go trawling through his family history.

"Family history is interesting, Hugh, but does it really have a relevance to Ben's situation now?"

"That's what I intend to find out, Leah. I have a gut instinct that if we knew what drives my mother to overprotect Ben, then we would know how to correct that and move forward. I've been able to track Maria Cosgrave on social media. I'm meeting her tomorrow. "

I shrugged. Not that I didn't appreciate any help, no matter how off-beat, but I couldn't see how trawling through Della's childhood could help. I sensed that Hugh was looking for answers about his mother for himself, as much as for Ben. I wondered which brother was the worst off – the overprotected, or the under-loved. And I had thought them to be the perfect family. The Parrishes of Howth.

I looked across at the photograph on the dresser. Another perfect family. The Parrishes of Paircmoor. Me, Ben and the three children. Taken on the day Rob started primary school. I remembered every minute of that happy day. We were smiling. All of us. Proud. I almost cried out when I thought of the photo that might never be – of mother, father and four children. Taken perhaps when the embryo started primary school. All of us beaming with pride because the youngest in the family would be taking the first steps towards independence. But would Ben be there to take his place as father of this perfect family?

"He's stashing pills again," I blurted out.

Hugh paled.

"He had them locked in his desk. I'm ashamed to admit I rifled through his private office, but I'm glad I did.

Apparently his GP prescribed anti-depressants. He has three months' supply of pills stashed away."

"*Jesus!* Sounds familiar. You must talk to his doctor, Leah."

"Yes, I must. Difficult, though, since Ben has convinced everyone that what happened on Friday night was an accident and has refused counselling or psychiatric assessment."

"To my mind he's very volatile now. Very angry. Why can't they see that?"

I shrugged, knowing that Ben would be the essence of calm and rationality when he needed to be in order to get his own way. The trouble was, at that stage I didn't know what his own way was.

I no longer recognised the angry, spiteful man in Room 5 as Ben Parrish, the love of my life and the father of my children. All four of them.

CHAPTER THIRTY-EIGHT

Thursday 2nd December 2010

Hugh left for Wexford early the following morning. The children had clamoured around him, demanding hugs and a promise that he would be back soon. Their intense attachment to the uncle they did not know that well told me how much they were missing Ben. Maybe that's why I too felt sad as we waved Hugh off on his cross-country journey.

Back in the house, I looked at the clear-up needed after the breakfast, the washing and dressing of the children yet to be sorted, the stove to be cleaned out, lunch and dinner to be organised, hoovering and laundry to be done. I had a moment of empathy with Ben. This was his day-to-day life. Almost. He was spared the bulk of the mundane tasks as I did them before I went to the salon. Ben was essentially a baby-minder. I remembered back to Dublin, before our whole world fell apart, when Ben was working and I was at home with first Rob, then also the twins. Not for long. The twins had only been six months old and Rob three years when we moved to Paircmoor. But in that short time as a stay-at-home Mom I had felt truly fulfilled. The reality of unemployment and the threat of homelessness had been cushioned for me by the warmth of my babies in my arms, my love for them, their trust in me. I knew Ben loved them too with all his heart but, for him, it was obvious there remained a void in his life that only a career could fill.

And now? Now, my wonderful little brood was causing mayhem judging by the sounds drifting into the kitchen. Even Rob was shouting. I rushed to the twins' bedroom to find Anna standing up on her bed, trying to photograph herself with Rob's new camera. Rob was attempting to grab it back from her, while Josh stood beside her, defending his twin. It was hard not to laugh as I saw her pose this way and that. If Rob had not been so upset, I would have stayed watching, just to see how many poses she would strike.

It took a while to get them all back on an even keel, and longer again to get through the housework which had been piling up. Immersed as I was in domesticity, I decided to make a quiche for lunch, something all the children enjoyed. I had just taken it out of the oven when the doorbell rang.

I heard shouts of 'Uncle Hugh!' as the children rushed to the front door. I knew he could not be back from Wexford already. Anna had the letter flap open and was peeping through it. Her piercing squeal – her special Della squeal – told me who was there even before I opened the door.

Della was pale, her mouth a straight line, puckers around her lips that I had never noticed before. She was wearing a coat with a fur collar, into which she seemed to be shrinking. I couldn't understand how she had aged overnight until I noticed that she was not wearing any make-up. It was the first time I had seen her, barefaced, so to speak. The battleground seemed a little more even.

I held the door open for her. After the children had had their hugs, she straightened up and looked me in the eye.

"We need to talk," she said.

We certainly did. She had, of course, brought along a goody bag for the children which she let them see, then asked if I minded. I worried they were getting spoiled with gifts from Hugh and Della, but they needed the distraction from their father's absence. This time she had given them books, with interactive sounds for the twins and an audio and print for Rob.

"Uncle Hugh gone," Josh piped up. "On a *big* long spin."

Della looked at me and raised an eyebrow.

"To see an old friend," I answered.

It wasn't a lie. Just a bending of the truth.

"We were about to have lunch," I told her. "You're welcome to join us."

She nodded and began to lay the table while I tossed salad and cut up the quiche.

"Della, have you been to see Dad?" Rob asked.

"Yes, I have. The great news is that he'll be home soon. Isn't that good?"

"You know this for sure?" I asked, furious that the children's expectations had been raised.

"Of course he will. Why would they be keeping him any longer than necessary?"

"Have you been talking to the doctors, Della?"

She shrugged and looked away. I felt like pouring the salad dressing over her head. She was bluffing. Winding me up. I was sure Ben's medical team were talking only to him. I noticed Rob scrutinising us both. He obviously knew that all was not well between his grandmother and his mom. The child had more than enough trauma in his life without having him worry about that dysfunctional relationship. I smiled at him, then turned on my best smile for Della. She did not respond.

I tidied the table after lunch, settled the children down with their new books, and told them Della and Mom needed to have a grown-up chat in the lounge. Even as I said those words, I felt more like an errant pupil being brought before a headmistress, than an adult.

In the lounge, Della sat herself in Ben's armchair. It was upholstered in the softest, wine-coloured leather, and placed so that it was in line with the television and near the fire for cold winter evenings. Brought here all the way from our Dublin home. It was Ben's throne. Sacrosanct. Della knew that. I sat myself opposite her on the other side of the fireplace. She was dwarfed by the chair. I felt a nasty thrill of satisfaction at seeing her authority diminished. Or so I thought.

"We must start with an apology," she said. "Yours. To me. You accused me of being controlling and selfish. I am neither."

I did admit that what I had said yesterday was hurtful to her. For that I would certainly express my regret. But what about all the years she had undermined my position as Ben's wife? My right to be the one to share decision making *with* him. Not *for* him. And yes, I thought her attitude to mental illness, her reluctance to admit that Ben needed help, her need to cover it all up by hiding him away, could, quite rightly, be classed as controlling. As for the selfishness, I was conflicted on that one. Della was undoubtedly generous in material things. However, she was utterly greedy when it came to sharing her youngest son. I figured that unless I apologised we could end up sitting here, in our respective chairs, staring at each other for a long, long, time.

I squared my shoulders and went for it.

"If what you overheard me say yesterday upset you, Della, I apologise. I never meant to offend you."

"Of course you upset me! But nevertheless, I accept your apology."

Deuce. An insincere acceptance of a half-hearted apology. We needed to move on from there.

"I hope you can see things from my perspective, Della. I don't wish to interfere in family business but offering Ben and the children a home in Dublin, without even discussing it with me, was not fair."

"Oh, you're splitting hairs now. Admittedly, I didn't mention you by name in the invitation, but of course I assumed if Ben and the children were moving, you would be too."

That comment took the wind out of my sails. That was not what Ben had told me. What had she hoped by not including me? That I would stay in Paircmoor while she spirited my family away to Dublin?

"Whether you like it or not, Della, Ben needs help that neither you nor I can give him. I believe he should stay here and be treated by the doctors who are most familiar with his recent history."

"Don't be silly. Medical reports can be sent anywhere in this day and age. And he would certainly have access to more cutting-edge treatment in the city. If and when he wants it."

"What do you mean 'if'? He must have it, Della. Surely you don't want him to continue to struggle?"

"Of course not! That's why I suggested he leave Paircmoor. And he agrees."

Game, set and match to Della. Unless . . .

"You haven't got him to sign any documents, have you?"

She smiled at me. "Would I do that?"

I shrugged. "Would you?"

She stood. Grown-up talk over. I had been dismissed. Sidelined yet again. In my own home. On which she had paid the deposit. There was the catch. Her trump card. She had bought her way into our lives, and we could not afford the price of reclaiming our independence. Nor could we, as a family, allow her to dictate our future.

She walked out, but I continued to sit there for another few minutes, analysing our conversation and realising our attempt at a truce had not brought peace to either of us. I dragged myself up from the chair, battle-weary from fighting my mother-in-law, from the worry of Ben's health, and from the pregnancy that was now beginning to sap my energy and break my heart.

Della, as always, balanced being mean with being kind.

"You go visit Ben," she said. "I'll stay with the children. I know Hugh sometimes forgets to come back when he goes out."

I gladly accepted her offer as the afternoon was pushing on without any sign of Hugh returning. I hoped that meant he had made contact with the Cosgrave woman and that she had talked for hours and hours about Della, detailing the most awful scandals. I fantasised as I drove to the hospital about what secrets Hugh might uncover. Maybe Della once had an affair with a married man. Though she was unlikely ever to have shown that much passion. Perhaps she had cheated on exams or been charged with drink driving. Or shoplifting. I had to smile to myself as I pulled into the hospital car park. If I wanted a big black secret to hold over my mother-in-law's head, then I would surely be disappointed. Della was too bloody uptight to have ever stepped over the line of what was socially acceptable.

I went to the nurses' station before going in to see Ben. I stood there for a full five minutes before anyone appeared. I could see how understaffed the whole floor was and that it appeared to be a time when medications were being dispensed too. But I needed to ask them about my husband. The nurse who approached looked so young she could have been playing dress-up doctors and nurses. I felt old as I noticed her unlined skin, trim figure and sparkling eyes. At that moment I knew my own middle age was waiting around the corner for me, getting ready to pounce.

"Excuse me," I said. "I know you're busy but I would like to talk to someone about my husband, Ben Parrish. He's in Room 5."

"He's making very good progress, Mrs Parrish."

"So, his scans and X-rays. Are they all clear?"

The girl shifted from one foot to the other. She looked down, avoiding my gaze.

"I think you should speak to Mr Parrish," she said.

"No. You tell me, please. Has his heart been damaged? I'm entitled to know."

"And your husband is entitled to confidentiality. We have to respect that, Mrs Parrish. Talk to him."

I stood there, not knowing what to do. It was easy to infer that the staff were under instructions from Ben not to discuss his condition with me. As things stood, he was the patient and he was entitled to confidentiality. But his doctors should also be aware of his full medical history, past as well as current. Even if that was the last thing Ben wanted.

The nurse smiled at me.

"Rest assured he's making a good recovery, Mrs Parrish. I'm sorry, I have to go now."

I watched her disappear into a ward. As I made my way towards Ben's room, I felt I had, in the kindest way, been pitied. I wondered if she guessed that I did not trust Ben to tell me, or them, the truth. That I was far more concerned about his mental health than anything else. She probably did. The nursing staff dealt, day in day out, with every aspect of the human condition.

Ben was sitting out in his chair, watching the TV which had been placed so high up on the wall you had to bend your head back to view. He looked brighter. Even a little stronger. He was watching a news bulletin.

"Can you believe what this asshole is saying?" he asked.

I laughed. This was more like the Ben I knew. He blamed all politicians for the state of the economy and frequently shouted at the TV when they were on. He was not alone in that.

"Listen to him! He's saying the economy is showing green shoots! Where is he coming from? The highest unemployment figures ever, a constant stream of emigration, the country on its knees, and this clown is talking about green shoots. Maybe he's smoking them!"

I sat on the side of his bed. He switched off the TV and turned towards me. He frowned.

"You look tired, Leah. And a bit pale. I'm sorry I've put you through all this worry. It must be a nightmare time for you."

I took his hands in mine. My Ben was definitely back.

This was the time. The perfect opportunity to tell him about the almost-foetus. About our fourth child. We could make the decision together. I squeezed his hands.

"You know I'm tough, Ben. I can cope. We'll get through this together."

He pulled his hands away from me.

"What are you saying? That I'm not tough enough? That I'm not able to cope? Is that what you think?"

Jesus! What a sudden turnabout. The volatility Hugh had also spotted. I really needed him to answer the questions the nurse had effectively prevented me from asking.

"That's not what I said, Ben, but now that you mention it I do think the strain of losing your job and the change in our circumstances has hit you very hard. There's nothing wrong with needing an extra bit of help to get through rough patches. I asked the duty nurse about your current state of health but she was very evasive."

I felt anger radiate from him but I stayed sitting close to him.

"I'm glad to hear that," he said, "because I specifically asked that my treatment not be discussed with anybody but me. I knew you'd be sticking your nose in. And Hugh. I told you that I'll be going back to my GP. Isn't that enough for you?"

"Doctor Kelly thinks you're taking the medication he prescribed, doesn't he? Do you think he should know you're stashing it? Why would you do that?"

He left his chair and sat on the bed beside me. His anger deflated as quickly as it had blown up. He put his arms around me and laid his head on my shoulder. He was shaking.

"I don't know, Leah," he whispered. "I don't know. I

promise I'll talk to Doctor Kelly. I trust him. But I don't want to get drawn into the hospital system. Going to clinics to see people who don't know me at all. Being labelled. I'm just a bit depressed. That's all. Nothing we can't cope with."

I held him until he stopped shaking. That took some time. I told the embryo inside me that Daddy was not well enough to hear about it yet. Nor was he in the right frame of mind to discuss the question of the house in Howth. But both discussions would have to happen soon. Very soon. Before it was too late to take control.

CHAPTER THIRTY-NINE

If circumstances had been different, Hugh would have thoroughly enjoyed his walk along Curracloe Beach in Wexford. The sky was grey, the sea dark and restless, but the beauty of the seven-mile stretch of sand was stunning. He licked his lips, salty with spray the stiff breeze carried shoreward.

"Wasn't this where *Saving Private Ryan* was filmed?" he asked Maria Cosgrave.

"That's right. There was huge excitement while the film crew was here. That was back in 1997."

Hugh stood and looked out to sea. To where the grey sky met the grey ocean. An appropriate setting for his grey thoughts. Yes, he had come here to try to get an insight into his mother's childhood, but he had not been prepared for what Maria told him. He had no doubt she was being truthful. Two years Della's senior, Maria was a striking older woman. More remarkable than her appearance was her zest for life. The wonderful energy she radiated. Her kindness. Her honesty.

"Della and I used to spend a lot of time here," she said. "Especially during the winter when the place was all ours.

We used to search the shoreline for treasure."

He tried to imagine my mother as a carefree child. The picture did not fit with the woman he knew.

Maria checked the time on her phone.

"I'd say my dad should be awake by now. He hates anyone knowing he takes a nap during the afternoon. As if a ninety-four-year-old is not entitled to a rest."

Hugh followed as she led the way towards the woods. Her father, long since retired from his job as gardener/handyman for the Roaches of Curra Manor, lived in the heart of the woods. His cottage was situated in a clearing, the ivy-clad walls blending in discreetly with the surroundings. Hugh was surprised to see triple-glazed windows and a solar panel on the old building.

"He refused to leave here and come live with me in the town, even after Mam died, so I decided to make it as comfortable as possible for him," Maria explained.

"Beautiful setting," Hugh said.

It would indeed be spectacular in spring, carpeted with bluebells and snowdrops, but it had a bleak beauty in the fading light of the November afternoon.

Maria knocked on the door. A dog began to bark.

"That's Toby," she said. "He's a sheepdog, as old and toothless as Dad. No need to be afraid."

The door opened. Dog and man peeped out. James Cosgrave's face was weather-beaten and time-worn but the pale blue eyes were alert. The dog gave one more bark and then disappeared back into the cottage.

"So you're Della Roache's eldest son," he said, offering his hand to Hugh. "I remember you when you were little. You were always asking questions."

Hugh took the old man's hand.

"I haven't changed," he said. "I'm still asking questions."

"I know. Maria told me. Come in and sit down."

James led Hugh and Maria into the kitchen and sat them next to the blazing log fire. He settled himself into the rocking chair across from them. His gaze was steady as he looked at Hugh.

"So you want to know about your Uncle George," he said.

"Yes, please," Hugh answered. "In fact, I didn't know my mother had a brother until Maria told me today. I had always believed Mom was an only child. She never told me otherwise."

"She was only four when her brother died. Maybe she doesn't remember him."

"Maybe," Hugh said, not wanting to openly disagree with James, but he did not believe that.

"Maria told me you were the one who found George. His body, that is."

He nodded, then bowed his head. Not before Hugh saw sadness dim the old man's bright eyes. It was as if he was reliving the horror of the moment. When he lifted his head again, there were tears in his eyes.

"He was a lovely lad, your Uncle George. He spent a lot of time in the woods here. There was a particular oak tree he loved. It's around 100 years old now. He often climbed that tree and sat up there. He was a dreamer. But one evening he took a rope with him. I found him next morning. He was fourteen."

They were silent, the three of them. Hugh thought of the vulnerable fourteen-year-old George. Depressed. Needing support. Misunderstood. How tortured his life must have been. How lonely his death.

"Your mother adored him," Maria said. "I remember her trailing around after her big brother whenever she got the chance. He was ten years older than her and she hero-worshipped him."

Hugh put his hand in his jacket pocket and took out the photo Maria had given him. Even though his mother had only been four when the picture was taken, it was safe to say the little girl holding hands with Maria was a miniature version of Della Parrish as she now was. And the boy standing behind them, George, was like a twin to Ben. The same dark hair and eyes. The same indefinable aura of sadness. George Roache, Ben Parrish. Peas in a pod. Hugh looked up at Maria.

"So why did she not tell us about him? Why no photos? I don't remember her ever visiting his grave. It's as if, for her, he never existed."

"Not her fault," Maria said. "You knew your Grandfather Roache. You must remember how strict he was. He ruled the roost with an iron fist. What he said went. To his way of thinking, his son had disgraced the family name, so he banished him from their history."

Hugh shook his head. Leah had been right. His mother's family history was like an excerpt from a Victorian novel. For crying out loud, it wasn't that long ago. Sixty-four years. Surely there would have been some understanding of mental illness and how to treat it.

"How can you deny someone's existence?" he asked. "Especially your child's. That's not just puzzling, it's downright cruel."

He heard James give a disapproving huff.

"Before you judge your Grandfather," he said, "remember all this happened in a different day and age.

Suicide wasn't decriminalised in Ireland until 1993. And then there was the moral aspect. You know your grandfather was a very religious man."

Hugh shrugged. Yes, Grandad Roache had attended church regularly but Christian kindness had never been part of his make-up. He had been twenty years older than Grandma Roache so he certainly belonged to another, less enlightened era.

"You have to agree, Dad," Maria said, "that old man Roache was harsh. Della was afraid of him. Terrified that she might inadvertently break one of his rules."

"Well, she broke the strictest rule of all, didn't she?" the old man said. "She asked him about George's death. That was your fault, Maria."

James stared at his daughter. Maria shifted uncomfortably in her seat.

"Well, yes, Dad, I suppose it was my fault. But I don't regret it. George was her brother. She had a right to know how he had died. And he had a right to have his life, short as it was, acknowledged."

James' chair creaked as he sat forward, glaring at Maria.

"You interfered in something that was none of your business. You stirred up a lot of trouble then, and you're doing the same again now."

Hugh sensed the spark of anger pass between father and daughter. He felt awkward, sorry that his enquiries had seemed to stir up old disagreements. He moved to stand up.

Maria waved to him to sit and turned back to her father.

"Who was going to tell her?" she asked. "Her parents? You? The people who whispered behind her back? The ones who said there was a streak of madness running through the Roache family?"

She stopped suddenly, realising the Roache blood ran in Hugh's veins.

"Sorry . . . I don't mean . . . I didn't mean . . ."

Hugh smiled, breaking the tension that had suddenly seemed to grip the room.

"Aren't we all that little bit off-kilter? Isn't that what makes the world interesting?"

"Maybe so," James said. "But Della paid a high price for asking her father about George. He sent her to boarding school within days. Off up to Dublin. You lost a friend, Maria, and Della lost her childhood. We never really saw her here again, did we? Not mixing with the likes of us anyway."

They were silent then, the old man staring into the fire as if reading history in the flames.

"I was at the burial," he muttered eventually. "Dug the grave and helped lower young George's coffin into the ground. Not here. The cemetery is twenty miles away. Not even marked with a gravestone."

He picked up the poker and stirred the logs. Sparks crackled, flames made a whooshing sound, the dog snored as it slept at James' feet, the clock on the mantle ticked away the minutes.

Hugh felt transported back in time. To a graveyard, twenty miles from here, to a furtive burial of the brother Della never spoke about. The uncle he had never had a chance to meet.

James turned towards him.

"Your grandfather wasn't a cruel man, Hugh. I watched over him at his son's graveside as he wept bitter tears. He was devastated by George's death and the manner of his dying. It was different times. That's all."

Hugh nodded. There would be no point in telling the old man that the damage Grandfather Roache caused was not buried with George. He understood now. He knew why Della had always been so protective of Ben, why she tried her best to cover up his vulnerability. To deny his need for psychiatric care. To never, ever, mention her brother George. The shame was part of her DNA. It was plain Dad had not known about George either. He would have brought it all out into the open. And maybe, just maybe, he would have understood Ben better and loved Mum more.

Hugh stood up. He could find death and burial records online. At some stage he would erect a headstone to commemorate George Roache's short life and tragic death. For now, he needed to get back to Paircmoor and talk to his mother. And to Leah. He offered his hand to James Cosgrave.

"Thank you so much for your help, James."

"You're welcome. Are you going up to the Curra Manor before you leave?"

"No. I'd better make tracks. It's a long drive back."

"There's a young couple there now. And a gang of children. It seems like a happy place again."

"That's good. Thank you, James, for seeing me. I appreciate it."

"I hope you'll let the ghosts of the past sleep in peace now," James said, before turning back to gaze into the flames.

Maria walked Hugh to the door.

"Thank you too, Maria," Hugh said. "Do you mind if

I keep this photo of George? I'll send it back to you when I get it copied."

"You're very welcome, Hugh. Feel free to call anytime you're in the country. Do tell Della we were asking for her. She's always welcome here."

"I'll tell her."

As he walked away, Hugh was sure that Della would never want to come here again. Nor would he, but he knew that the shadow of Curra Manor would always travel with him.

CHAPTER FORTY

It was past eleven o'clock when I heard Hugh's car drive up the avenue of Cowslip Cottage. I went to open the front door, worried that he might knock and wake the children. As I watched him walk towards the cottage, I noticed the droop of his shoulders. If body language was anything to go by, his trip to Della's home place must not have gone well.

"That was a long drive," I said, as he made his way into the hall. "You must be exhausted."

"You bet, Leah," he said as he followed me into the kitchen and sat at the table.

He did indeed look tired. His skin had a yellow tone as if he had paled underneath his tan. I sat down across from him.

"I was about to offer you hot milk, Hugh, but would I be right in thinking you need something stronger?"

He nodded. I went into the lounge, poured a whiskey and put it, and the bottle, on the table in front of him. He emptied the glass in one long swallow, then refilled it. I felt my stomach knot with tension. What in the hell had happened in Wexford?

"Did you meet Maria Cosgrave?"

"I did. And her dad. James Cosgrave. He dug the grave for Della's brother. My uncle. Ben's uncle."

"Her brother? You mean her uncle? Della was an only child."

"No, as it turns out. She was not. Her brother's name was George."

He picked up the glass of whiskey, looked at it, and put it back on the table again. He began to talk, telling me what he had learned of George's life and death. Of how the memory of the boy had been banished from the Roache family history.

"So Maria Cosgrave told Della how George had died. Is that right?"

"Yes, Leah. That's how, when she was fourteen, Mum found out that her brother had died by suicide. After talking to Maria, she went straight to her parents and asked them if it was true. That's when they sent her to boarding school in Dublin. They banished her from her home as effectively as they had erased her brother's memory."

Hugh reached into the pocket of the jacket he had hung over the back of his chair. He took out a photograph and pushed it across the table to me. It was black-and-white. Old, with a sepia tinge. I had to hold it up to the light to see it properly. My breath caught in my throat as I looked at the boy in the photo. He was standing behind two girls, one of whom was obviously a very young Della Parrish.

"George?" I whispered.

Hugh nodded and reached for the glass of whiskey.

"You want one?" he asked, holding the bottle towards me.

I needed a drink but, damn it, I was pregnant, wasn't I? And shocked. I shook my head.

"The likeness is uncanny," I said. "That could be Ben standing there. Or Rob – if he was older."

"You see? That's the answer to our questions. Della has buried the memory of her brother and his death so deeply she cannot recall him. By protecting Ben, who in every way seems to be a clone of George Roche, Mum feels she is looking after her brother and saving him from himself."

I could not help my derisive laugh. I did not want to be unkind to Hugh but this psychobabble was just giving Della a free pass and not bringing us any nearer the truth.

"For heaven's sake, Hugh, she was fourteen years old when she discovered how George had died. Of course she remembers. But obviously she agreed with her parents that it had to be hidden. Just like she tried to deny Ben's illness when he was in his teens. And now she's trying to whisk him off again. To brush all unsavoury mental problems under the carpet."

Hugh nodded. When he looked at me, I could see the pain in his eyes and I regretted speaking so harshly to him.

"I think the truth is halfway between both our views, Leah. Yes, Mum's attitude to mental health is unacceptable but you must allow for the fact that she was indoctrinated at a very young age."

"And chose not to change when she became an adult. A mother."

"Maybe so. I'll give you that. But I don't believe we have a right to judge her. At least not until we speak to her."

I felt ashamed. He was right. I was being judgemental. Self-righteous. Della was hurting. She also had a very devious streak.

I shrugged. "I don't want to be unfair, Hugh. I know the good side of Della too. The generous woman, the grandmother who loves her grandchildren very deeply. And her sons."

"Well, one son anyway. But we know why now, don't we?"

"In a way. But I don't agree that discouraging Ben from getting the help he needs is necessarily loving him. Besides –"

I stopped speaking suddenly. I had been about to say that, as a mother, I could not understand her favouring one child over the other. That I loved and respected all my children equally. What a hypocrite! I laid my hands on my tummy and felt the barely perceptible bump. The embryo. Our fourth baby. How could I criticise Della when I did not have enough love in my heart for this child?

"Besides?" Hugh prompted.

I looked across at him and saw that his hurt was etched on his face. It resonated with my pain. I knew, deep in my gut, that I had more than enough love for my baby. But it was too much struggle. Ben, the salon, the twins soon starting kindergarten, and Rob moving on to senior infants. All money, money, money. But I ached with longing to hold this baby in my arms. To protect and nurture it.

Tears rose from the well of sadness inside me. They streamed down my face, hot and salty. Through a blur of tears I saw Hugh stand up and come around the table to me. I stood and walked into his open arms. He was as tall as Ben but more solid. Comfortable to lean into. I felt warm and safe in his embrace. Cossetted. Looked after. When I noticed his eyes brim with tears, I knew he needed comforting as much as I did. I reached up and stroked the tense muscles of his shoulders. He pulled me closer. I heard his breath quicken, felt the heat from his body. My body answered the unspoken question by moving even closer to him, by raising my face to his for the kiss we both longed for.

But, before that happened, over his shoulder my eyes fell on the family photograph. The one of Rob's first day in Primary School. The smiley, perfect family one. The picture that reminded me of what we were and what we could be again. I stepped back from Hugh, bumping into my chair and almost knocking it over.

"I'm sorry, Hugh. Sorry, my fault. Just feeling very vulnerable at the moment. Sorry."

"Stop apologising, Leah. We're both a bit all over the place now. Anyway, I don't normally drink whiskey. My fault."

"No. Nobody's fault. We didn't do anything wrong, did we? Mutual support when we needed it. Done and dusted now."

"Agreed."

"We'll talk in the morning. About Della. And George."

"Yes. We'll do that. Sleep tight, Leah."

I quickly turned my back on him, checked on the children, then went to my bedroom. Our bedroom. Mine and Ben's. I lay there, listening to Hugh's footsteps as he left the kitchen, went to the bathroom, then the click of the lock as he closed the door of Rob's room. I pictured him lying in Rob's bed, wearing only boxers, probably silk, his strong arms and muscled chest, bare. I longed to be there with him. To finish what we had almost begun. It was a while before I could fall asleep.

The guilt, Leah Parrish. Oh, the guilt!

CHAPTER FORTY-ONE

Friday 3rd December 2010

I meant to be up early the following morning. To get, as my mother used to say, a hold on the day. Maybe do some spring cleaning, floor polishing, ironing, baking. Anything that would keep me from thinking about the events of last night. Anything to make me forget how good it felt to be in Hugh's arms. Anything to erase the guilt and the dread of having to face him this morning.

The children were already in the kitchen by the time I went in there. I got out a pot and began making their porridge.

"Uncle Hugh asleep, Mom," Josh announced. "He making snores. Like this." He snorted while the other two laughed.

"*Shh!* Don't wake Uncle Hugh," I said. "He's very tired after his big drive yesterday."

"How much longer before I can go back to school?" Rob asked.

"When Daddy home again," Anna said.

"I didn't ask you, monkey face," Rob said. "I was talking to Mom."

Disappointed by Rob's nastiness to his sister, I quickly turned around from the cooker. Anna's eyes were brimming with tears. I should have expected this row. It had been waiting to happen since the children's routine had been so disrupted. I went to the table and sat beside Rob.

"Rob, you must apologise to Anna. That was not a nice way to talk to her."

He reluctantly muttered an apology but I could see how upset Anna was. Her big brother was her hero and his criticism hurt her.

"I know we're all missing Dad so we must help each other," I told them. "That means not calling each other names."

"We have to say names, don't we?" Rob said. "How else could we call someone?"

"Don't be doing the smarty," I told him. "You know I meant we must not use bad names."

He nodded agreement. Rob as a five-year-old kept me on my toes with his logic and his sometimes alternative ways of looking at life. I was suddenly struck by the idea that his teens might be a very challenging time for all of us. I reached out my hand and ruffled his hair, loving him for his seriousness and his innate kindness. He tossed his head, not liking to have his hair messed. I smiled at him.

"You'll be back in school next week, Rob. Either Monday or Tuesday. I'll do some homework with you after breakfast so that you can keep up with the class."

"It's okay, Uncle Hugh did my reader with me and he showed me some very cool maths. And coding. Computer coding. I think that's what I'll do when I grow up. Like Uncle Hugh."

The mention of Hugh started Josh doing his snoring act again and sent the three of them into fits of laughter. Josh could end up on the stage. Or in film.

"*Oh, shit!*" I said as the smell of burn filled the kitchen.

I ran to the cooker and removed the pot of charred porridge. Even with the pot scraped out and soaking, the extractor on and a window open, the place still reeked of burn. I suddenly realised the twins were having great fun chorusing '*Oh, shit!*' while Rob laughed at them.

"Everything alright here?"

I turned from the sink to see Hugh standing in the doorway. He was barefoot, wearing jeans and a shirt. The shirt was unbuttoned, obviously hastily thrown on. Pot scrub in one hand and burned pot in the other, I couldn't help staring at his chest. Just as I had imagined it. Pecs like his did not come without a lot of hard work. Lucky Piper, getting to snuggle up to him every night.

"Leah! Are you okay?"

I jumped guiltily. Lust and burnt porridge made very inappropriate bedfellows.

"Yes, Hugh. Fine, thank you. Just a burned pot and a few squabbles. The usual morning routine."

I was aware that he was staring at me, a frown on his forehead. I wondered if he regretted our closeness of last night. Or felt guilty, like I did. He must have, because he began to button his shirt.

"How about you make coffee," he said. "And I'll do some eggs."

I nodded, glad not to have to start over making porridge.

"Who's for scrambled eggs and toast?" he asked.

There was a chorus of "me, me, me" from the children. I raised an eyebrow, knowing that they would probably have turned up their noses if I had asked.

And of course they cleared their plates, as I did too.

"What's the secret to your perfect scrambled eggs?" I asked.

He grinned at me. "If I told you, it wouldn't be a secret anymore, would it? I'll just tell you it involves magic."

"There's no such thing as magic," Rob said. "It's just a trick."

I wished, not for the first time, that he was more child and less analytical adult.

"Of course there's magic," I said. "How else could a tiny seed grow into a massive tree, or butterflies have beautiful patterns on their wings? We live in a very, very magic world."

"I agree with your mom," Hugh said. "There is magic. But I agree with Rob too, because there are tricks. Like this."

He took a coin from his jeans pocket and after some deft hand movements and a stream of patter, the coin appeared behind Josh's ear. Magic! The kitchen rang with the children's hearty laughter.

"Something my dad taught me," Hugh said to me.

I nodded, smiling.

On that morning, watching my children smiling, their eyes shining, hearing their laughter, I did indeed believe in magic. And just to confirm it, a burst of winter sunshine broke through the clouds, bathing the kitchen in an ethereal light. I looked across at Hugh. His eyes told me he felt it too. The magic of that special moment in time.

They were leaving Ben's room as Della walked up the corridor. A train of medics, all following in the tracks of the man she assumed to be the head consultant. He had that air of authority about him. Doctor Nyhan, one step behind the great man, nodded to Della as she passed by.

Della tapped on her son's door, then walked in, nervous now that something else had happened to Ben. He wasn't in the room. Then she heard the most extraordinary of sounds. Through the closed door of the bathroom, she heard the gush of water, presumably the shower, and the deep tones of Ben's voice as he sang 'You Raise Me Up'.

She sat on the side of his bed and smiled as she listened to the full-throated, if not very tuneful, singing from the bathroom. That was the sound of a happy man. A man with a future. A man with a successful life ahead.

When the gush of water and the singing stopped, Della tapped on the bathroom door.

"Ben! Mum here. Make sure you're decent when you come out."

"Hi, Mum! Be with you in a minute."

He was fully dressed when he came into the bedroom. Smiling. Definitely thin, but he seemed more energetic.

"You're looking well," Della said. "When I saw all the doctors leave your room, I was worried something had happened to you."

"Something did happen, Mum. I'm cleared for going home. Isn't that great news?"

Della stood up from the bed and walked across the room to get the visitor's chair. The task gave her time to think. To frame her words in such a way that Ben did not fly into one of his tantrums. She placed the chair beside his bed and watched as he began to take clothes from his wardrobe.

"Terrific news, Ben. Are you free to go now?"

"No. I must wait for a prescription. But they shouldn't be too long. I'll ring Leah now to come and collect me."

"Don't do that. You'll ruin the surprise. I'll drive you to the cottage."

Ben turned to look at her, a frown on his forehead. Then he nodded.

"Yeah. Maybe you're right. I'll just turn up."

He took his travel bag from the wardrobe and began packing. As he went from bedroom to bathroom and back, Della waited her chance to broach the topic she must discuss with him. She had already spoken to her solicitor in Dublin that morning and everything was in hand for sorting all the legal and tax implications of signing the house in Howth over to Ben. The tenants in the quayside apartment had received their notice to quit, so her new pied-à-terre was on track too. Everything was in place except Ben's acceptance of the offer. She cleared her throat.

"Ben, stop fussing around and sit down for a moment. We need to talk."

He took the children's drawings and his phone from the top of his locker. He looked at his phone for a moment, thought about turning it on, decided against it and put it into the front pocket of his bag with the drawings. He turned to face his mother.

"If this is about Howth, I will discuss it with Leah. We'll make the decision together."

"Of course. I accept that. And I'm not trying to pressure you into making a decision. I just wanted to know what you thought of the idea in principle. Is it something you would consider? If Leah agrees."

Ben sighed and sat down, for what he hoped was the last time, in the chair beside the window.

"I know what that house is worth, Mum, even in recessionary times, and you're gifting it to me. Very generous. But how come you seem quite comfortable with cutting Hugh out of his inheritance? Talking of principles, that doesn't seem very principled to me."

Della leaned forward in her chair and tried to make eye contact with Ben. He continued to stare out the window, deliberately not engaging with her.

"You're being unfair, Ben. You should know I wouldn't overlook Hugh. He will get the equivalent in other assets and investments. I told you, your father left me well provided for. He would want me to do this."

Ben shrugged and finally turned to face her.

"Would he? Do you really believe that? He'd probably say, like he always did, that I'm a dreamer. That I need a good kick up the backside to get me going. Remember that?"

Della nodded. Gavin had been an insensitive clod at times. Especially when it came to the way he spoke to Ben. And the cavalier way he conducted his extramarital affairs as if his wife didn't either know or care.

"Yes, I remember, Ben. He meant well. Sometimes he lacked understanding."

Ben laughed. A mirthless sound. "He's had his way now. I got a really good kick up the arse as I sat in the cave, the tide rushing in to get me. I don't ever want to go back there again, Mum. There will have to be changes."

He stood up and came to stand in front of his mother. He took her hands in his.

"Mum, I do appreciate everything you've done for me. I know it has cost you more than money. You've devoted a big chunk of your life to looking out for me. I love you for that. But –"

"But you want to take control of your own life. Right?"

He nodded. Della smiled at him. She felt like singing 'You Raise Me Up' with abandon herself. She had heard Ben say that there would have to be changes. That could only mean he intended leaving Paircmoor behind to move back to Dublin. The fact that he said he needed to control his own life was a guarantee that he didn't want Leah to call the shots anymore. And nobody knew better than Della how stubborn her youngest son could be when he made his mind up. He had proved that by marrying Leah in the first place.

She closed her eyes for a moment and pictured the children running around the garden in Howth, Ben yachting in the harbour when he had downtime from what would be his very successful architecture practice. Keeping the Parrish name alive and respected into the future.

Ben tugged on her hands. "Come on, Mum. They'll be a while getting my paperwork sorted. Let's go to the cafeteria for coffee and cake. My treat."

Della's step was light as she and her son walked to the hospital cafeteria. Ben was, at last, becoming the man she had always known he could be.

CHAPTER FORTY-TWO

I rang Ben. My husband's phone was, as usual, turned off. I brought the children into the hall and dressed them in their coats, hats and wellies. The morning was cold but the winter sunshine still shone. A run in the garden would burn off some of their excess energy. I put on my own coat and pulled on my boots. The garden was big, two acres. The wildness of it made it an exciting place for the children but not somewhere they could be allowed to play unsupervised.

I heard Hugh walk into the hall from the kitchen. The children set up a chorus, asking him to come out and play with them. I smiled at him. The more I got to know him, the luckier I thought Piper was to be married to him.

"Do you mind if I borrow one of Ben's jackets and a pair of boots?" he asked. "I left San Francisco in such a rush I forgot about how damp and cold Irish winters can be."

"Help yourself," I said, showing him where the coats and boots were kept.

"Uncle Hugh," Rob said. "We're growing a big Christmas tree, and Dad's going to put loads of lights on it. I'll show you."

"For Santa," Anna said.

I smiled as I watched the four of them walk ahead of me into the garden. The tree the children were so excited about was only about three feet tall, but it would look nice decked out in fairy lights for Christmas.

The sound of a car driving up the avenue distracted me. As soon as I saw the stickers on the car, I realised who was calling. And why. There was to be a Presidential election on the following Tuesday. I had forgotten all about it. It didn't make any difference to us, since we had not yet got around to registering in the Paircmoor electoral area, so we would not be entitled to vote here. The car pulled up beside me and a woman with a bundle of leaflets in her hand got out the passenger door. I recognised her from seeing her around the village but had never spoken to her before.

"We're canvassing for Evelyn Thurley for President," she said. "Can we count on your vote next Tuesday?"

"Sorry. We haven't registered yet so we can't vote. Thank you for calling though."

"That's a pity. You know, I suppose, voting in Paircmoor takes place in the National School, so your little boy won't have any school on Tuesday."

I hadn't known that. Rob would be furious. He had missed enough time now.

"How is your husband?" she asked.

"Well, thank you," I answered, wondering just how much she knew.

"I'd better move on," she said. "Don't forget to register your vote here. Looks like we could be in for a General Election very soon."

I waved to her and watched the car drive away, before following Hugh and the children. I knew I would find them in the area the children call the playground. Shortly after we had moved in here, Ben had begun to clear the back garden. The part overlooked by the kitchen window. That way we, or mostly he, could keep an eye on the children while working in the kitchen. He had started the project full of enthusiasm, hacking away overgrown shrubs, felling two trees that were blocking light, putting in a swing and slide, making three little seats and a picnic table from the sawn-off trunks, and painting them in vivid colours. There was a small flower bed, a bit dreary and neglected this time of year, and an area where Ben had dug drills so that the children could grow vegetables. In pride of place was the Christmas tree, soon to be lighting Santa's way to Cowslip Cottage. I felt a knot of sadness in my throat, remembering how happy Ben had been planning this play area, what fun we all had there. When had he stopped being happy? And, shamefully, why had I not seen happiness and fun slip away?

Hugh was crouched down on one of the little seats. Just as well it was a solid ring of timber. I laughed when I saw him.

"Just following orders," he said. "What Anna says, goes. I don't like the way you're enjoying my discomfort. I think you should sit too."

Anna, from the swing, shouted at me.

"*Sit down, Mom! Watch me go high!*"

It was Hugh's turn to laugh as I gingerly lowered myself onto the red stool with the white spots.

"Looking at this," Hugh said, "it's easy to see how creative Ben is. Not having the opportunity to use his talents must be so frustrating for him."

"Absolutely. He has great plans for renovating this

cottage but, unfortunately, the cost is prohibitive at the moment. Anyway, I think he has lost interest."

I watched Rob and Josh poking the earth with sticks. They were fascinated by snails and I knew they were searching for them. They loved them as much as Anna dreaded them. There would be the usual furore if they found one and chased her with it.

"We need to talk, Leah. There are decisions to be made."

I took a deep breath. I was shocked. Was he about to make an issue of last night? I was horrified by the possibility that my moment of weakness could become public knowledge. More specifically being brought to the attention of Ben or Piper. I had really thought Hugh and I were at ease with each other this morning. How wrong was that?

"Decisions about what?" I asked, none too politely.

"About George Roache. Della. The whole mess I uncovered in Wexford. How do you want to handle it? Do you want to tell Ben yourself or do you want me to tell him?"

I sighed with relief. Della's secret history I could cope with, one way or the other. The timber of the little stool was cutting into my bottom, even through my coat. I squirmed, trying to find a comfortable position. More uncomfortable than the stool was the fact that, after a morning where there had been magic and laughter, I now had to face reality again. Of course Ben would have to be told about Della's secret brother.

"I'm not sure what to do, Hugh," I said. "It's your family history. Parrish business. But then, Ben is my husband, and the fact that there may be a genetic factor in his depression is surely my business too."

"Exactly. Like it or not, you're part of this family."

"That's a first. I've never before felt myself accepted as a full family member."

He reached over and caught my hand.

"I know that now. I'm sorry I didn't realise. As far as I can figure out, the only way we can all work through this situation is to do it together."

"Are you including your mother too?"

"I'm just making a suggestion. Do you have a better one?"

I took my hand away from his. I felt anger begin to churn in my gut. Against Della, her family secrets, her pride, her selfishness and her snobbery. Yes, I would like to sit down and confront her, face to face. To point out to her how damaging her behaviour had been. To Ben. And to Hugh also. I would like her to realise how totally wrong and irresponsible she had been. How deceitful. But, even as the angry words formed in my mind, I knew they would not help Ben. And with that thought came the admission that I was, yet again, being judgemental. Della, without doubt, had been damaged by her overly strict upbringing. It was unfair to blame her or to think she would ever deliberately do anything to harm either of her sons. A shiver ran down my spine as I wondered if my children would, at some stage, look back on their childhoods and think that *I* had failed them.

A yell from Anna brought me back to reality. She had jumped down from the swing and was being chased by the boys. They had not found any snails but they were each holding a wriggling worm in their hands, trying to dangle them near Anna.

I went to stand up but I was cold and stiff from sitting on the low stool and I couldn't.

Hugh looked at me and laughed.

"I think we're stuck," he said. "We're way too old for such low places!"

He held his hand out to me. I took it in mine and wondered at how I had, for so long, found him annoying. I had a brief flash of how close I had come to kissing him last night. I knew, in my heart, it had happened because we had both been upset and needed comforting. But here, in the cold light of day, with my children around me, I realised we were playing with fire. I loved Ben. Hugh loved Piper. And that was that.

"We'll make a gallant effort to stand," Hugh said. "On my count of three, go. *One! Two! Three! Go!*"

We managed to get to our feet by leaning on each other. We rose, laughing, still holding hands.

"You see," he said. "Together is the best way. Don't you agree?"

I nodded. Yes, together as friends. As brother-in-law and sister-in-law. As family. The Parrish family.

No doubt the George Roache and Della situation was so deep-rooted and complex that it would take a combined effort to find a way ahead for all of us. We would have to put bitterness and recriminations aside and talk it all through together. I smiled at Hugh, wishing that the togetherness didn't involve Della.

"Together it is, then. All of us. Don't know how we'll organise that though."

"Leave it to me," Hugh said.

"I will." I turned and called to the children. "Who wants hot chocolate!"

The boys dropped the worms and Anna stopped yelling.

We all trooped back into the house.

We had just finished our hot chocolate when the doorbell rang.

Anna scurried into the hall and made her trademark shriek.

Hugh rose from his seat, ready to run after her. "Is she alright, Leah?"

"She's fine. That's just the way she announces her grandmother's arrival. I'd better let Della in."

I went to the hall door. Della stood there, a pale and frail-looking Ben by her side. I could not believe that Ben had not let me know he was coming home. There was a glint of satisfaction in Della's eyes. Her mouth pursed as if to hold back a laugh. My anger welled up again, and my promise of consorting with the enemy for the common good wavered. Could either of these two men, my husband or my brother-in-law, not see that Della was manipulative, bad, selfish, evil? I ran out of adjectives at about the same time my anger ran out.

Walking past Della, I threw my arms around Ben and hugged him tight, not even letting go when the children clung on to his legs.

Ben was back home with us, his family. That was all that really mattered.

The children could not bear to let their father out of their sight for the rest of the day. When he needed a rest in the afternoon, Hugh and Della took the children out to the woods. I was glad of the chance to have Ben to myself for a little while. He looked very tired as he threw himself down on our bed. I pulled the duvet up and tucked it in around him.

"Well, how does it feel to be home?" I asked him.

He smiled at me, that lazy smile I loved.

"I missed you, Leah. I've been missing you for a long time now. And I'm sorry. So sorry. We have a lot to talk about. To sort out."

I stroked his hair back from his forehead. His eyelids drooped.

"We have forever to talk, Ben. You just rest now. I love you."

His eyes closed. I sat beside him, stroking his hair until I knew he was in a deep sleep.

I tiptoed out of our bedroom and into the kitchen wondering what I would cook for dinner. I assumed Hugh and Della would be eating with us. It would have to be something quick to prepare. I thought of one of Ben's favourites – sausage casserole. Maybe not the healthiest but definitely tasty. I checked in the fridge. I had sausages, bacon, tomatoes, mushrooms, onions, stock cube and I could snip a sprig of thyme from the pot of herbs growing outside. I smiled as I anticipated Della's reaction to bangers and mash. If she didn't like it, she could go to her hotel.

As I chopped and peeled, I let my mind drift into the past, to when my mother used to make this dish. How she used to hum as she cooked. How happy she would be to see her grandchildren relish it, as I used to when I was young.

And then, completely out of the blue, just as I was popping my largest casserole dish into the oven, it hit me. That thought, that worry, that unanswered question I had managed to bury for so many years.

I sat down at the table, oven gloves still in my hand, and trembled as all the doubt and uncertainty rushed back at me out of the past.

"Who's my daddy?" I had asked.

Again and again, I asked. And again and again Mam had not answered. She used to distract me with a question of her own, a treat, a story. That worked while I was little.

"Who's my father?" I asked as I got older.

"You don't need to know," she would say.

I eventually stopped asking. But I did need to know. I do. Was he a rapist? Was he a relation? Did he even know I existed? Mam, like me, was an only child. Her parents were dead now. I had no one to ask. Was my father someone in authority? A teacher, a cleric? Was he dead or alive? Who was he? And who the hell am I?

Shaking, I stood up to put on the kettle. Coffee. My solution for life's crises. The need was so urgent I spilled some on the counter as I spooned it from the jar into my mug. I knew, of course, what had triggered this regression. It was Della, and the revelations of her secret past. It was a shock to realise that Mam, my loving, loyal, wonderful mother, had been as cruel and selfish as I considered Della to be. Where was the difference? Their silence had damaged us both, Ben and me.

I forgot to put milk in my coffee and burned my tongue. The pain brought me back to the here and now, and to the knowledge that burying the question of my parentage again would not be a healthy option. I could imagine my children at some date in the future, wondering who their maternal grandfather had been and why they had not been told about him. Tongue stinging, I made two big decisions. One, I would use all the resources available to me to research my background and discover who my father was. Two, I would be less judgemental of Della. Condemning her would mean condemning Mam. That I would never do.

As the oven was on for the casserole anyway, I decided to use the extra oven space to make bread and butter pudding for dessert. When that was in the oven, I peeled a mountain of potatoes, all the time humming so that I could not hear my inner child crying and asking who my daddy was.

CHAPTER FORTY-THREE

Della dithered a bit about staying for dinner, even before she knew we would be having sausages. Hugh persuaded her to stay. I suspected that he had decided to have the big family powwow, sooner rather than later. Seeing how much brighter and stronger Ben seemed after his rest, I thought it was probably a good idea as long as the children were in bed first. They insisted on having Ben read their bedtime story. I looked in on them, the twins on Ben's knees and Rob sitting on the bed beside him as he read to them. Yes, yes, yes, there were problems to be faced, but the love I saw in that tableau of a father and his three children, had the power to overcome any difficulties. It was obvious how happy and secure the children were with him. How protective and loving he was with them. I was filled with hope that he would welcome baby number four with the same generosity. All I had to do now was find the right moment to tell him.

Back in the kitchen Hugh was again trying to persuade Della to stay. She was standing behind her chair, her coat draped over her arm.

"You know I don't like driving late at night, Hugh. I'd prefer to go now."

"You're comfortable with night driving when it suits you, Mum."

"Stay here if you like," I offered. "You can sleep in Rob's room if Hugh doesn't mind taking the couch."

"Or I can drive you to your hotel if you want," Hugh said. "The important thing, Mum, is that you stay for a while. I've booked to go home tomorrow. I'll be flying out from Dublin in the afternoon."

I was taken aback. Hugh had not mentioned that he would be leaving so soon. To be fair, he had responsibilities in San Francisco. His job. His wife. He would be glad to escape. He must be weary from the Paircmoor Parrishes and all their dramas.

"We have some very important things we need to discuss before I go," he said to Della. "I would appreciate you waiting until Ben has put the children to sleep. Is that alright with you, Mum?"

Della looked suspicious. Even a little afraid. Her glance flicked towards me and then away again. She turned and went back into the hall. I heard the closet door open and a hanger rattle as she hung up her coat. I knew it must be imagination, but somehow she seemed smaller and frailer as she came back into the kitchen and sat down at the table.

I brewed coffee. By the time it was ready, Ben was back in the kitchen and sitting at the table opposite his mother.

"Seems ridiculous," Ben said. "But I could swear the children have grown in the week I've been away. They'll be up and gone before we know where we are."

I noticed a frown on Hugh's forehead. A trace of sadness, and I wondered if he wanted children of his own. He would be a wonderful dad judging by the way he was with our kids. I saw his expression change to concern as he focussed on Ben.

I made sure everyone had coffee before sitting myself down beside Ben. Hugh and Della sat across from us at the long kitchen table.

"Are we right now?" Hugh asked.

It was obvious he had appointed himself chairperson of the meeting. When we all nodded, he leaned forward, looking Ben in the eye.

"Ben, I've asked Mum to stay here for a while. I've something very important I want to tell you both. It's not going to be easy, so I think the best bet is to tell you where I was yesterday and what I discovered on my trip."

"*She* said you were meeting an old friend," Della said, nodding in my direction

Hugh's frown deepened. "*She* is Leah, Mum. We're not starting this discussion with animosity. Believe me, we're going to need all the co-operation we can muster to sort through things."

Ben made a sound that was halfway between a laugh and a derisive jeer.

"What *have* I been missing while I was in hospital?"

"It's what we've all been missing," Hugh said as he turned to face Della. "I went to Wexford, Mum. I spoke to Maria Cosgrave and to her father James. They gave me this."

He reached into his shirt pocket and placed an old photo on the table in front of Della. She sat staring at it. Head bowed. Not moving. Barely breathing. Colour draining from her face.

I sat on the edge of my chair, worried that Hugh's direct method of confronting the past might be too much for Della to cope with. Ben looked puzzled. He reached across to turn the photo towards himself. Hugh put a hand on the picture, preventing Ben from seeing it.

"Before you see it, Ben, there's something you should know about Mum's family in Wexford. About our grandparents."

I could see Ben's mood changing. I caught the spark of anger in his eyes.

"What's all this cloak and dagger, Hugh? Can't you see you're upsetting Mum?"

Della lifted her head and reached for the photograph of herself aged four, her friend and her brother. She held it in front of her, the picture shaking as her hands trembled.

"Where did you get this?" she asked Hugh.

"Maria Cosgrave."

"She was always the same," Della said. "Couldn't mind her own business."

"She was a good friend to you, Mum. She still would be if you let her."

I watched a red flush spread up Ben's neck. He was getting upset. I wished that Hugh would get the story told. Even though I was sitting here with the Parrishes, I still felt I did not have a right to voice an opinion without being invited. I would, though, if I saw Ben getting any more agitated. Or Della. Tears filled her eyes as she stared from the photo to Ben.

"For fuck's sake!" Ben said. "Will somebody tell me what's going on?"

I reached for Ben's hand and took it in mine. His palm was sweaty. I had enough of the pussyfooting around. I took a deep breath and opened my mouth.

Della beat me to it.

"It's my story so I'll tell it my way," she said.

"*No!*" Hugh contradicted her. "It was your secret, but it is *our* story, our history, our heritage. Me and Ben. The children. It affects Leah too."

Della ignored Hugh's interruption. She ignored me also and addressed Ben directly as she told him about her childhood in Curra Manor and how she had idolised her big brother George.

"But –" he said and she held a hand up to stop him.

She told him of her friendship with Maria Cosgrave and how they used to play together. How her father was authoritarian and ruled the Roache family with fear. And then she stopped talking. I could feel Ben's hand shake as I held it.

"Why did you never speak of him before, Mum?" he asked. "Why did your parents never mention him?"

She shrugged. A helpless gesture absolving herself from any responsibility.

"I was only four when he died," she said.

"Oh! That still doesn't explain the secrecy. Why did –"

"Suicide," Hugh said.

The word seemed to reverberate around the kitchen. It was as if everything had been sucked from the room, cups, cooker, chairs. The vacuum left had been filled with the word, the deed, the awfulness of suicide. Suicide. *Suicide.*

"At fourteen years of age," Ben whispered. "Why?"

"Probably untreated depression," Hugh said. "It wasn't recognised in those days."

I felt Ben stiffen. I started also. It was if Hugh was pointing out a direct link between George's condition and Ben's. He had definitely picked up the American trait of openness and lost the Irish habit of softening the impact of bad news with indirect hints and clues.

"How?" Della asked. "I mean, what did he do to end his life?"

I looked at her in surprise. Did she really not know how George had taken his own life? I sensed vulnerability in the way she stared into Hugh's face, waiting for an answer to her question. It was clear she wanted to know as much as she dreaded hearing.

"Did Maria not tell you?" he asked.

"She told me to ask my father. I did. That's when he sent me to boarding school in Dublin and threatened that he would disown me if I ever spoke of George again. So I didn't."

Hugh nodded. It was an explanation. Of sorts. Della had gone on to university, read history and arts, graduated with an Honours degree. She was an intelligent woman. Her traumatic childhood was an explanation for keeping her secret. Maybe. An excuse, never.

"George hanged himself," Hugh said. "In the woods, near the Cosgrave cottage."

Della put her arms on the table and laid her head on them.

Ben reached across and grabbed the photograph. He stared at it, then stood and took it over under the spotlight lamp beside the dresser. His face was pale when he looked up. He walked back to the table and sat.

Della seemed to have got control of herself now and was again sitting up ramrod straight, head held high.

"I see now," Ben said. "This is all about me, isn't it, Hugh? You think I inherited George's genes. That manic depression and suicide is my inevitable fate."

"Don't be ridiculous, Ben. Yes, you're hardly going to deny you went through depression in your teens. But you had treatment in the Booly Clinic and look how you prospered after that. There's no excuse now for being secretive or ashamed about mental problems."

"Is that what you think, Hugh? That I'm a fucking mental case? Why are you dragging all this up now, just when you're about to escape back to your plastic life?"

Della looked from one to the other of her sons.

"Boys!" she said. "There's been enough sadness. Please don't argue. I am upset yes, but I also feel liberated. I loved my brother. He was gentle and kind. And so protective of me. I could never explain my father to you and how afraid of him I was. At the same time I adored him and always strove for his approval. I should have let go that fear and the promise of silence I made to him. I brought it into my marriage with me, into your childhoods and adolescence. It's time to let it go now."

"So, you never told Dad, did you?" Hugh said.

Della shook her head.

Ben still had the photo in his hand. He seemed mesmerised by it. I wondered now about the wisdom of exposing him to this family tragedy on his first day out of hospital. He had been so happy just thirty minutes ago but now his shoulders were stooped and when he looked up, his eyes flashed anger.

He glared at Hugh. "Well done, big brother. You've stirred the shit here and left us with the fallout."

Della reached her hand across the table to Ben. "No, Ben. Don't be angry with your brother. He acted in the interests of the whole family. I appreciate that, and you should too. If you need someone to blame, it should be me."

Ben pushed back his chair and walked around the table to his mother. He stooped and kissed the top of her head. He went to the door.

"The photo," Hugh said. "I'd like to take it with me."

Ben glanced from the photo in his hand to Hugh, then silently turned his back and went out, the picture still in his hand.

Della got her coat. Obviously she was not going to stay the night.

"I'll drive Mum to her hotel in town," Hugh told me. "See if I can get accommodation there too. If not I'll just head for Dublin."

I nodded, understanding that he needed to look after Della, but suddenly realising how much I was going to miss him.

"The children," he said. "I'm so sorry I have to leave without saying goodbye to them. Give them a hug from me."

"I will. And you take care, Hugh. Thank you for all your help."

He opened his arms to me and I gladly stepped into that embrace, safe in the knowledge that Hugh and I were friends. There for each other in a warm, supportive way. And we always would be.

We held on to each other until a discreet cough from Della alerted us to the fact that she was standing there, waiting for Hugh. I walked over to her, intending to say goodnight but when I saw how exhausted, pale and helpless she looked, I automatically put my arms around her. Then Della, the self-contained, snobby, devious, proud woman I had come to dread, became a vulnerable old lady as she laid her head on my shoulder and wept.

"Do excuse me," she muttered, as she straightened up and wiped her eyes. The raised chin told me Della was back.

"You don't have to go now," I said. "Stay until the morning."

"I must."

Then she was gone. Hugh followed, head bowed.

I walked to the hall door. Hugh stood on the step and faced me.

"I'm sorry, Leah. Maybe I should have left the past buried with George Roche. I hope I've not made things worse for Ben."

"Truth is always best," I said, and then kissed him on the cheek.

I waved them off but neither waved back. They had already left Cowslip Cottage behind.

I locked up, tidied cups into the dishwasher, turned off the lights and went to bed.

Ben was asleep, the photograph of his Uncle George on the pillow beside him. Even in sleep, he looked troubled. I lay there watching the rise and fall of his chest as he drifted into deep sleep. I thought over the events of the night. Della's shock. Ben's anger. Hugh's confusion. I didn't know if the truth was worth all that suffering. Could this be why Mam never told me who my father was? Could she have been protecting me from a fact I would not accept, but could not change?

What I did know for certain, as I lay tossing and turning until after four in the morning, was that the consequences of digging up all this hidden history would reverberate through our lives for a long time to come.

CHAPTER FORTY-FOUR

Saturday 4th December 2010

I awoke the following morning to silence. Not a whisper in the bedroom. Not even the usual creaks, groans and sudden clicks that were the voice of Cowslip Cottage. I was alone in the bed. For a moment I wondered if I had dreamt that Ben was home from hospital. Then the memory of last night's revelations about Della's secret brother and his suicide came back to me. Ben had been angry with Hugh. Upset.

I reached for my phone on the bedside locker. It was nine thirty. I jumped out of bed, noticing that Ben's pyjama bottoms were thrown on the chair. I called his name. Still not a sound. I threw on my dressing gown, shoved my feet into slippers and hurried to the kitchen. Empty. Silent. No Ben. No children. I raced to their bedrooms, the twins first, then Rob. Empty. Beds unmade. Heart thumping in my chest, I went back to the kitchen. There was ware in the sink. Four cereal bowls, so the children had breakfast and Ben had eaten too.

I held on to the back of a chair as I tried to control my racing thoughts. Panicking would not help me find the children, but all I could think of was Ben's anger and upset last night. Could he be thinking logically this morning? Was he capable of looking after the children? Were they safe with him?

Even as that thought entered my head, I knew how treacherous it was. And yet, when I searched the other rooms, I found them empty. A quick look out the kitchen window told me the children were not at the swing. I ran out the front door. The shed where we stored firewood and fuel for the stove was to my right. A little behind that, hidden by shrubs, was the quaint old shed with the dry-stone walls and corrugated-iron roof. In there we kept every bit of bric-a-brac we couldn't find space for in the house.

I had no idea why I should search the firewood shed, but I went there anyway. The door was difficult to open. I had to give it a good shove as it was swollen from all the recent rain. When I eventually got in, there was nothing to be seen except logs piled up against the wall and several bags of coal. I came out and started to head towards the old shed. I was suddenly brought to a halt as I glanced towards the avenue. The jeep was gone.

I stood there. Unmoving. Paralysed with fear. Ben had taken the children. Where to? Why? In milliseconds my mind recalled a plethora of horrific news reports. The awful things that had happened to other families when fathers took their children. Sometimes mothers too, but mostly fathers. Upset fathers. Troubled fathers. Terrified children. Dead children. Other families. Always other families. Other children. Not mine. Please God, not mine! And as well as all that, Ben should not be driving so soon after having a heart attack.

I screamed as I ran back into the house. I was calling on Mam to help me, help the children, trying to remember where I had left my phone, what I would say to the police when I made the 999 call. The bedroom was the last place I recalled having my phone so I raced there, almost tripping over the bedside rug as I grabbed my phone from the locker where I had left it.

I blinked when I saw it. The message I had been too sleepy to notice when I woke up. My fingers shook as I pressed the icon. It was from Ben. Sent at 8.45 am. While I had been snoring my head off and he had been kidnapping my children. I had to sit on the bed because my legs would no longer hold me up. I tried to read his words, but all I could see were mental images of my beautiful children. Rob, so solemn, so clever. Josh, full of fun. And Anna, a force of nature. My babies. Tears burned my eyes. They splashed onto the screen. I wiped them away with a corner of the duvet. I took a deep breath. I must read this message. The gardaí would need to know. It might give a clue as to where he had taken the children.

Then I heard it. The sound of an engine. A car pulling up outside. Car doors opening and closing. The excited laughter of children. Ben's voice telling them not to wake Mom, that she was very tired. I slipped into the lounge and peeped out through a slit in the curtains. There they were, the three children and Ben, complete with Christmas tree strapped onto the roof of the jeep.

I went back to the bedroom, threw myself onto the bed, and buried my face in the duvet. I cried with relief, and also with shame that I had suspected Ben of kidnapping our children. That I had even considered him capable of harming them.

When I dried my eyes, I took myself and my phone into the ensuite, locked the door and read Ben's message.

Hi sleepy-head, hope you had a good lie-in. You must be exhausted after the past week of hospital

visits and looking after the children on your own. I'm taking them into the farmers' market in Paircmoor to buy our Christmas tree for the house and a new set of lights for the garden tree. See you later. Enjoy your rest. Love you. XX

I looked at the calendar on the phone. Of course! It was the fourth of December. The day we had always gone and bought the Christmas tree. We had done so ever since our first Christmas together. I had forgotten about the tree, Christmas decorations and twinkling lights. Ben had not.

I vomited. Maybe because I was pregnant or more likely because I felt such self-disgust. The bile of my shame stayed with me. It burned deep inside, making me feel worthless, despicable. How could I have doubted him so much? All I knew for certain was that my betrayal must remain a secret. Yes, another secret. It would destroy Ben, and doubtless end our marriage, if I told him I had believed him capable of . . . of . . . I had to force myself to acknowledge the unthinkable, so that I could look at it, own it, and bury it in my subconscious. I had thought Ben capable of murdering our children.

There. That's how bad I was.

I texted him back.

Thanks for the rest. Just getting up now. Going to have a shower. See you soon. Love you forever. XXX PS: you should not be driving so soon after coming out of hospital!

Then I pressed send.

I went outside to the front of the house after my shower. The day was cold but bright and, for a change, not raining. The tree was still strapped to the luggage rack on top of the jeep. It was beautifully full and, I reckoned, so tall it would tip the ceiling in the lounge unless there was a chunk cut from the bottom. I smiled as I thought of the artificial tree Mam used to bring down from the top of her wardrobe every Christmas. It constantly shed its plastic needles, until finally, the year I married Ben, a new tree appeared in Mam's home. I had thought the old one had been dumped, but as I cleared out her flat after her death I had found the old one, still on top of her wardrobe. I had kept it and brought it with me to Paircmoor. I'm not sure why. Probably to remember the Christmases Mam and I had spent together. Warm, sharing times. Fun times, when Santa always, miraculously, brought me the best of surprises.

I followed the sound of laughter and went to the old shed. I stood, unseen, to one side of the doorway and watched Ben and the children as they poked around, pulling out boxes of decorations. Anna had a string of tinsel draped around her shoulders and Josh was wearing a headband with antlers. I guessed Ben was searching for the tree-stand. He always forgot where he had stashed it away the previous year. I glanced up to the roof rafters of the old shed, to where I had slotted Mam's bare-branched artificial tree. It had been no less magic to me than the big tree was to my children. Someday I would take it down and tell them about it. I took a step inside the door.

"Try behind the deck chairs," I said to Ben.

He turned around and grinned. His face, like the children's, was glowing with excitement.

"Thank you," he said. "What would I do without you? You know me so well."

I smiled up at him, praying that he did not see shame reflected in my eyes.

Anna and Josh ran towards me, while Rob came to the

door at a leisurely pace. They were all full of news, wanting to tell me about the tree they picked and how they were going to decorate it. Ben pulled the stand out from behind the chairs and gave me the thumbs-up sign.

"Sorry I slept so long," I said. "You should really be resting after all you've been through. And you should *not be* driving."

He put down the stand, caught me by the two arms, and looked deep into my eyes. So deeply I was afraid he would see the poison in my soul.

"I'm done with resting, Leah. That's just a half-life. I want to meet life full on. Challenge it. Control it. And I'm perfectly capable of driving. You don't think I'd do anything to endanger the children, do you?"

I heard the fervour in his voice, the passion, the determination. There was no doubt that Ben was tired of being buffeted by fate and was ready to stand and fight. It might be that he now realised how close to death he had come. Or perhaps it was hearing how his Uncle George had given up on a life so tragically young. Or he might be buoyed by the idea of returning to Dublin, to live in that great big house in Howth. I wondered where this battle was going to take us, or if his new-found enthusiasm would last. But one thing was certain, I would be by his side, trusting him, whichever direction life took us.

"Group hug!" Anna ordered.

I stooped down and picked her up. She shoved a Santa hat skew-ways on my head. Ben picked Josh up, while Rob stood in between us. We had a Parrish family group hug, right there in the quaint old shed.

I glanced up again in the rafters, at the remains of Mam's old tree. I smiled, silently thanking her for sprinkling this moment with angel dust.

CHAPTER FORTY-FIVE

I was in the kitchen in the afternoon, sorting through laundry, when there was a ring on the door. Ben and the children were in the back garden putting lights on the little tree. I went out to the hall to open the front door. Della stood there, looking pale and unsure of herself. It was as if she was waiting for an invitation.

"Come in, Della," I said. "Ben and the children are out in the back garden. They're all a bit manic because the Christmas tree goes up today."

"I know. Fourth of December. I brought trinkets for the children to hang up. If that's alright."

She held a bag in her hand, and for the first time I felt she was really asking me if she could give them to the children. I thanked her and she put the bag on the counter.

"Can I help?" she asked, as she looked at the stack of laundry I had strewn on the kitchen table.

"If you feel like doing some folding with me, that would be great."

We worked silently side by side for a few minutes, the folded stacks of clothing piling up. I guessed that folding unironed clothing must be painful for Della. She was a fanatic about ironing. Or, more correctly, having someone else iron for her.

"How is Ben?" she asked.

I heard a nervous quiver in her voice. I smiled to reassure her.

"He's actually better than I've seen him for a long time. Pity we don't have Christmas every month. He's as excited as the children."

Della dropped the towel she had been folding and sat down.

"Thank God," she said. "I was so worried after last night."

"You mean telling him about your brother George?"

"Well, yes. It must have been a shock for him. It certainly was for me."

I pulled out a chair and sat beside her. I could see her tremble. She was beautifully made-up today, hair perfect, nails freshly manicured, yet I could see the frailty through the veneer.

"I believed I was doing the right thing by saying nothing to my husband or sons about George's suicide. It was a burden I was willing to carry for them. You understand that, don't you, Leah?"

I nodded. I did. Or I thought I did at that particular moment.

She bowed her head. "I think of George every day. He showed me the only kindness I knew in that house in Wexford. I always felt I was being disloyal by tacitly agreeing to banish his memory and his name as if he had never existed. Yet, I couldn't find the words to break the silence."

"That's understandable, Della. You didn't have a choice when you were young. You can never forgive others if you don't forgive yourself first."

I cringed at my glib trotting out of a thought for the day I had read somewhere. Leah the hypocrite. How was I ever going to forgive myself for not seeing how Ben had been suffering through unemployment and isolation out here in Cowslip Cottage? For thinking he had taken the children from me? That he would harm them.

Della nodded her head slowly, as if I had spoken sincere words of wisdom instead of the trite hypocrisy I was spouting.

"You're right," she said. "But I should have taken responsibility when I grew up."

The clock ticked, the lavender fragrance of the fabric softener I used on the clothes wafted around the kitchen, winter sun shone through the window. A peaceful, domestic scene. How deceptive. Both Della and I were in inner turmoil, prisoners of our secrets.

"We all have secrets, Della. Things we decide, rightly or wrongly, never to share. And maybe, after all, some things are best left unsaid."

"Hugh didn't leave me with that choice, did he? I do wish he had been more tactful. Not his forte. But once Ben is alright, then we can work through it."

I caught her arm and took her over to the window. Outside, in the play area, the children were helping Ben wind a string of lights around the little Christmas tree. Anna was wearing more decorations than the tree and the boys, including Ben, had Santa hats. They were all laughing as Ben placed a star on top of the tree. I saw him pick up the plug for the lights, fit it into the outdoor connection box, and screw the lid down. He headed off in the direction of the back door, the long lead of the connection box in his hand.

"Come on," I said to Della, leading her towards the back hall.

Ben opened the door as we got there. He looked at both of us with concern first, then obviously realised we not at loggerheads.

"I was just going to call you, Leah," he said. "Almost time for the switch-on. Great that you're here for it, Mum."

I smiled at Della and raised an eyebrow. She nodded and smiled back. Yes, Ben was happy. Unharmed by the resurrection of Uncle George Roache. Unhaunted by ghosts of his mother's past or by her need to have kept it all secret.

Anna yelled. She had spotted her grandmother. We all walked over to the tree and counted down from ten. Dusk was beginning to fall as Ben flicked the switch in the back hall. The little tree twinkled and flashed red and green and blue bursts of colour. Josh and Anna squealed and ran around the tree, while Rob rearranged the lights into a more symmetrical pattern.

We watched them for a while and then Della turned to me. "I'd best get going," she said.

"Why don't you stay?" I asked.

"Thank you, Leah, but I have things to do in Dublin. I'd rather go now."

"*Stay, Della! Stay, Della!*" the twins chanted.

"I'll be back before Christmas," she told them. "And remember, be very good because Santa will be watching."

At the mention of Santa, Rob gave the same slow, lopsided smile I so loved in his father. But it was too grown up. Too knowing for a five-year-old. I hoped with all my heart I was mistaken, and that Christmas would continue to be magic for him. At least for a few more years.

The children, and Ben, the big child, said their goodbyes

to Della. I heard them start to sing as I walked back into the house with her. She whispered to me that she had things in the car for the children. Christmas presents from Hugh.

"He asked me to give them to you. Do you want to put them under the tree or keep them until Christmas morning?"

The tree in the lounge was not yet decorated and, besides, I couldn't see the twins leaving the parcels unopened until Christmas Day.

"I'll go out with you. We'll hide them in the old shed."

Hugh had really pushed the boat out. The boot of Della's car was packed with gift-wrapped parcels. Three of the boxes were much bigger than the others, all with big red bows tied around them.

"Tricycles for the twins and a new bike for Rob," Della said.

It was amazing how Hugh seemed to know exactly what they wanted. He would be such a great dad someday.

We carried the parcels, big and small, to the old shed. The walls were crooked, the corrugated-iron roof rusted, but the inside was dry and had plenty of hiding spaces. I put the big boxes into the empty space behind the deckchairs where the tree-stand had been. The other parcels we put into a black refusac and stood it between the lawnmower and the roll of wire mesh Ben had bought when he had the notion to get chickens. I wondered why he had changed his mind. I also wondered why I had never asked him.

"Safe from little prying eyes now," I said as I locked the shed and walked Della to her car.

She sat in, leaving the driver's door open.

"Thank you, Leah. For understanding. And for not . . ."

She closed her door and let down the window. "Take care of yourself. Make sure you get plenty of rest and that you're eating well."

She started the car and drove off without giving me a chance to answer. So, was she telling me she knew about my pregnancy?

Ben needed to know. And my doctor did. I must make an appointment to see the GP. Although, I would have to give Ben time to absorb the news of his Uncle George before telling him we would have another mouth to feed. Or not.

I went out to the back garden to join my little crew of carollers who were now singing their own version of 'Silent Night'. The lights reflected in their shining eyes, their faces glowed with happiness. I knew mine did too when Ben stood beside me and put his arm around my shoulders as we belted out 'Jingle Bells'. A crescent moon rose in a clear sky. A new moon. A new start for the Paircmoor Parrishes. All six of us.

I felt so happy I almost caught Ben's hand and put it on my tummy. I almost introduced him to his fourth child. Almost.

I was setting the table for tea when Mags Hoey rang. I answered immediately, thinking there must be trouble in the salon.

"Hi, Mags. Something wrong?"

"Leah! Of course not. Tina and me are the A team. Leah's Salon is buzzing. How is Ben?"

"Good. He came home from hospital yesterday."

"I heard he was at the Farmer's Market with the children this morning. Amazing to think it's just over a week since he was rushed to hospital."

I should have known. Viv Henderson would have had prime view of the market and would have spread the word.

"Anyway," Mags said, "I'm ringing about my Pavlova."

"Really?"

"Yes. You must have heard about it. It's my signature dish. I'm making one this evening and thought, now that Ben is home, you might be able to call over to me. I have takings to give you too. You know I don't like having much cash in my house. Not safe."

"I understand," I said, even though I did not.

Paircmoor seemed to me the safest place in the world. We often forgot to lock the cars, or even the house, before we went to bed, yet none of our belongings were ever touched. Paircmoor crime was limited to untaxed tractors and the brewing of Gobnait Slevin's scalp-scalding lotions.

"I'll pop over to you, Mags, when the children are in bed. I'm looking forward to some Pavlova!"

As soon as I put down the phone, I began to regret having made the arrangement. Because Mags had been so helpful to me since Ben's 'incident', I felt I had to go when she asked, but Ben was just out of hospital. The poison inside me bubbled again, bringing with it the thought that maybe I was afraid to leave the children alone with him. Angry with myself, I went to the lounge where Ben and the children were decorating the big tree. Even from the hallway, I could get the scent of the freshly cut tree and hear the children's laughter. There was Christmas music playing in the background and Ben was humming along as he put decorations on the treetop. He sensed me watching from the doorway and turned towards me. He looked at ease, content, as the children were too. I would have been happy too, if I had not felt so guilty. So disloyal. I pushed the awful feelings back into their hiding place and smiled.

"Mags Hoey has just been on the phone, Ben. She wants me to pop in to see her tonight. She has cash for me. And Pavlova."

Ben grinned. "Doesn't get any better, does it? Money and meringue."

"It's okay with you so? I won't go until the kids are in bed and I won't stay long."

The smile left Ben's face. He looked at me, a puzzled frown on his forehead.

"Of course it's okay. Since when do you have to ask permission?"

"Well, you're just out of hospital."

"Yes, thank goodness. And I intend never having to go back there again. You seem very uptight, Leah. Go to see Mags. Have a chat. Relax. Stop taking all the worries of the world on your shoulders. Just bring some Pavlova home for me."

Josh grabbed my hand then and pulled me over to the tree to admire the decorating he had done. Anna, draped in the skirt of the Christmas tree stand and wearing a little drummer boy decoration in her hair, insisted that I admire each of her decorations individually. Rob was absorbed in his job of helping sort out the tangled lights while Ben was humming as he worked. Happy.

He was so right in his observation. The only tension in the room was in my head.

I went back to the kitchen to finish getting tea, making potato cakes, emptying the dishwasher, sweeping the floor, keeping so busy that I did not have time to think. Time to feel guilty.

***

Mags enveloped me in a warm embrace as I stood on her doorstep. She looked very well. So full of vitality. At least I had no worry that running the salon was too much for her. She seemed to be thriving on it.

"Come in, come in, you skinny little thing," she said. "Sit down at the table there. I'm going to put extra cream on your Pavlova. You need meat on your bones."

"How's Claire?"

"She's fine. Doing a bit of romancing now. About time for her. She's so finicky."

As I sat at the table she prattled on, telling me about the week's events in the salon. Judging by the size of the bundle of cash she handed me, the best thing that ever happened to Leah's Salon was the disaster, turned opportunity, of Minnie Curran's scalded scalp. Or maybe the attraction was curiosity about Ben's dramatic rescue from the cave. A topic of conversation and speculation, according to Mags. Whatever the reason, customers were pouring into the salon.

"Here, before I forget . . ." Mags said, handing me a folded sheet of paper. "Tina made that out. It's the list of products we need to re-order. You can do that from home now, if you'd prefer not to go in."

"I'm very grateful to you, Mags. And to Tina too. I couldn't have coped without you both."

"Don't be daft. Of course you would. You're one of life's copers, Leah."

"You think so? But I'm not, Mags. I'm not. I'm . . ."

I had to stop talking because tears choked my words. I allowed them to because I felt secure with Mags. My surrogate mother. Also because I could no longer accommodate the sheer volume of fear, guilt and unhappiness inside me.

"I should be happy now, Mags. Relieved that Ben is home and in such good form. That the children are happy and healthy. That the salon is doing so well. But I'm not. I'm anticipating disaster at every turn. I'm afraid. What's wrong with me, Mags?"

She placed the two plates she had been carrying on the table, sat beside me, and put her arms around me. The tears and fearful words kept pouring out of me.

"One minute we were living the dream in Dublin, the next Ben was made redundant. One minute my mother was crocheting cot blankets for the twins, the next she was dead. One minute Ben was looking after the children, the next he was smashing a vase and running out the door into a storm. What the hell, Mags? How can I ever trust life again? Or trust Ben?"

Mags got up and went over to her counter. She opened a drawer, took out a box of tissues and put them on the table in front of me. I grabbed a bundle and began to mop my face, thankful that at least I hadn't been wearing mascara. Not even waterproof would have survived my tsunami of tears.

Mags patted me on the back. "Cry as much as you need to, Leah. It's unhealthy to keep it all inside. You'll feel better for getting it off your chest."

She was wrong there. Had I really said out loud that I could not trust Ben? That made me feel worse. Mags knew about Ben and Ellen Riggs. I assumed everyone in Paircmoor had heard the rumours. She probably thought my trust issues were about him being faithful. But they went a lot deeper than that. He had hidden his teenage suicide attempts from me. Also a three-month stay in a mental health facility. He had learned well from Della.

"We've just discovered that an uncle of Ben's committed suicide when he was fourteen years old. First we heard of it. It was never spoken about."

"That would have been some time ago?"

"The nineteen forties."

"Then, of course it wasn't spoken about. Neither was sex, pregnancy or homosexuality. Different times, Leah. Why is the information about Ben's uncle upsetting you now? Do you think there's a link to what happened to Ben last week? On the beach, I mean."

Of course there was a link. George had obviously suffered from depression and so did Ben. But that's where the similarities ended. Ben's suicide attempts were classic cries for help. George's suicide was a rejection of help. I smiled at Mags.

"Vera and Walter Sanquest put my mind at rest on that score. They found him sheltering in the back of the cave, trying to escape the tide. What he did that night was foolhardy, and even stupid, but he didn't intend ending his life. He's paid a big price though."

"So did you."

Mags pushed one of the plates, loaded with a massive slice of Pavlova, in front of me.

"Start on that while I pour your coffee. You need a sugar hit."

I didn't need sugar, but what I did need was Mags to care enough to fuss over me, to hold me while I cried.

But I began to eat her delicious Pavlova, heaped with fruit, smothered in cream and drizzled with a rich butterscotch sauce.

"This is just divine," I told her, and I didn't object when she placed a second slice on my plate.

"I suppose you'll be thinking of coming back to the salon now that Ben's home?" she said.

I wondered if I had misjudged. Again. Was she finding the extra responsibility too much?

"I was hoping to take a few days next week at home. If that would be alright with you and Tina?"

"Of course it is. I told you we're managing fine. And Ben will have to ease himself back into the school run and all that routine. You do know the Presidential election is Tuesday and voting is in the National School – so Rob will have a day off."

"Yes. I've been told. I need to get a bit of organising for Christmas done too. Hopefully we'll be very busy in the salon in the run-up to the holidays."

Mags smiled. "See! Better already! You're looking forward. Taking control. My Pavlova never fails."

She handed me a carefully wrapped plate.

"This is a Pavlova for Ben. I hope he likes it and that it gives him a lift too."

I hugged her, knowing that if she had served up bread and butter, it would have a positive effect. Mags' caring imbued everything she did with warmth. It gave me the courage to face back home to Cowslip Cottage, and to whatever twists and turns of fate awaited me.

CHAPTER FORTY-SIX

Sunday 5th December 2010

Ben had been delighted next morning when I told him I was going to take a few more days off work. It was a treat to sit down to Sunday lunch that day without having to worry about organising the coming week's housework. I had made our favourite dinner, roast pork and apple sauce with roast potato and roast veg drizzled with honey. As flavoursome as it was calorific.

"Am I going to school tomorrow?" Rob asked.

"You are," I told him, "but you have a day off on Tuesday."

"No! I don't want to miss more school!"

"Everyone will, Rob, because the school will be closed. Adults will be going in there to say who they would like to be their new President."

Rob nodded, loaded some food on his fork, put it down again.

"What's wrong with the old President?"

Ben laughed. "You might well ask, Rob! But, since you will have Tuesday off, and so has Mom, I think we should all do something special. What do you say, gang?"

Anna clapped her hands, and so did Josh, forgetting he was holding a spoon. By the time I had the splatter of gravy and mashed potato wiped up, suggestions on how to spend the day were ranging from a trip to Disneyland to visiting the famous caves in the next county.

"I've the best idea," Ben said. "How about we go to Dublin to see Della? We could look at the Christmas lights in the city too."

I stopped mopping up instantly. The children were squealing with excitement but I was stunned. He should have spoken to me about it first. How Della-like of him.

"That would be a very, very, long spin," I said.

"True, but we can share the driving, can't we?"

"I mean for the children, Ben. It's over three hours."

"We can stop halfway," Rob said. "In a garage and get juice and go to the bathroom."

"There!" Ben said, smiling at me. "That's sorted. We'll go to see my mother."

"She said she has things to do. Are you sure she'll be there on Tuesday?"

"Yes, I am. I rang her last night."

Game, set and match to Ben. I looked around at all the happy faces. The children would see me as a spoilsport if I objected. And I really was glad to see Ben taking the initiative. Planning something fun. The children would think so anyway. I'd had enough surprises though. I would talk to him about it later.

After I had served up Mags' Pavlova, Ben sat back in his chair and stretched.

"That was great, but I think we need a bit of exercise now. How about a walk on the beach, Leah? Are you up for it?"

As soon as I heard beach, I was on instant alert. Beach, cave, storm. Why would he want to go back there so soon?

"It's much too cold, Ben. I agree we need a walk, but not by the sea."

"I must go. I need to thank those people. The Sanquests."

My heart stopped beating, and for a second or two I thought it would not restart. Yes, he must thank Walter and Vera, but not until I had told him about my pregnancy first. Or until I warned the Sanquests not to mention that they already knew about it.

"Who are the Sanquests?" Rob asked.

"The people who helped Daddy when he tripped over the branch in the dark," I said quickly. "They called the ambulance to take him to hospital."

"I'd like to say thanks to them too," Rob said.

"You can't see them now. They're away. Visiting their son. They told me they would be gone for two weeks."

My God! I was good at this lying business. I didn't even have to think about that one.

"How about a walk in the woods?" I suggested so brightly that I didn't recognise my own voice.

To my immense relief, Ben agreed.

We had the wood trail to ourselves. The children ran on ahead of us, indifferent to the cold. They stopped every so often to pick up bits and pieces. I knew from experience that I would have to empty their pockets of leaves, sticks, stones and the odd feather or two when we got home. Their voices carried on the still air as they ran along, and their breaths rose in white puffs. I noticed that Rob looked back often, just to be sure we were there. I supposed that it was natural after his routine had been so upset, but it saddened me to see him show signs of insecurity.

"Do you think Rob is alright?" I asked Ben. "He seems

to have taken your stay in hospital harder than the twins. Not that the twins don't care. It's just that Rob is more . . . I don't know. More tuned in to other people's feelings."

"More sensitive?"

"I suppose."

"More like me."

I stopped walking and took Ben's arm so that he stood to face me.

"Are you calling me insensitive?" I asked him.

"Of course not! It's just that you're – pragmatic, I suppose. And that's not a criticism. Of either you or me. Who we are, and how we live our little slice of life is predestined long before we're born."

I frowned, wondering if Ben had, after all, gone for a soul-searching counselling session in the hospital. Or else if this line of fatalistic thinking had been influenced by the revelations about his mother's brother.

"Are you upset about your Uncle George?" I asked. "Learning like that, out of the blue, must be a huge shock for you."

"It was. When I first found out. But that was a long time ago."

"What! What do you mean by a long time ago?"

He was looking at me, as if trying to decide whether he should answer me or not.

"What in the hell are you saying, Ben? That you pretended to be shocked by what Hugh discovered in Wexford?"

Before he could say anything, we heard Rob call to us. When we turned to look, he was walking towards us, a worried expression on his face.

"Why did you stop walking?" he asked. "Is there something wrong? Are you sick, Dad?"

"No, Rob," I reassured him. "Nothing wrong at all. Dad and I are just chatting. Enjoy your walk. We're right behind you."

He looked at both of us for a moment, his eyes dark in his solemn little face. Ben smiled at him. Rob smiled back and then skipped down the path ahead of us. As we followed him and the twins, I thought how great it would be if a smile could fix everything in the grown-up world too.

"So, Ben," I said. "Tell me about it. How you knew about your Uncle George."

He shrugged, as if it was a matter of no consequence.

"Ireland's a small country, Leah. Not too many secrets here."

"Really? You made a good job of keeping this secret from me. So how come Hugh didn't know?"

"He doesn't live here."

I gathered from his glib answer that he was going to make me drag the information out of him.

"When did you find out? "

"When I was in university."

"How?

He sighed. I was annoying him but I needed to know what was going on. Looking back to Hugh's revelation two nights ago, it was apparent that Della had been shocked. She believed she had kept the secret of her brother safe from both her sons. Except that wasn't true for Ben.

"Look, if you must know, Leah, I started going out with a girl in uni. In first year. A law student. As it happened she was from the same area in Wexford as my mother. She knew our family history. All about George and the mad streak in the Roache family."

"Don't disrespect your uncle like that, Ben! So, didn't your mother realise that this girl could have told you about your uncle?"

He shrugged. "She probably would have, had she met her. But I was hardly going to strike up a serious relationship with someone who believed I was crazy."

"I still can't see why you didn't speak to your mother about it. It wasn't fair to allow her think you had never heard of George."

He looked at me and I could see the dark shadow of hurt in his eyes. I wished I had phrased that better.

"I'm sorry, Ben. That came out all wrong. I just meant that you've carried this secret alone for years. I can understand that you felt you were protecting your mother. And maybe Hugh also. But why didn't you share with me?"

Rob was looking back again. I waved at him. Ben caught my hand as we walked along.

"I was afraid I would lose you, if you knew."

I entwined my fingers with his, feeling how warm his skin was, even in the cold.

"I know now. I know about your stay in the Booly Clinic and your suicide attempts. About your Uncle George and his suicide. I'm not going anywhere, Ben. I love you. I always will."

We were nearing the turn on the path and dusk was beginning to fall. Just as I was about to call the children back, I saw a couple come around the corner and begin to walk towards us. They had a yappy little dog with them. I was too far away to see clearly but I was pretty certain the dog had a blue ribbon in its hair. Pilot. The Sanquests' dog. My own recently spoken words about honesty and lack of secrets echoed in my head. Mocking me. I panicked. Should I just blurt out to Ben, here and now, that I was pregnant? That I would have told him earlier if he hadn't marooned himself in a cave at high tide. If I had not, even for just a second, entertained the idea of aborting the baby.

The children were running towards the Sanquests. The twins loved dogs. Every so often they ran a campaign of nagging, hoping to break down our resistance to them getting a puppy. We told them we would when they were old enough to care for it themselves. In the meantime, they launched themselves on every dog they met. Like they were doing with the Sanquests' dog now.

Ben was looking ahead, squinting in the fading light.

"The dog, Leah. I've seen it before. I've heard that bark. It belongs to the woman I met the night of the storm. The woman who lives in Cliff House."

"Vera Sanquest," I said.

"Well! There's a coincidence. I was meant to meet them today, after all. Is that her husband with her? Walter, isn't it?"

"Yes, it is. And Ben, there's something you should know before you talk to them. I told them . . . I-I thought they were away visiting their son."

"Hold it, Leah. Looks like Anna is making a nuisance of herself with the dog. I'd better run ahead and sort out the situation before the dog loses patience with her."

"No, no. I'll go."

I started to run but after two strides my foot caught in a tree root which had been camouflaged by fallen leaves. I fell face down into the mulch. It smelled of death. I felt a pain in my back and something sharp cut my outstretched hand. Ben rushed towards me and helped me to stand.

"Are you okay, Leah? Are you hurt?"

My first thought was that karma was teaching me a lesson. *Woman lies to children about husband tripping over a fallen branch. Woman trips over a fallen branch.* I gingerly felt around my back, put weight on first one leg then the other. Nothing broken.

"I'm fine, Ben. Go get the children."

I stood and watched as he strode towards the Sanquests. Towards what could well be the end of my marriage when they told him about the baby. I began to walk. Why would they mention the pregnancy? Would it be, 'Hello, Ben. Nice to meet you again, and are you looking forward to the birth of your fourth child?' I wasn't sure if they had seen me fall. That would surely cause Vera concern for the baby she knew I was carrying. I began to walk more quickly. Ben had kept secrets from me, hadn't he? And anyway, he hadn't been in a fit state, post-hypothermia and heart attack, to tell him about the pregnancy. I braced myself to fight. To protect my marriage, my children, our future. Ben was shaking hands with Walter and Vera, obviously thanking them. They were chatting, smiling. No sign of shock or anger in Ben's stance.

Vera looked towards me as I approached the group. She held her hand out to me.

"Hello, Leah. It's so good to see Ben out and about so soon. And what beautiful children you have!"

"Us have no dog," Anna said. "Mom and Dad say no, no, no."

Josh repeated a few more no's for good measure. I began to explain that we had decided to wait until they were older. That the children would have to look after the dog in order to teach them responsibility. I waffled on as long as I could about dogs. Then I brought up the Presidential election. I was willing to discuss any topic under the sun as long as it did not relate to pregnancy. I was aware Ben was giving me a puzzled look. He stooped down to the children.

"One last rub for Pilot now," he told them. "Mr and Mrs Sanquest must take him home and put him to bed. It's getting too cold for him."

"Him has a coat," Anna said.

"He must have his supper and go to bed," Walter said. "But maybe Mom and Dad will bring you to visit him sometime. You would all be most welcome."

"Thank you," Ben said. "And of course I'll always be grateful for what you did for me when – when I needed help."

Rob, who had been quietly watching on, spoke up now.

"I want to say thank you too," he said. "It was very good to ring the ambulance for Dad when he fell."

Walter took his hand and shook it.

"You're more than welcome, young man. And don't forget to come out to our house to visit Pilot. He will be delighted to see you."

"And me," Anna and Josh said.

Walter and Vera laughed and said their goodbyes.

Just as they were walking away, Rob called after them. "Mom said you were gone away to see your boy. That you would be gone for a long time."

Vera and Walter glanced at each other and then at me. Ben was looking at me too. Even in the November cold, I felt sweat trickle down my back. Vera nodded towards me. She narrowed her eyes as if trying to work out why I had lied. She smiled at Rob.

"We *will* be going to see him in two weeks from now. Mom just got the times mixed up. We'll spend Christmas with him and our grandchildren."

"Will Pilot be going too?"

"No, Rob. Our son lives in Australia. Too far away for Pilot. He'll be staying with my friend while we're away."

I breathed a sigh of relief as I watched them walk briskly away.

As soon as we got home, I washed and dressed the cut on my hand, which was not near as bad as it had felt at first. In fact, it was quite a small scratch. The pain in my back was still niggling though.

When the children were in bed, Ben and I went to the lounge to watch television. I was worn out from the shock of learning that Ben had known about his Uncle George since before I met him. Another secret he kept from me. And why in the hell was I now taking a leaf from his book of passive lying? Why could I not just tell him I was pregnant? Was I protecting him or myself? And from what?

"I think I'll have a bath and an early night," I told him. "I feel tired."

"That's probably from all the fresh air we had today."

"Probably," I agreed.

"I was delighted to have met the Sanquests. I owe them a lot. I'm glad you were mistaken about them being away."

He was holding my gaze. Daring me to admit I had lied about the Sanquests.

"Take a rest in the morning," he said. "I'll take Rob to school. I'll take the twins with me."

I was about to object when I realised it would be good for both of them. It would serve also to stop speculation about Ben. I kissed him on the cheek. I was weary. I needed all the rest I could get, especially with the trip to Dublin coming up on Tuesday.

"I'll do that. Thanks, Ben. "

"Night, Leah. No more dishonesty from now on. Agreed?"

I nodded agreement and went to bed, too tired and too confused to figure it all out.

CHAPTER FORTY-SEVEN

Monday 6th December 2010

For the second morning in a row, the house was quiet when I woke. I remembered that Ben was taking Rob to school. I had meant to be up to say goodbye to Rob. To make sure he had everything he needed. That thought made me cross with myself. His father could look after him very well. It was just a matter of me allowing him to do it. There was certainly something different about Ben since he had come home from hospital. To my mind he was more confident. More assertive. More positive than I had seen him for a while. I, on the other hand, felt tired, confused and just a little bit out of control. It was almost as if we had swapped places. At least I didn't have to worry anymore about my husband chatting up the beautiful Ellen Riggs at the school gates.

I was having breakfast when Ben and the twins arrived home.

"Us going to school soon," Anna announced.

"Yes, you will," I said. "Bet the teachers are looking forward to it already."

I smiled as I looked at the two of them, fireball Anna and little comedian Josh. The teachers in the kindergarten would have their hands full.

Ben caught them both by the hands

"Right, guys. I'm going to turn on morning TV for you. Mom and I have things to talk about for a little while. Okay?"

They ran on ahead of him into the lounge without a backward glance. I felt a moment of sadness that they were already starting to grow up. To pull away from me. I got up to make fresh coffee, wondering what Ben needed to talk to me about. It made a change to have him initiate a discussion. It also made me a bit nervous. I had two mugs of coffee ready when he came back into the kitchen. He sat down opposite me.

"I need to talk to you about Dublin," he said.

"I told you, Ben. I think it's a long spin for the children. There and back in one day is a bit much. Besides, I would find that drive too taxing, and you can't drive that distance either. You're just out of hospital."

"We can share the driving. And better yet, we could stay over for a night. Mum would be delighted and she has plenty of space."

"If you want to do that, you should leave the trip until Friday. Rob has missed too much school already."

"He's bright. He'll catch up."

"That's not the point, Ben. Besides, I'll probably go into the salon Thursday to Saturday. I told you how busy they've been."

He sighed and put down his mug on the table. "Right. No overnight stay if you say so. But the reason I want us all to go up there is to let you and the children get the feel of the place."

"What are you talking about, Ben? I'm *from* Dublin. It's in my bones. And it's not unfamiliar to the children either."

"Not Dublin. Howth. *The Parrish House*, specifically."

Now I knew what this was about. His mother's plan to lure him back was working. I had to remind myself that I intended keeping an open mind about our future. That it was good to see him looking forward.

"So, Ben, cards on the table. You're not happy in Paircmoor. You want to move back to Dublin. Your mother's offer makes it possible now. How am I doing?"

He smiled at me. "Sharp as a tack! You always were. But, it's not just about me. I know you love it here and that you've worked really hard to establish your salon."

"*Our* salon. I couldn't do it without you."

He frowned. I knew he felt I had patronised him. It was true that I could not have gone out working if he had not looked after the children. But there was the nub of at least one of his problems.

"The point is, Leah, that besides fresh air and a clean environment, Paircmoor has little to offer us as a family. And before you say it, yes, coming here was a joint decision. I *did* think it the right choice at the time."

"And you don't now?"

"No. Not for me. Not for the children."

That statement took me aback. "Is this your way of telling me stay here, while you and the children move back to Dublin?"

"Of course not! Don't be so touchy. But you must agree that in Dublin the children would have better educational opportunities. And I would have more chance of picking up work. Firms are beginning to take on staff again. Very slowly, but it's happening. Paircmoor won't wake up for another fifty years. If ever."

I nodded. There was some sense to what he was saying,

though I didn't agree that the children would be better off in crowded classrooms. The small numbers in Paircmoor were a big advantage. But that was just up to primary level. They would have to travel from here to attend second level in the town and even further for university when the time came. I noticed, despite his denials, that he had it all worked out for himself and the children, but no mention of how he saw me fitting into his vison for the future. Or even if I did.

"The point is, Leah, Mum has everything in place now. Just waiting on our say-so to sign the house over to me. Then she will be moving to the quayside apartment as soon as it's renovated. We're being handed an opportunity. It would be mad not to grab it. Though a touch of madness is also part of the Parrish legacy."

I decided to ignore his oblique reference to George Roache. One problem at a time.

"Yes, I know it's a very substantial house. Extremely generous of your mother to sign it over to you. Generous of Hugh also not to insist on his share. But because of its size the overheads must be huge. Heating, electricity, maintenance. I dread to think what it costs to run."

"But once we have sold here, we would have a nest egg to tide us over."

"Where would that leave me, Ben? Cowslip Cottage is fifty-fifty ownership. I would want my name on the deeds of the Howth house. I'm not sure your mother would like that."

"We can always add your name once the rest of the legal work is through. It's a straightforward procedure. Does that mean you would consider moving? What about your salon?"

"Oh, I'm not saying anything other than that I'll

consider it. There are so many things to take into account. One of them being the god-awful name on the house."

Ben laughed. "You mean you wouldn't like living in *The Parrish House*. Nearly as bad as Cowslip Cottage."

I ignored that jibe. Nor did I even hint at the fact that we might soon need a bigger house to accommodate our growing family. My back was still aching after my fall yesterday. At least I assumed the pain was from the fall. It was gone past time that I saw my doctor. And certainly time that I told my husband that he was about to become a father for the fourth time. If that was what he wanted. What I wanted.

I looked at Ben. His eyes, so dark but with a sparkle in them today, were mesmerising. That tingle of physical attraction to him I had first felt had not diminished over the years. And yet, I didn't know him at all, did I?

"I'm going to make an appointment to see the doctor today." I said. "Do you want me to make an appointment for you?"

"No, thanks, Leah. I'll go to see him sometime next week. There's no hurry. The hospital gave me what medication I need for now."

"Like what?"

Ben looked askance at me, as if deciding whether to answer or not.

"Blood thinners, cholesterol medication if you must know. And sleeping pills since I had a lot of trouble sleeping in hospital."

He didn't say his treatment was none of my business, but I understood the implication from his defensive tone.

"Your turn now," he said. "Is your back still giving you trouble? You must have pulled a muscle when you fell yesterday."

I nodded. Words stuck in my throat. I told myself I needed to check with the doctor first. To find out if all was well with the pregnancy. That it would be upsetting to Ben to confront him with yet another choice to make. At least until he had fully recovered from his ordeal.

Truth was, I didn't want to share my news with him. I believed that, at that time, Ben could not cope with another child. And I knew, in my heart, I could not cope with a termination.

Stalemate.

The doctor's surgery was packed. As usual. He was the only GP for the extensive catchment area surrounding Paircmoor. The magazines were always last year's, so I had brought my book with me. I tried to read but it was difficult to concentrate on my novel as the room buzzed with conversation, coughs, sniffles, and whinges from children. The noise suddenly stopped as the secretary came to the door to call the next patient.

"Leah Parrish, please. The doctor will see you now."

I felt fear in the pit of my stomach. Suppose he said I was about to lose the baby. Suppose he said I was having twins again and then we would have five children to feed, clothe and educate. All the supposes tumbled around in my head as I followed the secretary down the narrow corridor and into the consulting room.

Doctor Kelly waved me to a seat without lifting his eyes from his computer screen. He was obviously looking up my chart. Not much to research, as thankfully I had been very healthy since arriving in Paircmoor. Eventually he raised his head.

"It's a while since I've seen you, Leah. What can I do for you?"

Much to my shock and embarrassment, I felt tears in my eyes and my words were strangled by a tightness in my throat. What could I say? *I'm pregnant – I want the baby but not now?*

Doctor Kelly pushed a box of tissues towards me, then sat back in his chair. "Take your time, Leah."

I thought of the packed waiting room outside and of the growing baby inside me. I did not have time and neither did the doctor.

"I'm pregnant."

"Ah! When was your last period?"

"I'm not exactly sure. Ten or eleven weeks ago."

"You've done a test?"

"Yes. Positive."

"How are you feeling?"

"Good until yesterday. I fell. On my face. But I've got a pain in my lower back since."

"I see. I'll do a quick examination and then I'll need a urine sample. Hop up on the couch, please."

Examination, urine and blood samples done, I sat in front of him again. I had the illogical fear that he could see right into my head and would judge me for the fact that I had considered, even if just for a short time, terminating this pregnancy. And might yet have to. Apart from the fact that Doctor Kelly was a middle-aged man with traditional views, abortion was not available in Ireland. Not at that time. And I wanted, needed, my baby to be alright.

"Is the baby okay?"

He nodded and smiled at me. "Yes, indeed. You have a healthy nine-week pregnancy. I think you may have pulled a muscle when you fell. Nothing a bit of rest won't cure. I'll book you in for your scan in the hospital just to be sure. The secretary will be in touch with your appointment."

"Thank you, Doctor. There's just one other thing. My husband, Ben. I'm sure you've had notification from the hospital about his recent accident. If it was an accident."

He narrowed his eyes as he looked at me. He seemed wary.

"How *is* Ben?"

"Good. More positive, I think. But I'm worried about telling him of this pregnancy. I know you've prescribed anti-depressants for him. Could the –"

The doctor's hand shot up, palm towards me.

"I'll have to stop you there, Leah. As my patient, I guarantee you one hundred per cent confidentiality. Ben is also my patient, so I owe him exactly the same. I cannot, and will not, discuss his treatment with you. Unless with his permission, which I don't have. I'm sorry."

I felt as if I'd been slapped across the face. There were so many things I had wanted to ask him. For instance, if he knew that Ben had been stashing his anti-depressants, not taking them. If he had been made aware of Ben's past history, both his own and his Uncle George. If the depression was likely to take over his life again and lead him to another overdose, another slashed wrist. Another brush with death on a tide-swept beach.

The doctor's stern look and clipped words left me with no option but to pick up my bag and coat to leave. I looked back as I reached the door. Doctor Kelly was concentrating on the computer screen again. Next patient, I assumed. His attitude made me angry as well as worried. I needed to know exactly what Ben's mental condition was. How could we make a measured decision about returning to Dublin if his battles with deep depression were rooted in his childhood home? The only thing I knew for certain was that he undoubtedly loved Rob and the twins with all his heart and soul. But I did not know if he had the capacity to share that love with another child.

I needed time and space to think. To ease the hurt of the doctor's professionally correct, but cold, rejection of my plea for advice. The salon was my place of refuge and today, being Monday, it was closed. I passed by the turnoff for Cowslip Cottage and headed for the salon.

I made myself a coffee and sat there in the empty salon, in the dim December light, letting the coffee go cold as I reviewed the disaster my life had become. My husband, I had to admit, was a liar. Not that he overtly lied to me. He had not, and probably never would, tell me the full truth. And yes, he had now informed me about his past episodes of depression, about his family history. But only because circumstances forced him to.

I sat there for a long time, wondering what else was going on in Ben Parrish's head and who I could turn to for help.

That was the day I realised that, while first puberty, then unemployment, had exacerbated Ben's difficulty, the real trigger had been his genetic inheritance through the Roache line. I shook with fear as it finally dawned on me that my children, my beautiful Rob and my darling twins, my vulnerable inch-long foetus, all shared that same bloodline. Also I had no idea what I had brought to them through my unknown father's line. Of course, it was different now. They could be monitored, counselled, medicated if needed. But I could not be inside their heads.

Just as I had no idea what was happening inside my husband's head.

CHAPTER FORTY-EIGHT

Tuesday 7th December 2010

We were on the road to Dublin by seven o'clock next morning, three sleepy children in the back of the jeep. I was tired after the early start, but Ben was so full of energy that I felt no guilt in having a snooze as he drove. I didn't wake until the jeep stopped at a service station. I woke to the children chattering and laughing in excitement. We were at our halfway stop and they could now have their promised juice and treat.

The car park was full with trucks, camper vans and cars. People on the move. These modern-day oases off the motorways always fascinated me, wondering where people were going, and why. In fact, I could have asked the same questions of myself. Yes, I was about to visit Ben's childhood home in Howth, but was I going to inspect my future home?

Taking the children to the bathroom and shepherding them to a table for their snack allowed little time for soul-searching. I took over the driving when we got back to the jeep, glad that traffic was light. The nearer we got to Dublin, the more excited the children became. And as we headed north from the city towards Howth, they started a chorus of '*Are we there yet?*'.

"Not too far now," I assured them. "We'll soon be in Della's house."

"Dad's house too," Rob said. "Cos he lived there when he was small."

"I was born there," Ben said. "And I stayed there until Mom and I bought our own house."

"Were you borned a baby or a daddy?"

Anna's question sent Rob into a fit of giggles. Josh showed his solidarity with his brother by joining in. That sent Anna into a sulk, until Ben distracted them by telling them about the seesaw he and Hugh had in their garden when they were young.

Concentrating on my driving, I was unprepared for Rob's next question.

"Where did my Granny Scally live?"

Granny Scally. My mam. Rob had been just three years old, little more than an infant, when my mother had died. They had been close. She, more than anyone, recognised that Rob valued quietness and calm above all else. "He's one of life's thinkers," she used to say.

"Granny Scally and I used to live in the city," I told him.

"Where? Can we go there today?"

"No, Rob, we can't," Ben told him. "The place where Mom used to live when she was small is gone. People needed to build shops and offices there, so they took away the houses."

"Oh! Where did you and Granny Scally go then, Mom?"

Where indeed? I was already married and living with Ben in my four-bed detached in a nice suburb, when the inner-city flats were demolished. They should have gone years before that. They were shabby, damp, increasingly a hub for social problems. And yet, it had been a good place to grow up. Mam and I were an integral part of that underprivileged community. Lacking in money and educational opportunities but blessed by supportive friends and neighbours. Ben was not saying anything. I supposed he was leaving it to me to tell Rob what I wanted him to know. What I could allow myself to remember.

"Granny Scally went to live in a new house, Rob. A very nice one."

"I don't remember it."

"You were very little then."

Yes, Rob had only been two when I was pregnant with the twins. Busy with my family and my social life. Mam had been rehoused outside town. In an area she was unfamiliar with, beside people she did not know. If I had visited her more often, if I'd had her around to our house on a regular basis, if I had been the type of daughter my mother deserved, I would have seen how unhappy she was. How lonely. How sick she was. Her death certificate attributed her passing to pancreatic cancer. I saw it in her face the day she came to attend the twins' christening. The jaundiced skin, the lifeless eyes, the deep sadness, the knowledge that she would not live to get to know the twins or see her beloved Rob grow up. That was also the day I acknowledged that my selfishness had contributed to her dying. Leah Parrish, née Scally, always the guilty one.

"What do you remember about Granny Scally?" I asked Rob.

"She smelled nice. And she read me stories and did funny voices. She used to sing to me too."

Ben and I exchanged glances, amazed at how much detail Rob remembered. I made a mental note to talk to Rob about my mother in future, just as often as I spoke silently to her.

"That's why Mom is such a good singer," Ben told the children. "She inherited her lovely voice from Granny Scally."

"Me too!" Anna said. "I'll sing."

She did. The same line over and over. '*Twinkle, twinkle little star, how I wonder what you are.*' Or words to that effect.

I was relieved to see *The Parrish House* come into view.

The room Della had ushered me into was roughly the area of the flat where I was reared. It had built-in wardrobes, an ensuite bathroom and a window overlooking the extensive back garden. The place where Ben had played on the seesaw with Hugh, and where he was now kicking football with his children. I walked to the window and looked down. From my vantage point, Ben looked healthy and happy, infused with a zest for life I had thought lost for good. Sounds of laughter drifted up, the children's light and carefree, Ben's deep and hearty. A glorious chorus, and a very powerful argument for agreeing to move here.

"Ben enjoyed having all this space to himself as a boy," Della said.

"This was his room?" Lucky boy.

"Oh! I forgot that you hadn't seen it before."

"I never got past the kitchen, Della."

I sat down on the double bed and looked around, taking in the chest of drawers, the bedside lockers, the order and neatness, a few discreet paintings. There was no trace of Ben in this room. It was pure Della. She sat on the bed beside me.

"I'm sorry," she said. "I could have, should have, been more welcoming to you."

"No need to apologise, Della. I *do* realise it was difficult for you. You had a different view of the type of woman your son should marry. Let's leave it at that."

"That's kind of you, Leah, but I can see now how much damage leaving things unsaid has caused. I resented Hugh for what I saw as interference in my family history. But it is, in fact, also his history. And Ben's. I owe them an apology too."

I turned my head to look at my snobby, cold, mother-in-law. What I saw was a vulnerable old lady, confused, sad, and, I thought, genuinely regretful.

"Della, every family has secrets. Everyone has regrets. I'm sorry too, for not making a greater effort to bridge the gap between us. But the future can be different, can't it? And because we're being completely honest with each other from now on, I should tell you the Scally family also has a secret. I don't know who my father was. Or is. My mother simply refused to tell me."

"I know."

"Ben told you?"

"Yes. He told me before he proposed to you."

"Is this why you were so against Ben marrying me?"

"No! I just felt . . . Well, because of his history of – you know – depression, that maybe he shouldn't marry at all. That he was not ready for the responsibility of a baby already on the way. And also, in truth, I felt you and he had little in common. I've made a lot of mistaken judgements."

I could have said 'ditto' to that, but instead I sat there speechless. Ben had never told me he had discussed my father with Della.

She lowered her head, refusing to meet my eyes.

"Now that I've learned more about Ben's background,"

I said, "I think I'll try to trace my own father. It may be important information for the children in the future."

"Your mother was obviously protecting you, Leah. Believe me, you need to think carefully about this. About whether you want to rake up the past. The truth isn't always liberating."

"You've changed your tune very quickly. I thought you appreciated all this new openness Hugh stirred up. Why are you warning me? It's as if you know something horrendous about my father. Do you?"

"Of course I don't. How could I?"

That was true. Della Parrish had moved in very different circles to my mother, and probably to my father also. They would have had no reason to interact. My intrusion into the middle-class circle was an aberration that reverberated uncomfortably in our supposedly classless society. That discomfort still sat there, an unbreachable gulf between me and my mother-in-law.

"Your mother was a lovely woman," Della said. "You must miss her."

I wished Mam could be there to hear those words. I remember being so proud of how she had reacted with dignity when Della spoke down to her on the few occasions they met. In a way, they were alike, Della and Mam. Both the keeper of secrets.

"I miss her every single day," I said.

Suddenly she smiled at me. "See the bottom drawer in the chest? The one with the lock and key."

I looked to where she was pointing and immediately thought of the locked drawer in Ben's desk in Cowslip Cottage, containing the three bottles of anti-depressant. A cold feeling came over me. Had Ben locked his stash of pills away here when he had been a teenager? Just like he was doing now?

"Young Ben's secret place?" I asked. "For his private things?"

"It was sacrosanct because it was where he kept his diary. Or I should say diaries. Something the psychiatrist in the Booly Clinic recommended for him. I have no idea how, but it worked, didn't it?"

"Did it?" I asked, flabbergasted yet again at Della's ability to see things as she wanted them to be.

Just then I heard a commotion as Ben and the children climbed the stairs.

I stood up and loosened the belt on my jeans a notch. I would soon need the next size. I saw Della glance at my tummy, eyebrows raised, but I had no intention of confirming her suspicions before I had told Ben.

The children burst into the room, cheeks glowing, followed by an equally shiny Ben.

"We're going to the village. For lunch," Rob announced.

"Pizza an' ice cream," Josh said.

"Me too," Anna chorused. "C'mon, Mom. C'mon, Della."

Della looked at me and laughed.

"I think we had better leave the house tour until later," she said. "We can't miss out on pizza and ice cream."

I saw love for my children reflected on her face. I smiled at her and took her hand as she stood up. It was worth it to see the surprise on Ben's face. I winked at him and the raised eyebrows were quickly replaced by a smile.

That smile lasted through lunch, a visit to Howth Market, a stroll up to the Castle, and a brisk walk along Claremont beach so that the children could let off steam and the adults allow the stiff breeze blow away those trials and tribulations light enough to be carried on the wind.

Dusk was already starting to fall by the time we packed the children into the jeep again. When I finished strapping them in, I sat into the front passenger seat, assuming Ben would drive. Della had driven her own car down to the village and was parked beside us. I saw that Ben was talking to her. He walked over to the jeep, opened my door, and leaned in.

"Would you mind if I went for a quick walk along the cliff path? Just for old times' sake. Best view in the world from up there."

"You won't be too long, will you? The children are getting tired. Besides, we promised them we'd show them the lights in town."

"Sure. I'll be an hour and a half. Tops. Mum is leaving me her car, so she'll be travelling back with you."

I got out of the jeep and looked up at Ben.

"Translation: you're going to walk the loop. It will take two hours because you will stop to take photos of Ireland's Eye and Lambay Island. Despite the lack of light."

Ben grinned. "Well guessed."

"No, Ben. It's not a joke. You're just after a heart attack. Please don't go too far. And don't climb."

He gave me a peck on the cheek, turned his back and strode away.

I was still looking after him, wondering if I should go and drag him back, when Della got into the jeep.

"He's looking so well, Leah, don't you think? Thankfully the 'revelations' have not had an adverse effect on him."

She threw a furtive look in the children's direction. They were all too full of pizza and fresh air to bother listening to the conversation in the front of the jeep. I tied my safety belt, then turned to my mother-in-law. There was pleading in her eyes. A need for reassurance. I made a snap decision.

"Della, I think you should know that the reason Ben has taken the news of your brother George so well is that he has known about it for a long time."

I started the jeep and concentrated on driving back to The Parrish House. The children chatted amongst themselves but not a word passed between Della and me until we pulled up outside her house.

"How long have you known?" she asked me.

"Since Hugh came back from Wexford. Just about the same time as you."

She got out of the car without saying a word. I followed on in silence, knowing that I had already said too much.

CHAPTER FORTY-NINE

Ben could not help but smile when he saw Leah and Della sit side by side in the front of the jeep. It looked like peace had broken out between them. Or tolerance at least. He waited until the jeep disappeared from sight, then he turned back and walked to his mother's car. Traffic was building as he headed towards town but he should still make his five o'clock appointment with ease. He had travelled this route so often in the past he knew several shortcuts if needs be. He was casually dressed. Wearing a suit would have aroused Leah's suspicion. The last thing he needed.

It was just gone ten minutes to five when he drove onto the familiar street and parked in the lot at the back of the building. Concentrating on finding a space, he had not noticed the changes to his former workplace until he walked around to the front door. The big feature window with *Walton, Walton & Meade, Architects* stencilled in gold lettering, had been replaced by a revolving door, above which a discreet sign read *Walton Architects & Design*. Ben frowned. Edward Meade must have been put out to pasture. Della had not mentioned it. But then he had not told his mother he was coming to his former workplace.

He pushed through the door and into a bright reception area, all glass and mirrors. Neither the old reception desk, nor the old receptionist, were anywhere to be seen. A young woman, dark-haired, groomed and manicured to perfection, sat behind the semi-circular counter, a meticulously shaped eyebrow raised as she looked at Ben.

"How may I help?"

"Ben Parrish. I have an appointment to see Mr Walton."

"Oh! Yes, Mr Parrish. Mr Walton is meeting with clients at the moment and he apologises for the delay. He'll see you shortly. Would you like a coffee while you wait?"

"No, thank you."

"Take a seat, then. You'll find reading material on the coffee table if you want it."

The first five minutes of waiting he spent looking around, taking in the changes in the decor. No wonder Edward Meade had gone. He would have found the feature black wall and modern art unbearable. It was edgy, Ben thought, but not very original. He spent the next five minutes flicking through a few of the design magazines. He checked his watch. He had been waiting for ten minutes and getting anxious. He would give it another five and then remind Ms Raised Eyebrow at the desk that he was here. He stood to stretch his legs. It would have been good to walk along the cliff path. So much of his youth had been spent there. He knew every twist and turn, every rise and fall of that walk. Each ebb and flow of the tide that had called to him so often. A soothing voice when the noise of his thoughts had been too raucous to bear. The soles of the trainers he was wearing squeaked as he walked on the polished concrete floor. Embarrassed, he sat. And waited. For another ten minutes. He was worrying now that Leah might ring, fussing to know if he was alright. He took out his phone and switched it off.

A door at the opposite end of reception opened. Ben saw Garry Walton usher a couple out of his office and accompany them as far as the front door. He looked away. Garry was an upstart. A prick of the highest order who would not have been employed there except that his father, Charles, owned the company. Ben felt his anger rise as he remembered how Garry Walton had never pulled his weight on any project, told tales to his father, blamed others for his mistakes, came and went when it pleased him. He took deep breaths. Garry didn't matter. It was Charles he was here to see. A gentleman. A great friend to Dad when he had worked here.

Garry approached the couch where Ben was sitting. He must be thirty now but still looked mid-twenties. The swagger was new though. He held his hand out, and Ben stood and shook it.

"Ben! Nice to see you. Sorry for the delay. What can I do for you?"

"Nothing, Garry, thank you. It's your father I'm here to see."

"Dad? You're a bit late then. He retired six months ago."

Ben started. Fuck! True, when he rang to make the appointment, he had asked to see Mr Walton. But he had meant Charles. Not the poor excuse for a Walton standing before him now. Why had Mum not told him Charles had retired?

"I'm surprised your mum didn't tell you. She was at his leaving do."

It took all Ben's self-control not to show his anger. He forced a smile.

"Really? And I see Edward Meade's name is gone off the sign. Is he retired too?"

"He is. About time. Edward's ideas are very last century. So, how are you? I believe you had a caving accident recently."

Jeez! How did he know? Paircmoor was a whole world away from here.

"I'm very well, thank you, Garry. I'll be getting back to work again."

Garry stared at him. From top to toe. From windblown hair to sandy trainers. Ben cringed, deeply regretting his decision to come here at all.

"As you can gather, Ben, I'm at the helm now. My focus is on the top end of the residential market. You know what they say, every recession throws up new millionaires. It's certainly true. And they're spending on their des res. No expense spared."

"Well, congratulations. Glad to hear the company is thriving. I –"

Garry's hand shot up to stop Ben finishing his sentence.

"Ben, if you've come here to ask for a job, I'm sorry. The answer will have to be no. I respect your skill set, but it wouldn't fit with our current profile. I explained all that to your mother only a few days ago."

Ben shoved his hands into the pockets of his jacket. Otherwise he might have punched Garry Walton in the smug face. He shook his head.

"No, no, Garry. Actually, I have plans. I've been head-hunted by an American firm."

"Oh! Good luck then."

"I just dropped by to say hello to your father for old times' sake. Do please tell him I was asking for him."

Garry pulled up the cuff of his shirt and looked at his watch. A Rolex from what Ben could see.

"Sorry," he said. "Must dash. I've a planning meeting to attend. Drop by if you're around the area again."

Then he was gone in a flurry of self-importance.

Ben left, eyes cast down, avoiding the interested stare of Ms Raised Eyebrow.

Traffic was heavy when he drove out onto the street. He would be late back. Leah might be worried enough to drive down to the village when she got no answer from his phone. He turned it on. The lesser of two evils.

All the way back, his anger simmered. Why had his mother had not told him Charles Walton and Edward Meade had retired? Or that she had canvassed for a job for him? She could have saved him humiliating himself. And why had she mentioned the 'caving' accident in far-off Paircmoor? On another planet. Was everyone in the country talking about Ben Parrish, he of the sandy trainers and obsolete skill sets? He imagined Della begging Garry-pigging-Walton. Asking him to give her poor, half-mad, half-drowned, half-alive son, a job. Please, please, please, take him. Nobody else will. And Garry had said no.

Ben shook his head in amazement. His mum was only paying lip service now to the Hugh-driven policy of openness and honesty. The fact was, she'd had no alternative as far as acknowledging her suicidal older brother, George Roache, was concerned. Hugh had dragged George's sad spirit back from his place of peace. Exposed him to the scrutiny and censure of the next generation. And for what? Truth? It was certain Della still held a headful of other secrets she would never reveal. All day, every day, she had to guard each word she said in order to protect her cache of secrets. No wonder she was so uptight. So controlled. She was the obsessive keeper of secrets. Another victim of the Roache propensity towards insanity.

His phone rang. It was Leah. He was stuck in a line of traffic, six kilometres outside Howth. He was humiliated. Angry. He turned off his phone.

It was dark outside and getting very windy. Echoes of a stormy night in Paircmoor when Ben had gone for his ill-fated run. I shivered and then had a stern word with myself. My husband was no longer the distraught man he had been on that night. Eleven nights ago. Such a short length of time to pull himself up from the depths of despair that had driven him towards the raging tide.

"He's gone for ages." I said to Della.

She was making coffee for us both. Getting out cups and saucers. Milk in a jug. No mugs or milk cartons on *The Parrish House* table. The twins were upstairs, having a nap, while Rob was in Hugh's room reading one of the dozens of comics Hugh had hoarded there since his boyhood days.

"It's a long walk, Leah," Della said. "And you can be sure he'll meet people he knows along the way."

"*Hmm.* I suppose."

I looked at my phone. It sat on the table in front of me. I knew Ben would be annoyed if he felt I was keeping tabs on him. I was. It was too soon after 'the incident' to have him out, alone, in the dark, on a clifftop. I picked up my phone and keyed in his quick dial number. It rang. At least he had it turned on. Then it stopped ringing. I rang again. Straight to voicemail.

Della put my coffee in front of me.

"I don't know what's going on," I said. "His phone was ringing but then it suddenly stopped. I wonder if I should drive down the village. Make sure he's alright."

She sat down opposite me and began to slice the cake she had brought to the table.

"Just sit there and drink your coffee while the children are asleep. Getting them all ready for bed before you travel was a good idea, but exhausting. The twins are little firecrackers, aren't they?"

I laughed. That was a polite way of describing the hyper behaviour of the excited pair. They had giggled and wriggled their way into their nightclothes.

"You could, of course, stay the night. No need to disturb the little ones. Let them sleep on."

I heard the note of yearning in her voice. I understood. This big house must be very lonely for her with nothing but echoes from the past to fill the empty rooms. And what a wonderful home it would be for the children. All three, or maybe four, of them. Earlier, Della had brought me from room to room, from the study to the drawing room, dining room, the five bedrooms. She had stuffy names for rooms that were, in fact, light-filled and full of potential. I could not help imagining the changes I would make, the colours I would introduce, the life and laughter the children would bring to *The Parrish House* in Howth. The house which needed to again be a home. But the decision was too big to rush into. And it would have to be made by Ben and me. Alone.

I smiled at Della. "Next time I'll make sure I pack for a sleepover. They would love that."

"Thank you," she said. "Thank you so much."

The key rattled in the front door. I breathed a sigh of relief as Ben came into the kitchen.

"I was getting worried about you," I said.

"Sorry. I met a few people I know. I was chatting."

I exchanged glances with Della. She had been right and I had been unnecessarily worried.

"Mum, I bumped into Garry Walton. He told me his father and Don Meade have left the company. Big changes since I was there. You never told me."

"I forgot what with one thing and another."

"You forgot you were at Charles Walton's retirement party? You must be getting a bit bothered, Mum. Anyway, where are the kids? We'd want to be hitting the road."

I sensed tension between Della and Ben. I stood up. I would go get the children, give them their supper, go through their bedtime routine with them and then put them in the jeep. That should give Ben and Della plenty of time to sort whatever was bothering them.

I was just to the top of the stairs when I heard Ben's footsteps behind me. I turned to look at him and he was smiling. Relaxed. I realised then that I was the uptight one.

Because the children were already in their nightclothes, it took only thirty minutes to feed and take them to the bathroom. They were very much awake and excited about driving through the city to see the Christmas lights.

"I'll be down to Paircmoor soon," Della said, as the children hugged her.

"Why don't you stay for Christmas?" I asked.

"Thank you, I'd love that. But I've already promised Hugh I'd go to him. Next year. Maybe Hugh and Piper could come to Ireland and we'll all have Christmas together. It would be fun."

Yes, it would be fun. And fun was what the whole family needed so badly. And maybe, by next year there would be another little Parrish for Santa to visit.

I looked back as we drove down the avenue. Della was standing on the top step, a lonely figure. I waved. The children waved. I noticed Ben did not. Maybe it was because he was driving. And maybe not. I didn't ask and he didn't say.

After the magic of the city-centre lights, the children fell sound asleep. So did I.

I didn't wake until we were crunching up along the gravelled avenue of Cowslip Cottage.

CHAPTER FIFTY

Wednesday 8th December 2010

I had another lie-in on Wednesday morning. It was as if I was the one recovering from hypothermia and a heart attack while Ben looked after me. I slept right through the children's breakfast, nor did I hear the front door close and the jeep start up as Ben drove Rob to school. I woke to a kiss on the forehead from Ben and the twins bouncing on the bed.

"Ben! Has Rob gone to school? You should have woken me!"

"No. You need the rest. You're back to the salon tomorrow, aren't you?"

"I'd better. It's been so busy there, Mags and Tina must be exhausted."

"I'm sure they could manage for another while if you need them to. You're looking very pale. Do you think you might be anaemic?"

I leaned back against my pillows and looked Ben straight in the face. Tried to read his expression. To see a sign that he was asking me if I was pregnant. Did he know? Why else would he ask about anaemia? He was aware I had needed iron supplements to treat anaemia during both of my pregnancies. But no. How could he know? Unless. Unless Della had said something to him. I was certain she knew. And I was just as certain I didn't want to mention the pregnancy to Ben. Until the time was right.

"Maybe I *am* anaemic," I said. "The doctor took a blood test yesterday."

"How is your back?"

"Much improved, thank you."

He clapped his hands to get the twins' attention.

"Listen up, you two, we must look after Mom. She's tired. Deal?"

The twins jumped into bed, one on either side of me. I cuddled them close to me, kissed Josh on his silky hair, and Anna on her mop of blonde curls. Ben put his hands underneath the duvet and began to tickle their toes. The laughs of the twins were loud enough to raise the ghosts of the workhouse from their rest. Ben and I looked at each other and shared the acknowledgement that here was another precious moment we would remember when we were old, and the twins grown. I filed it away with the other treasured memories, like when Rob took his first step, the first scan of the twins.

Ben took the twins to the kitchen to get my breakfast ready while I reluctantly got out of bed to face the day. I was conflicted about going back to work. It was good that the salon was busy. Hopefully the increased business would continue, at least until Christmas, to tide us over that expensive season. And after Christmas? Who knew? The increased custom was most likely driven by curiosity about Ben's brush with death. A form of onlookers at a roadside crash, with the added benefit of a hairdo thrown in. And how ungrateful was I? People in Paircmoor had been very kind and genuinely concerned. And yet, as I showered and dressed, I wished with all my heart that I could stay at home with Ben and the children. All we needed was a lotto win. A big one.

They had made me coffee, boiled egg and toast. The twins had set my place at the table with an array of spoons and two pots of jam. They stood either side of me when I sat.

"Thank you so much," I said. "This is beautiful. You're the best."

Ben served up the food and then dressed the twins in their coats and hats. It was a sunny day, but cold.

"I'll take them out to the back garden," he said. "We can keep an eye on them from here."

"We fix the tree for Santa," Anna said and Josh nodded in agreement.

They ran into the back hall ahead of Ben. I went to the window and watched as they began to pull bits of weeds and drape them on the tree. Ben was issuing instructions I could not hear, but I knew he would be warning them to stay in the play area, not to go near the stone wall, and no fighting. I hoped that someday my children would realise how lucky they were to have such a loving father.

I sat back down at the table and thought about the advice Della had given me to forget about my father. My absent father. The man who had rejected Mam and me. Maybe she was right. Why would I want to know about him? I didn't need him. And Mam had her reasons for not wanting me to know. That's what frightened me. What had she been trying to protect me from? Was he violent? Criminal?

"Hey! I slaved over that egg and you're letting it go cold."

I started as Ben came back into the kitchen.

"Sorry," I said. "I was just thinking about your mother."

"Good or bad thoughts?"

"Good actually. I enjoyed yesterday. It was my first time really seeing the house. You were so lucky to have been reared there."

"Was I?"

"Well, of course! It's a beautiful house."

"Now you said it. It was a house. Space for all of us to live our separate lives. Enough scope for loneliness and isolation."

He was standing at the counter, pouring a coffee for himself.

"Do you want a top-up?" he asked me.

I shook my head. I was aware that this could be a breakthrough moment. That Ben might truly open up about the depression which had plagued his teens.

"Come and sit down, Ben. Tell me all about when you were young. You know, until quite recently all I've had was the sanitised, privileged upbringing version. I envied you."

He remained standing, looking out the window at the twins as they played.

"I explained the family dynamic to you before, Leah. Dad had Hugh. Mum had Dad. I'm not sure you understood how difficult that was for me. I had my books and sketches. I even had a few friends until I reached my mid-teens. But then, when all hell broke loose inside my head, all I had left was an overwhelming feeling of worthlessness. Self-hatred. Failure. And that house which became a prison."

I stood up and walked over to the counter to stand beside him. I slipped my arm around him as we both looked out on our children playing happily together. I was confused. Yesterday, I been convinced that Ben was happy to be in Howth. So much so that I was considering moving the family back there for his sake.

"But yesterday –"

He interrupted straight away.

"Do you remember I said I had met Garry Walton?"

"The prick, as you always used to call him when ye worked together."

"Exactly. He's even prickier now. It turns out Mum told him about my – my misadventure in the cave. She had also asked him for a job for me. Completely without my knowledge or permission. He rejected me. The reason being, he explained, that my skill set wouldn't fit with their 'current profile'."

"Oh, the prat!"

"Yes. Thanks to my mother's interference, I had to stand there and suffer the sneers of that scumbag. It was utterly humiliating."

"But your mother meant well, Ben. She was just looking out for you."

He took a step away from me.

"She was, as always, trying to control me, Leah. You saw her reaction when I told her I had met Garry Walton. She was cool as ice. Not a trace of guilt or remorse that she had gone behind my back. Not a hint of an apology for telling Garry Walton my private business."

I nodded. No denying that. Della had more or less shrugged off the mention of the Waltons.

"So what are you saying, Ben? I'm confused now. I thought what you wanted was to move back to Dublin."

"Just because I don't want to be in Paircmoor, doesn't mean I want to go back to Howth. And yes, *The Parrish House* is a substantial property in a lovely area. A good place for the kids to live. But the personal price is too high as far as I'm concerned."

"It's your inheritance, Ben, even if you're getting it early. She's gifting it to you."

His eyes were glittering with either anger or tears. I wasn't sure which.

"You don't understand, Leah. I can't go back there. It would be like reliving my childhood over again. And the nightmare of my teens. Letting her make decisions for me. For the children. For you. Never knowing what secrets she was keeping or how she was manipulating us behind the scenes. Anyway, I thought what you wanted was to stay here."

"What I want, Ben, is for you and the children to be happy and safe. And despite what you think, that's what your mother wants too. I know now you've never settled here. And I do realise it's fantastic for the children but, looking to their future, as you say, we may need to move to a city with secondary schools and a university. Better employment prospects for you too."

He wrapped his arms around me. I leaned my face against his chest and felt the warmth from his body and the steady beat of his heart.

"I'm sorry, Leah. Sorry to have put you through so much. Sorry that I can't support you and the children. Sorry I'm not the husband you deserve or the father the children should have."

I placed my fingers gently on his lips to silence him and tightened my arms around him as we held each other close.

"I love you, Ben Parrish," I muttered into his chest.

"*Oh, bloody hell!*" Ben yelled.

He pushed me away from him and ran out the back

door. I ran after him and almost tripped over the mat in my hurry. Ben was racing towards the ditch, where Anna was balanced on the top of the stone wall and Josh was clambering up after her. I looked at them in horror, knowing that the four-foot-high structure was unstable. It was a dry-stone wall, constructed many years ago without the use of mortar. Securing it had been on our to-do list for a long time. Anna swayed as stones under her feet began to shift. In one long stride, Ben reached the wall, grabbed a twin in each arm and stepped back just as a section of the wall collapsed in a heap of dislodged stones.

Anna began to cry. I ran to her. She was snuggled into Ben's shoulder, her little body racked by sobs.

"I sorry I broke the stones, Daddy."

"Me sorry too," Josh said, crying in sympathy with his sister.

Ben rocked both of them in his arms, holding them tightly.

I joined them and mouthed a thank-you to him.

He smiled at me over their heads.

"You know I'd never let them come to harm," he said. "I'll always protect them."

I smiled back at him, secure in the knowledge that wherever the future led, Ben would be there to wrap his strong arms around us all.

I rang Mags. Yes, the salon was very busy and, yes, they could do with extra help tomorrow.

"The organised people are getting their Christmas cut and colour now. We'll be delighted to see you tomorrow. You'll need to stock up on products too."

I rang off, promising to go in early in the morning to

get orders organised. I was delighted that the salon was continuing to build custom, but I was also disappointed that Mags did not suggest that I take the rest of the week off. I would miss Ben and the children so much. I could have told her I was taking the extra few days off – but needs must. I might have to keep Mags on-side and the salon going for a long time yet. A move to Howth looked like it was firmly off the cards.

Ben had put the twins down for a nap. I checked the fridge and cupboards. We were fairly low in basics. I would need to stock up for the next few days. Back to the old routine of cooking dinners the night before because I would be too exhausted to cook when I came home and the children would be too tired to eat by the time it would be ready. I had to tell myself I was lucky to have this source of income. Doubly lucky not to have to pay a mortgage. And yet, as I wrote the shopping list, I felt anything but lucky.

I put the list on the counter and tiptoed down to the twins' room. Awake, Anna was a little madam, full of confidence. Asleep, she was a vulnerable baby. And Josh, happy-go-lucky, loyal Josh, was like a cherub as he slept. They were so beautiful, so precious, that I felt a lump in my throat that could only be tears. These babies, and Rob, already starting on the road to independence, were the best of Ben and me. It made me sad to have to miss any minute of their growing up. I closed the door softly behind me and went back to my grocery list.

Ben was in his office. He said he had a few emails to sort out. I thought of the anti-depressant bottles locked into his drawer. I should have taken them away. Flushed them down the loo. But then, that was what Della did, wasn't it? Controlled him. Made decisions for him. Still, I must make sure that he went to see the GP next week.

I had lunch almost ready by the time Ben came back into the kitchen.

"Did you hear the news?" I asked. "Evelyn Thurley didn't need our votes. She won the presidency by a landslide."

"Good on her. But we should make sure we're registered for the next election."

As he pulled out a stool from underneath the counter, he noticed the grocery list.

"How about we all go to collect Rob after school. Then we'll go to town to shop. We'll have tea out because it's your last day before going back to work. And it's my treat."

I wasn't about to argue. Yes, it would be an extra expense, but the salon was bringing in more money. I appreciated the fact that he sensed tomorrow would be hard for me. I hugged him.

"That sounds good, Ben. Did you know there's a nice little park near the hospital? I went there a few times when you were in. Just to get a breath of air. I wonder why they keep hospitals so warm."

"To knock all the patients out. They're easier to manage when they're asleep. Just like the twins."

We both laughed and my heart sang. Ben Parrish was smiling, laughing. Being the man I had fallen in love with so long ago.

"If you take the children to the play area in the park, I can get through the shopping quickly. Then we can decide where to go for tea. Okay with you, Ben?"

He nodded then glanced at the clock.

"Look at the time! I'll wake the two mini demolition experts while you finish getting lunch ready. Then we'll collect our little professor and hit the town. Finally scotch the rumour that I died in the cave last week."

I wasn't sure that I appreciated his black humour, but I loved his laugh. I felt myself swept up in the energy he exuded.

Life was good for the Parrishes of Paircmoor as we collected Rob from school and headed off to town.

CHAPTER FIFTY-ONE

I dropped Ben and the children off at the park in town, and made my way to the shopping mall. Luckily the supermarket was quiet, so I got through the shopping quickly. I packed the groceries in the boot and returned the trolley to the bay.

On impulse, I went back into the mall. It was a fine evening, with about another hour of daylight left. The children would be enjoying themselves in the park. I had noticed a new pop-up shop in the mall, a riot of tinsel, glitter and everything Christmassy. It would be a good place to pick up a few surprise presents for Christmas morning.

I bought three big Christmas stockings, and a handful of glittery things to put into them – a bracelet for Anna, a plastic hammer and saw for Josh and fancy pencils and pencil case for Rob. Stereotyping maybe, but I knew these were the things they would treasure more than the expensive toys. I would put them in with the groceries and hide them in the old shed tonight before I went to bed.

I parked in the hospital grounds. It felt so good to look up at the first floor, to the window of Room 5, and to know that, for us, the nightmare was over. It wasn't that

I was fooling myself. I knew there was a long road ahead, of talking, possibly medication, certainly counselling. Not just for Ben, but for the two of us. We both had childhood issues to deal with. Both obviously had problems communicating. It was beyond belief that we had lived together for over six years, had three children, and a fourth on way, and still we nurtured secrets. I had not yet told Ben about my pregnancy. And what was it he had not yet told me? I had no idea but I did believe there was something. I turned my back on the hospital, certain of only one thing. Ben and I loved each other and we would work through our problems in time.

I walked to the park, stopping for a moment by the wooden bench under the oak tree. So recently my place of refuge from the hospital. Litter was still strewn about, but the despair I had felt when I had last sat there was gone. I stood for a while at the entrance to the playground and watched the children play. The twins were on the low swings, Ben behind them, pushing each in turn. Anna, of course, was swinging highest. I smiled. Josh was swinging along at his own pace, smiling. I admired his ability to live in the moment, to suck every ounce of enjoyment out of life. Rob was on the climbing frame, standing up on the platform on top, chatting to another boy. They could have been two old men standing at a bar counter, shooting the breeze. I wondered what they were talking about. No doubt about it, school was benefitting Rob greatly as far as his social development was concerned. It was so good to see him make a new friend. I was conscious of baby number four, nestling inside me. Boy? Girl? Feisty? Playful? Born. That's all it needed to be.

Ben looked up and saw me. He waved and smiled.

Twee, I know, but I did get a tickle in my tummy, a skip of my heartbeat. I waved back and went in to them.

Dusk had fallen and street lighting had kicked in by the time we got to the restaurant. There was much discussion about the menu until eventually we all decided to have chicken and chips. I asked Rob about his new friend.

"He's not new. Elliot's my friend in school. His mom's my teacher."

"Oh! Miss Tracey has a son?"

"Yes. But his dad lives in the town, so he spends some time here too."

"I see. Why don't you invite Elliot to come out to Cowslip Cottage to play with you sometime?"

"I did."

"I'll clear it with his mom. Can you pick him up someday after school, Ben?"

Ben didn't answer. He had a faraway look in his eyes. I guessed he had not heard any of that conversation. My new-found euphoria took a little dint. Just a little one. I accepted we had a long way to go before Ben was fully rehabilitated. But I knew, with every fibre of my being that we would eventually get there.

If there is anything I detest more than grocery shopping it is putting the shopping away when I get home. I left most of the bags in the boot of the jeep that evening, taking in only the perishables. The children were tired, and all in need of a good wash, so I filled the bath and put the three in together. Ben sat on the edge of the bath, supervising. I put the seat down on the toilet and sat watching and listening to their chatter. Anna discovered that if she squeezed her rubber duck underwater, air streamed out and made beautiful heaps of bubbles with the baby bath I had added to the water. They all had a go and there was much laughing and bubbles with miniature rainbows reflected on them. Ben eventually pulled the plug before they turned into three little prunes.

I went to the kitchen to get their milk and rice cakes while Ben dried the twins and put on their pyjamas. Rob went off and got himself ready for bed before coming into the kitchen to me.

"Do you think Dad is all better now?" he asked.

I was surprised by the question and wondered why he had asked.

"What do *you* think, Rob?"

"*Hmm*. He's not cross anymore. Elliot said that Dad swam away out into the sea in the dark and that a helicopter had to fly down and pull him out of the water. Is that true?"

I shook my head. Obviously there were still some dramatic rumours around Paircmoor about Ben's dice with death.

"Rob, I told you what happened. He went out for a run and tripped over a branch in the dark. An ambulance, not a helicopter, brought him to hospital. You know that's what happened, don't you?"

He thought for a moment before answering. Then he nodded.

"Yes. The Sanquest people called the ambulance, didn't they? Not a helicopter."

"Exactly. And it may take a little while for Dad to get really strong again, but we'll all help him, won't we?"

"Sure. Can I have jam on my rice cake?"

I had been just about to say no, when I changed my

mind. Having the gumption to confide his worry in me deserved a dollop of jam.

Supper was a quick affair because it was getting late. Tooth-brushing, a trip to the bathroom, and they were all in bed. I tucked Rob up while Ben read the twins their bedtime story. Rob was reading one of Hugh's comics which Della had allowed him to keep.

"I think I might make cartoons when I'm older," he told me. "Animation. Not just drawing."

I had no doubt he would. Or that his Uncle Hugh would pave the way for him into the world of computer technology.

"You can be whatever you like when you're older, Rob. Don't forget to enjoy being young though. And don't stay reading too long now. Love you loads."

"Love you too, Mom."

I kissed him on the cheek and breathed in the scent of baby bath. One of the most comforting smells in the world.

I switched off the main light in his room, closed his door and went to say goodnight to the twins. They were asleep already. Ben was sitting at the end of Josh's bed just watching his children sleep.

"They're angelic, aren't they?" I said as I eased myself gently onto Anna's bed.

I looked at them both, Anna was lying on her back, her arms flung out, curls framing her face. Josh peaceful, a slight smile playing around his mouth, his dark lashes, incredibly long, casting shadows on his face.

Ben stood up, smiled and held his hand out to me.

I took his hand and we went back to the kitchen. He helped me bring the rest of the shopping in from the jeep.

We worked in silence as we put things in the cupboards and fridge.

"What's this?" Ben asked, holding up the Santa bag with the Christmas trinkets from the mall.

"Just a few bits and bobs for Christmas morning. I must put them out in the old shed with the other things Hugh bought."

"I'll put them out for you later. I've a few jobs to do there anyway."

I handed him the bag and we finished putting the shopping away. Tired then, I sat down. I should get the children's clothes ready for the morning and make Rob's school lunch. I felt too exhausted. Baby number four was wearing me out. Maybe because I was getting older. Or perhaps all the stress of the past couple of weeks was taking its toll.

Ben frowned as he looked at me.

"You look tired, Leah."

"I am. I think I'll go to bed soon. I need to make an early start in the morning. Things to catch up on before the salon opens. Would you be okay with dropping Rob into school? I'll take him on Friday morning to give you a break."

"Sure. Go on. Scram. I'll heat your milk and bring it to you."

I had just got into bed when Ben arrived in with my mug of milk and put it on my bedside locker.

"Don't stay up too late, Ben. I'll be leaving here at half past seven in the morning. That will give me an hour of peace and quiet in the salon to get the orders done. I'll call you before I go."

I lifted my face for a kiss. He leaned down and stared at me for a moment.

"You really are your mother's daughter, Leah. So strong and honest. So much to offer. I love you for it."

It was a puzzling little speech. I hadn't realised Ben had such admiration for my mother. Nor was I either strong or honest at that particular time. My bafflement disappeared when he kissed me, softly at first, then with an urgency my body responded to. Just as I was about to pull back the duvet for him to join me in bed, he stood up.

"Drink your milk before it goes cold. Sleep tight."

Then he was gone. I set my alarm for six thirty, then picked up my milk to drink it. The skin already forming on top gave my stomach a turn. Besides, I ached for sleep. My eyelids were already drooping. Not wanting to hurt Ben's feelings, I took the mug, still full, into the ensuite, emptied the contents down the loo and flushed.

As I snuggled under the duvet I wondered, if I would ever, ever, understand the enigma that was Ben Parrish. Kind enough to bring me hot milk in bed, yet not trusting me enough to allow me to help him through his sadness.

Ben turned off the television and wandered into his office. A one-time dairy. A cowshed. He switched on his computer. There were no new emails. Why should there be? He thought of writing some. But who would want to hear from him? Ellen Riggs? No. She was gone from Paircmoor and out of his life. Back to where she belonged. Into the arms of a man who could give her the life she deserved. He could email Garry Walton. Tell him that all the staff who had bowed and scraped to him because he was the boss's son, had called him Wanker Walton behind his back. Let him worry that they still do. But the prick was so arrogant he would probably laugh it off.

Maybe he should mail Hugh. Ask him to leave George Roche at rest. To give their uncle the peace he had craved so much that he had hung himself. But there was no talking to Hugh once he was on a mission. He would rake up every last skeleton in the Roache/Parrish family in an effort to explain his defective brother. That was it, wasn't it? He needed to pin down the faulty Roache gene that had taken George's life, skipped past Hugh, and fucked up Ben. To hell with Hugh and his billionaire brother-in-law.

He logged off and sat for a moment listening to the house. Cowshit Cottage was never silent. It was an uneasy place, full of whispered memories. He had made plans for renovations. All drawn up and ready to go. Walls blown away, roof raised, and glass, glass, glass, to let the light in and the ghosts out. All he was short of was money. And a job. Plus a life.

He left his office and tiptoed into his bedroom. Their room. His and Leah's. She was sleeping soundly, lying on her back, her arms flung outside the duvet, her blonde hair fanned out on the pillow. Anna was a perfect clone of her mother, except that her hair was curly where Leah's was straight. Still beautiful, his Leah Scally, the little hair stylist from the wrong side of the city. The woman his mother never wanted him to marry. Ben stooped down and kissed her forehead, then picked up the mug from the top of her locker and turned off the bedside lamp she had left on.

Back in the kitchen, he put Leah's mug in the dishwasher and then stoked up the stove. It would be a long night. He picked up the key to the old shed from the hall table and made his way out there. As soon as he opened the door, he got that feeling again. Calm. Security.

The first day he had set foot in this shed, he had felt as if it welcomed him. Fanciful as that seemed, time had proved his instinct right. Maybe it was the compact size, the crooked walls, the tendrils of ivy that poked through the corrugated roof. Or maybe it was that the space was his. Leah ventured in there only at Christmas time to sort out the decorations. Whatever the reason, he felt comfortable there, and breathed a sigh of contentment as he set about his task.

He got the trikes and bicycle out from behind the deck chairs, and ripped the packaging with his Stanley knife. There was some assembly to be done on Rob's bike. That did not take long. Then he tipped over the refusac full of Christmas gifts Hugh had bought for the children. Box after box tumbled out on the floor. Some tied with red ribbons, some with silver wrapping, others in Santa paper. Extravagant. Typical of Hugh. Next he found the Christmas stockings Leah had bought, and put the trinkets in. Gifts ready, the hard work began.

It took a long time to string all the lights around the inside of the shed. Next he hauled the tatty artificial tree, which had belonged to Leah's mother, down from the rafters. It looked moth-eaten in its bare state but wound around with bell-shaped lights and a star on top, it was beautiful. He smiled as he thought how Granny Scally would love it. She was partial to glitz.

He took a last look around before turning off the light. The twins' trikes were one on either side of the tree, multi-coloured ribbons decorating the handlebars. Rob's bike, balanced on the stabilisers, was standing to the side. The parcels were strewn around the floor and the stockings hung from the rafters. Low enough for the children to reach. He turned off the main light and hit the Christmas-light switch.

Ben laughed out loud. He had done it! He had turned the old shed into a Christmas Grotto! It shone and twinkled with red and green reflections. The lights bounced off the metallic frames of the bike and the trikes. He imagined the children's reaction when they saw it. How magical it would seem to them. How special it would make them feel.

He turned off the lights, locked the door and went back into the kitchen. The fire in the stove had burned down but the room was still warm. He poured himself a drink. A whiskey. He had earned it. As he sat by the dying embers, glass in hand, he thought about his own childhood Christmases. How they had always been a disappointment. Not because he had been deprived of material things. He never was. But he had not felt the joy, the fun, the magic. Yuletide had been something he endured, rather than enjoyed. Until tonight. He could not wait to see the children's faces when they saw their custom-made Christmas Grotto.

He went to their rooms. They were all asleep. Innocent. Beautiful. Precious. He poured another drink for himself and brought it into the lounge with him. He toasted the ghosts of Cowshit Cottage, knocked back his whiskey in one swallow, lay down on the couch, and slept.

CHAPTER FIFTY-TWO

Thursday 9th December 2010

I heard my alarm through a fog of sleep. I reached out my hand and turned it off. A few seconds later, realisation trickled through. I must go to the salon. Still half asleep, I rolled out of bed and headed for the bathroom. I was in the shower before I fully awoke and realised Ben had not been in the bed when I got up. In fact it seemed his side of the bed had not been slept in. I rushed through my shower, quickly dried off and threw on my dressing gown. I double-checked in the bedroom before I left. Ben's side of the bed was cool to the touch and undisturbed.

I headed for the kitchen. No sign of him there. I remembered him sleeping on the Queen Anne chair in the twins' room the last time we had a row. I tiptoed in, being careful not to make any noise. Anna was a very light sleeper. It was much too early for her to be up and about. In the dim glow from the nightlight it was plain to see that Ben was not there. Nor was he in Rob's room. I would not allow myself to panic until I had searched the lounge and his office.

The lounge was in darkness. I switched on the tall lamp just inside the door. Then I saw him. Lying on the couch, his long legs hanging out over the arm on one end, his head propped up on the other arm. Still dressed in yesterday's clothes. I stooped down next to him and heard his breathing. I could see his eyes move inside his lids. I stood there watching, wondering what he was dreaming about. He was frowning. The stubble on his face, paradoxically, made him look boyish. Vulnerable. I gently touched my fingers to his cheek. His skin felt cold. I went to the hot press, got a rug and put it over him and switched off the lamp. I would let him sleep on, finish his dream, and call him before I left.

Time flew past with getting the children's clothes and food for the day organised. I barely had time for a slice of toast and a quick coffee before dressing myself. It was already seven thirty. I went into the lounge and gently shook Ben by the shoulder. He jumped up. Startled.

"Hey! Sorry. I had to wake you. I'm leaving now. Why did you not come to bed last night?"

He rubbed his eyes, still not totally awake.

"I told you I had a few jobs to do in the old shed. It was late when I finished. I didn't want to disturb you."

"I left everything ready for the children. It's all I the kitchen."

"Good. Thank you. Stop fussing, Leah. I can manage the children. Go to work."

I didn't like his prickly tone but knew him long enough to admit that morning was not his best time. I gave him a quick kiss on the cheek. I thought for a moment I smelled alcohol on his breath but knew I must be imagining it. Silly idea. He never drank on week nights. Not much on weekends either. As I picked my bag up off the kitchen table, I realised my phone was still in our bedroom. I dashed in there, picked up my phone and popped it into my bag. I noticed the mug was gone from the locker top, so Ben must have been in the bedroom last night. So thoughtful of him not to wake me. I was ready to go except to say good bye to the children. I looked at the clock. Seven forty. They could have another twenty minutes sleep if I did not disturb them. I put three tiny kisses on my fingers and blew them in the direction of their bedrooms.

I peeped into the lounge in passing. Ben was still standing where I had left him. At least he was awake.

"Eight is time enough to call them," I said. "I'll ring later."

I dashed out the door, not waiting for an answer. My car was reluctant to start. I cursed and tried again. Thankfully the curse worked and the engine ticked over. I looked back towards the cottage as I turned the car. Ben was standing at the door. Hand up to his eyes as he was caught in the headlights. I waved to him. He did not respond. I got the message then. Ben did not want me to go into the salon. He resented me having a job to go to, while he had none. As I drove out onto the road and headed in the direction of Paircmoor village, I wondered where the loving Ben of the past few days had gone. Who was the real Ben Parrish? The caring man, or the boorish boy-man?

I parked in front of the salon, and sat for a moment, listening to the clicks of the cooling engine. It was at times like that, challenging, frightening times, I usually had my one-sided conversation with Mam. I didn't want to talk to her now. Not while I was still angry with her for not telling me about my father. Could I talk, one to one, to Della? Ask her if this was how Ben had behaved in his teens. Up one minute. Down the next. No. Della still wanted to deny that

Ben needed help. Psychiatric help. Hugh. I could talk to him. Ask for his advice. And I would. Tonight.

That decision made, I locked the car and faced my first day back in the salon post 'the incident' which had landed my husband in hospital.

Ben waited at the door until he could no longer hear the sound of Leah's car or see the twin arcs of light created by her headlights. It was a cold and damp morning. He shivered and headed back inside to the warmth of the cottage. The embers in the kitchen stove still glowed from last night's stoking. It was blazing in minutes. He looked at the table and saw that Leah had bowls and spoons laid out, the cereal boxes standing in a neat row on the counter. An organiser of bowls, spoons, boxes and lives. That was Leah.

A glance at the clock told him that the children would be up and about soon. Not enough time for him to shower and shave. He had caught a glimpse of himself in the hall mirror. A pathetic sight, still dressed in yesterday's clothes, a shadow of dark stubble on cheeks and chin. He shrugged. Pathetic was his default style.

He heard some sounds coming from the twins' room. Anna was up and about and ready to tackle the day. He met her in the hall, already on her way to the bathroom, Josh in tow. She ran towards him.

"Daddy! Him won't let me brush his teeth."

"Anna, Josh can do his own teeth after breakfast. Can't you, Josh?"

"Can too."

Rob emerged from his room, rubbing his eyes and yawning.

"Dad, can I go to the bathroom in Mum's bedroom? Anna and Josh will be ages here."

Out of the mouths of babes. Mum's bedroom. It was. Cowshit Cottage was all Leah. He nodded to Rob.

"Get a move on, guys. I've a surprise for you before we go to the school."

Anna and Josh clapped their hands, while Rob, obviously in dire need, ran off to 'Mum's bedroom'.

Ben poured cereal into bowls and sat at the table with the children as they ate. He looked at them each in turn and knew they were his greatest achievement in life. His only achievement. They were so beautiful, so clever, so precious. So vulnerable.

"What's the surprise, Dad?" Rob asked.

"Guess."

"A puppy," Josh said.

"*Him sleep in my bed!*" Anna said, making sure she got to make the first claim.

Ben shook his head. "No. Not a puppy. Mom and I explained that you must be able to look after a dog yourselves before we get one. You're still a bit too young. Besides, no matter what age you are, the dog won't be sleeping with anyone. He'll have his own bed."

"I bet you're going to say Della is coming here for Christmas."

Ben looked at Rob, at his solemn little face and mesmerising eyes.

"Not that either, Rob. Don't you remember she said she was going to America to see Uncle Hugh? Next year though, we will all be spending Christmas together."

"In America?"

"We'll see."

"That's what you always say when you really mean no."

So! Rob was beginning to see life as it is, not as it should be.

Ben smiled at him. "You'll just have to wait and see, won't you. Now, c'mon all of you. Get dressed quickly. It's surprise time!"

There was no having to tell them a second time. Leah had, as always, laid their clothes out at the bottom of their beds. Anna was almost as independent as Rob already, but Josh still had to have a lot of help. He held up his arms so that Ben could slip on his sweater. The upturned little face was so innocent, so trusting, so loving, that Ben's breath caught in his throat. When the sweater was on, he held his son close. Josh was the cuddler. The one who needed to give and get affection. The one who needed most protection.

Rob came into the room, his school uniform on.

"Are we ready for the surprise now?" he asked.

"Jenny must get surprise too," Anna said, as she got her toy donkey, Jenny, her new best friend, from the bed where she had tucked it in last night.

Ben looked at each of his children in turn. He had never felt as intense a love for them as he did at that minute. It was the purest of love, his for them, theirs for him. He demanded nothing more of them than that they be safe. They demanded nothing more of him than that he keep them safe.

"Put on your coats. It's cold where we're going. Then follow me."

They did. Out through the kitchen, the hall, across the front garden, past the coal shed, until they reached the old shed. Ben stood at the door and put the key in the lock.

"Ready?"

There was a chorus of yeses. He was ready too. He turned the key, opened the door and flicked the switch for the Christmas lights.

The children stood still for one moment, transfixed by the twinkling lights. Then they rushed inside, the twins to their trikes, Rob to his bike. Ben watched them, their faces glowing with happiness. It had been worth all the work last night.

Rob suddenly stood still, a hand on the saddle of his bike, a frown on his forehead.

"But it's not Christmas yet," he said.

"Is so!" Anna said. "Santa bring this to me."

Yes, no doubt about it, Rob was well on his way to becoming someone who would search in vain for logic in an illogical world, order in the chaos of existence.

"Rob is right," Ben said. "Santa has not come yet. Uncle Hugh left these presents. See the Christmas stockings hanging up? There are more surprises in there. From Mom."

"Can I take my bike out? Cycle it a bit down the avenue."

"No, Rob. Not now. You can do that later. It's very cold today. How about I make hot chocolate and marshmallows before we go to school."

"*Yummy, yummy!*" Anna and Josh rubbed their tummies, as they always did at the mention of hot chocolate.

"I'll go and make it and bring it out to you. Play with your things until I come back. And no fighting."

Ben closed the door of the old shed behind him as he left. He stood for a moment listening to the sound of his children's laughter. Even Rob had shed his solemnity and joined in the happy chorus.

It took Ben a while to organise the drinks. Milk was a bit scarce. There had been just about enough to make the three drinks. Between Leah's hot milk habit and the twins' cereals, they could well justify grazing a few cows in the back garden. Except there wasn't a whole lot of grass out there. There wasn't a whole lot of anything except bleakness.

Feeling his anger rise, Ben deliberately channelled his thoughts towards his children. Nothing mattered now, but to get the hot chocolate out to them, hear their laughter again, see their smiles. Then they could get on with what the day held in store.

Stocktake done, I sat and looked around the salon. Mags and Tina had run a tight ship. The place was sparkling. The appointment book full. It was just eight forty-five so I had time for a coffee. I got out my Stephen Pearce mug, noting that it was exactly where I had left it when I was last here. I was a bit paranoid about anyone else using it. Mam had bought it for me, shortly before she died. It was a connection to her I clung onto, even when I was not talking to her. I made my coffee and brought it into the salon. I glanced again at the appointment book and wondered how they had turned things around so quickly. It was ridiculous to think that every new customer came in here just to hear about Ben. All they had to do was go to Henderson's pub, shop, garage, post office, to find out all the details, plus added extras. Whatever the reason, I was very grateful.

They arrived together, Mags and Tina. Mags had a

new energy about her. An air of authority. And Tina looked as graceful and unflappable as ever.

"Welcome back!" they chorused.

"How's Ben?" Tina asked.

"Thank you! Ben's good. A bit to go to full recovery yet, but he's on the right road."

They both hugged me. I felt tears well in my eyes as Mags enfolded me in the comfort of her embrace.

"I'm so, so, grateful to you both. But tell me how in the name of goodness you managed to triple business in such a short period of time."

"Three things," Mags said. "First there was Ben's accident. That brought the curious here. Then there was Minnie Curran, terrified you would sue her for slander, telling anyone who would listen that Leah's Salon was the best in the country. And then there was Tina!"

I looked at Tina. She seemed uncomfortable. Reluctant to look me in the eye.

"Go on, Tina," Mags urged. "Tell her."

I heard Tina's intake of breath. I began to worry.

"I'm sorry, Leah. I know I should have asked permission but I didn't want to disturb you."

"Oh, for heaven's sake, child," Mags said. "I'll tell her. Tina set up Facebook and tweeter accounts for Leah's Salon. That's how we're getting a young clientele in and also people from the catchment area. All thanks to Tina."

I was stunned. I hadn't realised that cyber-reach would be so effective in the rural area. So much for urban/rural prejudice. I hadn't even thought of setting up a personal Facebook account, let alone one for the business. I smiled at Tina.

"Well! Tina, I don't know what to say. Thank you so

much. It must have taken you a lot of time. I really appreciate it."

"I enjoyed doing it, Leah. And I'm happy it brought in new custom. And Mags, I've told you loads of times, it's Twitter account. You tweet on a Twitter account."

Mags shrugged her shoulders. "Whatever! It worked anyway."

I was just about to tell Tina that I would pay her for the extra work, when the first customer of the day arrived. Quickly followed by two more.

There was an awkward moment when Mags and Tina looked to me for instructions.

"You're the manager, Mags. Manage. Tell me what you want me to do."

Mags didn't need to be told twice. She was in her element organising customers and staff, chatting, meeting, greeting. There was little chance for me to think, but when I got a break I decided that I could afford to spend less time in the salon in future, and more time at home with my children. And my sometimes childish husband.

I rang Ben at elevenses break time. There was no ring. Phone turned off again or else he had forgotten to charge it.

There were ten precious minutes when the salon was empty except for a blow-dry Mags was finishing off. Tina and I sat side by side at the little counter in the kitchenette.

"I can't thank you enough for the online work you did for the salon, Tina. There will be something extra in your pay this week."

"No need. It's practice for me. I'll be applying for computer science after my Leaving Cert. It's what I want to do."

"Yes, there *is* a need to pay you for your work. My son is very interested in computers too. I think he'll definitely make a career in some area of computer technology. Gosh! He's only five. I'm definitely a pushy mother!"

We were both laughing when Mags came in.

"That woman just told me there's something big going on in the area because Garda cars and a couple of ambulances passed her on the way here."

"Must be a car crash," I said. "I hope it's not too serious."

The salon phone rang. I told Mags to sit and have her lunch and I went to answer. It was Viv Henderson. Lady Paircmoor herself.

"Is that you, Leah? It's great that you're back again. How is your husband?"

"Good, thank you. What can I do for you, Viv?"

"It was Mags I wanted to talk to."

"She's having her break. Can I take a message?"

Viv hesitated.

"Just tell her the rescue helicopter is gone over towards Pouldubh Head. You know, that cliff on the headland just past the beach. That usually means trouble for some poor soul."

I had to bite my tongue. Viv wallowed in other people's troubles. Just the suggestion was enough for her to start spreading the word.

"I'll tell Mags, Viv. I assume you have your usual Friday appointment. See you tomorrow."

I was just putting down the phone when I noticed a blue light flashing outside the salon. The door opened. Two uniformed gardaí stood there. One male, one female.

"Mrs Parrish?" the woman asked. "Leah Parrish."

I found the strength to nod but not to stop the scream that sounded in my head.

"Does your husband drive a black jeep? 04 D 54321Y?"

My legs lost their strength. I reached behind me for a stool. Mags came to stand beside me. She put her arm around my shoulder. I felt strength flow from her to me.

"Yes. That's Ben's jeep. Has there been an accident? Is he hurt? Are the children alright?"

They exchanged looks. The man and the woman. He spoke this time.

"A jeep of that description was seen going into the sea off the Pouldubh Headland. Emergency Services are on the way there now. Is there someone you would like to call to be with you? "

"My little boy Rob, is in school in Paircmoor. Is there someone with the twins?"

I heard the garda take a breath. It quivered. He pursed his lips and I knew he was trying to be strong. To behave like he had been trained to do in tragic situations. I didn't want him to answer. I wished the scream in my head was louder so that I could not hear his words.

"We checked. Rob didn't go in to school today."

Mags reached down and took my shaking hands in hers.

"The twins," I whispered.

"They are with their father. So is Rob."

The salon began to spin, the mirrors and sinks dance around. The place went dark, just as the strong arms of the garda held on to me and prevented me from hitting the ground.

I remember being led to the Garda car. Mags telling me she would look after the salon. Giving Hugh's and Della's numbers to the female garda sitting beside me. Asking her to make the calls. They wanted to take me to a Garda station, but I insisted on being taken to Pouldubh Head.

A black wind howled around the headland, whipping the sea into peaks and troughs of angry tide. The jeep, they told me, was on the sea floor beneath the cliff. Under thirty feet of rolling, bitingly cold, North Atlantic. Five fathoms deep the Coast Guard said. But I still hoped. I had given life to my babies. I believed I could will them to live again.

There were divers. And boats. Helicopters overhead. Doctors on standby. Squad cars. A priest muttering words of consolation I was not ready to accept. And everywhere, all over that bleak headland, blue lights flashed, vehicles came and went. I saw a camera with a zoom lens pointed in my direction as I sat in the squad car. People spoke in whispers around me. I ached. Every cell in my body yearned to hold my babies. To run my fingers through Anna's curls, to watch Josh's grin, to see Rob's beautiful dark eyes. To hold them close to me and feel their warm breaths on my face, their soft skin next to mine. To tell them everything would be alright now that Mom was here. To feel Ben's arms around me, telling me he was looking after the children. Keeping them safe.

I saw Vera Sanquest, Walter by her side. She was talking to two gardaí. Pointing towards the headland. I jumped out of the squad car, the garda rushing after me.

"Vera! Did you see them?"

When she turned towards me, I saw that her face was ashen. She was crying.

"I'm sorry, Leah. So sorry. I should have known."

Because I was in shock. Because everything I lived for

was lying five fathoms deep. Because Vera was crying as she spoke, I did not immediately understand what she was saying. A garda, a gentle woman, repeated the words until I followed the sequence of events. Vera had been driving out onto the Paircmoor road when Ben and the children passed by in the jeep. She waved but got no acknowledgement that Ben had seen her. He seemed strange. Distracted. Focused only on driving, very fast, straight ahead towards Pouldubh Head. The glimpse she had of the children made her think they were asleep. She felt uneasy, so followed him. She arrived at Pouldubh Head in time to witness Ben accelerate as he drove the jeep over the cliff edge.

"I'm sorry, Leah. If I had rung for help instead of following. If I had stopped him on the road. If . . ."

Her words faded into the background of my consciousness as a pain gripped my belly. It ripped around my lower back. I bent forward, my breath stopped by the intensity of the cramp. I felt life seep from me. The foetus. The fourth baby. I was losing the only member of the family Ben had not murdered.

"My baby!"

"How far gone are you, Leah?" the garda asked.

"Eleven weeks. Twelve. I don't know."

She got on her radio straight away and called over one of the ambulances. I tried to stop them taking me away, but I was haemorrhaging and destroyed by grief. I was lifted into the ambulance and put on a drip. The siren sounded and the ambulance sped away from Pouldubh Head. Away from my babies.

For the second time that day, I left my children without saying goodbye.

NOW

CHAPTER FIFTY-THREE

Two years later
Sunday 9th December 2012

"*For the second time that day, I left my children without saying goodbye.*"

The words leave my mouth and are swallowed by silence in the County Kerry Community Hall. I am standing on the stage. Centre of attention. The object of pity. Here to tell our story. Mine and Ben's, Rob's, Anna's and Josh's. I am the only voice they have now. I secure the microphone back in the stand. My pain is raw. It still has a razor edge that tears me asunder.

I look down from the stage at my audience. Someone sniffles. Maybe they have a cold, or maybe the sniffler is weeping out of sympathy. Or fear. Someone who has doubts. A person who can draw parallels from their own experience, who dreads that my tragedy could become theirs. That is the reason I stand here, in front of all these strangers, the images of my dead babies on the screen beside me. There is always that one sniffler.

I hear some foot-shuffling and sense embarrassment in case I break down in floods of tears. Doubt about whether it is appropriate to clap or not. The usual discomfort around grief. I mean to take a deep breath. Form a coherent sentence. Put people at ease. Instead my eyes are drawn to the screen. It shows a photograph Ben had taken of the children in the back garden with their Christmas tree. Anna, laughing, wearing her flowery raincoat and a Santa hat, Josh, making a funny face for the camera, Rob, arranging lights on the tree. Five short days before they died. Before they were murdered. Before Ben drove them to their deaths on Pouldubh Head. My throat tightens with emotional pain that is more agonising than any physical pain I have ever felt.

The tap, tap of high heels tells me Cora Sheehan is making her way onto the stage. Cora organised this evening. She contacted me, invited me to tell my story in this community hall that is a clone of so many others I have visited. And now she is rescuing me from the silent agony that is robbing me of my voice.

She stands beside me at the podium and leans towards the microphone.

"Ladies and Gentlemen, thank you for your attention during Leah's telling of her harrowing story. I'm sure you appreciate how difficult it must have been for her. And how very brave."

There is tentative applause, which grows in volume until the hall echoes with the sound of peoples' support. Part of the enthusiasm is a release of tension. A sliver of normality in the twisted world of familicide. A word far too small to encompass the depth of horror of the crime.

Cora covers the microphone with her hand and turns to me.

"Are you alright to go ahead with questions, Leah, or do you want to wind up now?"

How many times in the past two years had I longed to

give up? To stop the pain by drawing the comfort of nothingness around me. But I was blessed, or cursed, with my mother's chin-up, keep-going genes. I nod to Cora and she angles the microphone towards me.

"Thank you for being so attentive, Ladies and Gentlemen. My story is difficult to tell, and also, I realise, difficult to hear. I'll take a few questions. If there is anything you want to ask, just raise your hand."

I waited a moment. It always takes that beat of time for a brave soul to be the first to raise a hand. It is usually someone mid-thirties, female, confident. Often that person is a reporter from a local paper, or increasingly, an online journalist. I see a hand being raised towards the front. She fits the profile of questioner number one.

"Karen Levy. First of all, I can't say how much I admire your courage. I'm sure I speak for everyone here when I say that."

I smile my thanks as murmurs of agreement ripple around the hall. Images of myself flash before me. Lying on my bedroom floor, banging it with my fists in despair, tears and snot streaking my face, my hair uncombed and tangled, my body unwashed, my heart broken, my soul tortured. My only wish to lie there until I die. The antithesis of courage.

"My question, Leah, is why do you think your husband allowed you to live?"

Whew! This one isn't messing about. Straight for the juggler. I notice heads turn to look at her. Probably because it is a question they want to ask, but never would. I take a deep breath.

"If you remember, Karen, I mentioned in my talk that Ben brought hot milk to me the night before . . . the last night. I didn't drink it. He turned on the dishwasher before he left the house, so any traces of a drug that may have been in the mug, were washed away. It is possible he meant to drug me and take me, as he did the children, to Pouldubh Head too. Or maybe he wanted to make me suffer the agony of the survivor. I have no way of knowing now. That is the cruellest part. There are so many questions and few answers."

Karen Levy looks set to ask another question. It would probably be about the funerals. I do not want to answer that question. Not now. Not ever. I notice a hand being raised towards the back of the hall. I nod in that direction.

"It must be a great consolation that the children were too sedated to know what was happening to them?"

I nod. "Toxicology analysis confirmed the children had been given potentially lethal doses of the sleeping pills Ben had been prescribed in the hospital. And, as I said, they did appear to be asleep when Mrs Sanquest saw them. Even though autopsies confirm their cause of death as drowning, they were most likely not conscious when the car entered the water. I pray they were not. And the answer is yes. It's some consolation."

I long to run. To race off this stage and keep going until I have no more breath left in my body. No more nightmares. No more suffocating grief. No more touting my tragic story from pillar to post so that someone else will not have to go through this torture. Because they will, won't they? Nobody believes it will happen to their family. I didn't. Not until I had to go to the morgue, Hugh by my side, and formally identify my babies. And their father. Their murderer.

"Who do you blame? Your husband? His doctors? His mother?"

No-one ever asks the other question. *Do you blame yourself?* But that's the answer they most want to hear.

The questions come from a man sitting in the front row. Directly in front of me. He is white-haired, middle-aged, stocky. I meet his direct gaze and know he is neither curious nor judgemental. He cares.

"If you had asked me that question two years ago, I would have answered yes to all. I blamed the professionals for not recognising the need for intervention, his mother for covering up Ben's mental health problems. Most of all I blamed myself. I lived with him. I saw his mood swings. I believed him when he said he would talk to the doctor. I was the children's mother. The one who gave them life. The one who should have protected them to *my* last breath, not *theirs*."

"And your husband?"

"I hated him. With as much passion as I hated myself. I was so consumed by hatred that even the good memories were tainted."

"But you don't still feel the same?"

I turn to look at the screen. They look back at me. Rob, concentrating on aligning the Christmas lights, his eyes so beautiful. They were Ben's eyes without the darkness of tortured thoughts. Anna, her boundless energy reflected in her smiling image. Those curls, that beautiful blonde cascade of hair, escaping from underneath her Santa hat. And Josh, his grin so full of devilment. How can I tell these strangers that Ben had been there with them, laughing and having fun? Loving them. Because he did. I know he did. And yet, even as he had decorated the tree with them, brought them to Dublin, played with them in the park in town, he must have been planning to kill them. I had hated him. Sometimes, I still do. And yes, hatred hurts the hater, but his crime, his unspeakably evil, premeditated crime, is unforgivable. The man was still waiting for his answer.

"I am working towards hating what he did," I said. "But not hating him. It's a slow process."

I close the image and click to the next page. A list of contact numbers flash on screen. Help lines for mental health professionals. Confidential phone lines for emergency situations. Or when you just need someone to listen.

A young girl in the second row raises her hand. I notice her eyes are puffy. She is probably the sniffler.

"How did you get through the trauma and come out strong enough to be able to carry on? To give talks to groups all over the country like you do?"

Innocent girl. What makes her think my nightmare is over? That I don't wake screaming anymore when I dream of the jeep plunging over Pouldubh Head, carrying Rob and the twins to their deaths? When I dream of them under thirty feet of water, trying to claw their way out of the jeep, and I'm trying desperately to claw my way in to them, while Ben laughs manically at all of us. Strong? How? Why? But, yes, yes. I can be strong when I need to be. For the snifflers. For the people in danger of walking unknowingly into the same nightmare that has now become my life. That's why I'm standing here in this quaint little hall in Kerry on the second anniversary of what has become known in the media as the Pouldubh Tragedy.

I smile at the girl. "Believe me, I have a long way to go to being strong again. But, yes, I have moved on from the crippling first year after the funerals. I've had tremendous support from my husband's family, from friends, from the

Paircmoor community, and from the counselling services I attend. Talking. That really helps. And having people listen, like you all did tonight. It's so important to talk to family, to friends, to professionals. Get past the idea of shame or embarrassment where mental health is concerned. If you feel that life is a struggle, if you suspect that someone close to you may be suffering, *please*, *please*, *please*, ring one of the numbers on the screen. *Don't wait.* Don't think it will all work out without intervention. Sometimes it does. Many times, it does not."

There are still upraised hands. I have had enough. I have told them the truth. I have exposed myself to humiliation and judgement so they can be warned. I know from experience I will be asked why I allowed Ben to be buried with the children, why I still have a relationship with Ben's mother. Why I didn't realise what stress he was under. It's as if some people believe that Della deliberately reared her son to murder his children. That I purposely ignored the signs and symptoms of his breakdown. His loss of humanity. His capacity for evil. I don't want to explain myself anymore. Because I cannot. There are no explanations. I want to go home.

Cora to the rescue again. She trots towards me, a huge bouquet of flowers in her arms. She presents them to me and says a few words of thanks. Applause breaks out. They're standing now and I feel like a fraud. I glance down and see tears on the sniffler's cheeks. I feel an urge to go to her and put my arms around her. All I can do is hope that something I said will send her in the right direction. One that doesn't lead to lifelong agonies of regret and guilt.

"I'm sure you need a coffee after all that," Cora said.

"Follow me."

I close my PowerPoint presentation, shut down my laptop and pick up the notebook. Then I follow Cora, the applause still sounding as I leave the stage. She leads me backstage again to where she has freshly brewed coffee ready for me.

"You'll have biscuits," she says.

I take a chocolate digestive.

"Eat up. I'll just hop outside and make sure the projector and screen are properly stored away. And the chairs."

She scuttles off leaving me a lovely moment of silence. Digestive eaten, I take out my phone and key in the number.

"Everything okay?" I ask.

I nod as I listen.

"I'll be leaving here in the next few minutes. I should be home around eleven."

I agree to all the instructions about being careful on the road and not to drive too fast.

I find Cora, still on-stage, directing tidy up operations. I offer her my hand and tell her I must get going. She ignores my hand and hugs me.

I had parked my car earlier at the rear of the hall. I slip out the back door and point my fob in the direction of the car. When the lights flash, I see that there is a woman standing by my car. The sniffler. She turns towards me as I approach.

"Sorry if you think I'm stalking you," she said. "But I just want to thank you. I've finally decided to look for help. I'm a victim of domestic violence. I have two little girls. I'm not going to wait for him to turn on them too. Listening to you has given me courage. Thank you."

Like a wraith, she disappears into the night. I should call her back, support her, thank her for making this visit worthwhile. Make sure she knows that Ben had never, ever, raised a hand to me or to the children. But why would I want people to think well of him? Make excuses. There are none.

I put my laptop into the boot of the car, take off my coat, fold it and put it on the back seat. The beautiful bouquet of flowers Cora had presented to me go on the passenger seat. Beside it I place the notebook. I look at the two items for a moment, thinking there is something appropriate about the arrangement. Then I sit in and drive home.

I haven't even put my foot over the doorstep of Cowslip Cottage before Mags is in the hall, her face anxious.

"Ha! It's only ten minutes to eleven. You drove too fast!" she says.

I laugh. As ever, there is something warm and comforting about being nagged by Mags.

"I had a clear road," I say. "How has he been?"

"Like a little angel. Why wouldn't he be with three angels up above to look after him?"

That's another thing I love about Mags Hoey. She always speaks about Rob and the twins. Not in a morbid or apologetic way, but with love, and lack of the awkwardness most people feel at the mention of their names.

I walk down to the bedroom which had been Rob's, Mags trailing after me. The nightlight is on, casting a mellow glow around the room. I tiptoe to the cot. He is lying on his back, dark curls framing his face, his arms flung out. He is a restless sleeper. Like Anna. He has dark brown eyes, just like Rob, and an impish smile that is pure Josh. He was the embryo. The foetus. Baby number four. The one I didn't want. The one I almost lost. The one who fought to stay with me, to grow to full term. Now eighteen months old. He is the essence of his siblings, and yet he is uniquely Reuben. Hopefully he is also what is good in Ben and me. I reach out my hand and gently touch his hair. He gives a little wriggle and settles down again.

"Night, night, Reuben," I whisper.

I follow Mags back to the kitchen. My nose twitches as I get the aroma of her homemade pizza.

"Sit," she orders, waving me to the place she has set at the table.

I do as told. Through the open door I catch sight of the packed boxes in the hall. I begin to shake and doubt my decision.

"Oh! Mags! Am I doing the right thing?"

She places a plate of pizza in front of me. I know she will nag until I have eaten it all. She continues in her quest to 'put meat on my bones'.

She sits down opposite me, elbows on the table. She looks me straight in the eye. So few people do. They cannot cope with the suffering they see there.

"Look here," she says. "A swanky apartment in Dublin City centre is a pretty good start to the New Year, Leah. Della has been very generous."

"But it's not my home, Mags. It's Della's apartment. The one she had intended living in before Ben changed all our lives. I don't know why I agreed to take it."

"We've been through this again and again. You need to move on, Leah. There are too many reminders here. And before you say it, I know you're not trying to forget your children. You never will. But what you need to carry with you is how they lived. Not the way they died."

I look at Mags. She is still the busy, bustling little woman I had first met and didn't altogether like. Now, I love her like she was my mother. Maybe Mam has organised for Mags to be with me when she cannot. I smile.

"What will I do without you, Mags?"

"What do you mean, without me? I'll visit you in Dublin of course."

"I'll hold you to that, Mags. I'll come down here and drag you back with me if necessary. Maybe I should wait until after Christmas to move."

"Hugh and Piper and their baby are coming to see Della in Howth for Christmas, aren't they? You and Reuben will have a grand time. You haven't changed your mind about keeping on Cowslip Cottage, have you?"

"Yes, of course I'm keeping it. Reuben will have to be told soon enough about his brothers and sister. It will be good to show him where they lived. I couldn't leave Paircmoor behind anyway. Not even Viv Henderson. Everyone's been so good to me. Besides which, who'd buy Cowslip Cottage? People say it's cursed. Maybe it is."

"Stop talking daft and eat up your pizza!"

It's after midnight as we stand at the front door. Both reluctant to say goodbye.

"You have the spare keys to the cottage?" I ask for the third time.

"Yes. Don't worry about it. I'll look after it for you."

"I know. Thank you."

"And the salon, Leah. You're sure I can't pay for –"

"Mags! I haven't set foot in that salon for two years. You've made a great success of running it. If anyone is entitled to have their name over the door, you are. You'll have to deal with Viv Henderson when the lease is due for renewal, but the equipment and the client list are yours."

We hug. A say a quick prayer this won't be the last time I feel the comfort of Mags' arms around me. That's a lasting curse Ben has left me. I can't feel the joy of the moment because I'm too aware of the fragility of life. The randomness of death.

I watch her walk towards her car and wait for her to turn towards me. Mags always has the last word.

"Reuben," she said. "I often wondered why you chose that name for him."

"The bible. Old Testament. Reuben was Leah's son."

"*Hmm*. I didn't know you were religious."

"I'm not."

Mam had not been religious either but she had chosen the name Leah for me and told me the bible story about Leah being married to Jacob while he was also married to her beautiful sister Rachel. But Mam had no sister. Not that I knew of. Maybe the answer has something to do with my father. I don't know. And that's the way it will stay. For now.

"Take care!" Mags calls. "I'll go see you as soon as you've settled in."

I wait at the door until the sound of her car fades into the distance. It is a still night, yet the trees in the avenue sway as if dancing to their own music. I can hear the river hiss as it rushes under the bendy bridge. I have no doubt the workhouse ghosts are wandering restlessly along the banks of the river. Behind me, Cowslip Cottage whispers its story in groans and creaks. Then I let it all pour out into the night. The hate, the anguish, the fear of striking out alone, the guilt. Oh, Leah Parrish! The guilt!

I wipe my tears, go back into the kitchen, collect the key I keep at the back of the cutlery drawer, and take the notebook with the green cover from the counter where I had left it. Then I walk over to the old shed and put the key in the door. It's the only one. I have not had a duplicate cut for Mags. I open the door and switch on the light. It hasn't changed. Not since the forensic team were here, fingerprinting and whatever else they had to do. Not since my children spent their last few hours here. Not since Ben had spent his last night turning it into a Santa's Grotto for them. The toys are still strewn around the place. Jenny, the toy donkey Hugh had given Anna, lies abandoned on the floor. Proof positive that Anna had been asleep, unconscious, when she was put into the jeep. She would not have left Jenny behind had she been awake. Rob and Josh must have been asleep too when Ben strapped them in and drove them to their deaths. Rob's bike is showing signs of rust. The ribbons on the handlebars of the twins' trikes are drooping and dusty. Mam's artificial Christmas tree continues to wilt.

I look at the notebook with the worn green-leather cover. Ben's diary. The one he left out here for the gardaí to find. Or maybe for me. A suicide note of sorts. And yes, I have read it, every single word so many times that I can recite it verbatim. Some entries are in pen, some pencil, fading now. The writing is copperplate at times and at others the script sprawls and tumbles over the pages. It starts from when Ben had been made redundant and then it continues on in crests and troughs of hope and despair, right up to the morning he and the children left their make-shift Christmas grotto and went to their deaths. Reading it has allowed me to see inside his head, to plumb the depths of his depression. But it has not brought me the explanation I desperately needed, that one word, one sentence, to tell me he had been motivated solely by a twisted kind of love for the children. It did enable me though, to tell Ben's story in his own words, so that other people will, in future, recognise the signs I missed. I turn to the last page.

The children are excited. Happy. Sleepy. It is time.

Yes, it is time. I place the diary back up into the rafters. Rueben may want to read it sometime in the future but I will never open it again.

I stand motionless. Listening intently. Staring into the dark corners. Holding my breath. There is no echo of Rob's gentle voice. No whisper of Anna's constant chatter or Josh's giggle. Nothing. Nothing. Nothing. I call their names. Not just with my voice. I call them with my heart, my soul. *Rob! Anna! Josh! Why, Ben? Why?*

A cold breeze blows through the shed. The door bangs shut. I hear the key rattle in the lock. I freeze. Was that the force of Ben's anger? I catch the inside handle and tug. It doesn't budge. My heart thumps with fear. Reuben! He's on his own in the house! I tug with the strength of desperation. The door opens. I lock the old shed and know it will be the last time I will ever go in there.

I rush back inside to check on Reuben. He is still lying on his back, sound asleep, a smile on his face. He is indeed, playing with the angels. I smile too.

I put four little kisses on my fingertips, one for Rob, one for Anna, one for Josh and one for Reuben. I blow the kisses to my sleeping babies.

The End.

Printed in Poland
by Amazon Fulfillment
Poland Sp. z o.o., Wrocław